THE RINGMASTER'S REVENGE

THE RINGMASTER'S REVENGE

BOOK 1: CIRQUE DU NOIR

ROMANTIC SUSPENSE NOVEL

THEMATIC DISCLAIMER

This book is intended for mature audiences only. This is an Adult Romantic Suspense novel with explicit themes and extreme situations.

CONTENT / TRIGGER WARNINGS:

Reader discretion is strongly advised for content that includes:
Explicit Sexual Content
Human Trafficking
Abduction & Captivity
Graphic Violence: Associated with Organized Crime
Non-Consensual Drugging
Explicit Language & references to Trauma

READER COMFORT:

For your peace of mind, this story contains:
NO Sexual Assault
NO Cheating

For the kids who realized Nancy Drew was too good and the Hardy Boys were too clean. To those who wanted to see the detectives cross the line, trade their flashlights for darkness, and find a mystery worth losing themselves in.

TABLE OF CONTENTS

PROLOGUE:

ROSALIE

FOUR YEARS AGO - AGE 21

Ducking into the ladies' room, I check that I'm alone before locking the stall door. The slip of paper burns a hole in my palm. Memorizing the room number, I read it one more time before shredding it into tiny pieces and flushing it down the toilet. I don't want the poor waiter, who discreetly passed it to me while circling the ballroom, to get in trouble. After all, information is power.

With all the grief I've gone through tracking down a professor, blackmailing him into telling me Martín's location, and setting me up with a contact on the inside, I'm not about to let this opportunity go to waste.

Slipping my gloves back on, I quickly check my appearance in the mirror. I'm not a bad-looking girl, but tonight my outfit puts casual Rosalie to shame. My long hair is curled in loose beach waves, gently framing my face. A simple yet tasteful gold chain locket dangles from my neck, complementing the dangling gold earrings peeking from beneath my dark hair. It naturally guides the gaze toward my sweetheart neckline.

The shimmering maroon dress drapes loosely over my shoulders before tapering in, accentuating my hourglass figure and long legs. My favorite feature is the thigh-high slit that allows for a comfortable breeze, a slight tease, and, most importantly, easy mobility. You never know when you might get in a pinch and need to flee quickly. And finally, the *pièce de résistance*—two elbow-length matching maroon gloves—to class up the outfit, but also to remove any evidence of fingerprints.

With one last splash of water, I cool my nerves and steel myself for meeting the devil himself—Martín Gonzales, ringmaster of Circo del Sol.

Knock, knock.

The door opens; the space filled with none other than Martín. Clearly, he wasn't expecting me, but he was expecting someone.

Martín Gonzales is a porky, middle-aged man who sports one of those gross pornstar mustaches. Originally from Baja Sur, Mexico, he grew up on the streets and has contacts with all the major gangs and cartels that run the peninsula. After joining the circus as a kid, he traveled and eventually took over as the ringmaster of Circo del Sol.

"To what do I owe the pleasure?" Martín slyly grins.

I lean seductively against the doorframe, popping a leg forward, showing a hint of the slit. As intended, Martín leers, skimming down my body with a sweeping gaze.

"Well, I was actually looking for someone," I purr. "Are you the infamous Martín Gonzales?"

His eyes make their way back up to mine. "Depends on who's asking?"

"Oh, just little ol' me, Señor. I've heard so much about you, and after seeing the show yesterday I *had* to meet you in person." I smirk coyly. "See for myself if you're as magnificent at activities outside of the ring as you are in it."
Letting the implications linger, Martín takes the bait.

"Well, Bella, you're in luck. I'm Martín." He extends his hand to my gloved one, drawing it in for a kiss. "And you might be?"

"Rosa." I lie, batting my eyelashes in what I can only hope appears seductive. "May I join you tonight, Señor Martín? I think you'd very much enjoy my company."

Sliding the door open, he steps to the side, and waves me in. "Sí, sí Bella, come on in. I'm sure we can find some way to pass the time." The sexual undertones hang thick in the air.

Fake smile plastered in place, I push down the acid threatening to make an appearance and slink past him while he turns to lock the door.

His suite is more lavish than your standard hotel room. It has a lovely sitting area fitted with a plush couch and matching chair surrounding a small coffee table. Tall windows frame one wall, providing a stunning view of the ocean. The corner sports an upscale minibar, featuring a few full-sized bottles of wine, whiskey, and tequila. Around the corner is a door leading to the master bedroom and en-suite.

Making myself at home, I perch on the loveseat, crossing my legs at the ankle.

"Shall we take this to the bedroom, Bella?" Martín asks while gesturing around the bend.

"Actually, Señor—" I start to reply before he interrupts.

"Bella, por favor, with how well you and I plan to become acquainted, just Martín will suffice." He insists.

"*Sí, gracias.* I was actually hoping we could start with something a bit more...

refreshing—perhaps a drink while I get to know the man behind the *maravilloso* Martín." I lean forward, drawing his eyes to my cleavage while he absently agrees.

"A great idea. What's your poison, Bella?" He makes his way to the bar. "We have some fine red wine imported directly from Italy or a white from one of my vineyards in Napa Valley."

"Perhaps something stronger?" I suggest. "I'm partial to good tequila myself."

"Ah!" He claps his hands in delight. "A woman after my own heart! I too appreciate a fine tequila or mezcal." He reaches into the mini freezer, grabbing two frosted tumblers. Tipping two fingers' worth of tequila into each glass, he walks back to the couch, passing me my drink and joining me on the loveseat.

"*Gracias, Señor.*" I continue with the formalities, hoping it gives the illusion of power and control to this slimy man.

"*De nada,* Bella."

"Before we get too comfortable, would you mind helping me with my shoes?" I sigh dramatically, draping my leg across his lap. His gaze immediately trails from my cleavage to the slit splitting at my thigh. "My feet are *so* tired from standing all day." My dramatic flair borders on cringy, but he's eating my act up like a starving lion served a gazelle on a silver platter.

Setting his glass on the coffee table, he starts just above the knee—sliding his hands down my calf to the tiny clasp at my ankle.

"Of course, it would be my pleasure." He replies with a creepy smirk. He lingers for a moment too long at each dip and curve.

As he fusses with my shoe buckle, I tug gently on the middle finger of my glove, slipping it off and dropping a discreet pill into my palm. He motions for the other leg just as I finish removing the other glove, providing the perfect opportunity to set them down on the coffee table while he's distracted by my feet and increasing skin showing.

With a skilled sleight of hand, my palm successfully drops the little pill into his tequila—dissolving before it can hit the bottom of the glass. *Success*! Now, to make sure he drinks the whole thing.

Martín takes the liberty of starting to massage my foot. It could have been considered kind had he been anyone else. A sleazy guy like him can turn any innocent action into a repulsive affair.

Keeping my sex-kitten persona at the forefront, I force a soft, breathy moan from my lips. Pointing my toes, I place one foot on his chest, leaving my other foot resting on his lap. As the massage continues, Martín's touch wanders up my calf.

A few more stretches and moans, and he's ready to go. I switch to a more aggressive tactic. I pull my feet from his grasp, placing my tumbler on the coffee table next to Martín's long forgotten drink.

I really need him to finish his drink before my entire plan's ruined.

Pressing on his shoulders, I shove the bile down as I straddle his lap. Making a show of tossing my curled hair over one shoulder, I lean forward and whisper into his ear. "So, Señor, are we having fun yet?"

Martín chuckles darkly. "Oh, we're just getting started, Bella."

With both palms on his chest, I apply a little pressure to

get his attention on me. "I must admit, there is another reason I was looking for you tonight—beyond attempting to seduce you."

Martín eyes me with a grim chuckle. "You make it sound so formal. Are you in some kind of trouble?" His hands move north, gripping the outsides of my thighs.

"No, no, nothing like that! I actually have a proposition for you." Digging my claws into his chest, I bring my lips close to his ear. "I believe you can start my interview now."

He pulls back. "Interview? What would I even be interviewing you for?" He squints skeptically.

Still straddling his lap, I lean, doing a full backbend to pick up his drink and placing it between my tits for him to take with his mouth. He eagerly wraps his lips around the edge, shooting the remaining liquid in one giant gulp.

"I'm not hiring right now," Martín chokes out, the tequila burning his throat. He leans closer to bury his nose where the glass was, focused solely on the promise of sex.

"You might not be, but I couldn't help but notice you are all alone in the center ring." I walk my fingers up his chest, leaning closer to his ear, taunting him. Teasing him. I bite my lower lip, in a practiced seductive pout. "Not a ringmistress in sight. It must be lonely not having a sexy little thing hanging on your arm to help keep the audience interested. A man with your kind of power should have a whole harem of mistresses at his feet."

Our game of cat and mouse begins, dancing around being insulting and insinuating that he cannot do the job of ringmaster on his own, while actively laying the framework for Martín to come to his own conclusion that a ringmistress would be a welcome addition to his circus.

"Oh, really now? And I don't suppose you know anyone with the qualifications who might fill this void?" he asks, still quite distracted by having my tits so close to his face and my pussy hovering just out of reach of his now fully erect cock.

"Actually," I purr into his ear, "I am more than qualified. I can do all the tricks: splits, flips, acrobatics." I lower my hips just enough to brush the tip of his dick with my gyration.

"And you seem to enjoy the sight of me in a dress."

"Hmm, you make a good point." He slurs, the drugs slowly taking effect.

"Let's make a deal," I encourage, needing to speed this

negotiation along before he's rendered completely unconscious. "I get to perform in one show with you. If it goes well, you hire me as your full-time ringmistress. If it goes horribly, I'll disappear and no one will be any the wiser."

Nodding off, it takes increasingly more effort to hold his head upright. "Seems fair to me," he slurs. "Meet me at the big top one hour before showtime. Give them... my business card... at the entrance... they'll show you back."

I smile, my first genuine one of the evening. "Wonderful. I'll need your business card then, Señor." I continue purring.

"Oh, Bella... enough business... that is talk... for the... morning." He leans in, sloppily taking my mouth in his. Within minutes, Martín's lips falter and he slouches forward, passing out on the couch.

Phew. I was getting worried about how long he'd been conscious. My mouth desperately yearns for mouthwash and a mint.

Phase one of my plan is complete. Now it's time to execute phase two.

I hop off his lap and shudder, trying to shake off the fact that he was touching me only seconds earlier. Sliding my gloves back on, I slip my arms under his armpits—dragging him awkwardly along the floor toward the master suite. I strip him, mess up the sheets, and half-tuck him in. Throwing his clothes in a haphazard pattern on the floor, I create a scene that implies we were too passionate to care where they fell in the heat of the moment.

Grabbing his boxers off the floor, I run some water in the bathroom—making it look like there were more bodily fluids involved than there actually were. I turn on the shower, running it for a few minutes while I get to work on rumpling the towels. Everything alludes to a passionate round two in the shower after round one.

You're probably wondering, *Rosalie, why are you going to such extreme lengths to pretend like you had sex with Martín?*

One, I am absolutely not actually putting out for this man. He's *the* worst of the worst. *El Diablo* himself.

Two, despite not actually doing it, I need Martín to *believe* that we had a splendid night filled with heat and passion—so when I execute phase three of my plan, he's primed and ready to extend a full-time offer for ringmistress.

Stripping off his last sock, I swipe a business card from

his wallet—leaving the room looking like Vikings ravaged it. I quietly exit the hotel and make my way out the back stairwell to my car.

Phase two is complete. Now to begin the last steps of infiltrating Circo del Sol and taking out their ringmaster.

A FEW DAYS LATER

Navigating the Las Vegas Strip, I pull up to Circo del Sol. Taking a few deep breaths, I steady myself as my sweaty palms grip the crisp business card. Despite having used my burner to call and run through the plan countless times with my mentor, Joaquín, I'm nervous.

What if he doesn't remember me? Or worse—what if he does and figures out I played him? My inner monologue panics.

A huge part of my plan banks on Martín remembering right until the end of our conversation from a few nights prior. If he doesn't remember enough, I'll have no leverage. But if he remembers too much, I'm dead.

Brushing aside the doubt, I march to the rear entrance like I own the place, flashing the business card to the uniform on duty. He examines the card. "Is Señor Gonzales expecting you?"

"Of course! He's the one who gave me the card and directions here, silly." I flirt a little, putting extra emphasis on batting my eyelashes.

With a rough nod, he waves me through. "It's the big tent on the right. Can't miss it."

I dip my head in an appreciative nod, scurrying through to find Martín.

He isn't at the entrance like he said he would be, but I assumed as much since he likely forgot all about our little "arrangement." Pulling my coat a little tighter, I venture forward in search of him.

"Excuse me, miss, but we're closed." A heavy Spanish accent calls out.

"Oh, hello. I'm actually here for Señor Gonzales. He's expecting me," I reply.

"Ah, sí, Señorita, he's over there getting ready for the

show." The man gestures to the other tent flap, revealing dressing rooms and makeup stations for the performers.

Slipping past the next set of flaps, I finally spot him. Martín Gonzales is perched in his director's chair, sitting in front of a mirror outlined with bright Hollywood-style lights. A clown is finishing his makeup touches when I confidently stride up behind him, dropping a kiss on his cheek.

"Hola, Señor Martín," I coo into his ear. "Did you miss me?"

I nuzzle his neck lightly. He stiffens. He definitely recognizes me, but there's also a hint of confusion. *Perfect.* He makes eye contact with the makeup artist, dismissing her with a sharp nod.

"Bella, what a pleasant surprise. I didn't expect to see you again so soon." He falters, still trying to grasp what the fuck is going on.

Spinning around, I climb onto his lap, straddling the director's chair, letting out a fake boisterous laugh. "Oh, Señor, always so modest! I had a divine time. I haven't seen stars like that in ages." I continue, laying it on thick. "Surely you had a good time, sí?"

Quickly regaining his composure, "Sí, yes, of course I did. It was a night I'll never forget."

I hold back my snicker. Too bad he can't remember the night to begin with! I pull out his business card, fluttering it in the air. "Phew, then I hope you're ready to uphold your end of our bargain."

"Ah, yes, of course. I'm always a man of my word." He claims with false confidence. "Just to make sure we both understand, what were the terms of this agreement exactly?" His mask slips, his voice lilting up with the question. Clearly, he doesn't remember what we agreed to, but is too proud to admit it outright.

"Oh, Martín. How you make me laugh!" I playfully slap his chest. "Tonight, I get to be your ringmistress! And even though you don't know it yet, you'll be standing in the ring with me by your side for a *very* long time." I smile sweetly. "Right, Señor?"

"Yes, of course, Bella." He laughs uncomfortably, the emotion fleeting so quickly that I would have missed it if I weren't paying close attention. "Let's get you ready for the show then."

After a quick twenty minutes, I am ready to take the stage. The makeup artist added a few enhancing dashes of color to my face. My torso is now covered in a gold sequined shirt with a petite red tailcoat on top. My outfit's a perfect complement to Martín's black top hat and red coat—the female version with a black skirt and tall boots in place of his dark pants.

I spent the next hour and a half twirling by his side—acting like his arm candy, all while adding my personal flair to the role.

I joined some of the acts, participating in the clown's Three Stooges act, pretending to push the human cannonball, and doing handstand splits while acrobats flipped above. Anything to enhance the performance and wring extra laughs from the crowd.

Overall, the night goes off without a hitch. The house loves me and the show. Sweat glistening and a little out of breath, we close the production out with a unified "Thank you!" while I'm perched on Martín's shoulder for a joint bow.

The lights turn on and the doors open for the crowd to file out. Martín places me on the ground before he scoops me back up and twirls me around in the heat of all the excitement. "Well, Bella, that certainly was a show!" His mustache inches up in a wide grin. "I believe drinks are in order!"

We whirl around and make our way to the cookhouse. It takes us a while to get away from the other acts. They keep welcoming me to the show—asking where Martín has been hiding a beauty like me and where he discovered such talent. After the bartender pulls us some drafts, Martín and I make our way to the back corner.

"So, do we have a deal?" I ask, hopeful the performance sealed the deal.

"I think we might be able to work something out." He drops his voice and wiggles his eyebrows.

"Oh, Señor, I thought we already did." I playfully deflect, "I think the crowd enjoyed having a ringmistress thrown into the mix, no?"

"Sí, they did. I know my crew did for sure. If you want the ringmistress position, it's yours. There are some rules and responsibilities you'll have to take on as part of the circus family, but they're nothing outrageous."

I can't hold back my genuine grin as I shake Martín's

sweaty hand. "Looks like you've got yourself a ringmistress, Señor."

Phase three of my plan is complete.

1

ADRIANO

PRESENT DAY - AGE 28

Staring at the ceiling of my trailer, I force myself to stay in bed until the sharp beeps of my alarm sound. I'd love to say the alarm was to wake me up, but with how horrible my sleep schedule is, I am always awake long before it attempts to rouse me. With a deep sigh, I roll off my bed and begin getting ready for the big show.

With a quick cold shower and towel dry, I lean over in front of the backlit mirror that all the trailers come equipped with. I loosely run my fingers through my dark wavy hair, giving it a halfhearted attempt at styling it, before covering most of it with my deep purple top hat. Donning my standard black button-up and black jeans, I'm almost ready to go. Unlocking my large oak armoire, the doors swing open to reveal a deep purple tailcoat. The sleeves and edges are smattered with an array of golden thread. Embroidered swirls and abstract shapes dance up the arms. The fabric looks new, but the lining tells a story of how well-worn it is. At a glance, you'd never notice the different trinkets tucked in the inner pockets or that there's a protective thin layer of Kevlar sewn between the fabric layers.

Tucking my sidearm into my belt, I throw on the coat before lacing up my black combat boots, slipping a small knife into the side—just in case. In my line of work, you can never be too careful.

Ready to get the show on the road, I exit and navigate between the trailers, listening to the other acts and families getting prepped and ready. Their comfortable chatter washes over me while they secure their outfits.

Tonight is opening night in New Orleans—our home base and my favorite stop for our bandwagon of misfits. It's the closest place that feels like home. Humidity and the smell of beignets greet me as I approach the cookhouse, where we gather for meals and special occasions as a family—a wild circus family, but family nonetheless. A burly man, whom we affectionately call Chef, manages all the food our staff eats. Keeping over one hundred twenty people well-fed on the road is not a small undertaking, but he makes it look easy.

With this being opening night, there are extra items on my to-do list; the most pressing is a meeting with St. Francisville College's professor, Monsieur Jacques. Prior to any of our "special" shows, it falls on the ringmaster's shoulders to meet and greet the school's professor.

Stepping through the curtain to the backside of the cookhouse tent, I amble up to the stools lining our traveling bar. Nodding to Spike, our resident bartender, as his tattooed arm reaches across the bar and sets a freshly mixed Sazerac on the counter. After dropping off the drink, his spiky blue mohawk disappears toward the kitchen. He knows better than to hang around during any of my meetings.

Monsieur Jacques is already waiting for me, a smoked Old Fashioned in one hand and his other resting on a short stack of manila folders.

With a grunt, I slide into the empty seat, extending a greeting. "Pleasure to see you again, Monsieur Jacques."

"Oh please, Adriano, we share way too much history to observe such formalities." He chuckles, gripping my hand tightly before letting go. "Tell me, how has the last batch of recruits been performing?"

"You know I can't disclose details, but as always, your picks are exemplary." I reply, sidestepping some of the more implied questions. Giving my glass tumbler a swirl, I ask, "What have you got for me tonight?"

Monsieur Jacques grins and slides the small stack of folders over, each one containing information on a potential circus candidate.

"I think you'll be very pleased with this batch. Not only have they aced every lesson in the classroom, but they've set record scores!" he exclaims.

Lifting one eyebrow, I peer skeptically from beneath my hat's large brim. Besides being fashionable and helping the crowd distinguish who the ringmaster is, this hat has served me well in hiding unwanted emotions from enemies and business partners.

"I'll be the judge of that, but I'm eager to see them in action. Thank you for passing this along." I rise, ready to be done with this mandatory reunion and get back to my job. "I'll be in touch after the show for any follow-up items. Otherwise, take your time, finish your drink, and enjoy the show, Monsieur."

"I look forward to hearing from you, Adriano. I appreciate the hospitality."

Turning, my tailcoat swishes behind me as I exit the tent. It's almost time to get in position. Julianna, my right-hand gal, announces loudly over her bullhorn, "Get to places. We're on in five."

Detouring, I stop and see my favorite wild cats, Raj and Shiva. These gorgeous Bengal tigers have been with me since they were cubs, bought from Jin Mingh, the prick ringmaster at Cirque du Neige out of Canada.

Over the years, we've forged an unbreakable bond. When we first bought them, I spent countless hours training them and perfecting tricks. After all, being ringmaster wasn't always my career path. And they were welcome company after my family left.

A few quick pats on their heads, and I make my way toward my starting spot.

The house lights dim to pitch black. I close my eyes, assuming my stage persona of puppet master extraordinaire. The hum of smoke machines starts, pumping dark furls of smoke as I take my place on the center stage. Blue, purple, and white lights circle sporadically throughout the high top, briefly highlighting the unfamiliar faces of the entranced mass before honing into a single stream and falling onto my hat. The light illuminates the golden-trimmed coat, casting mysterious shadows on my face as the wisps of smoke finish curling around my feet, dissipating into the atmosphere. This is it. The beginning of the show that kick-starts the rest of the evening's performances.

A hush falls as the crowd waits in anticipation for my signal. I have their sole attention. Sole control as the ringmaster, their ringleader. Tilting slightly, I peer from under the plum brim, my gaze lingering on the group of young faces in the front row.

I take a deep breath and announce in a resonant voice, "The things you are about to see may be disturbing, enchanting, and even magical..."

Whoosh!

Two tall, stoic clowns appear in black and white jumpers with striped, frilly collars encircling their necks, creating a blend of Cruella De Vil meets Pennywise. Like yin and yang, their cheeks sport monochromatic flames. Each clown lights a match, placing it in front of their painted lips and blowing giant fifteen-foot flames toward the stands like twin fire-breathing dragons. Each flame sets a separate ring ablaze, casting shadows on Raj and Shiva's fierce faces. They leap through the fiery hoops with synchronized roars. Their incredible striped coats are licked by the sparks, but never catch fire. Landing with grace only cats possess, they pad to my sides.

The music pauses. My hands rest on either large cat's head. A grin takes over as I announce, "Ladies and gentlemen—welcome to Cirque du Noir!"

Entry of the Gladiators' tune echoes softly, adding to the anxiety and anticipation, building into a musical symphony. Trumpets blare as the shrill of flutes fluttering down the scales gets layered in. I lift my head, the light hitting my face for the first time. Stretching my arms wide, I cue the acts to begin their circus routines. The steady beat of the snares and hi-hats thumps through the big top, music in full circus swing. The spotlight expands, highlighting the act surrounding me. My faithful tigers circle me before stepping off to rest on their podiums on the sidelines.

"Tonight, in our big top, I'll be your host, Ringmaster Adriano, and I'm pleased to introduce our fabulous team of acrobats, the Flying Frenchmen! Among them, we feature the Stupendous Shirleen, tackling the tightrope."

Above my arms, teams of flying trapeze acts somersault through the air, barely scraping past Shirleen's long pole as she balances delicately on her tightrope over a hundred feet in the air. They leap from one hanging bar, flipping and twisting before reaching their partner's outstretched arms hanging by their knees on the bar opposite them. Shirleen's bright amethyst and pearl-white tutu sticks out in contrast to the tent's dark color, her glittery makeup catching the light and casting little dots on the canvas. As she reaches the middle of the tightrope, the trapeze acts flip by once more, but this time, on either side of her pole. Midair, they breathe out smaller flames than the opening clowns, setting Shirleen's balancing pole aflame. The crowd goes wild as she arches backward, shifting the firestick to her mouth, and executes the perfect backbend.

The spotlight drifts from the rooftops back to me. Stretching my arms lower and turning in a circle, I guide the audience's attention toward the next act.

"Introducing our resident horse whisperer, the Magnificent Madeline Schumann! The Schumann family hails directly from Denmark and has been training horses for over three generations. Their Lipizzaner's have bloodlines tracing directly back to Napoleon himself. Their beautiful white coloring and smaller stature make them the perfect breed to perform tricks and jumps for you tonight."

A dozen white horses donned in sleek black armor with magenta plumes in their manes and tails gallop laps around the arena. Madeline steps forward as she directs them from the ground. One of our younger foals trails behind them, mimicking their prancing steps. Acrobats vault on the horses' backs—executing perfect handstands and synchronized pyramids while galloping around. Two large stallions break apart from the group, executing perfectly timed leaps and kicks. Six split off from the group to dance: rearing in unison and moving in synchronized patterns before disappearing through the tent flaps.

"Entering the big top next, we have our merry bandwagon of clowns!"

Three tiny clown cars zoom into the ring, zipping around like a Mario Kart race and throwing objects. The blue car hits a banana peel and spins out. The driver emerges, his cheeks painted white with large blue tears. Scratching his frizzy blue hair, he kicks the tires with his massive shoes, sometimes missing them completely, before trying to get it running. To his despair, it just sputters and honks. Dramatically, he pops the hood. A torrent of clowns erupts from the engine compartment, followed by more from the trunk, ultimately releasing upwards of thirty clowns. After producing upwards of thirty clowns, the blue car roars to life, racing backward out of the ring, pursued by the giggles of clowns on foot.

Ellie and Babar enter, their large flapping ears and leathery gray heads dressed in matching sparkly headdresses. The royal purple and black headbands shimmer as the light dances across them. The centers of their massive foreheads feature a large white star, with amethyst gems on each corner. They're magnificent, marching around the arena, trunks swaying with the music. While two delicate ballerinas sit nestled behind their ears. Ava and Avery, siblings like their elephants, shine just as brightly from their steeds. Having grown up together, their relationship was just as strong, if not stronger, than mine with Raj and Shiva.

Ellie's trunk raises in a majestic arc to hold hands with the tiny ballerina. Ava's black tutu matches Ellie's sparkly headband. Avery performs a similar move on Babar, all four of them moving in sync with practiced ease.

One of our most renowned magicians, Mystical Merlin, steps into the arena. The spotlight focuses on him as he entertains with a handful of illusions and surprises. Each more enticing than the last. After a few more tricks, it's time for the grand finale. The greatest act of all time.

"One of the greatest masters of illusion, the Great Harry Houdini, once performed the largest disappearing act of all time. He put a ten-thousand-pound elephant into a box and magically made her disappear! Tonight, prepare to be even more amazed, as the Mystical Merlin makes *two* massive elephants vanish before your very eyes!"

The spotlight expands, illuminating the entire stage, with an additional light on each elephant. They step up, placing their enormous feet on separate reinforced podiums. Rearing up, Ellie and Babar brace their feet together and await their cue.

Raising their trunks in a trumpet-like pose, letting out a loud toot of excitement. They reach across the podium, interlocking their trunks like they're preparing for a game of tug-of-war. The music pauses. Silence echoes through the big top as the greatest act known to man prepares to take place. Instead of being placed in boxes, Merlin has both elephants standing in the open, lit up like Christmas trees.

With a wave, smoke forms at his fingertips. His lips move as he utters unintelligible words, a witch casting a spell. The anticipation is palpable. Each person is perched on the edge of their seat.

With a few jarring gestures, Merlin shouts, "Ten... Nine... Eight... Seven..."

The crowd joins in for the final countdown. "Six... Five... Four... Three..."

Every eye is glued to the stage, bouncing between the statuesque elephants and Merlin's smoking hands. "Two... One... EVANESCO!!" he bellows.

A collective gasp echoes throughout the tent as both Ellie and Babar, along with Ava and Avery, disappear with an audible *poof* of smoke.

The stands erupt! Leaping to their feet, clapping and hollering with awe and delight. This part of the show is always a hit. Even though I still haven't quite figured out how Merlin makes the giant beasts disappear, it's a true testament to his showmanship and mastery.

"Ladies and gentlemen, thank you for joining us! As always, it's been a pleasure, and we hope to see you again soon!"

The acts emerge from backstage and filter into lines for a deep, theatrical bow. Even the horses join in, executing a well-rehearsed dip.

The last of the lights turn on, the tent doors open, and the acts exit with a majority of the crowd. It's time for my least favorite part: Recruitment.

As one of the largest circuses in North America, Cirque du Noir is also one of the three largest trafficking operations. We mostly focus on firearms and money laundering, but dabble in a multitude of illicit activities.

Large operations like ours require manpower to keep business running, so we partner with universities for recruitment. We don't work with the entire college, but rather with a handful of trusted professors who scout for promising students with skills we need. The faculty is equally invested in quality placements. After all, we fund a significant portion of their salaries and pensions.

Their job is to identify the most exceptional talent and funnel them to the show under the guise of 'extra-credit'. Once they're in the tent, it becomes an exclusive job fair. Each visiting circus makes its pitch and extends offers to their desired recruits. Even though the students ultimately choose their post-graduation path, we get the first look at the best and brightest.

The regular crowd departs, leaving Monsieur Jacques standing shoulder to shoulder with a fellow professor. They hover next to the remaining students, ensuring they don't sneak out with the rest of the stands.

After confirming the masses have left, I turn to the future of our organization, ready to deliver my stale, practiced recruitment speech. I spin tales of the amazing opportunities available if they join our outfit—traveling, a family, and of course, a padded paycheck. Only a handful of seniors are aware that this pitch is really an opening to join one of the three most powerful syndicates this side of the pond. The circus is only a portion of our day-to-day work, and the high pay isn't for their tightrope skills or juggling abilities—it's for their silence and loyalty.

Jumping into the standard song and dance, I skim their youthful faces snagging on familiar pale blue eyes.

A pit forms in my stomach, cold and sudden.

No, it can't be.

They swore they'd keep him away from this life. From me.

Maybe I'm mistaken? I mean, it's been years, but the resemblance is uncanny. Same blue eyes. Same wild curls. Here. In the one place he was never supposed to find. But there in the third row is the one face I never thought I'd see again—my little brother, Sammy.

2

ADRIANO

On autopilot, I finish delivering the spiel, ignoring the tightness in my chest. My thunderous heart rate threatens to run away like a freight train. I skip the Q and A, nodding abruptly to the professors, dismissing them.

Swiftly disappearing behind the curtain, I lengthen my strides—doing my best to exude calm and collected, while my insides are churning with turmoil. I can't show any emotion. No weakness. I race to my trailer, slamming the door behind me.

Scanning and confirming that I'm alone, I rip off my top hat and frisbee it onto the bed in rage. I rest my sweaty forehead on the door. Fists clenched. Jaw tight.

"Fuck." I chant the swear like it's my new religion. "Fuck, fuck, fuck!" I slam my fist into the door. The comforting sting grounds me enough to get my head on straight.

Walking to my makeshift desk, I shove the student folders from Jacques aside, flipping open my laptop. The dull glow illuminates the dark room as I start up my VPN and follow Julianna's instructions to secure a private connection. My fingers tap away as second nature takes over. Julianna may be a tech guru, but I've learned enough to hold my own on the web.

Pulling up St. Francisville's roster, I unravel the threads of information—disabling firewalls and security systems, desperately searching for a name I didn't think would ever re-surface.

I click on the first profile. This kid clearly isn't related. He has wild red hair and wiry glasses, not Sammy.

"Dammit," I mutter under my breath.

I click on the second profile. My breath is trapped in my lungs. The whole world spins out of focus as I stare at the face of my now-grown baby brother.

"FUCK!" I roar, scanning the rest of his profile frantically.

The breath I'd been holding slowly seeps out with a hiss.

God dammit! At least he doesn't have our real last name listed. Maybe the school doesn't know our relation? The odds are 50/50, since we look related—similar height, build, and facial features. But thankfully, Sammy takes more after our mom, while I resemble a younger version of my father.

Mom and Dad promised—they swore—that he would be kept out of this life. That was our deal. I get them out; they keep him out.

I recline in my chair to stare at the ceiling, needing a break from those familiar eyes staring back at me.

Fuck.

I need a plan. Maybe it isn't too late to keep him out? Maybe he's clueless about the recruitment program, the circus, or this life. But with him here, I'm skeptical.

Typically, kids aren't recruited until their senior year, but the odds that some professors already suspect Sammy's real identity are pretty damn high. They all deal with me regularly during our recruitment sessions. There's no way at least one of them wouldn't see our resemblance.

Gulping in a few deep breaths, I force the panic away, locking it deep in my gut's vault. Hunkering down, I force my brain to think logically about the situation. Reaching out to him directly is out of the question.

I can't contact the school directly. If they don't know Sammy's identity already, that would definitely trigger them to dig deeper and find our connection. Any special interest I show in a prospective recruit immediately flags to the recruiters that they need to be prioritized and added to the additional after-hours extracurricular program—where they provide extensive additional training and preparation for joining the "business."

Rubbing my palm on my sternum, I try to ease the strain threatening to pop. I have to think of something. There's no other choice. I resign myself to an evening of brainstorming. I'll keep him out of this life no matter what it takes. I did it once before, and I'll gladly do it again.

Moving my elbows from my knees, I drag my fingers through my hair, tugging hard. The dull burn does nothing to numb my pain. I squeeze my eyes shut, seeking even the briefest reprieve from my torment.

What the fuck am I going to do? I have to get Sammy as far from this shit as possible. Looking at my mirror, an idea forms.

When my parents had first gotten out of "the life," I used to pick up postcards from our travels and write them letters. I never sent them, but it helped me feel closer to them, even though we're estranged. As I got busier, I continued to collect cards, but quit writing on them.

Flinging my oak cabinet open, I unearth an old shoebox from the far back corner. Rummaging through my collection of photos, I find one that is perfect to get the message across. With my shitty handwriting, I scrawl one word.

"RUN."

There's nothing else I can say that won't just add to Sammy's pending danger.

Needing someone who can slip in and out of the shadows, I know I'll have to recruit someone to help execute my plan. Julianna, my right-hand gal, is the perfect person for the job.

Julianna and I met under extremely unconventional circumstances. While I was shadowing Armond, the old ringmaster and my predecessor, at sixteen he decided I was mature enough to attend our first auction. Yes, you heard correctly. My first trafficking auction was at the ripe age of sixteen. As much as I respected Armond as a kid, he was a crazy motherfucker with no concept of preserving childhood innocence or age-appropriate activities.

At the auction, I was reeling—sick to my stomach—confused as to what was going on. Armond never explained where we were going. He simply said, "Get in the car," and away we went. Over the years I'd grown used to acting more like an enforcer than an apprentice. Most of the time, we would pull outside of some shady warehouse or a rundown home. Imagine my surprise when instead, we wound up at a gorgeous mansion swarmed by people dressed to the nines. Without an explanation, Armond ushered us inside, his mask of indifference plastered on as we entered one circle of hell. It was unnerving and stuffy. Each patron exuded arrogance and entitlement. Following him along, we meandered deeper into the bowels of the mansion.

Girls of all ages were lined up for sale, but most of them were roughly my age or slightly older. As we walked through the house of horrors, at the end of the line was a small girl dressed in a modest white tunic. She couldn't have been more than ten years old—significantly younger than any of the other victims.

While many of the others were cowering or crying, this little girl stood ramrod straight. Her head tilted so her wild red hair covered as much of her face as possible, leaving only a tiny slit for her to peer through. The only signs of life were the soft rise and fall of her chest and her eyes flitting around. She watched each buyer like she was waiting to pounce. Analytical. Intelligent. Vulnerable.

A short, plump man with a twisted sneer was circling her. His leering stare promised a future filled with pain and suffering—a future that he would take great pleasure in. I stopped in my tracks, unable to break eye contact with this strong soul. Armond, noticing my interest, leaned over. "See something you like?" He asked in a hushed tone. "Didn't take you for one who liked them young."

I grimaced quickly, schooling my features, trying to

outwardly hide my disgust as much as possible. Flicking my gaze to his while trying to keep the girl in my sights, I quickly devised a plan.

"That one. I *need* that one," I said, pointing.

"Jeez, kid, I don't usually buy the young ones." He tried to play it off as though that made him holier than the other perverts here purchasing humans like livestock.

"She's. Mine." I growled, my resolve resolute. I didn't care if I had to buy her myself. She wasn't going home with anyone but me. She'd never survive anyone else buying her. "Where do I go to pay?"

Armond looked me over, amused. "You might just have what it takes to be ringmaster yet, kid. I'll tell you what, let's see if we can strike a deal before the auction begins. A special private sale. It'll be my gift to you."

I nodded in agreement, keeping my fists clenched at my side. I wasn't able to help everyone here, but at least I could spare her. We went and found the man who was running the sale, and after some harsh negotiating, he agreed to keep her off the auction block for a steep price. Apparently, the whole thing caused outrage among the other buyers, but Armond didn't give a shit and wasn't a man you trifled with; so by extension, neither was I.

Once we got back to the circus grounds, Armond sent her to my trailer, no different than if he were giving me a puppy. He didn't care what I did with her. She was mine, a fucked-up present.

She was quickly adopted into our family. My parents easily accepted her as their own, while I easily assumed the role of her overprotective big brother.

She stayed in our family trailer until I took over as ringmaster. Then she was given a choice: she could stay and work for me at Cirque du Noir or she was free to leave. I would've happily funded her fresh start and made sure she was safe, but Julianna would hear nothing of the sort. Her loyalty runs deep, and she insisted her home was with me—with us—at the circus. If there was anyone who would understand the importance of keeping someone as far removed from this life as possible, it was her.

Dialing, she arrives at my trailer moments later, waltzing in with a single knock.

"Hey A, what's up?"

"Jules, can you make a delivery to Professor Lockrin at St. Francisville?"

"I mean, sure. I can do it first thing tomorrow morning." She shrugs nonchalantly.

"No!" I declare, louder than intended. Rubbing my temples. "Sorry, I really need this delivered tonight. Please. She won't be expecting you, but I need you to convince her to assist us without too many questions."

"You look like shit. What's going on?" She takes in my disheveled appearance and. "You know you can tell me, right? I can tell when you're lying, and right now, you look like you're halfway between puking and passing out."

"Not now, Jules. I'm fine. Just tired and need this taken care of ASAP."

She flops onto the edge of my bed, concern wrinkled on her forehead. "Alright, I'll drop it for now. What exactly do you need me to do?"

Within the hour, we've hashed through logistics, finalized details, and set the plan in motion. I stand in the doorway until the Louisiana heat sticks my shirt to my back, watching as Julianna's taillights vanish around the bend, the red eyes swallowed by the night.

3

ROSALIE

Sweat drips off my brow as I throw one last combination at the heavy bag hanging behind my trailer. Four years of circus life and I still start every morning trying to punch Martín Gonzales's face off an inanimate object. It's cheaper than therapy, and Joaquín swears it keeps me sharp.

My trailer is strategically located at the farthest edge of the grounds. It conveniently allows me to come and go freely undetected.

At first, Martín tried to have me spend nights with him, but after enough excuses, he quickly grew bored with the fruitless pursuit. It wasn't too hard to stay out of the way until he was distracted with his flavor girl of the week. Thank God.

The travel, the spotlight, and the circus lifestyle are addictive. Four years of smiling for Martín Gonzales while mapping every dark corner of his empire. While Martín focuses on perpetuating his illicit dealings, I've been busy running my own operation. Hunting and plotting.

I mostly keep to myself. At least I did until Anna and Phillip joined the show a few months ago. They're the most talented trapeze duo I've ever witnessed. The way they move in sync—flipping, twirling, and effortlessly catching bars—speaks to an expertise that only comes from years on the circuit. They claim to have recently come out of "retirement," but their skill level says otherwise. I suspect there's more to their story, but I don't mind; we all have secrets.

We instantly connected. Anna took one look at me, a loner even in a crowd, and decided to take me under her wing. Between her warm eyes and caring soul, it was impossible to keep her at arm's length. She persisted, joining me for meals, my morning runs, and including me in their practices. Before long, she had become my best friend and mother figure. Her husband, Phillip, is broody and quiet, but when he's with Anna, he comes to life, constantly brushing against her and stealing kisses in private. They're easily the cutest couple I've ever seen and the closest thing I have to family.

Finishing my workout, I slide the burner phone from its hiding spot under my bed, checking to see if Joaquín, my old mentor, called for our weekly check-in. The ex-operative for the *Cuerpo de Fuerzas Especiales* (FES), the Mexican Navy Special Forces, has been my anchor. After choosing to "retire" on the beach, he happily spends his days fishing, running a local MMA gym in Tijuana, and assisting me with planning my side quests. It is through his contact, nicknamed *Le Fantôme*—The Phantom, that I've successfully built a name for myself. They're extremely organized and have infiltrated numerous trafficking rings.

Turning on the dark screen, I check the battery life and place it on the charger. I never know when I'll get a message from the Phantom and need to be ready. They're constantly changing their number, communicating via cryptic texts: an address when an auction rescue is needed, followed by another with an estimated number of victims expected on-site.

Satisfied that I haven't missed anything, I lay out my worn yoga mat on my trailer floor and sink into the familiar routine.

It's up to me to figure out the logistics of getting to the girls and setting them free. Oftentimes, I'll collaborate with Joaquín on the planning stages for a mission. Le Fantôme is always three steps ahead of me, sending a second address for after a successful extraction. I drop the group at the designated coordinates, often an abandoned house or warehouse, where one of their network contacts helps the victims with housing, warm meals, and new identities. The entire network is an extremely well-oiled machine, which makes waiting to take down Martín worthwhile.

The familiar ache as I stretch helps me find my center. Focusing on my mission. My purpose. Even though I wanted to strike now, patience is key for success and ensuring the whole ring gets dismantled forever. In the meantime, I enjoy helping wherever I can.

Moving into downward dog, I focus on my breathing, repeating my mantra to never fail again, remembering my early mistakes and vowing to learn from them. In the beginning, I insisted on waiting with the girls at the drop-off point. I couldn't help worrying and wanting to make sure I wasn't delivering them to another fucked-up sale or buyer. But at my second drop-off, the woman meeting the girls scolded me, lecturing me on how I was putting the girls in greater danger by hanging around. It was easier to track and trace me to the girls, and having the concrete link between us was an unnecessary risk. The kind woman reassured me, and after that, I had to trust the network to handle things.

Finishing my cool-down, I roll up my mat and hop in the shower. You'd think after years, Martín would trust me enough to involve me directly in the trafficking side of the business. However, he's kept me at arm's length. I've spent years hinting that I not only knew about Circo's illegal dealings, but was interested in participating. Roughly two years in, he found himself short-handed, one of our usual drug runners was sick. Martín let me do the drop, and since then, I've been picking up as many odds and ends as possible for the drug side of things. I still haven't directly seen the trafficking front or met anyone higher in the food chain.

Until finally, it happens.

We'd just finished our Houston shows and had a few days to pack when Martín calls.

"Bella, I have a job for you."

"Sí, Señor? I'm just about to head over to the big top." I answer, assuming it has to do with our pending travel.

"I have a meeting with some business associates. I usually attend alone, but I need you by my side this time."

"Of course, when is it?" My heart speeds up. *This was it!*

"Tomorrow, 6:45 PM. You'll meet me at the Manoir Hotel, just outside of Houston, at the restaurant inside. Don't be late."

Click.

4

ADRIANO

With my plan to handle Sammy's surprise appearance in motion, I pace the length of my trailer, the residual adrenaline of the situation refusing to burn off. Moving to the small bar, I pull out the rye and the absinthe and begin mixing my favorite drink: a Sazerac. You can't grow up in New Orleans and not have a soft spot for whiskey. The harshness may repulse some, but to me, it tastes like home.

I haven't even finished stirring the first glass when my phone vibrates on the counter.

Martin

Meeting tomorrow at our usual spot?

Me

Of course.

Sí, see you then.

Tomorrow. The Manoir Hotel. Neutral ground. Same song and dance every quarter: smile, shake hands, and pretend we're civilized while we carve up the continent.

The meeting tomorrow isn't a social call. Every couple of

months, we meet with the ringmasters of the other two largest circuses—*Circo del Sol* and *Cirque de Neige*—to ensure the peace holds and to discuss new business ventures. Cirque du Noir handles everything east of the Mississippi plus the state of Louisiana. There are other circuses in North America, but they're smaller and report to one of us.

Swirling the glass, I swallow down the last dregs of whiskey before moving back to the bar, pulling out another bottle.

The East Coast is profitable. We spend our summers circulating the north, escaping the sweltering southern heat before working our way south to avoid the New England cold. Every year we rinse and repeat, moving our caravan of trailers up and down the coast. This coastal route gives us control of many major ports—Boston, Miami, and our home base, New Orleans. Our real asset is Washington D.C. Having the country's capital in our territory allows us unique access to lucrative off-the-books contracts with the alphabet organizations. We move and distribute weapons and firearms.

Martín and I generally keep our businesses separate, each sticking to our own territory. They're deeply involved in drug trafficking and money laundering—a natural fit since they border Mexico. I supply him with firearms, while he ensures my region has high-quality drugs. Personally, I dislike them, but people will use them regardless, so I might as well ensure the product is safe. More importantly, the ability to supply high-quality substances—and know who uses them—gives us leverage over politicians and other public figures.

Martín is no different than the other scum from the underworld, equally as driven by greed and depravity. The real problem is he's is the kingpin of human trafficking. Anyone for sale passes through his network in one capacity or another. His reach is extensive and relentless.

Under Armond, Cirque du Noir exclusively dealt in the black market. Since taking over, I've decommissioned the skin trade. It's a volatile business, and honestly more work than it's worth. Between managing pimps, vetting buyers, and maintaining a steady supply, it's a hassle—not to mention immoral as fuck. Julianna has a particular aversion to it, and after watching Armond's clients and the twisted appetites of the political underbelly, that was the first network I dismantled and repurposed. It's a secret I keep under lock and key.

I peel off the purple tailcoat, hanging it in its designated spot in the armoire. The Kevlar lining catches the lamplight, a heavy reminder of the price of peace. Swallowing a long sip, the rye, absinthe, and bitters burn going down like liquid New Orleans.

I've worked tirelessly to transition deals to legitimacy. Diversification is good for business, and old-school crime is riskier now more than ever. Digital footprints, paper trails, and increased intergovernmental collaboration make true invisibility impossible. We're still moving drugs, weapons, and laundering money, but it's slowly becoming a smaller percentage of our portfolio.

I sigh, taking another swig before calling Julianna. As usual, she picks up in one ring.

"Yes, A?" she answers robotically, always efficient and straight to the point.

"Our meeting with Circo del Sol is tomorrow, 19:00. Will you be able to make it?"

Jules ponders for a beat. "I've got to handle something first, but I can meet you there."

"Good. Anything on our… side project?" I inquire discreetly, unsure if anyone is listening on her end.

"Nothing to report. Still running down some leads."

"Keep me updated. Thanks, Jules."

"Always. Cya tomorrow, A."

Click.

Finishing my second drink, I kill the lights, stretching out on the bed. The comforting scents of rye and cedar permeate the trailer. Hopefully, tonight I can finally get some rest, a break from the nightmares and flashbacks that consume my thoughts.

Tomorrow, I'll sit across from Martín Gonzales, smile like a gentleman, and pretend I don't care that he still trafficks skin. Tomorrow, I'll lie to him the way I've lied to everyone else for years.

The mattress creaks under me like it's laughing, but the alcohol does its job and the darkness consumes me, while the low, steady tick of my clock continues counting down until tomorrow's song and dance.

5

ROSALIE

After spending what I'm sure would be considered way too long getting dolled up, I finally pull into the hotel parking lot exactly on time. Crossing the parking lot, the hairs on the back of my neck stand; the sense of being watched crawls up my spine. Scanning, I spy the most handsome man I've ever seen. The definition of tall, dark, and dangerous.

He leans nonchalantly against a sleek Ferrari. A tousled mop of curls falls over a face carved from sin. His dark eyes are pools of mystery guarded by thick lashes that promise ruin. He flashes a million-dollar smile, sending a jolt of heat pooling in my thighs. With a shake, I remind myself I'm here for business, not pleasure. Even though this adonis will definitely be starring in my fantasies later tonight.

Scurrying into the hotel, I navigate the lobby toward the hostess. "The Gonzales party."

"Of course. Right this way, Miss." She grabs a menu and leads the way through the low-lit space. We pass the normal tables and enter a smaller private room tucked off the main dining area. The hunter green walls are smattered with Renaissance-era art. Soft glows come only from the candle centerpieces. A round table is nestled in the center of the room with four chairs surrounding it.

Martín is already waiting with a tumbler of amber liquid in hand. It really is the perfect meeting spot. Everyone has a clear view of the door while having their backs to a wall.

Before the others arrive, I turn to Martín, "So what's this meeting about anyways?" I ask. I don't want to mess up my first meeting with the big players.

"Nothing you need to worry about, Bella. You're here to be seen, not heard."

I hold my tongue at his dismissive 'Bella' and push again. "Can you at least tell me who we're meeting with?"

"Another circus. The Ringmasters of Cirque du Noir." Martín says, dismissing me with a wave of his hand.

The remainder of our wait is spent in in silence. Martín's edgy behavior slightly out of character as he fiddles constantly with his drink. I'm perusing the menu when Martín snaps to his feet.

"Señor and Señorita Devereaux, pleasure to see you again." He smiles, hand outstretched to his associates.

Holy shit. No way.

Joining us is none other than the sex-on-a-stick from the parking lot with a stunning redhead on his arm. She's tall with a slim, runway figure. Her wavy hair is pulled into a slick ponytail that trails to her petite waist. A foreign green monster brews in my stomach.

Mirroring Martín, I stand. The height difference between us quickly becomes apparent, my neck tilting up to meet our guest's eyes. I'm not extremely short, a comfortable five foot two, but his six foot one puts him almost an entire foot taller than me. His massive hand dwarfs mine as he politely brings it to his lips, kissing it with a glimmer of mischief. Praying that my cheeks aren't decorated in a deep shade of pink, I introduce myself. "Rosa, pleasure to meet you, Señor."

"Adriano," he rumbles, his voice even deeper and sexier than I'd imagined. "And this is my sister, Julianna." He motions to the gorgeous woman at his side. Our handshake lingers slightly, the chemistry electric between us. I quickly shake it off and greet his sister.

The green monster inside me does a tiny flip of joy. His sister! They look nothing alike, but *phew*! Relief cascades through me knowing I don't have to compete with those long legs.

Drinks ordered, pleasantries finished. They don't waste another breath before jumping straight into business.

"So, Martín, how are things going on the West Coast?" Adriano asks, leaning his elbows casually on the table.

Martín busies his hands with tucking his napkin in his lap. "Oh, you know how things are. Busy as usual, but good.

My supply lines are... reliable."

Adriano smiles, but it doesn't reach his eyes. "Reliable. Always good to hear. My contacts in D.C. are looking to expand their contracts this year. We're moving significant numbers and I believe we'll need an additional shipment in a few months." He glances pointedly at Martín. "You're still only managing direct imports from down south, yes?"

"Yes, of course. You know it's better to cut out the middleman when dealing with these cartels. Keeps them honest and the product of the highest quality." Martín really means it's cheaper and gives him more control. More power over the empire he imports. It's all about dollars and image with him. Quality is just a lucky side benefit.

Julianna sits politely, quietly observing us with a subtle, skilled eye. I would've guessed Adriano brought her here as arm candy, much like why Martín brought me, but I can tell she's actively listening. Adriano occasionally defers to her while remaining the main representative of their group. The two men continue chatting about drugs and laundering as casually as most people discuss the weather.

Adriano's hand brushes against my thigh under the table. My breath hitches as I try to ignore the heat coming from him. *Surely that was an accident.* His focus never leaves Martín, the conversation carrying on.

"Wonderful. I'll let you know when we'll need an extra order. Any changes to your orders coming up? I have some unique items coming over the next few months you might be interested in."

"Actually, I think we'll be cutting back our usual order this month..." Martín slips in, almost hoping Adriano will glaze over the statement.

Adriano's eyes narrow, stripping away the layers of masks Martín has plastered on. "Oh? Do you have too much inventory? I thought business was *reliable.*"

Martín bristles. "It is, yes, but I also want to make sure I'm not overstocking. You never know when some cartel leader will be taken out and no longer require our services."

"You're sure that's all?" Adriano leaves his question open-ended, baiting Martín to see how much information he'll give away.

"Sí. It's just for next month; then we'll re-evaluate and see if we need to increase our order again."

He brushes me again, lingering for long enough to know it wasn't an accident. The room shrinks as my chest tightens. Needing a breath of fresh air, I excuse myself to the ladies' room.

Wandering down the hall, I find the bathroom and make a beeline for the sink. The cool splash of water on my wrists and face provides a temporary reprieve from the heat that's been building since Adriano smirked my way.

What the heck, Rosalie. You know better than to be flirting with a goddamn ringmaster! They're awful—all of them. And Adriano is no different. I chide myself.

It's physical attraction, that's all. It's completely normal to be affected by such a gorgeous man. After all, it has been forever since I've been intimate with anyone—apparently too long. With a deep breath, I vow to make time to remedy the situation later.

The bathroom door swings open, my head jerking up as my pep talk is interrupted.

None other than tall, dark, and handsome himself saunters into the woman's bathroom without a care. Confidence rolls off him in waves and makes me question if I'm even in the right bathroom.

"Such a pleasant surprise running into you here." He says, the words slipping smoothly off his sinful lips.

"This is the women's room. I belong here—unlike you," I retort, not caring about the consequences of speaking so rashly to a ringmaster.

Adriano barks out a laugh, the mesmerizing sound drawing me closer. "Oh, chérie, I belong wherever I want to be." He replies with a glint of amusement.

He prowls a step closer to me, instinct driving me back until the wall kisses my spine. I tip my chin up, arching to maintain eye contact as he crowds my space.

"You, little bird, have no business hanging around a man like Martín." The words curl from his tongue, honeyed by a Cajun lilt.

Baring my teeth in a sneer, breath sharp on my lips, I snap back, "You're one to talk—"

His palm catches my cheek. Not rough. Sweet. Tender. My words die in my throat as his hand slides to the nape of my neck, drawing me flush against his unyielding chest.

His other arm braces beside my head, caging me in, his

dark mop of curls spilling forward. When he's smiling like this, he almost has a boyish charm about him. His lips brush against mine, promising ruin. A night of passion filled with more orgasms than a girl can handle.

My knees weaken. His hand drops from the wall to my waist, dragging me closer until his heat brands the curve of my hips. He places a searing kiss on my lips before pulling back. "Do you want me to stop?"

My traitorous body refuses to deny him, my head shaking side to side, every nerve ending flaring with anticipation. "I need your words, Cher."

"Please, don't stop."

The thin tether on his control snaps. His mouth claims mine. At first, a soft exploration, then relentlessly, his tongue plunders like he owns every corner of me. I can clearly feel his cock straining to be free from the fabric of his dress pants. Gasping, my body betrays me as I rub myself against the thick bulge. The friction sparks low and hot, every nerve screaming for more.

He pins me, his body unyielding, allowing me to take what I need.

I writhe against him, climbing higher, grinding desperately in search of relief. It's so close, yet just out of reach. My nails rake his chest, searching for something solid to ground me. A high, helpless sound rips from my throat—a wordless beg—part plea, part surrender.

Adriano doesn't move. Not until my pitched whine breaks into a ragged gasp.

"Please, Adriano."

His hips snap forward, grinding hard against my clit, the jolt of friction nearly undoing me. I'm *so* close. My orgasm is almost at its peak, but I can't quite reach the pools of pleasure I'm after.

His fingers thread through my hair, tugging my head to the side as he leans down, inhaling deeply like he means to consume me. A shudder spreads through my body as I careen closer to release.

He trails hot nips up my neck until his soft lips nibble my earlobe, dragging it between his teeth. A low growl rumbles through him, vibrating into my skin.

"Come for me, chérie."

His command slams through me, detonating the tightly

wound coil inside. It's all I need to tip over the edge. Pleasure crashes in waves, brutal and exquisite, tearing a muffled scream from me as I bury my face in his chest. His grip steadies me, strong and sure, while the aftershocks ripple until I'm nothing but trembling limbs and shuddering breaths.

He slows, grinding to a lazy halt. His touch gentles as though he hasn't just wrecked me with only a few words.

My forehead stays planted on his chest, his scent wrapping around me as I come back to earth. Out of breath and dazed, I'm grateful for Adriano's strong grip. Without his hold, I'd be a puddle on the tiled floor.

Silence permeates. Only the thrum of my heartbeat and the weight of his hand deftly caressing my neck remain. He tilts my chin up, stealing a kiss soft enough to confuse me — danger wrapped in tenderness. His stare softens, and I glimpse something more beneath the steel before I remember who I'm standing in front of.

Reality slowly sets back in. Where we are, who he is. The magnitude of what just happened crashes into my chest. The shame of how I hadn't only allowed it, but had basically begged for it.

I start to shake with fury. My fists, originally grasping his shirt for balance, switch to grips of embarrassment.

"You motherfucker," I fume, putting on my meanest glare. "Just who do you think you are? Coming in here like you own the place!"

Adriano chuckles, "Oh, *mon petit oiseau*, my sweet little bird. You weren't complaining a second ago when you were coming."

With a smirk, he simply turns and leaves the ladies' room. The door shuts with a soft thud and I sink down, burying my face in my hands and elbows on my knees. *What on earth was that, Rosalie?* I chide, resuming my internal beratement.

Trying to make it slightly less suspicious that Adriano and I were gone at the same time, I give myself a moment to settle, getting back into the headspace of a cunning ringmistress before heading out to the group. Adriano's amused eyes track my every movement as I approach, my body aware of his looming presence.

"Ah, Bella, you seem a bit flushed. Perhaps you're under the weather?" Martín asks as I approach the table.

"I must've eaten something that didn't quite agree with me. Apologies for the disruption," I reply. Quickly, I slide back into my chair, thighs still trembling. Daring a side glance at Adriano, he lifts his glass in a mock toast, eyes glittering.

Game on, asshole.

6

ADRIANO

The Manoir Hotel rose before me—more stately manor than a traditional hotel, its quaint feel a deceptive front. Tall, Greek-style pillars line the entire building, giving way to imposing windows along the first floor. Known for its ironclad discretion, it's perfect for meetings where everyone pretends they're civilized.

I'm leaning against my rental car, waiting for Julianna, when she walks past. A stunning goddess.

Her form-fitting black dress has the sides cut out, revealing a smooth tanned waist. She exudes class. Modest, but enticing. She calmly scans the area, clearly checking for someone. Her breath hitches slightly when she notices me, eyes dilating before she straightens and confidently enters the hotel.

Interesting, I muse. Perhaps after this meeting I might have to find out where a certain Latino dream is staying.

Julianna arrives in her beat-down Honda Civic. Despite offering to get her a better vehicle, she insists that having a car that blends in is more important than something flashy and fun. She steps out, looking the part of a powerful ringmistress. She curled her wild red ponytail into giant waves and paired it with one of her favorite green dresses. I'm still daydreaming of a certain raven-haired beauty, but Julianna is stunning in her own right. On the surface, it's easy to mistake her for a simple accessory. That's just one of the reasons why she's the perfect second-in-command. People underestimate her, overlook her, and most importantly, are looser-lipped around her pretty face.

She greets me with a side hug and slides her arm into mine.

"Long time, no see."

She huffs out a breath of air. "Yeah, yeah, let's just get this over with. I was in the middle of running down a lead and got wind of a big auction coming up soon. I'm hoping Martín can spill some details and I can get back to work." That's Jules—all business, no nonsense. She really should loosen up a little, but she's too driven and focused to find value in relaxing.

We head inside to find our usual spot in the back of the hotel restaurant. As the hostess guides us through the maze of dimly lit tables, my sights fall on Martín. As usual, he's dressed to the nines. His greasy mustache twitches rapidly as he stands to greet us, but my focus isn't on him. It's stuck on the woman beside him—the petite curvy siren from the parking lot. Feigning politeness, I shake Martín's hand, barely registering his touch, my gaze locked on hers.

We settle into our seats, Julianna on my right, Rosa on my left. Martín immediately launches into his usual monologue.

Halfheartedly listening, I focus on Rosa. Watching her fight to keep her composure the moment our skin touched was delicious. My cock jerks against my zipper as I envision how responsive her other reactions must be.

Unable to contain myself, I brush against her leg—the temptation to know how her soft skin feels is more than a man can take. She stiffens, every muscle drawing taut over her slim frame at the contact. I carry on the conversation, reading her every reaction as I continue to subtly tease and taunt her under the table.

Had she recoiled or moved her leg away, I would've let it be. After all, an unwilling partner is the last thing I'm attracted to. But she stays, leaning slightly into my touch—so subtly I'm not even sure she's aware she's doing it. The slight parting of her lips, the soft breathiness, the pink flush climbing her neck makes her even more enticing. Despite acting professionally, my touch affects her.

When the little sphinx excuses herself to the restroom, I can't help but follow her like a lost puppy. It's like my body is already addicted and willing to do anything to get another fix.

After our steamy session in the ladies' room, I slip into my chair. Julianna shoots me a knowing glance, slightly accusatory. Not because I'd just been with Rosa—she doesn't care who I sleep with. She does care, however, if the girl I'm interested in happens to be part of the largest trafficking ring west of the Mississippi—possibly in all of North America.

Martín continues gabbing, thankfully noting nothing amiss.

Rosa finally returns from the ladies' room looking flushed but composed. She spends the remainder of the meeting unusually interested in her drink, preferring to nervously swirl it around instead of meeting my eyes. Seems my little bird is shy with an audience.

While allowing her to hang in the background of the conversation, I keep my focus on Martín. I don't want him to notice my infatuation with his ringmistress, but I have a feeling he's already piecing the puzzle together. Despite his oafish act and being a pig of a man, his dark eyes betray glimpses of the cunning intelligence working behind the scenes.

With our drinks finished and no further business to conduct, Julianna and I politely excuse ourselves. After all, we have other shit to do. Martín extends his sweaty paw for a shake. Before letting go, the ringmaster pulls me in close.

"So, Adriano," he says, dropping the formalities, clearly more relaxed as liquor floods his bloodstream. "There's a *very* big opportunity in a few weeks."

I lean in closer to hear his hushed tones clearly. He's piqued my interest. "What kind of opportunity are we talking about?"

"The kind that offers more beautiful girls than Señorita Rosa—for a price, of course." Martín's mustache curls, damp from his drink.

I quirk an eyebrow in Julianna's direction. "When and where?"

"I can't disclose that right now, but if you are interested and plan to attend, I can send you the details prior to the event."

"Surely you can at least tell me if it's near Houston." I pry further, pressing him. "I need to make sure I'm in the area so I don't miss the show."

"Ah, sí, it will be around the Houston area," Martín confirms. "I take it you'll be in attendance?"

"Why, of course, we wouldn't miss this one for the world." I give the handshake one more pump and retract my hand sharply. "Always a pleasure doing business with you, Monsieur Martín. The merchandise never disappoints." The lie sticks to the roof of my mouth.

I'm so distracted mentally juggling the logistics of keeping the circus nearby until the auction, that I almost miss how Rosa's eyes have changed from soft and sweet to sharp and curious. Obviously, she isn't involved in that side of the business if Martín is keeping it out of her earshot.

I plaster on my best laissez-faire smile and pull her close, planting a kiss on the top of her delicate hand. "Pleasure meeting you, Cher. Hopefully we'll be seeing more of each other." I tack on a cheesy wink.

Rosa blushes and turns her head away from Martín to hide her reaction. "It was a pleasure, Señor Devereaux. Until next time."

Mon Dieu, this woman is going to be fun.

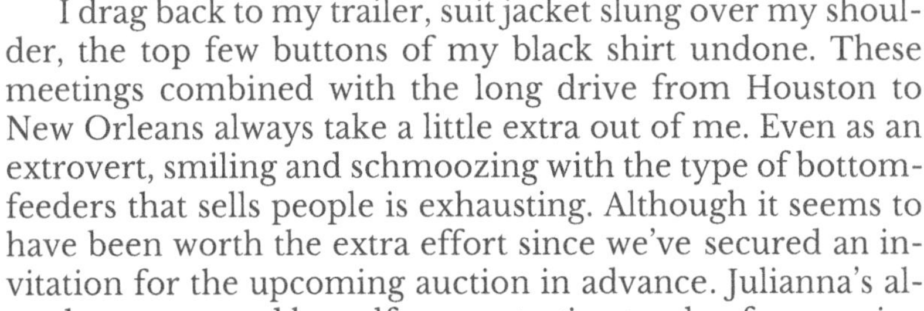

I drag back to my trailer, suit jacket slung over my shoulder, the top few buttons of my black shirt undone. These meetings combined with the long drive from Houston to New Orleans always take a little extra out of me. Even as an extrovert, smiling and schmoozing with the type of bottom-feeders that sells people is exhausting. Although it seems to have been worth the extra effort since we've secured an invitation for the upcoming auction in advance. Julianna's already sequestered herself away, starting to plan for rescuing the girls.

Reaching for my keys, I wiggle the doorknob only to find it unlocked. My gut twists. *Who the fuck has been messing with my trailer? I swear I locked this.* A jolt of adrenaline hits my spine.

My internal alarm bells ring, my gut twisting in anticipation. With a deep breath, I throw the door open and storm into my private space. A young man whips around at my desk mirror. The surrounding lights frame him in their bright glow. Squinting, I recognize the lanky build from the show in New Orleans. *Fuck*. It's Sammy.

I gawk at my younger brother, shocked to see him in the heart of the danger I'd warned him about. *Why the fuck is he here?*

Pain slices through me as I take in the boy I once knew, who is now a young man. Even staring at him, it's difficult to separate them.

Despite our six-year age gap, I've always been protective of my little brother. He was the cutest kid—bright blue eyes and sandy hair like my mother, with the same curly texture that my father and I share.

The Sammy before me is more man than boy. His curly hair's disheveled. Purple bags are etched under his sockets. He's dressed decently, but looks like shit. Stressed and utterly lost.

"Why were you at the show?" I demand.

"Seriously? That's what you care about? No, 'Hey Sammy, how ya been?'"

"Samuel." He flinches at the use of his full name. "Why were you at the show?"

He shoves his hands deep in his pockets, shoulders curved inwards. "It was part of some extra credit assignment for class. I didn't know we'd be dragged to the damn circus."

"What class?"

He mutters incoherently. I step closer. "Sammy. What class?"

"It was for a gym class."

My eyebrows pop up. "Just a normal gym class? What wild athleticism could you have possibly displayed to make them flag you as a circus candidate?"

"It was a gymnastics course..."

"Sammy! What the fuck!" Outrage leaks into my expression. "You know better! Of course someone would notice you! You're the son of goddamn acrobats!"

"I did everything to stay under the radar, A! I was doing poorly enough that I *needed* the extra credit! What more could I do?" Sammy bursts, the tension in the room rising.

I clear my expression, trying to act devoid of all the turmoil swirling in my chest. "You need to leave."

His face drops, his whole body deflating. "Was this from you?" He extends his arm, holding the postcard Julianna delivered to St. Francisville.

I don't answer, cocking my head to the side, letting the silence do the talking for me. Obviously, the postcard was from me. The photo on the front features the circus, *our* circus. It's a classic artistic shot of the show mid-swing. At first glance, it looks like another cheap gift shop item, but hidden in the background, a small acrobat duo flips between bars. The smiling man with extended arms catching the lovely woman midair was none other than our own parents.

"Were the others too?" he presses.

"What others?" My mouth goes dry.

"I'll take that as a no."

"You should head west. The East Coast isn't safe for you anymore."

His eyes bulge. "But I've got class! I have nowhere to stay. No money. What the hell! I'll just lay low until the end of the semester and decline any more extra credit."

There isn't time for explanation, debate, or emotion. Instead, I walk to my oak cabinet and pull out a duffle bag. I never know when we'd have to leave abruptly for one of Julianna's missions or an emergency, so I keep the go-bag stocked at all times. It isn't much, but it's better than the ratty backpack he has slung over his shoulder.

"Here. This should help with the money part," I whisper, handing him the bag. "You can't go back to school, Sammy. It isn't safe. Trust no one. I'm sorry. Good luck."

He reluctantly takes the worn strap, not quite sure how to respond, alternating between disappointed and angry. There isn't enough time to explain our situation, but I know he isn't safe at Cirque du Noir. There's no way for me to protect him and keep him under the radar at the same time. Too many older acts could recognize him. He has to go. Now.

He sighs in defeat, accepting that I wasn't going to be more forthcoming about his situation. I don't even know the answers he seeks. Nowhere is really safe. He walks out of the trailer, both bags slung over his shoulders.

"Leave out the back. Avoid everyone," I whisper as I shut the door behind him. I'm not an overly religious man, but I send up a quick prayer for Sammy's safety and shoot a quick text to Julianna.

S. came to visit. I gave him my
bag. Should help you track him.

She responds almost immediately with a yellow thumbs-up emoji. She'll see that he's handled and safe, while I focus on finding out what's going on. In the meantime, at least the distance from me should help protect him. As long as he's not standing next to me, he has a fighting chance.

7

ADRIANO

Three hours and a tank of gas later, gravel crunches and I pull up to a house I paid for years ago but never visited. Nervously ruffling my hair, I brace for an awkward reunion.

It's been over ten years since I've seen my parents. *Will they recognize me? How will they react? How should I act?* Considering I regularly rub shoulders with criminals and drug lords, a family reunion shouldn't ruffle my feathers. Still, I can't fully silence my inner little boy who desperately craves a warm reception.

After warring for long enough, I finally muster the courage to exit the car.

The house doesn't look remotely like its listing had. While it was modest online, it could currently be the cover of a *Better Homes and Garden* magazine. Overflowing flowerbeds of tulips and wildflowers wrap around the yellow single-story house. Green shutters line each little window. It's the perfect picture of small-town USA. Quiet, well-maintained, and rural. The only thing out of place is the slightly ajar screen door.

Rapping twice, I impatiently wait for an answer. No response, not a peep. *Maybe no one's home?* There are no cars in the drive, so maybe they're both at work. With another loud thump, I try again. This time, the wooden door lets out a bemoaned *creak* as it swings inward.

Crossing the threshold, I call out, "Hello, is anyone

home?"

Only eerie silence answers. I flip a switch, but nothing happens. I flick it a few more times—nothing. Maybe the powers out? Or someone forgot to pay the electric bill?

I draw a few of the curtains to let in some sunlight. The interior is in shocking disarray. Drawers are half open, clothes are haphazardly strewn around, and the pantry has been raided. My nose revolts as I open the fridge to the pungent smell of sour milk and rotten eggs.

"Jesus Christ." I gag, quickly covering my nose and shutting the door with a grimace. A thick layer of dust coats every surface. No one has been here in at least a few months.

Continuing, I hunt for clues. There must be some indication of what the fuck is going on.

Wandering down the hallway, I peek behind a door with a doodled "Keep Out" sign mounted on it. A neat stack of cardboard moving boxes labeled, "Sammy's Room," rests in the corner. Other than the dresser and bed, everything appears to be waiting for a mover more than abandoned. Hope flickers in my chest. *Maybe they're moving?* For one stupid second, I let myself believe Mom finally convinced Dad to downsize. A normal family doing normal things... yeah, that's a possibility.

The shared bathroom is no better. The shower curtain hangs open revealing no toiletries. Soap's dried on the dispenser, and the empty toothbrush stand made it clear the room hadn't been used in a while.

The master bedroom—AKA my parents' room, is at the end of the hallway. This room is only slightly bigger than Sammy's. The closet is littered with bare hangers. A few smaller boxes are stacked in the corner of the room, but not nearly enough to have their entire room packed away.

Venturing further, I enter a small office. A medium desk dominates the room, paired with an imposing filing cabinet and safe. This room is the least packed but is still relatively organized. A single brown envelope rest on the desk, its dust imprint ingrained in the wood. My heart drops at the embossed logo in the bottom corner.

"Fuck," I mutter. "You've got to be kidding me."

Brushing the dirt aside, I pop the two metal tabs, gently shaking out the folder's contents: a letter and stack of photos.

> "It seems we weren't clear enough the last time.
> If you want to avoid an unfortunate accident, you'll do
> as we ask.
> Disappear, or we'll make you.
> Follow these instructions EXACTLY and we'll consider
> sparing you."

The bottom of the note is torn off, the critical directions missing. My blood pressure rises. My breath shallow as my chest tightens. My vision tunnels into a red haze as I fall into a fit of rage.

"FUCK!" I roar, grabbing the nearest object and throwing it into the wall. With a kick, I send the rolling chair flying across the room and proceed to tear the office apart. Dark spots take over as I'm thrown into the recesses of my memories.

⎯⎯⎯⎯⎯ ••●◉●•• ⎯⎯⎯⎯⎯

AGE THIRTEEN

My parents were one of the best trapeze duos in the world. Their skills seemed to have skipped me and went straight to my younger brother instead. They were practicing their normal evening routine while I headed to Armond's trailer.

Armond, our old ringmaster, had taken me under his wing. I didn't know it at the time, but he was molding me. Preparing me. Up until this point, all our time had been spent on legal activities. No blurred lines or illegal exposure.

As I approached his door, a woman barged out—eyes bloodshot, tears streaming down her face as she pulled a bangled scarf over her head. Before I could ask what was wrong, she'd disappeared into the night.

Weird. Not dwelling on it, I eased the door open to my ringmaster's quarters only to find his back to me. He was towering over a rumpled man kneeling before him, sniffling at his feet.

"I'm sorry, Armond, please, it won't happen again!" He groveled.

In a foreign deep tone, my ringmaster replied coolly.

"You're right. It won't happen again. Don't worry, your family will be well taken care of."

The man slumped forward, his shoulders slouching in resignation. Armond's hand snapped up with the speed of a predator. *Pop*. The man crumpled at his feet. A small, precise red dot appeared in the middle of his forehead.

Armond lowered his arm, nonchalantly wiping the pistol barrel on his coat, re-engaging the safety and tucking it into his waistband. Flipping open his phone, he wasted no time ordering "cleaning services" to his quarters.

Shocked, I stumbled backwards, suddenly not comfortable turning my back on this man I'd considered family. I reached behind me, frantically fumbling for the door handle, but as my fingers got a grip on the knob, my shoes let out a stifling squeak. Armond whipped around, instinctively reaching behind him as we made eye contact. His deadly expression immediately lifted, replaced with wide-eyed recognition.

"Shit, Adriano, I didn't see you there." He removed his hand, approaching me with cautious steps.

"I-um, I'm sorry I was j-just stopping by to see what we were w-working on today..." I stammered, my stutter revealing how electrified my nerves were.

Armond schooled his expression into the perfect face of neutrality. "Of course, of course. How long have you been standing there?"

I tried to think on my feet, but also realized that lying and getting caught would be way worse, I told him the truth. "I'm not sure... It doesn't matter though; I won't say anything to anyone! I promise."

"I'm sure you wouldn't. Come, walk with me." He guides me outside.

I shoved my hands deep in my pockets, warily following him out of his trailer. Despite being out in the open air, I could hardly take a full breath. The pumping sound in my ears grew louder as we got closer to the edge of the grounds. Armond slid open a trailer door and sat on the threshold, patting the space next to him. We we're far enough away that we wouldn't be overheard but could still see people bustling about.

"You know, I was about your age when I learned what the circus actually is." He sighed. "But even then, I was too young. Too innocent. Clearly, we share more in common than I'd care to admit." He looked out at the grounds we'd claimed as a temporary home.

"Adriano, you know I think of you as a son, right? And I can't shield you from our world. Even so, I wish you hadn't had to see that."

"And what exactly did I see?" I whispered quietly.

"I thought you saw nothing?" He arches an eyebrow at me. "But if you *had* seen something, you would have seen a man on the receiving end of justice. That man was stealing. Not just from me, but from us—the circus, your parents, even you."

I shook my head, even more puzzled than before. "How could he be stealing from me if I don't have anything to steal?"

"One day, I'll explain everything. Until then I'll give you the choice. Are you ready to learn about the family business?"

"You mean the circus? I already know everything about it."

Armond chuckled, his sharp gaze aimed directly into my soul. "Not the circus, Adriano, the whole business. Our real business."

Nodding hesitantly, I silently agreed, not fully understanding what I'd signed up for, but terrified of what might happen if I refused his offer.

After that, my training changed. Instead of computer work, he'd take me to meetings. As I got older, the types of "meetings" evolved from mostly formal boardrooms to shady warehouses and unmarked docks. My evenings were filled with the screams and tears of anyone Armond declared an enemy. Each encounter etched another dark mark on my soul as I fell into a world that no one knew existed.

Forcing deep breaths, my brain slowly regulates, allowing rational thoughts to seep through the haze. If nothing more, I know two truths:

Truth #1: Armond's been out of the game for quite a long time. No one knows my parents are alive except him, and there's no way he would've come for them.

Truth #2: There's no evidence of a struggle or altercation. Therefore, they must be alive, be it captured or on the run. Either way, I could find them.

My parents were badasses. They grew up like Sammy and I did; embedded in the syndicate culture of violence and survival. So for them to run, it must have been a credible threat. The pit of worry gnaws at my stomach, concern for what drove them away consuming my thoughts.

Wiping the beads of sweat off my forehead, most of my angst and anger is finally worked off, leaving me with a clearer head. With a defeated sigh, I pull out my phone, speed-dialing to the one person I can trust to help unravel this mystery.

"Hey, it's me. I need one more favor..."

Julianna's voice comes through the other end of the line. "Just tell me when and where, A. You know you hardly need to ask."

"I need you to find my parents. They're MIA."

"Done. I'll get right on it."

I hang up and stare at the torn corner of the note still clutched in my fist. Whoever wrote this just declared war on my family. What they don't know is they also just declared war on me. And unlike my parents, I fight back.

8

ROSALIE

After our normal practice, I'm finally able to relax, joining Anna and Phillip for dinner. Filling my stomach, I enjoy their light-hearted banter, regaling tales from "back in their day."

They are like the parents I've always wanted—vibrant, funny, and clearly in love. Even with Phillip's broody tendencies, he's always attentive and dotes on Anna. It's the kind of love that withstands the sands of time.

Anna chatters about a new flip she wants to try. "Please, Phil, we can practice it over the net. It'd be something new to add!"

She's practically vibrating with excitement. Phillip, on the other hand, seems less than amused. "We've talked about this already. No. It's too dangerous and I'm not letting you hurt yourself just for the show." His protective nature slips through, leaving no room for argument. Typically, he isn't a controlling man, happy to stand back and support Anna's blossoming creativity, but he seems to have a hard line for anything he's deemed "too risky." Seeing her face drop a little, he softens, wrapping one of his big arms around her, pulling her onto his lap. It's intimate. Sweet. He turns her chin toward him, dropping his voice to a soothing purr. "We aren't young pups anymore, *mon amour*. We can try something similar, but I wouldn't survive if you got hurt because we were reckless." He presses a kiss to her forehead. "Please, spare me the guilt?"

My heart thuds at their tenderness. Anna's eyes sparkle as she relents. "For your sake, I'll find something else to try.

But mark my words, we'll try it one of these days. We'll just slowly build up to it." She turns to me and winks, pressing a quick peck to his cheek as he sets her back on the bench.

"I've got to rig some more ropes before the show, but I'll see you ladies later." He heads off.

"Well, I can't say I didn't try," Anna sighs. "He's lucky he's so damn hot when he's intense, or we'd never do anything fun."

My mind drifts to a different intense man. One who's been occupying way too many of my thoughts lately. Pressing my legs together, I try to shift discretely, needing to alleviate some of the pressure building.

"Oh, I've got to know what you're thinking about," Anna interrupts my mini daydream. *So much for being discreet.* "I'd know that look anywhere. Who's the man, sweetie?"

It's unfair how intuitive she can be, as though her years of parenting have made her a psychic. "It's nothing serious. I've only met him once, but he was... intense?"

Sensing my internal conflict, she probes thoughtfully. "Does the intensity scare you?"

"No, it isn't so much the intensity... He's gorgeous, powerful, and it doesn't help that he has those stupid side muscles—you know, the ones in addition to the sexy six-pack guys get—obliques." I motion to my sides. "But his job means he's involved in some... less scrupulous activities."

"Ah, so you're conflicted because you're attracted to him, despite your brain telling you to stay away."

"Something like that."

"Well, honey, do you know for sure that he's involved in these things?"

"Not exactly. I mean, I know he's involved in some stuff, but those aren't deal-breakers for me... It's the potential *other* stuff that would be."

"It seems like you should give the poor boy a chance to at least explain himself. If he's got you blushing like that after only meeting him once, it's worth pursuing and seeing if it could grow into something great. Besides, that's a lot of pressure riding on a maybe." She squeezes my arm affectionately. "You'll figure it out. Just give it time."

I'm exhausted. Sleep has evaded me for the last week. Tossing, turning, waking up in a hot sweat. Dreams played out the many different fantasies I'd conjured, featuring none other than Mr. Sexy himself—Adriano. Cold showers weren't enough to hold the heat between my thighs at bay. My subconscious refuses to acknowledge the hard facts: Adriano is a dangerous man. Conscious Rosalie knows this; however, subconscious Rosalie is obsessed with the adonis. Even entertaining a random hookup to take the edge off doesn't sound appealing. Only one man is occupying my mind.

Trudging to my trailer, I find a large box and a smaller bag waiting on my bed with a handwritten note taped to the top:

'Meeting tonight at 7:00 PM
717 Mayberry Drive
Wear the dress. Don't be late.
-M'

Opening the paper edges reveals a neatly folded, maroon dress. Holding it up, I ogle my reflection in my floor-length mirror. It's stunning. Elegant. The soft, stretchy material is designed to hug in all the right places. I slip it on and marvel. It should probably be creepy that Martín knows my exact size, but honestly, with how perfect this dress fits, I don't even mind. The high Grecian-style neckline makes it modest but flirty. The matching four-inch stilettos with delicate clasps to hold them on my ankles complete the goddess look.

I fist pump the air, breaking into my signature happy dance. This was it! The opportunity I've been waiting for since I joined Circo del Sol. The one I've spent so many countless hours training for.

It had taken me years to hunt down Martín Gonzales's name. After my cousin's death, I spent two years running around Mexico, infiltrating different cartels, gangs—really anyone who might have information regarding her disappearance.

I quickly mastered the art of interrogation, learning that having my opponents underestimate me was my greatest strength. Joaquín had my back the entire time, lending me his resources, planning expertise, and training.

I'd made a name for myself: *El Cuervo Libre*—The Free Raven, an assassin and vigilante. My actions remain laser-focused on achieving my goals to avenge Carmen and free anyone that I found being trafficked along the way.

Those who got in the way or withheld information ended up dead.

Those who were oppressed and sold ended up liberated.

After working through dozens of operations, I finally got the name of the asshole who initially ordered Carmen's kidnapping and sold her. The big man himself—Martín Gonzales.

Now that I had a name, Joaquín and I mapped out a plan to get close to him.

Based in San Diego, Circo del Sol is just over the border from TJ. With the amount of daily foot traffic that crosses between Mexico and California, it wasn't hard to find a ride into the US. One of Joaquín's contacts whipped up fake documents and before I knew it, I was outside of the gate for Circo del Sol's evening show, tickets in hand. It was time for step one in executing Martín's demise.

As per Joaquín's training, I needed to observe my prey in his natural habitat. Learn everything about his routine, strengths, and weaknesses before determining the precise moment to strike.

Ticket in hand, I methodically wandered the grounds, cataloging every detail. Each night, the big top came alive. Sitting out of view, I observed Martín as he took the stage. His black top hat matched his slick black mustache and shirt tucked under his red tailcoat. Golden buttons barely held in his pudgy gut and matched the golden frills that lined his shoulders. He stepped out with a sleek baton in hand, ready to direct the show.

The circus began—acrobats twirled above, clowns indulged the house with physical comedy, a human cannonball launched out of the tent, and the horses and lions did tricks while the crowd went wild. In a flash, the show came to an end. The lights dimmed, Martín thanked us for attending, and with a dramatic bow, he dismissed the house.

For the next year, I followed Circo del Sol, trailing up and down the West Coast, taking careful notes. Outside of show hours, I discreetly followed Martín, noting his schedule and contacts.

After the performances in larger cities, I noticed something different. San Diego, L.A., and San Francisco all had a handful of the crowd, mostly college-aged, who'd linger after the curtains closed. I began to loiter longer, only leaving when security came too close to catching me.

Finally, the Vegas show provided the perfect opportunity. Before the show, I found the perfect hiding spot with a good vantage point and low foot traffic. As the show came to an end, I excused myself early and went to my newfound hiding spot.

Just as I expected, after Martín dismissed the regular crowd, a smaller group remained. Martín confirmed everyone else had cleared out, shook hands with the adult of the group, and launched into a short speech spinning tales of life on the road. He ended the sales pitch with an offer: Come join Circo del Sol. When they'd finished classes, if the professors thinks they're worthy and they're interested, all they need to do is reach out to their professor—they'll get in touch with him to schedule your exclusive interview.

My ears perked up. The professors knew how to contact Martín. Finally, I had a plan. Now, I just had to find one of these special professors.

Thankfully, the professor pulled through and I was able to "seduce" Martín with the intention of dismantling his operations from the inside. But ever since he'd let me join the show as his ringmistress, I'd been kept at arm's length from the trafficking side of the business. It was frustrating, but I was patient. Waiting for exactly this opportunity.

It's already 6:15 PM. I have to hurry if I'm going to get ready and make it to the venue on time. If we're meeting another one of Martín's business associates, I definitely don't want to keep them waiting.

Despite rushing, I arrive at exactly 6:58 PM. Instead of another hotel, I find myself gawking through security at a ridiculously oversized McMansion. *Is this a private meeting?* Security interrupts my puzzling as I pass him my clutch.

"Password, Ma'am?"

My forehead wrinkles in confusion. *Password? Martín*

never mentioned a password?

"Umm, I'm here at the request of Señor Martín Gonzales? He didn't mention any password..."

"No password. No entry." He gruffly barks.

I can feel the color draining from my face. I can't mess this up. Not when Martín is finally taking me seriously and including me in more important meetings.

"Please, Señor. I'll just call him, and I'm sure he can clear up this misunderstanding," I plead, trying not to cause a scene.

"There's nothing you can do. Move along." Security begins, only to be interrupted by a harsh, familiar voice.

"Julio, let the lady through. For God's sake, she's with me," Martín commands, emerging from the giant doors behind the guard.

Immediately, the guard's demeanor shifts from aggressive guard dog to submissive puppy. "Of course, Señor Gonzales. Apologies for the misunderstanding." He passes me back my purse and a black masquerade mask.

Martín dismisses the guard entirely, taking me by the elbow and ushering me inside.

As much as I'd like to take the time to admire the vastness of the house, he quickly brings us down a hallway to what appears to be a ballroom filled with high cocktail tables. Other masked patrons sport fancy drinks and are engaged in friendly conversation. Martín swipes a champagne glass from a tray and passes it to me. Turning us away from the crowd, Martín leans in, whispering in a hushed tone. "Enjoy the evening, Rosa. Look pretty, make people comfortable. We'll catch up in the morning."

He rushes away, leaving me stunned, holding a glass of untouched champagne. Spinning, I carefully take in my surroundings, trying to deduce what type of event this could possibly be. My gaze gravitates past the other guests toward the back tables. A tall, lean masked figure is on the edge drinking alone. Despite his face being half covered, I'd recognize that chiseled body anywhere. After all, it's been the object of many forbidden fantasies since the bathroom incident.

His aura projects dark and dangerous enough that the people are intentionally sticking to the opposite side of the room to avoid crossing his path. His crisp black suit sends a tingle pulsing toward my thighs. Unlike everyone else who is chattering happily, he seems like he'd rather be literally anywhere else.

Our eyes lock. Even behind the mask, his stare is possessive, as though he's already mentally stripped me bare. I can't break eye contact, my feet compelled to him on their own accord.

I came here to burn this empire down. And he's looking at me like he's about to light the match.

Well, here goes nothing.

9

ADRIANO

Five hours of highway and one stupid password later, I'm standing in an ostentatious ballroom pretending I'm pleased to be on the exclusive guest list. Too many times I've put on a monkey suit and pretended to support Martín's fucked-up endeavors.

Based on the cocktail tables and how everyone is milling around, you'd almost mistake this for a networking event. Cocktail in hand, I loom in the shadows, waiting for the main event. I won't have more than one, but fuck, I need something to help take the edge off this sordid affair.

Usually, Julianna's with me as a buffer, working the room and gathering intel. But instead, I'm alone until she walks in.

She systematically scans the room until her chocolatey eyes land on mine. Champagne flute in hand, she glides over to my corner. Her sexy heels click softly. Her maroon dress is poured perfectly over every curve. She's breathtaking.

The crowd parts and my cock forgets we're in hell as the object of my secret obsession approaches. Then reality slams back: if she's here, she's one of them.

My mind reels with possible excuses for her attendance, but ultimately my gut sinks knowing she's involved at all with this world. I shake my head in an attempt to erase my disappointment. Of course she's involved. Martín is literally the host. As his ringmistress, there's no way she isn't involved in his dirty work.

Ahem, "Fancy meeting you here, Ringmaster." She offers

formally. "I didn't expect to see you tonight." Her Spanish lilt coats every word, sweet as honey.

"The feeling's mutual, little bird. What brings you here?" I probe, still trying to deduce her purpose for attending. "Did Martín bring you to window shop?"

With a sultry laugh, she replies, "Oh no, Señor Gonzales insisted I come, then disappeared on me. Perhaps you could keep me company instead, since we're both alone?" She leans closer and rests her hand on my chest; her fingertips daintily stroke my lapels.

The casual intimacy of her touch is a welcome distraction. The forbidden pleasure immediately countered by the bitter knowledge that this sweetness is a beautiful mask, concealing her intentions for attending.

The large ballroom doors thud shut at 7:15 PM on the dot.

"Ahem—ladies and gentlemen. Thank you for joining us tonight. We have some special merchandise, curated specifically with you in mind." Our host announces. "Please, follow me and we shall begin."

I glance at Rosalie, who is watching the announcer thoughtfully. She places her arm in mine. "Shall we?"

"Of course, Cher, lead the way."

We're funneled through a large, ornate archway, winding downstairs toward the basement in a tight spiral. The dim lighting flickers, mirroring candlelight and setting a grim ambiance.

Rosa grips my arm tighter. I assume it's so she can balance easier. Her sexy stilettos are more fit to be over my shoulders than for traversing concrete.

We reach the bottom of the spire and the space opens into a long room. Cages barely large enough to turn in line one wall. Narrow. Bare. Medieval. In front of each cage, a terrified young girl stands at attention, bound in place by large iron manacles, forcing their arms behind their backs in a submissive stance. They're dressed in crisp white garbs—enhancing the image of their innocence.

Inspections begin. Strictly looking, no touching, but it's uncomfortable nonetheless.

Rosa's nails dig deep into my arm, supporting what must be close to her full weight. Her knees wobble subtly, and despite having a mask on, I can see the color draining from her face as she registers the horror before her. *Interesting. Maybe she isn't familiar with this business after all.* I think, happy to support her while she finds her footing.

It doesn't take long for her to lock her knees and slam on a mask of indifference. Her vice-like grip hasn't loosened, but no one else noticed her visceral reaction. Moving us deeper into the room, I feign interest in the merchandise. It's important I know exactly the number of girls and their general descriptions. Since I can usually only get away with purchasing about a third of them outright, I create a mental catalog of the others so Julianna can track them down later.

Typically, this is when having Julianna around is the most beneficial. Not only does she get first-hand information on the buyers and the girls, she also puts on an Oscar-worthy performance. Any girls who look like they're unlikely to make it through the first night or are under a certain age, Jules adopts the role of a spoiled rich woman who simply *must* have "that one" or else she'll just die. It's cringy to a point, but pretty damn effective. Since we're such big players at these events, by making her interest known for a specific person early on, the other bidders often won't even bother bidding against us. They know that whatever she wants, ultimately she will get, so why bother running up a tab. It helps us keep costs down and opens our budget to save extra girls directly from the auction.

Unfortunately, despite suspecting that Rosa might be disgusted by this business, I don't know her well enough to trust that she could take Jules's place in our dynamic duo.

We follow the procession of inspections. Because this auction is a *special* event, there are more buyers and girls than usual. Typically, there are fewer than twenty people on the block, but tonight's event features closer to forty people for sale.

Rosa clings to me like a lifeline, her nails carving shallow half-moons into my skin. Her perfect stoic mask reveals nothing about her true feelings, but those curved claws act as constant reminders of her secret discomfort. I like that she chose me to be her support. My body craves the proximity, and being around such helpless victims raises my protective hackles.

For tonight, I'm the only thing keeping her upright in this nightmare. By tomorrow, I'll likely be another monster instead.

10

ROSALIE

I thought the worst part would be the masks and the champagne. I was wrong. The worst part is the smell when the ballroom doors close behind us: fear, concrete, and something metallic that coats the back of my throat like blood.

It takes me longer than I'd care to admit to figure out exactly what type of function this was. This was the perfect embodiment of watching wolves in sheep's clothing. The fancy gowns, the alluring masks, the sweet cocktails. Everyone was masquerading around with an air of entitlement and money. Snobs who are as likely to be walking the red carpet or attending a gala were buyers.

Never did I expect that Martín would go from my first formal meeting with another circus to throwing me into at an auction almost overnight.

At first, seeing Adriano sent a rush of heat to my core. He was even more dashing in all black. The sharp edges of his suit cut perfectly to his slim frame. When he extended his arm to me, I was fool enough to be flattered that among all the other beautiful women present, he was choosing me. Tamping down the butterflies, I naively accepted his invitation and ignorantly walked straight into the lion's den.

It wasn't until we rounded the last steps to the basement that I realized what was going on. Over the years, I've had my share of up-close and personal experiences with victims of trafficking. But until now, I've never actually seen firsthand what the sales process entailed.

The air shifts, growing heavy and stale—a metallic tang of fear seeping through. Despite the bright lights, it feels darker, dimmer. The incessant muffled music from the ballroom above now pulses like a mocking heartbeat.

My knees almost give out at the horrors before me. Cages. Torturous metal confinements line the walls. Worse than the empty cages are the poor girls forced to stand outside of them. Still bound but exposed to the crowd. The scent of cool concrete, expensive cologne, and the raw, coppery scent of panic permeates the space.

The sharp points of my stilettos dig into the hard floor; the restrictive satin of my dress constricts my chest. Adriano's steady, warm grip is the only thing that keeps me upright as the trauma from my youth is thrust forward. The scene doesn't just remind me of Carmen; it's the realization that this was the type of hell she must have endured.

AGE TEN: TIJUANA, MEXICO

The house was fragrant with sugar and cinnamon. Perched on a stool, I watched my older cousin, Carmen, knead dough for her infamous *conchas*—a sweet, shell-shaped bread. Even though it was midweek, I was home from school with a slight fever—making the already relentless heat feel even hotter, and I was dying from boredom.

"Pleaseee, Carmen! I'm feeling a million times better!" I begged, desperately wanting to help.

She quirked her eyebrows in a mom-like fashion. "You're sick, Rosita, and should be resting. Tía would be upset that I even have you sitting in here, let alone if I let you help."

While accurate, her valid point didn't dissuade me from nagging relentlessly. "But Carmen, I'm totally fine. See!" I jumped to the floor, doing a little dance—wriggling about as though movement was proof that I was no longer ill.

Laughing at my foolish moves, she left the mixing bowl, kneeling down to bring her chin to my forehead. "Hmm, you aren't burning up anymore. I'll tell you what, go wash your hands. I'll finish the dough, but you can help mix the ingredients for the cinnamon topping. Okay?"

"Yes!" I squealed with joy, crushed her in a quick hug, and raced off to the bathroom.

Buzz. The doorbell sounded, a sharp interruption.

Perhaps Tía Maya or mama came home for their lunch break? I hurried, but before I could make my way back to the kitchen, Carmen rushed to the door, her face suddenly blanched against her tan skin. "Rosita," she whispered. "I need you to stay in the bathroom for a little while." The door buzzed again, louder this time. "It'll be like when we play hide-and-seek. You have to do an extra good job at hiding, okay?"

She glanced over her shoulder at a scraping sound at the front door. "No matter what you might hear, I need you to stay here. Don't open the door and don't make a sound."

She was scaring me. Her usual friendly demeanor was gone, replaced by a hard, serious exterior. "Promise me, Rosalie."

Sniffling a little—partly from my runny nose, partly because I was scared. "But Carmen, you promised I could help you…"

She forced a smile. "Please, Rosita. If you're extra quiet until I come back, I'll let you pick an extra concha. Think of it like a special challenge." Even though she was in a hurry, she knew my favorite game of hide-and-seek, and I was always excited to play.

Being too young to understand the seriousness of the strain behind her smile, I agreed. What kid doesn't want more of their favorite *pan dulce*?

A few minutes passed with scuffling and thuds from the kitchen. Then silence.

I waited. Curled under the sink, my little muscles ached from being squished. Eventually, the faint ringing of the oven timer beeped, signaling the conchas were ready. Carmen would come get me soon.

She never came back.

For three years, we desperately clung to hope that she'd return to us safely. I'd spent countless nights wishing on shooting stars, and praying to any god who would listen—

offering anything I could in exchange for her safe return.

The guilt and ache in my chest consumed me day after day. I missed her. Missed how each morning she'd braid my hair. Missed how she'd patiently help me with my homework. Missed her warm laugh.

Then the *policia* came.

My mama and tia's broken wails echoed the horrors the officers delivered.

My precious, wholesome Carmen had been found. Her body was dumped like common trash in a ravine outside the city, battered and bruised. Her once luscious curves deteriorated, starved to skin and bone. The closure I'd thought I wanted turned out to be the catalyst for true anguish.

How can I be expected to simply mourn and move on when she died protecting me?

Our family was devastated, stuck processing our grief and withdrawing from each other.

It was at her funeral, staring at the closed casket, that I made a vow: I wouldn't just mourn Carmen. Better than revenge—I would avenge her by taking out the sick assholes who preyed on the young and innocent.

The tragedy of what happened to Carmen is part of the baggage I still haul around. The weight sometimes feels too heavy to bear. But I'd never dwelled on how horrific the process of being sold and bought would be. These girls haven't even been assaulted yet, but the trauma from simply being inspected is enough to make my skin crawl. My determination to dismantle their trafficking ring is cemented even further in my resolve.

Forcing the memories of Carmen down, I lock on a calm exterior, letting raw, cold determination take over. An emotionless mask that matches our black masquerade masks. I wouldn't fail these girls. I couldn't. I follow Adriano deeper into the hall of horrors, memorizing every masked monster and every chained girl. Le Fantôme will get the list, then I'll come back to save them all.

And then I'm coming back to burn this place to the ground with or without him in it.

II

ADRIANO

Bidding for our first fifteen-year-old girl begins. A young blonde with plaited braids is brought on stage. She fixates on the floor, likely wishing it could swallow her whole, while the announcer introduces her for bidding. This "special" auction maintains a specific theme: young virgins. I cringe at the reality that enough twisted fucks exist to warrant these "specials."

Raising my paddle, I kick off the bidding at a crisp $100,000. It's a declaration. I'm not just bidding; I'm marking my territory.

"Do we have $150,000?" The auctioneer rattles on. A man in a tux that is one size too small puts his paddle in the air.

The auctioneer gestures to him and turns back to me. "$150,000. Do I hear $200,000?"

I nod, accepting the new bid.

"$200,000 for this lovely virgin. Do I hear $250,000?"

A new bidder enters the fray. An elderly man who looks like he'd be more at home at bingo night than here. These poor victims can be sold to anyone for any purpose. Sadly, many are trafficked into some kind of sex work. A sheen of desperation to save her coats my skin.

"$500,000." I shout, the warning setting the tone: these are mine, back off. I've had enough of these stupid games and need to shut this shit down fast.

The auctioneer smirks with glee. "I have $500,000 from this gentleman; do I hear $600,000?"

The room is crickets. No one dares to raise a direct bid from me. They know a direct challenge is a death sentence for their businesses. Julianna would love nothing more than to dismantle their personal lives and businesses brick by brick in retaliation.

"SOLD!" the auctioneer bellows. "For $500,000 to number 144. Your merchandise will be available for pickup immediately following the auction."

Releasing a shallow breath, I glance down to find wide brown eyes staring at me. For someone so entrenched in this world, the shadows in her stare are far too heavy. They grow as she analyzes me, as though she's finally seeing the monster lurking beneath my facade. As much as I'd love to reassure her that my intentions are pure, I'm sure watching me drop hundreds of thousands of dollars to buy another person paints me in a pretty dim light.

I intertwine our fingers and refocus my attention on the next girl shuffling to the block.

The remainder of the auction is a blur. I successfully bought eighteen of the girls, which is more than the third I'd hoped for. Rosa likely thinks I run an eclectic stable on the side, but only a handful of girls remain to rescue later. I flip Jules a discreet text with the total so she can send transportation for the girls.

Just as the auction is winding down, Martín takes the mic from the auctioneer. "I know it's highly unusual, but we have a special surprise for last!" He rumbles to the crowd.

The host ushers the "surprise" to the podium. A surge of disdain boils my insides. *This motherfucker.* Rosa turns to me, panic flitting across her face as her other hand digs into my forearm to steady herself. Her pulse is hammering so hard it reverberates through my sleeve. I shut down all emotion. Now more than ever, I need to be formidable and ruthless.

Front and center are a set of twins, a boy and a girl. The spotlight highlights their tanned skin and kinky hair, a contrast to their matching outfits: a pale blue dress and a white shirt with blue pants. Clinging tightly to each other, their light eyes peer at the terrifying ring of masked strangers surrounding the podium.

"This unique pair hails all the way from the Dominican Republic. They're a ripe four years old and have never been separated before. We'd love to sell them as a duo, but if we must, we'll auction them off separately." The auctioneer babbles on, having taken the mic from Martín. "Bidding will begin at $500,000!"

Before he can jump into the usual banter of bidding, I raise my paddle and bellow, "Two million dollars."

Silence swallows the crowd, the entire room enveloped by the dark aura pouring off me. To most people, the millions we dropped at auctions was a ton of money, but for a multi-billion dollar business like Cirque du Noir it was barely a drop in the metaphorical bucket. My bid was ridiculously high, but the money wasn't what stopped their breath; it was the taste of danger I was oozing.

The auctioneer glances at Martín, seeking direction on how he should proceed. Martín raises an eyebrow, then dips his chin subtly, cueing him to accept my bid. A smirk crawls onto my face. I knew he had no choice but to accept my offer.

"SOLD! For the final price of $2 million to the generous buyer number 144." He concludes, joyfully setting his wooden gavel on the podium. "Your purchases will be available for pickup by the side entrance. Please don't forget to return your masks and paddles to security on your way out. Thank you for attending and goodnight!"

The crowd scatters, everyone trying to gather their things and get organized to collect their latest acquisitions.

I run my fingers through the top of my curls, a nervous habit that I can't seem to kick. Rosa slowly extricates her hands from mine, stepping back like I'm contagious. I know how this looks. I deserve her disdain. But fuck, it stings worse than any bullet I've taken.

She refuses to make eye contact with me, finding a sudden interest in the floor.

"Goodbye, Señor Devereaux." She mutters in a sharp hiss before she scurries off to security, disappearing without a glance.

Fuck. This was one of the most brutal events I've ever attended. Sure, they are always nauseating, but between Julianna's absence and Rosa's reactions, my insides were churning. Twenty girls were saved, but one woman just decided I'm the devil. Tonight, she might be right.

12

ADRIANO

We had just enough space in the vans Julianna coordinated to fit all eighteen girls, but we needed room for my two last-minute additions—the twins.

Leading them to my car, it takes some convincing, but they finally detach for long enough to load them into the back seat. Without car seats, I do my best to get them safely buckled before hopping into the driver's seat.

Ring, Ring.

"What?" Julianna's agitated voice booms through my car stereo.

"Hope I'm not interrupting."

She mumbles something unintelligible while multitasking with whatever she'd been working on.

"We had a surprise addition to our group. I need a place to send two four-year-old twins. A boy and a girl."

"Shit," Julianna swears. "I can find someone, but it'll take me a day or two. Most places aren't equipped to take on multiple young kids without notice. And I don't want to split them up... I can make some calls, but you'll have to hang onto them for now." She instructs.

"Not a problem. I'm bringing them back to the grounds, but keep me in the loop."

"Sounds good, I'll be in touch. Gotta go." She rushes, a loud bang echoing before her line disconnects.

The twins raw innocence and vulnerability struck close

to home. The guilt of bringing them deeper into this life is riding me hard. I'd spent my entire life trying to keep kids like these out of this path. Even as a younger man, I'd sold my soul to become this monster to give my own brother a chance at escaping it.

EIGHTEEN YEARS OLD

It was opening day, so we had opened the doors to the circus early for those who had purchased backstage tickets to come and watch the "behind-the-scenes" of circus life. The big top was bustling. My parents were doing their thing, flying overhead with an otherworldly grace, while they did final checks for sound and lights. Plenty of other adults and families were around monitoring the tent and visitors.

As usual on show nights, I was in charge of watching Sammy. At the exciting age of twelve, he was a constant chatterbox, babbling about everything and anything, and really didn't need that much supervision. Not thinking much of it, I'd left him backstage to watch our parents warm up while I used the restroom. He wouldn't go far, and besides, plenty of trusted adults were around to babysit him.

Scurrying off, I did my business and quickly stopped to grab some popsicles from Chef on my way back. I swear I was only gone for five minutes, *maybe* ten minutes max.

Stepping through the tent flaps, I made my way back to where Sammy should've been waiting. But instead of where I'd left him, he lay motionless on the ground. I rushed to his side in a panic.

His left arm was contorted at an abnormal angle and his right eye swollen. The hitched rise and fall of his chest was the only indication that he's still alive.

"Sammy! Wake up! Oh God. Help! Someone call for help!" I dropped to my knees in the dirt, scared to touch him without causing more damage. Purple bruises already tinging his pale complexion.

"Sammy, can you hear me? Come on, please wake up. Mom! Dad! Please, someone help. Hang on, Sammy, just hang on."

My parents, who'd just finished their set, rushed over at my screams. My mom dropped beside me and desperately clutched Sammy to her chest, begging him to wake up. My dad had his cellphone already plastered to his ear as he barked orders to some poor 911 operator. Before long, ambulance sirens penetrated the chaos, forcing everyone out of the way. EMTs loaded Sammy, carefully avoiding jostling his broken arm. His small face covered by a plastic oxygen mask, my parents loaded into the back with him, accompanying him to the hospital.

As they carried him on the stretcher, a small note clutched in his fist fluttered to the ground.

'Consider this a warning.
You think you can just waltz right in and take over,
but no kid like you deserves a seat at the table.
Drop out now or your "backup" here will go missing.'

My blood chilled. *What the fuck.* I shook as I snatched the note for a closer look. Nope, I had read it right. Some asshole was threatening me. Not only me, but my family. There was no question about what they were implying. Sammy wasn't safe here. No one was if they could do this in broad daylight. Clearly, being surrounded by over a hundred people wasn't a deterrent.

I was seething by the time I tracked Armond to his trailer, my temper sharpening with every step. Knocking once and flinging the door open, I marched into his space. The ringmaster was at his desk with a ridiculous pair of reading glasses perched on the bridge of his nose, surrounded by stacks of paperwork cluttering his desk. He caught the murderous glint in my stare, quickly setting aside whatever he was working on.

"Adriano, to what do I owe the pleasure?"

Wordlessly, I dropped the note on his desk and began pacing the room—stalking back and forth like a caged tiger. He cocked an eyebrow before picking up the letter. His jaw tightened as he skimmed the text. He reread it a few times before he took off his reading glasses, dangling the frames in one hand, while the other pointed at the crumpled sheet on the desk.

"What the fuck is this?"

My nails bit into my palms. "Someone beat Sammy to a pulp. He can barely open his eyes and his arm is broken. This was all they left behind"

He leaned forward, folding his arms. "So, what are you going to do about this?"

I paused my pacing, my head snapping up to glare at him. Gritting my teeth, I answered. "What am I going to do about this? Don't you mean what are *we* going to do about this?"

His hard, blank stare met me. "This threat wasn't for me. My enemies know better than to send empty threats my way. If I had to guess, this was them testing you. They've seen you by my side, but you've never given them any reason to fear or respect you."

I began to pace again, letting loose a laugh that would have made any madman proud. "Fear? Respect? HA! What the fuck, Armond. I've watched you kill men and never once have I cowered. My callouses have callouses from the pain I've inflicted on your behalf. I've bled and made plenty of others bleed. But I'm not in charge of shit! This threat is personal, but it doesn't make sense. What have I ever done to these fuckers?"

"That's where you'd be wrong, son." His voice softened slightly. "Did you really think I bring you along just to keep you busy? You're smarter than that. I have plenty of people I could bring to meetings if I simply wanted company—plenty with way better looks too." He chortled, pointing his finger at my chest. "No, Adriano, I have you along because *you* are the future. This is my way of preparing you. I can't be ringmaster forever and have no children of my own. I have to pick a successor and can't think of anyone better for the position than you."

Me? The ringmaster? My whole body went rigid. "Seriously? The fuck! You didn't even bother to ask me!"

"I don't need your permission, boy." He challenged, irritated by my tone and blatant disrespect. "Remember, I don't have to ask you for shit. You do as you're told."

I snapped. "And what has that gotten me? My family is in fucking danger because of you!"

"So do something about it." He growled. "Everyone in this life is in danger. Grow the fuck up."

By this point I'm spiraling. I didn't ask for this. He was right. I did exactly as I was told. When he said heel, I heeled. When he needed someone roughed up, I rolled up my sleeves. If Armond demanded it, I obeyed. Every. Fucking. Time. The perfect puppet, playing chess when I didn't even know a game was being played. Yet here I was, tangled in strings. I flopped into the chair facing his desk, slouching into the cushions.

"I don't know what I can do." I sighed in defeat, burying my head in my hands, my fingers tugging at my roots. "But I have to do something. I can't let my family get hurt. They did this in broad fucking daylight—surrounded by tons of people! It could even be one of our own, for fuck's sake, sitting right under our noses." My despair flared at the violation.

He seemed to contemplate my words, formulating a plan of attack. "I believe I might have a way to find out who's responsible. But are you ready to do what it takes to eliminate the threat? You need to set an example, so everyone thinks twice about crossing you."

"I don't think I have much of a choice. There's too much at stake to do nothing." I resigned.

"Well then, let's fix this mess."

I spent the next few days hunting down anyone possibly involved in the threat. The drive to protect and defend my family was more of an animalistic impulse than passion. But even with the immediate threats removed, I needed to guarantee that Sammy and my parents wouldn't be in danger with my new role determined. Their safety mattered more than anything else.

By the wee hours of the morning, Armond and I had come to an agreement. Now we just needed to tell my parents.

My parents were *not* on board with our plan. Not even a little. But Armond and I had already struck a deal: I would continue as his right-hand, enforcer, and goon until he was ready to retire. Then, I would take his place as the ringmaster of Cirque du Noir.

The trade-off for selling my soul, operating in the shadows, and committing to this path at such a young age is that he would grant my parents early retirement and my little brother's existence would be forgotten—erased from all circus life.

All the logistics had been sorted. An unfortunate "accident": no survivors, a fictional car fire, a forged police report—no evidence. With a few greased palms and our pull with some local law enforcement, no one would dig deeper, and my family would be declared "dead."

My parents would receive a lump sum of cash to help get their feet under them, but they could never come back to circus life. Blacklisted. No longer welcome in the circuit.

At first, my parents tried to refuse. Not to leave the life; after Sammy's injuries, that was an easy decision. They refused to leave me behind. But at eighteen, the circus and Armond already owned me. I'd seen too much, done too much, and knew too much.

So despite their protests, they had to do what Armond ordered. No one defied him, and that wasn't about to change. Hell, they were lucky he was helping them get out at all. No one left the circus; not unless it was in a body bag. The circus was for life.

Within the hour, we held the documents of three new identities:

Anna Jones, Phillip Jones, and Samuel Jones.

With the insurance money from their "accident," and my first paycheck they were able to purchase a small but quaint fixer-upper in a one-horse town in Louisiana. It was just far enough outside of the normal circus tour routes to be safe, but close enough that I could monitor them from afar.

They packed up as much as they could fit into one of our spare circus cars and left under the cover of night. Off to start their new lives with their new identities.

I grieved their absence, but this was for the best. This was the only way to protect Sammy and make sure he didn't get forced into this life. Once it was public knowledge that the future ringleader had a younger brother, he would have a permanent target painted on his back. Family was everything—but in this world, family was a fatal vulnerability. I wasn't about to have any weaknesses that could be exploited when I took over. Besides, keeping Julianna and myself alive was going to be hard enough.

••●● ● ●●••

As much as I wanted to keep the twins far from the circus, it was too late. They were already in too deep and the safest place for them now is under the protection of Cirque du Noir.

Checking the rearview mirror, the staggered street lamps sporadically illuminate their precious faces. They've reached across the backseat to hold hands, determined to stay together as they silently observe their surroundings. Since I couldn't convince them to separate, they're secured in the rear seat directly behind me and in the middle seat.

"Hey," I say in the gentlest tone I can muster. "My name is Adriano. I'm here to help." Hopefully, a warm introduction demonstrates my good intentions. They both stare wide-eyed back at me, tightly clinging together.

"I'm sure this whole thing has been really hard on you both, but you're safe now. You are safe and I'll make sure you don't have to be worried about getting separated." I babble on, trying to connect and reassure them as much as possible. "What are your names? Are you hungry? We'll be going to my home where we can get you some food and whatever else you might need." About halfway through my rambling, I realize that they might not even understand or speak English. *Duh! I'm such a fricken moron.* Digging into my memory, I dredge what little Spanish I know to help set them at ease.

"*Hola amigos.*" Their little ears perk up at their familiar mother tongue, still eyeing me warily, but actively listening. Quickly, I realize that's as much Spanish as I really know. *Merde*

I turn on some quiet tunes for the long, monotonous drive back to New Orleans. Before long, their soft snores echo from the backseat. The adrenaline from the auction finally subsides as they rest for the remainder of the journey.

We pull into the circus grounds. Before unbuckling them, I point to myself. "Adriano." Then I point to them and raise my shoulders, miming my question. When they're both out of the car, the little boy points his tiny thumb toward himself. "Daniel." Then he gestures to his sister, who has tucked herself behind him. "Maribelle." His strong stance belies the young boy inside, who is understandably terrified. Yet, despite this paralyzing fear, he courageously steps up as his sister's protector.

Acknowledging his gift of trust with a nod, I shuffle us toward the cookhouse to see what kind of food we can rustle up for their famished tummies.

All kids gravitate toward Chef. I'm not sure if it's because he closely resembles Santa sporting a jolly belly or because he always smells like food, but the twins take to him instantly. He whips together some mac and cheese with little bites of hot dogs cut up into it. The perfect meal for little ones. They dig in, clearly starving, and scarf down as much food as their little bellies can hold.

After they'd eaten their fill, their eyes glazing over from exhaustion, I usher them to our resident fortune teller, Baba's tent. A quick jingle on the makeshift doorbell and we're greeted by a lovely older gypsy woman. Right away, little crows' feet crinkle at the corners of her weathered face. Her wily gray hair is tucked under her magenta bandana, arms hidden by a slew of loose bangles.

"Hey, Baba. Sorry it's late. Odds you'd have space for these two for the night?"

Her smile grows. "Of course, Adriano, I always have room for a few more. They can stay as long as they need or want to."

"I appreciate it, Baba. I don't think they understand English, but figured that wouldn't be much of a problem. Keep me updated if it becomes too much. I'll check in on them first thing in the morning."

Unfortunately, she and her late husband were unable to have kids of their own, so Baba spent her youth traveling the world, collecting languages as easily as shiny trinkets. Over the years she's been an amazing foster grandma, always over the moon to provide a loving home. Our resident polyglot is the perfect candidate to connect with our little Dominican guests.

She steps aside, inviting the twins to explore their new temporary home. Their stiff, timid stances slowly relax as she jabbers in Spanish. Who knows, this might even become their new permanent home. Our resident fortune teller has the perfect temperament for raising them on the road, and it would be easier to keep them safe if they were raised here. Baba closes the tent flap behind them, her silhouette already kneeling to their height, arms open.

I hover in the dark until the lantern inside goes out.

Twenty kids were saved. One brother lost. One woman who thinks I'm the devil. And two four-year-olds who just learned the world is full of monsters.

Welcome to the circus.

13

ROSALIE

There isn't enough bleach in Texas to wash tonight away. I scrub my skin raw, settling for scalding water painting my skin a bright, angry red as I attempt to wash away the guilt.

I stood by and watched while people were sold to the highest bidder. Worst of all, the man of my earlier fantasies has morphed into the worst offender of everything I'm fighting against. He was fierce, competitive, and unyielding. My newest self-declared enemy.

He bought children. What kind of monster does that!

A tall, sexy monster. My subconscious mocks. *The monster who held you up when you nearly collapsed. A monster who purchased countless lives without hesitation.* I let the burning water absolve my thoughts, the heat loosening the knots in my stomach.

It might be too late to save every girl on my own, but I'm going after the twins. I'll find them, no matter what. My reflection hardens, the darker edges of my personality coming to the surface. I'm done watching. It's time to go hunting.

Hours later, I'm only a half mile from Cirque du Noir's site. My phone buzzes with a location from an unknown number. *Dammit.* I don't have time to help and save the twins tonight. For the first time, I decline the opportunity in pursuit of my own rescue mission. At least Le Fantôme is working tonight, hopefully rescuing the girls from the auction. Setting my phone to silent, I stuff my pockets with the essentials, secure my blade in my thigh holster, and begin the short hike toward the big top. My black tactical gear paired with my favorite combat boots helps me blend into the shadows—think old-school cat burglar meets modern special ops badass.

I'm ready for the next step: locate the twins.

Slinking to the backyard, I clamber over the defensive temporary barrier that encircles the grounds. Avoiding the security guards, I stick close to the perimeter, searching for the ringmaster's trailer. If anywhere is going to have a paper trail or clues about the twins, it would have to be stored in Adriano's personal space.

Much to my surprise, I don't find his trailer located at the center of the lot, like Martín's, but conveniently nestled near the back, slightly apart from the others.

Checking my watch, *4:00 AM. Perfect.* Adriano is probably off with one of his latest purchases, so it should be empty.

Double-checking that the coast is clear and hearing the soft hum of chatter and laughter floating from the cookhouse, I get to work. Slinking around, I do my best to avoid drawing attention to myself while I try the door handle.

Locked. *Humph*, of course it is. *Why can't anything be easy today?* Pulling out my tools, I get to work picking the lock, whispering sweet nothings to the cool metal, listening for the soft, distinct *click* indicating the mechanisms are aligned.

With the final peg in place, I hold my breath and ease the door open. The latches are silent and the lock simple. Thank God, or I would've wasted precious time, extra time the twins didn't have.

Tiptoeing through the door, I turn and ease it shut, making sure it stays unlocked for an easier escape. *"Phew."* I let out a small sigh of relief. Now for the next step of my plan— search Adriano's trailer for any clues about where he sent the twins.

I just need to locate where he stashed them and get them off the grounds. Once I have them, I'll text the Phantom and beg them to coordinate a last minute drop-off.

"Looking for something?" A deep voice startles me out of my thoughts.

Whipping around, my hand flies to my chest, the other instinctively hovering over the knife at my thigh. Looming in the shadows sits none other than the devil himself—Adriano.

He leans back in the chair, the casual sprawl looking deceptively relaxed. His black shirt hangs loosely with the top few buttons undone and a towel draped across his shoulders. His rolled sleeves show off intricate designs inked on his forearms. The short tendrils of wet curls are mussed from his fingers running through them. His deep brown eyes are disarming, instead of hard and sharp like at the auction; they're filled with amused curiosity. He's breathtaking. If it weren't for the fact that he's cut from the same cloth as Martín, he'd 100% be my type.

Oh, who am I kidding, he *is* my type. And he's even more handsome dressed down than in a suit.

I lift my chin, despite my nerves, and retort as confidently as I can muster. "Actually, as a matter of fact, I am."

He stealthily stalks toward me as I fumble for the door handle. With a growl, he grabs my wrists, placing them in one of his, pinning my back to the door. His lethal body trapping me beneath him.

A squeak escapes my throat as he crowds into my space, his breath hot on my neck. He murmurs, "Oh really? And what might that be?"

His other hand deftly traces the outline of my hips, trailing up to my waist until his thumb reaches my throat. Assertively, he collars my neck, squeezing the sides.

I shudder, a mixture of fear and arousal coursing through my body. I bite my lip, struggling to hold back a soft moan. His thumb presses just under my jaw, forcing my eyes to his.

"Last chance, little bird." His velvet voice drops to a forceful growl. "What are you looking for?"

14

ADRIANO

Throwing on a pair of gray sweats and leaving my towel draped across my shoulders to catch my hair's remaining droplets, I flop into my armchair with a *humph. Finally.* I don't expect to doze off, but my dreams are filled with a certain maroon gown.

My eyes fling open at a soft scratching at my door. Shrugging on a shirt, I patiently wait. It isn't every day that someone has the balls to try and enter my trailer uninvited, let alone twice in one night. Imagine my surprise when, of all people, the damn woman who has been haunting my dreams slinks through my door.

It seems my little bird has a few hidden talents.

She hasn't noticed me yet, so I savor taking in her fit body in all black. Her long hair is pulled into a tight braid, tempting me to tug on it. Her footsteps are light as she moves with intention.

Usually, I would be out and about, too restless to sleep, but after my hell of a day, I opted for a nap in my trailer instead. *Lucky me.* Had I been out, I would have never met my little minx in the wild. She finally eases the door shut, dutifully checking that it's unlocked. *Clever little bird.* Before I know it, I can't help but break the silence.

"Looking for something?" Her whole body stiffens and spins; her intelligent eyes scan for the source of my voice.

"Actually, as a matter of fact, I am." She tilts her stubborn chin up and stares right back at me. Most grown men struggle to hold eye contact with me, yet here she is leaving me equal parts impressed and amused by her little attitude.

"Oh really?" I hold back my snicker, "And what might that be?"

She refuses to answer. Her hand rests near a knife strapped to her thigh. I can tell she's warring internally on what the correct answer might be. After watching for a few moments, I decide I prefer her decisive and spiteful to deceitful and shy.

I clear the distance in two strides and catch both of her wrists. Raising them above her head, I pin her to the door. I have to lean my body away to hide my growing arousal. I will my cock to go down, but it has a mind of its own when it comes to my little bird. Caressing the curves of her throat, I loosely grip her fragile neck. She softens into my grip. It's so subtle I doubt she even realizes she's doing it. *God, she feels good*. I lean closer, entranced by her flowery scent. I hold back a groan as I harden even more.

"Rosa. What. Are. You. Looking. For?" I grind out.

She peers at me with determination, her bottom lip tugged between her teeth. *Fuck me, she's devastating.*

Clearly, she doesn't plan to answer me, and I have nothing to hide. Anything of value is digital, thanks to Julianna, hidden behind countless firewalls and shell companies. Not even the government has managed to hack in over the years.

I pry myself away, forcing my body to assume a nonchalant stance. Really, what's the worst she can find? Let her search.

15

ROSALIE

I refuse to answer the devil, even if he is hot as sin.

He raises a thick eyebrow and steps away. He says nothing more, opening an uncomfortable silence between us. My arms are still frozen above my head, forgetting that he is no longer pinning them. Slowly, I bring them to my sides. *Screw it*. I push past the awkwardness, making my way toward his desk.

Sitting in his office chair, my palms rubbing the mahogany wood, I shuffle through the papers on the desk. He sits in his armchair, a king on his throne, with his ever-watchful eyes trailing my movements.

After searching the contents of the desk drawers, I let out a frustrated sigh. Of course, I won't find anything. The devil himself is letting me dig through his stuff without so much as a complaint. Obviously, I'm searching in the wrong spots.

More desperate, I turn the trailer inside out. While Adriano quietly observes, unaffected by the mini tornado I'm leaving in my wake.

After checking almost every corner, I turn to leave. But as I reach for the doorknob, he's there. Hand covering mine, he pins the door shut. His chest presses against my back, powerful thighs anchoring me in place. His brooding silence pierces the night.

Unable to turn, I crane my neck, arching up to see his face. His other hand moves from the door frame to caress my cheek before sliding to my ponytail. With a firm tug, he forces my chin even higher, placing my lips inches from his.

"Find what you were looking for?" He rumbles.

"N-no," I stammer. My heart skips a beat in time with my stutter.

"Well, you did miss a spot," he chuckles. "Shall we look together, chérie?"

My stomach somersaults. The only area of the trailer I'd intentionally avoided checking was his bed, a neatly made, queen-sized mattress tucked at the far end of the trailer. With three sides flush against the walls of the narrow trailer, there's only one way on or off. There's no way I can risk climbing onto it without fear of getting penned in.

Despite him being the enemy, my body's already betraying me. Gray sweatpants should be illegal, and it should be a crime for any man to be half as gorgeous as the monster behind me.

No. I couldn't search the bed. If I end up there, I'm lost. There's no way I wouldn't end up bending to his every whim, likely begging for more. I try to conceal my body's reactions, but he knows. A relaxed smile teases his lips. I purse mine, refusing to give him an answer. A chuckle escapes past his lips, vibrating against my back.

"Don't look so nervous, mon petit oiseau." He smirks. "I'll only bite when those pretty little lips beg me to."

I'm sure I'm glowing beet red. How can he throw such frivolous, flirty comments around? It took me years to perfect the art of seduction, but with Adriano, it seems effortless. Electric.

He releases his grip on my hair, spinning me around so my spine is pressed against the door. His grip rests loosely on my hips. He's close enough for his breath to flutter across my lips.

"What exactly were you searching for, cher?" he asks. "Perhaps I can help point you in the right direction."

I fixate on his mouth, contemplating if it's worth directly demanding the twins' location. Then I remember his intensity. His ruthlessness. The way he dominated the bidding stops me cold. I nod slowly, lips sealed in a tight line.

"Oh, come on, what could you possibly be looking for other than me? Hmm?" he prods. "Tell me, and maybe I can help you?"

Reaching behind me, my grasp tightens on the doorknob. I just need a small distraction, and I can make a break for it.

"Ah, ah, ah." Adriano tuts, pulling my hips flush with his. "I let you search my space freely and without interruption, even offered to assist. Now it's my turn."

"You don't get a fucking turn. Just who do you think you are?" My temper builds.

He chuckles, a deep rumbling sound. "I'm the man whose trailer you broke into and tossed worse than any FBI raid I've ever seen."

His playful attitude toward my plight only stokes the fire in my lungs, and before I know it, I'm jamming my pointer finger into his chest.

"I only broke in because you are a goddamn monster! You bought over a dozen children—*children*! I don't have time to save them all, but you're going to tell me what you did with those precious twins or else!" I threaten, taking larger steps toward him, my finger still spearing his bare pecs. He continues to retreat, still holding my hips until his knees hit the chair. He tips backwards, sitting in the chair and pulling me down with him.

I'm seething, waiting for him to answer and doing my best to ignore the fact that I'm straddling his lap. His arms wrap around my waist, his palms lowering to rest on my ass, a palm on either cheek.

"Ah, there's that fire." He retorts, clearly amused by my outburst. "The twins? They're already gone, delivered to their new home by me personally."

I level up to a new tier of anger. "You motherfucker!" I grab the white towel from his shoulders, pulling it into a makeshift noose, slowly tightening and twisting it against his throat. "You're a goddamn monster!" I squeeze tighter.

He isn't fazed in the slightest. Instead of reaching to loosen my grip on his windpipe, his hand slides from my ass and delivers a firm swat. "You don't need to worry about the twins. You should be more worried about yourself."

"How dare you! I get to decide what I give a shit about, and right now it's those two innocent little ones." I retort, getting more irritated and turned on by his stubborn dominance. "Where. Are. They." I growl ferally.

Adriano pauses; I can see the wheels turning as he contemplates whether he should tell me anything or simply tell me to fuck off. "Why do you need to know? Did Martín send you to try and get them back?" An ominous flicker clouds his features, silent recognition that I might be working on my ringmaster's behalf.

"Now you listen here, Mister. You don't even know me, and I am *not* Martín's errand girl. Or anyone's for that matter." I reply, emphasizing my point by continuing to spear his chest forcing him back a step.

"That wasn't how it seemed at the auction. It seemed like you were acting the perfect part he gave you to play. Come now, what could be so urgent after our last meeting that you had to seek me out right after? If you had wanted to see me again, you only had to ask, ma chérie."

My rage boils to a tipping point. *The fucking ego and nerve of this guy!* "I'm not working for him, asshole. Now. Where. Are. They?"

Just as he looks like he's about to answer me, he surges to his feet. My legs snap from straddling his lap to locking around him to keep from falling. He hefts me effortlessly, throwing us onto the bed. I thrash, fighting to get free of his hold.

"No!" I exclaim. "I need to know! Adriano, please. They need me."

He cages me on the bed with his body, hovering on his elbows, to keep the brunt of his weight from crushing me. "You'll never find them, Cher. Let it go." His firm tone holds a certain finality.

I pound against his chest. The panic of not being able to rescue them shoots through my nervous system. A flood of emotions drowns me. Flashbacks of Carmen's broken body and her years of suffering without rescue bury me. She was a decade older than those two kids. That little girl would likely never make it to her teens, and the little boy is even less likely to. My breathing turns shallow as I get lost in the horrors of my own mind.

"Please, please, please." I plead, still pounding both fists on him with all my might. "Please, they need me... They're just kids."

Wet trails burn down my cheeks as I beg for his help. A hiccup bubbles, escaping my lungs as I break into heavy sobs. Trapped in my own personal hell loop, my mind breaks, flashing between images of Carmen's horrid fate and their terrified faces. He moves from his elbows, his full weight settling over me. His strong arms envelop me in a fierce hug.

"Shh." He coos under his breath. "Breathe, cher, take deep breaths."

My sobs slowly subside as he rocks me, rubbing circles on my back, and whispering calming French words. I don't know what they mean, but their gentle tone slowly breaks through the madness, softly soothing my hysteria. Another small hiccup escapes as I bury my face in his shoulder and softly plead once more. "Please... I'll do anything."

"Shh, baby." He settles me, anchoring me as the storm of my emotions passes. "Let's get some rest, and we can talk more in the morning."

Rolling to his side, he curls around me, the move protective and possessive, flipping me so I'm tucked under his arm as the little spoon. I'm exhausted from the stress of the auction, the adrenaline of the rescue mission, and the emotional turmoil of failing to locate the twins before it's too late. *I can't stay; I need to go home.* I think I say the words, but whether I said them aloud or not, I'm not sure. He pins my legs with his and tugs a thick blanket over us, letting the darkness settle as I pass out.

My head pounds from dehydration. I wake trapped against a furnace. Tattooed arms clutch my waist. A heavy thigh's thrown over mine. Apparently, Adriano's a cuddler, his breath slow and steady against my neck.

Shifting slightly, I try to wiggle out from under him without waking him. The red numbers on the clock show it's still the wee morning hours, but between the drive and the shower I need, I have to get moving. Especially if I want to be back before Martín notices my absence.

"Stop moving," Adriano groans, his upper body constricting tighter around my torso.

I keep wriggling, trying to loosen his grip. "Let me go." I hiss quietly, trying to keep it down for the sake of my throbbing skull.

"Nuh uh, go back to sleep, little bird. It's too early." His raspy morning voice sends goosebumps crawling up my arms.

"I have to go! Martín can't know I was here." I push back.

Adriano slowly peeks open one of his chocolatey eyes, assessing me with a contemplative expression. "Martín really didn't send you?"

"No, *humph*. He doesn't even know I left the grounds." I huff, crossing my arms like a toddler throwing a tantrum. We'd already covered that I wasn't Martín's stupid errand girl last night, but clearly, Adriano wasn't convinced yet.

"And I should just let you go? You don't care to know more about the twins anymore?" He pulls away, gauging my reaction.

"Of course I still want to find the twins. But someone is being less than helpful in my search." I fume.

"You still haven't told me why you need to know, cher. What would you do if you did know their whereabouts?"

I shut off the faucets of my drained emotions to prevent another meltdown. "No one deserves to be sold, Adriano. But those kids, they're supposed to be protected by adults, not auctioned off like old farm equipment."

We size each other up, both trying to figure out the other's angle. Despite his behavior at the auction, the way he handled me last night has thrown me off-kilter. How could someone be so cold and calculating, yet also so tender and sweet? I wanted to tell him the truth—to tell him about Carmen and the depths of my own pain. I wanted to see if he could soothe it like he did last night. But I can't. He was the one buying people in the first place.

Seemingly satisfied by what he found in my expression, he releases me. I need to leave, regroup, and return when I can scout unattended. I throw my legs over the edge of the mattress.

"If you're so desperate to know more about them, stay. I can show you the grounds and I'll answer your questions as best I can."

Dumbfounded, I pause. "What?" *There's no way I heard him right.* "Are you serious? You'll tell me where they are?"

He leans back, his arms casually resting behind his head. Gray sweats hang low on his hips, his bare chest flexes with defined ridges and peaks on full display. His hair's messy from sleep, looking every bit the king in his domain, he pauses before answering.

"I never said I'd tell you where they were." He smirks. "But you never know what you may find."

Pondering how to respond, I clamber off the bed to the door, shaking my head to clear away the madness of his proposal. As much as I want to tell him to pound dirt, if there's even a slim chance to save them, I have to take it. "I can't stay... Maybe I can swing by later?"

"Anytime, ma chérie." He repeats, as though I would forget.

"Later then, Adriano." He lets me walk out of his trailer with his scent still on my skin.

Instead of driving all the way to Houston and Circo del Sol, I book a motel room near Cirque du Noir. As much as I'd hoped to find the twins last night, I'm not about to give up on them, and I'm too exhausted to drive for five hours.

The quiet thirty-minute drive at least gave me some time to process yesterday's events. The radio's chatter was too distracting, so I opted for silence. Never in a million years did I expect to spend the night with Adriano Devereaux, let alone in my state of despair. I'm *El Cuervo Libre* for fuck's sake. My name is feared as a ruthless assassin and interrogator; a death sentence traffickers avoid at all costs. But one measly auction and I'm acting like a hormonal girl?

Disappointment rolls through me. The winding roads allow my mind to wander, processing the pain of not finding the twins or rescuing the others. Hope threatens to bloom at Adriano's declaration to disclose their location, but I damp it down. Until I have them in sight, I can't afford to get my hopes up just to be crushed if I fail.

Checking into the motel, I opt for a quick shower, skipping my normal morning workout routine in favor of a nap. As my ear brushes the pillow, the resounding beats of Darth Vader's theme pierces the air.

"Hello, Martín." I answer my phone.

"Where did you spend the night, Rosa?" He gets straight to the point.

"I was in my trailer, as always."

"Don't play coy with me, girl. I saw your car leave in the late hours of the night, and you didn't come back this morning." He pushes. "You can go where you please, but I want to know where you ended up after your important debut last night."

My brain works overtime, digging for an excuse that'll keep me out of trouble and not raise suspicion.

He interrupts my musings. "I frankly don't care where you were, but I do care who you were with. Were you with a certain ringmaster by chance?"

"Umm, I don't think that's really important..." I trail off.

"I beg to differ. I love that you're feeding his obsession with you, but I expect that if you're taking time off to spread your legs for another circus's ringmaster, we'll come to an agreement."

Acid coats my stomach as I swallow the bile. "What do you mean?"

"Well, I think this is a perfect opportunity to get to know our partners more... personally. Obviously, as business associates, it's in our best interest to know everything we can about them. Especially someone as... *involved* as Señor Devereaux." He continues. "I couldn't help but notice he seems to have taken an interest in you, so it only seems natural to encourage this fling, but I want you to report anything of interest to me."

There it is. Of course he wants information on Adriano. Cirque du Noir is thriving and profitable. Based on Adriano's spending at the auction alone, I'd ascertain that Circo Del Sol is nowhere close to the same tax bracket as they are. We have money, sure, but not the amount of funding required to splash that type of cash around casually. Perhaps this can work in my favor. If I can convince Martín that I need time to "spy" on Adriano, then he won't force me to return while I hunt for the twins. With my renewed commitment to getting them to safety, I know I'll do whatever it takes to get there tonight. Besides, I'm sure I can find harmless information to pass along to subdue Martín for long enough to save the twins.

"Of course, Señor." I placate, using formalities to inflate his ego and distract him slightly. "Anything to be of service to Circo del Sol."

"Wonderful Rosa, I knew we could come to an understanding. Until further notice, you're on temporary loan to Cirque du Noir. I expect daily updates, Rosa. Don't disappoint me." He hangs up before I can respond.

On temporary loan. A spy for a snake, hunting a monster

who smells like home. I don't analyze the math of the disaster I've invited in—I just let the exhaustion pull me under.

16

ADRIANO

Waking with Rosa in my arms was a dream come true. Her meltdown provided insight to slowly peel away my mystery woman's layers. Her masks have masks, but last night helped piece together some of the parts that aren't adding up.

As much as I wanted to see her again, an auction was the last place I wanted our reunion to be. They're shady, dangerous, and where the worst kind of people congregate to indulge their heinous tastes. Having her included in that group made me nauseous. How could the woman who fell apart for me so perfectly be the same woman who bought and sold fucking people? Reconciling them as the same woman was a challenge.

I spent the next hour after she'd finally passed out watching her sleep. Waves of relief coated my tongue. Her outburst was a balm to my fractured soul. Deep down, I wanted her to be upset. To fight me. To demand better. As far as she knows, I'm an asshole who drops millions of dollars to steal children from their homes and sells them. I'd be more concerned if she *didn't* have an issue with that. Hell, sometimes even *I* struggle to reconcile the villain and the man.

Despite acting tough, my little bird is kindhearted at her core. She has to be based on her reaction to not being able to find the twins. She's fucking gorgeous. Perfect. Fierce. Confident.

Her sobs calmed, the lingering sniffles subsiding as her

breathing evened out. Wisps that'd escaped her ponytail curled gently around her features. A protective instinct grew in my gut as I watched her brows pull tight, fighting demons even in her sleep. Her periodic tossing and turning were paired with pained whimpers. Gingerly, I smoothed the wrinkles forming on her forehead, caressing her cheek and whispering sweet words of comfort to my sleeping beauty. Even though my heart broke as she was reduced to begging, I couldn't set her soul at ease. Telling her they were safe wasn't enough to calm her panicked nerves. A few times I was tempted to tell her they were here, but until I knew for certain that she wasn't trying to kidnap them for resale, I couldn't risk trusting her, not yet.

I should've made her leave, but with how drained she was from the long drive and the emotional strain of the day, I didn't think she was in any condition to drive. Instead, I gave into temptation and wrapped myself around her, drifting to sleep while strategizing about our next steps.

The rustle of blankets meets my ears. The alarm clock isn't going off yet and no morning rays are peeking through my window—so it's still early. I blink, slowly adjusting to the darkness as I realize someone's moving next to me. *Rosa.* I give one more squeeze before reluctantly loosening my grip. Obviously, I can't hold her hostage or force her to stay, even though we still have plenty of unfinished business to attend to.

I watch as she gets herself together and heads toward the door. Before she can leave, I have to tease her a bit. Just enough to tempt her to return later so we can actually sort this shit out. My half-baked plan from the night before was lost and muddled in my still-sleeping brain. So instead of trying to be sweet, I default to what I know will be effective. A taunt. A tease. Incentive.

"Come back later; I'll show you around." It isn't a commitment; nothing formal at least. It's a seed. The idea of a chance. Hope. It's enthralling to observe her stance change from determined to shocked and hesitant at my offer.

She isn't even gone yet, and I miss her already. We're not friends, let alone lovers, but I still can't help hoping she swings by later. Something about her is etched into my soul. I want to show her my world and get to know her more. See if we can put together those remaining puzzle pieces so her full beauty can shine.

Indecision flashes across her face. Her meticulous mind weighs the pros and cons of my request. She finally agrees.

"Later then, Adriano." My heart does a little flip for joy as she closes the door behind her.

With a big stretch, I give up on falling back asleep. Instead of staring at the ceiling until my alarm goes off, I get ready for the day. After sleeping with her in my arms, I feel like I've had a full eight hours of quality rest—something that hasn't happened in years.

Julianna texted saying she has Sammy with her and she'll send an update after they finish coordinating the post-auction rescue efforts. Relief floods my veins. Even though I'd known we could track Sammy, I couldn't help but worry about how he was getting on. Jules would keep him safe, and their being together helps set me at ease.

I settle in to take care of some admin. With Julianna on the road doing her usual vigilante activities, babysitting Sammy, and tracking my parents, the least I could do was handle her tedious overflow.

When she isn't coordinating our anti-trafficking network, Julianna is our in-house tech guru, handling mostly payroll and internet connectivity issues. This leaves me to worry only about the less legal activities, administrative duties, and any inevitable bureaucratic snags.

After spending a frustrating hour on payroll—a task that Jules would have handled in twenty minutes—I hunker down with a new steaming cup of coffee, ready to enjoy some peace and quiet before the regular circus chaos.

The morning passes like clockwork. In the circus, most of our work happens at odd hours. The mornings focus on practice and chores to keep the grounds clean and operating smoothly. Afternoons are when everyone has free time to handle their own business. Some folks run errands, some take naps, others use it as a time to play games or socialize. Just as I finish tending to Raj and Shiva, a familiar car pulls into the back lot.

I couldn't contain my elation if I tried. *She came.* My little bird actually showed. Making my way to her car, I school my features, hiding the rush of electricity seeing her causes my nerves. She hasn't noticed me yet; her lips are moving as she engages in a heated debate with herself.

Sauntering to the driver's door, I rap my knuckles lightly on the window and yank on the door handle. Her gorgeous gaze collides with mine, her hand flying to her chest.

"What the heck, Adriano! You scared the shit outta me!" She finally unbuckles, swinging her legs out of the car.

Chuckling, "You seemed deep in conversation, cher. I didn't mean to scare you." Holding the door open, I extend my hand like a proper gentleman. "Are you ready for the tour?"

"Tour? Surely you mean you're taking me to see those kids?" She snipes back, staring with a hard gaze.

I wait until she stubbornly huffs and links her delicate fingers with mine. Pulling her closer by her tiny trimmed waist. The quiet "*Oh*" that slips from those delicious lips strokes something deep inside me. Taking advantage of her surprise, I lean in, subtly inhaling her scent and whisper. "You'll have to wait and see. That all depends on how well-behaved you are."

Rosa's eyes flutter slightly, her breath hitching at the idea of being a good girl. *My good girl.* Snagging her keys and leaving her hand in mine, she tries to ignore the obvious sparks between us.

17

ROSALIE

You know the devil and angel that supposedly ride shotgun on our shoulders? Yeah, those little bastards. If it weren't for me being so lost in thought arguing with them when I arrived at Cirque du Noir, I might've noticed Adriano sneaking up on me.

Fine. He didn't technically sneak, but still, a girl needs a warning when a man like him is within a five-foot radius. *Maybe I should get him a bell?* My subconscious snickers, finding the idea of this mountain of a man being outed by a tiny jingle bell hilarious.

I'm reluctant to remove my hand from his. There's something about masculine hands. I'm not delicate or dainty. I sport callouses and tiny white scars from sparring and circus work. But Adriano's hands... *my God*. Massive, rough, and strong, yet he's intentionally cradling me with a gentle grip. It's like God followed my recipe for hot tamales when He made him. Because that's exactly what Adriano is—*sinfully hot*.

Needless to say, that's what I was arguing with myself about when he appeared at my door. The devil was swooning for the man who held me all night after I melted down, while the angel was pressuring me to remember he's the enemy and villain. Ultimately, I've landed somewhere in the middle where my body's thrumming, but my mind is determined to find the twins.

"Ready, cher?" Adriano's deep voice sends a tingle along my spine. "Cirque du Noir is nothing like your little Circo del Sol."

"Born ready. Let's see what you've got." The traitorous organ does a little jump in my rib cage at his pet name. Dragging me along, he winds us through the grounds toward the main entrance. "Where exactly are we going?"

He gives a nonchalant shrug. "The beginning. The best way to experience the circus starts the way everyone does— at the ticket booth."

"You going to make me buy tickets, huh? And here I thought this was a special tour." I feign hurt.

His twinkling eyes distract me from his luscious lips and sexy smirk. "It is, ma chérie, I promise you'll get the whole behind-the-scenes experience. Don't you worry."

We round the corner and make our way toward the temporary gates blocking the entrance. He moves the barrier and escorts me to the other side. Leaving the gate open, he spins me until I'm facing the gate. The heat from his body surrounds me as he reaches around and blindfolds me with his large hands. His low voice rumbles in my ear.

"Ready to see my world, sweetheart?"

With a deep breath, I play along. Letting the darkness block out my nerves and settling against his broad chest. It's too easy to pretend that I'm here for pleasure instead of business. "Ready. Let's see the goods."

He spreads his fingers, the light trickling in as my vision adjusts to the intrusion. I'm struck by seeing the circus for the first time like a normal patron. The banner above the entrance announces *Cirque Du Noir*, swirled out in an elegant cursive. The ticket booth and gift shop line the entrance way, mirroring the setup of Circo del Sol, the main difference being the imposing royal purple and black striped tent looming beyond the gates. Seven towering peaks pierce the sky. The tallest cupola in the center is nearly double the height, surrounded by six slightly shorter points. It spans the length of a football field, its massive presence stretching across the land. Their big top dwarfs Circo del Sol's.

My pulse hammers, not from the surprise, but from the realization of just how vast this operation is.

"This is incredible, Adriano," I say, keeping my tone light.

With a shake of my head, as though I can shake the awe loose, I refocus. *The twins.* I need to know they're close. I pivot to face him fully, minimizing the distraction of the tent. "I was hoping, maybe, you could introduce me to a few of your newer additions? Specifically, a pair of innocent twins?"

He smiles, but there's a guarded flicker in his expression before he replies. "We certainly have incredible newer acts, *ma chérie*. In fact, some of the best in the class. But we'll have to get to them later; for now, the tent awaits."

He pulls me forward with an easy strength that brokers no argument. Soon, my feet take over, physically drawn toward the deep purple canvas. Adriano trails behind, watching as I take it all in. The tent gets closer and I pause before the entrance flaps, which are currently closed since the show isn't on.

Until this point, I've been semi-lost in my own world, forgetting that I even have a guide. Despite joining Circo del Sol to avenge Carmen, I truly did love the circus. Its infectious lifestyle seeped into my bones until it became part of my identity. Part of who I am at the core.

Adriano shifts, assuming his ringmaster persona. He grips the corner of the tent flap, dramatically bowing and dragging it open. He dips with his arms wide; his other sweeping toward the door in a welcoming fashion.

"Welcome to Cirque du Noir, the most magical show on earth. Step right up."

His rumbling voice sends a shiver from the base of my neck, all the way to my toes. His charm and enthusiasm are contagious, making my palms sweat as the anticipation builds. Crossing the threshold, we're transported into another world.

The atmosphere is surreal. Despite being empty, the air thrums with a phantom energy lingering from the earlier crowds. We pass the rows of empty bleachers, heading straight to the short barrier that separates the crowd from the performers. The black, starry fabric shimmers with the overhead lights.

Adriano straddles the divider with ease, his long legs clearing it as if he's simply stepping over a sidewalk crack. My short legs, however, would need a miracle to make it across without taking out the entire fence. As I'm about to jump the barrier, he hoists me by the waist, Russian twisting me swiftly across his lap and the wall in one effortless motion.

I'm fit, but muscular. I pack a decent weight behind these curves. It doesn't matter how much I try to lose a few pounds; my love for tamales, enchiladas, heck, even a killer burger always wins out over saving a few calories. So the fact that he can manhandle me without so much as a grunt or an inkling of strain makes my lady bits damp. Dammit. He's attractive *and* strong. My shoulder devil adds another tally in the good guy category.

Gently placing me down, he casually swings his other leg over and leads the way across the dirt floor. "Most circuses use plastic or rubber flooring, but because of our animal acts, we dump layers of arena footing in here. The horses and elephants need the extra cushion." He explains. Under the center peak, a large stage commands the arena. Adriano guides me to the striped throne, the violet and black stars decorating the sides making it otherworldly. The podium is huge, large enough for a menagerie of beasts and acts to perform simultaneously. The lights above highlight a web of ropes and bars rigged for aerial acts.

"It's beautiful," I whisper, afraid to speak too loudly and break the trance.

"It's home." He agrees with a note of pride. He points to the podium. "What do you say, Ringmistress? Ready to see what it's like to be the center of attention?"

Entranced, I follow him to a discreet ramp that leads to the top of the stage. Ascending the incline, he gives me space to experience the heady illusion of complete control. I slowly twirl, taking my time to absorb all the sights around me. It isn't difficult to imagine what it'd be like during a show. The crowd of blurred faces. The spotlights. Acts commanded with a flick of my wrist. The illusion of control is intoxicating. The freedom to not be second fiddle to Martín and perform like a marionette. For a moment, I'm not Rosa from Circo del Sol; I'm Rosalie from Cirque du Noir—ringmistress of the greatest circus in North America. It's heady. Overwhelming. Exhilarating. I can taste how the control can be addictive.

"How does it feel, cher?" His deep voice penetrates my daydream. Closing the distance, he twirls me around, sweeping me into a lingering, subtle dip. He pauses, eyes locked on mine as he waits for me to respond to a question I've long since forgotten.

"Huh?"

"Tell me. How does it feel?" He repeats, our noses practically touching. "Describe what has you looking so pleased and distant."

Heat climbs my neck to my beet-red cheeks. The embarrassment of being caught lost in my own performance washes over me. The suaveness of this man is ridiculous.

"N-nothing, I just enjoy being the center of attention." I squeak out.

His eyes search mine, seemingly aware of the layers beneath my shallow answer. But he lets me get away with my lame excuse. Granting me some space, he shoves his hands in his pockets as he wanders around the stage slowly.

"Yeah, there's something about being up here that goes to your head. I wasn't always sure if ringmaster was where I was meant to be, but it quickly became addictive. Like second nature."

My eyes bug as I contemplate the weight of what he said. "Wait, you mean you weren't always meant to be ringmaster? Wouldn't you have been trained by your father?" It was common to pass the position to the next of kin. A bloodline that ringmasters took fairly seriously. Their legacy.

"No, I was chosen for the role, not bred for it." He answers somberly. "My predecessor, Armond, picked me as a teenager. I guess he saw potential or something. He had no kids of his own, so I was the next best substitute."

My heart pangs with empathy for young Adriano. His path was predetermined. His choices stripped away.

"Do you regret it? Ever wish you were doing something else, somewhere else?"

"Nah, the circus was always in my blood. And I spent years trying different acts, but none of them were my thing. That's probably why Armond picked me. It was easier to put me to work than let me run around getting into trouble." A goofy grin tugs at his mouth, lending him a boyish charm. That, combined with the twinkle in his eye, makes it easy to envision him as a mischievous teenager.

"Come on," He pulls me toward the ramp and out via the performer's entrance, passing a line of backlit mirrors and foldable chairs. "There's plenty more to see."

Exiting the big top, we enter another massive tent. It shares the same deep purple color scheme, but swaps the soaring peaks for a long, vaulted structure more akin to a hoop barn than a traditional circus tent. Flaps on the sides are rolled up to invite natural light and fresh air in.

Adriano pulls a banana from his pocket, giving me an amused smirk while I gawk at him with confusion.

"Any particular reason you have a banana in your pants?" I give my best saucy smile and wriggle my eyebrows.

"Oh, that's far from the only thing I have in my pants." He laughs. "A man has to stay prepared. Ya never know when you'll need a quick pick me up. Or have hungry elephants on your hands." We step deeper into the vaulted shelter, coming face-to-face with two of the cutest elephants I've ever seen.

Hearing our footsteps approaching, their oversized ears twitch in our direction. The gorgeous grey animals contentedly munch on heaps of hay. They're roaming freely. The floors are coated in deep layers of sand, keeping them comfortable and clean.

Moseying over, they fondly greet Adriano, ruffling his hair with their trunks before rummaging for treats.

"Meet Ellie and Babar, our resident Asian elephants." He nudges away their persistent trunks. "Do you want to try feeding them?"

"I'd love to, please. How do I do it? We don't have any elephants at Circo del Sol, so I've never been this close to one before."

He places half of the peeled banana in my palm. "You hold it out and let them wrap their trunks around the banana." He shows me with Babar. "You don't have to put your hand flat. Just hold it steady, and they take it to their mouths. Their very own built-in forks."

Mimicking Adriano's demonstration, I extend the fruit offering toward Ellie. She inspects me with her curious trunk, meandering until she reaches my outstretched fistful of banana. Folding her nose around the food, I'm floored at how graceful she is despite being the largest creature in the room.

"Hey, pretty girl," I coo. "How are you today?"

18

ADRIANO

T he giggle that escapes Rosa when Ellie's trunk delicately takes the banana and pops it in her mouth
stops me in my tracks. It quickly rises to the top of
my list of sounds I'm obsessed with. I never want her to stop
giggling unless it's replaced by those delicious moans she
makes when she comes.

Watching her absorb each experience today has been like
watching a caterpillar shed its cocoon, emerging as a free
butterfly. The shadows behind her eyes have begun to fade,
a fresh spark replacing it.

We spend the next half hour feeding the elephants until
we finally ran out of fruit and shuffle along to the next stop
on our tour route: the horses. Like every girl is at some point,
it seems Rosa's a horse lover. She lights up; her posture shifting from alert to completely at ease as the familiar sounds
and smells of the stable greet her.

With friendly nickers, the long row of box stalls comes to
life. The horses stick their white heads over the doors. She
greets each horse by the name etched on their plaques, pet-
ting their faces, and fiddling with their forelocks. She shines
with delight when I snag a bag of carrots from the designated
feed room—a separate temporary stall stuffed with grain
bins, hay, and treats.

Holding her palm flat, carefully keeping her thumb out
of the way, she gives a carrot to each thrilled pony. You'd
think they never got attention, even though I know Madeline

dotes on them like they're her actual children.

I lean on a bale of hay, content to simply observe her. The barn truly is a girl's happy place. I make a mental note to see if Madeline, nicknamed Maddy, would be willing to take her out during their next training session so Rosa can get up close and personal with these majestic beasts when they're in their real element, the show ring. Even to the untrained eye, the connection Maddy has with each horse is addicting to watch. They trust her implicitly and she showers them with affection and respect, like Rosa, who is freely pouring out love in buckets.

A shrill tone from my pocket interrupts.

"Wait here for a second." I instruct Rosa, before pacing until I'm out of earshot.

"Speak." I answer curtly.

"Boss, we've got a problem."

"What kind of problem?"

"It's the Marcello boys. They roughed up Marco pretty bad when he was doing a drop. Sent him back with a warning to stay out of their territory."

"Shit." I swear under my breath. "Does he need a doctor?"

"We've already sent him to Doc's place. What do you want us to do, Boss? We still have half a shipment to distribute, and Marco won't be healed for at least a few weeks."

I blow out a breath. There's never any rest for the wicked. Shrugging on my jacket, I make my way back inside. "I'll be there in an hour. Hang tight and don't do anything until I get there."

"Sure thing, Boss. Sorry to bother you."

"I'll see you shortly, Mario. Thanks for keeping me informed."

Rosa patiently waits for me next to the stalls. Her body language indicating it's no chore to ask her to hang out with the horses longer than intended.

"I'm sorry, cher. Something has come up that I have to take care of."

Her eyes widen, a mixture of panic and interest warring on her face. "Is everything okay?"

"It's fine. Just work. I'm sorry to cut the tour short, but you know how it is: duty calls." I step in closer, savoring the heat radiating off her body.

She doesn't retreat. "Maybe I could help? I'm quite

handy.”

The pink spreading on her cheeks makes me want to lean in further, but not wanting to overwhelm her, I let her off the hook. “Unfortunately, there’s not much you can do for this one. Come on, I’ll walk you to the car.” I extend my elbow.

We’re halfway to the parking lot before she tugs on my arm, pulling us to a stop. Her plump bottom lip is pulled between her teeth as she chews unconsciously. I raise an eyebrow, waiting while she musters the courage to spit out whatever’s on her mind. The second she chooses to be bold is visible as she straightens her shoulders, clearly gearing up for a fight.

“You never showed me the twins.” Her voice sure and accusatory.

Smirking, “No, I didn’t, did I?”

She yanks my elbow harder. I spin toward her. “You promised.” Her wicked finger’s poised at my chest.

“Duty calls, little bird. Besides, I didn’t promise anything more than a tour—which you got.”

“That wasn’t what you implied, Adriano, and you know it.” Her frustration oozes out of her pores. Her mind rapidly spinning to find the best way to solve her dilemma. “What if I come back again tomorrow? You can show me anything I missed, *specifically* the twins.”

My heart stutters at the idea of seeing her again so soon. Even though I know it’s a bad idea, my lips are moving before I can protest. “Sure, ma chérie. If you swing by tomorrow, I can show you the rest of the grounds.”

“Including the twins.”

“We’ll have to see.”

With a huff, she drops my arm, marching to her car before furiously flinging the door open. “You don’t have to be an ass all the time.” She misses grabbing the seatbelt in her tizzy. Reaching over, I slid the belt across her lap until the metal clicks.

“Drive safe, cher. I’ll see you tomorrow.” My amusement just makes her more petulant.

“Whatever.” She slams her door shut, tearing out of the parking lot, my smirk still firmly in place.

Watching her pull away, I let the warmth drain out of my soul. I fire up my Maserati, the engine's roar drowning out the memory of her laughter. By the time I hit the pavement toward Bourbon Street, Adriano the tour guide is gone and Ringmaster Devereaux has taken his place. There's no room for softness where I'm going. My blood pressure rises as I race to the historic quarter, mentally embracing the monster I need to be. The Marcello family may be the French Quarter's ruler for everyday bullshit, but ultimately, this is my turf. Everyone answers to me. And no one—not even them—gets away with assaulting one of my own.

Skidding to a halt in front of the old restaurant, I leave my keys in the ignition; no one in this city is stupid enough to touch what belongs to me. Besides, this shouldn't take long. Throwing the heavy door open, I ignore the hostess, heading straight to the back. White tablecloths hanging off square tables and flickering tiny candles set the perfect ambiance for a romantic meal are a blur. Passing the gaping patrons, I shove the double doors open. Line cooks scramble out of my way as I navigate the stainless-steel maze. Reaching a hidden door, I throw it open without bothering to knock.

Cigar smoke wafts through the space. The three middle-aged men sit around the card table, glance up, two of them already pointing pistols my way.

Sauntering to the empty chair, I loosen my jacket buttons and sit directly across from the Don—Carlos Marcello. Despite being part of the infamous Italian-American mafia, even Carlos knows better than to fuck with me.

Kicking back, I snag a cigar off the table, taking my time to cut it. Slowly. Deliberately. "Are the guns really necessary, Carlos?" I address the Don casually.

"Signore Devereaux, my apologies. You can't fault them for reacting when someone barges in." Despite the bravado, he gives a sharp nod to his men, signaling them to lower their weapons. "What can we do for you?"

I motion for a lighter. Sylvestro, his underboss, begrudgingly obliges—flicking open his Zippo and passing it to me. Still taking my time, I light the cigar, relishing their flaring discomfort and exhaling a slow plume of smoke before answering.

"I received a very interesting call this morning." Carlos remains silent, listening intently. Despite deferring to me out of respect, Carlos wasn't a man to be trifled with. He's single-handedly known as the "Godfather of New Orleans." He has his fingers in everything from drugs and casinos to borders and weapons—supplied by me, of course. He's a formidable man and typically, business is good between us.

"It seems one of your men thought it would be a good idea to threaten one of mine. Something about staying out of *his* territory. You wouldn't happen to know anything about that, would you?"

Carlos's fingers twitch subtly, the only outward indication of his brewing temper. He knows he's stuck between a rock and a hard place. By saying he didn't know, he admits he doesn't have as much control over his men as he claims to. But by admitting he knew, he'd be inviting a war. The circus doesn't do classic mafia bloodbaths. We're more strategic. Intentional. I control the supply of weapons, drugs, and cash for the entire coast. I'd simply cut him off and watch his resources bleed dry until a hungrier mobster takes his place. Cleaner. More efficient. Far more lethal.

"I wasn't made aware of any altercations. But I have a hunch it was one of the new outfits we've acquired. They have a few loose cannons in their ranks who haven't seemed to get the message that your men are protected here." He turns to Sylvestro. "Call Gino. Tell him to bring in whichever dumbass touched his man."

Sylvestro excuses himself, phone already at his ear as he carries out his boss's orders.

Before long, a single knock sounds at the back door, followed by a beefy man who I assume is Gino. His six-foot-four frame barely flexes any of his packed muscles as he drags in a gangly man by the collar.

"Don Marcello." His deep voice rumbles. "You requested our presence."

The Don enters his element, the full *Godfather* vibes oozing from his pores. "Your men are causing me problems, Gino. What did I tell you about letting them run amok in my city?"

The imposing man focuses sharply on the man he brought with him. "Something you forgot to tell me, Freddy?" The lanky man folds in on himself, muttering under his breath. Moving with more speed and grace than a man of his size should possess, Gino snatches Freddy by the neck, forcing his head up. "Try again."

"It was nothing. Some punk was peddling drugs in our corner of town. We took care of it."

Don Carlos waits, allowing Gino the chance to handle the situation. "You took care of it? Didn't think that's something worth reporting to me? You moron." He throws him to the ground, pinching the bridge of his nose.

"Let me guess," he says, addressing me directly. "This punk happened to be one of yours, Signore Devereaux?"

I nod sharply, not bothering with words.

"Fuck." Glancing at the Don. "Apologies, Don Marcello. We have some new guys we brought in from Alabama, and they clearly need a lesson in manners. I'll correct things immediately."

He points to Freddy, who is gingerly holding his throat, deep purple bruises already blooming around his throat as he stumbles to his feet. "Want me to take care of it, or do either of you want him?"

Freddy blanches, but smartly holds his tongue.

Don Carlos turns to me. "How would you like this handled?"

Letting out another puff on my cigar, I draw my Glock and pull the trigger smoothly, placing a single bullet squarely between Freddy's eyes. The life light dims as he slumps backwards.

"He's handled, but I'll be expecting a report from you both detailing your plan to prevent issues moving forward. Next time, I won't be so civil."

Typically, I'd drag something like this out, make an example out of what it means to threaten what's mine. As far as deaths go, it was a merciful kill. Quick. Painless. Better than what poor Marco will endure on his road to recovery. I'm busy enough without having to find time to torture some idiot for making poor decisions.

My threat lingers as I button my jacket with steady fingers, giving Carlos a final nod. "Carlos, Gino—hopefully we won't be seeing each other anytime soon."

Both men nod, promising they'd handle things as I exit the restaurant.

Death doesn't affect me anymore. It's simply another

part of my job. My life. After years of acting as judge, jury, and executioner, I'm simply numb to it. When I was younger, it used to claw at me. Nothing prepares you for the first pull of the trigger. For a while, I'd wake in a cold sweat, the stench of cheap beer and cool metal still palpable in the dark.

EIGHTEEN YEARS OLD

It wasn't hard for us to get confirmation on who was responsible for the note. Within a few hours, we had a name and last known address punched into our GPS. Armond and I pulled up outside of a dingy, rundown cottage that had clearly seen better days. The paint was peeling, the windows were jagged holes of broken glass, and the remaining shutters hung crooked like broken teeth.

Before stepping foot in this dump, I had already embraced the monster I was about to become. If there's a devil, he would cower from me. If there's a God, he was about to turn a blind eye. Because I wasn't weak and would happily embrace the role of executioner to protect my own. They had awoken a beast that no one would be able to put back in its cage and I didn't care—couldn't care.

Stepping over the piles of old newspapers littering the porch, we didn't bother knocking, just kicked the door in. I entered, gun first, followed by Armond. Clearing the dank space for immediate threats, I pushed deeper into the house. Turning, I stalked toward the living room. The place was a pigsty. Pizza boxes and booze bottles littered every visible flat surface. Musty furniture cluttered the already tiny space. It was a miracle we could find a path through the maze of garbage.

The TV played reruns of *F.R.I.E.N.D.S.* to a disengaged audience, unless you counted the two lackeys passed out on the couch.

The men weren't in much better shape than the house. One had his greasy hair tied in a man bun and his shirt coated in cheese puff dust. The other was a mess of grease stains, his pudgy stomach busting out of his wife beater that bore a closer resemblance to a crop top than a tank top. Obviously, these weren't the brains behind the threat. They're sheep that blindly followed instructions from their boss.

Unfortunately for them, I didn't care. The fastest way to root out their boss's identity and send the message that my family is off-limits was to use them. Strolling to the couch, I grabbed Manbun by the throat. He woke with a start, grasping at my forearm to get me to let him go, his loud snoring interrupted as he choked on his tongue. Armond wrapped a cloth around Crop-top's mouth, restraining his arms from behind the couch.

With him flailing about, I failed to see him flick open a small blade in his palm. He swiped at my arm, slashing across my upper arm—thankfully missing anything vital—but still drawing blood. *Fucking asshole.*

Now I wasn't a bulky guy, but I'm taller than most, with a deceptive amount of strength. Anger fueled me as I leveraged my height, lifting Manbun until he teetered on his tippy-toes. His eyes bulged as he fought to figure out what the fuck was going on. He looked panicked enough that I almost felt bad—almost.

"Who are you working for?" I growled, not wanting to waste time on pleasantries.

Manbun gaped like a fish, no coherent words formed as he tried to pry my fingers from his windpipe. I pinned him against the wall, his toes no longer touching the ground.

"I asked, who the fuck do you work for?" I loosened my grip just enough for him to gasp in a few gulps of air. He'd be of no use to us unconscious, and I needed him to start talking.

"Just s-some guy," Manbun squeaked out, the alcohol potent on his breath. "Never met him in person."

I eyed Armond skeptically. "Really? You expect me to believe that two rats like yourselves are freelancers? No goon in the world would hire you both." I squeezed a little tighter. "Let's try this again." I turned to Croptop, who was watching from the sidelines, struggling in Armond's grip. Pointing my gun at his knee, "Who. Do. You. Work. For?"

Manbun had gone silent, sucking in tiny breaths as he silently pleaded with Croptop.

"I am not a patient man. You have until the count of three before I start shooting. One. Two." I paused, but neither man looked ready to talk. "Three."

Bang.

Manbun jolted in my grip as Croptop let out a wail of pain, his knee bleeding onto the dusty floorboards. I'd given them a fair chance to answer me. It's not my fault they didn't want to be forthcoming. Armond continued to restrain Croptop as he rambled. "Okay o-okay, f-fuck man, I'll talk, I'll talk!"

Manbun jerked in my hold, doing everything he could to get more air before bellowing, "Don't! Jay, don't say another fucking word!"

"Fuck you, man! You try saying nothing with a shattered kneecap. I didn't sign up for this shit!" Croptop deflected.

"Name?" I coolly repeated.

"B-Brandon, Brandon Cobbs. I swear we were just following orders." He pleaded. "Please, you have to believe me!"

"Thank you for sharing." I looked at Armond. "Anything else we need?"

He grinned darkly. "Not that I can think of. I know where we can find Brandon."

"Perfect." I pressed my barrel to Manbun's forehead, squeezing the trigger, while Armond buried a bullet in the base of Croptop's skull. Both men slouched forward. Releasing Manbun, he thudded to the floor, leaving a dark smear where the bullet pierced his skull. Armond discarded Croptop's body onto the couch where we'd found them, then wiped his hands on his jeans, muttering something about how pigs would be at home in this place.

"Now what?" I asked, eyeing him suspiciously.

Whipping out a jagged hunting knife, he made his way toward Manbun, holding his ring finger in one grip and the blade in the other. He chuckled, "Now, we send a message to good ol' Brandon about what happens when you fuck with Cirque du Noir."

Your first kill is one you never forget. The detached stillness of a life draining away clings to you. No matter the circumstances, it changes you. Marks you.

We drove back in silence. Armond kept giving me side glances, clearly trying to determine if I was going to break down. I wasn't about to give him the satisfaction; that would have to wait until I was alone.

Instead of dropping me home, Armond brought me to his trailer. "Come in for a drink, son. You've earned it."

Settling into the silence, we both nursed our tumblers. The burning rye was a nice reprieve from my internal monologue.

Brandon Cobbs was a ringmaster at a smaller circus. I'd met him a handful of times at meetings with Armond. It's clear now that the other ringmasters knew I was the next in line for his position at Cirque du Noir. Because I always executed Armond's orders to the letter, never overstepping, they mistook my restraint for weakness. They assumed I would be easy to manipulate.

At first, that assessment had probably been accurate. The younger version of myself had a weaker stomach. I'd avoided as much bloodshed as possible. In the beginning, Armond was careful about how privy I was to the more gruesome tactics used to keep people in line, but I wasn't an idiot. I knew bad shit happened and had chosen to ignore it.

That option was no longer a luxury—not with my family on the line. I would go to the ends of the earth, sell my soul to the devil, then break into hell to steal it back before I forsook them.

••●●●••

THE NEXT DAY

Sitting in Armond's car, we munched on chips as we took turns watching Brandon's house. A medium box disguised as a delivery waits on his doorstep. Tucked inside the cardboard flaps is a message:

> I don't take kindly to threats.
> I suggest you quickly appoint a new Ringmaster and make your peace.
> See you soon – A

Two can play the love letter game. I don't think ol'

Brandon expected to be confronted by an eighteen-year-old boy who had already become a man. But here we were outside his home. Patiently waiting to pounce.

It's dinner by the time I can sneak away to visit Baba and the twins. After changing into casual jeans and a t-shirt, I swing by the cookhouse for four meals and a basket. Snagging extra napkins, I wind my way through the trailers toward Baba's large tent.

Being a fortune teller inherently gives you the right to be a bit.... Quirky. So, to no one's surprise, Baba is one of the few of us left who insists on living in a tent instead of a trailer. Despite our efforts to convince her that trailer life's way easier than having to assemble and dismantle your entire home every time we jump cities, she insists that having the extra space and flexibility to redecorate is her preference. A few of our older acts also kept to the tradition of tents, since they're really more mobile yurts than camping gear. However, most of them work with our larger animals, so it's easier for them to make camp close to their animals' than trying to maneuver a separate trailer next to their enclosures.

Knocking on the door, I'm greeted by a glowing Baba and the rhythmic thuds of tumbling blocks. "Adriano! Welcome! We weren't expecting you to visit so soon."

"I had to check in and see how our two newest additions are doing. Besides, everyone's gotta eat." I grin, holding out Chef's overflowing basket of goodies for her to see.

"Wonderful! Come in, come in. They just woke up from a nap and are playing in the living room." She waves me into her tent. The one upside to tent life is the space. Sure, you have to dismantle and rebuild in each city, but you also have unlimited space and can configure it however you'd like. Baba must've spent some time today redesigning her tent to be better suited to house two little ones instead of one elderly woman. She'd cleared out her "living room" and added a large area rug with plenty of space for the twins to romp and play safely. A makeshift twin bed is pushed against the far wall, donned with blankets and a few stuffed animals. A thin partition hangs to separate her bed from the main area, giving the illusion of privacy for the kids while still letting her hear them with ease. Crystals and dreamcatchers hang from the ceiling along with other miscellaneous trinkets that tinkle when the door opens—the only real sign that Baba is a mystic soul with a knack for contacting the other side.

The twins are currently playing with an old Jenga set that they're repurposing to build houses and little fences on the carpet. They're both significantly more relaxed than last night. It's amazing how resilient kids truly are. No doubt they'll need therapy and support as they get older, but they've settled into their new home with relative ease.

"Daniel, Maribelle, Señor Adriano *está aquí para cenar.* He's here for dinner with us. Let's wash up."

Not all trailers and none of the tents are equipped with bathrooms. We make sure to have the honeypots in a central area so everyone can easily access the washrooms and showers. Despite this, Baba keeps a small basin for hand washing. A clever setup, especially with potentially sticky kids running around.

Daniel eyes me, his guards slamming up at my intrusion into their newfound sanctuary. Maribelle shuffles to Baba, hiding in the folds of her skirts.

"Come, come, *mijos.* Adriano is a friend. *Un amigo.*" She ushers them to the basin before settling them at a coffee table that's doubling as a dinner table.

While she finishes, I unpack the basket. Chef's menu shifts with our coordinates. Tonight's specials are inspired by some good ol' Tex-Mex. I pull out a stack of cheesy quesadillas stuffed with black beans, fried bell peppers, and fresh *pico de gallo.* He packed bowls of sour cream and salsa with extra tortilla chips on the side. I place extra napkins and juice boxes at the kids' spots. Baba materializes a pair of bibs, and soon each child is safely tucked under their plastic protection. She's the perfect caretaker and based on how comfortable Daniel and Maribelle already are around her, I know I've made the right choice of leaving them here.

We spend the next couple of hours chatting, eating, and playing. The twins slowly warm up to me as the night wears on. As they start to yawn, Baba kicks me out so she can get them bathed and into bed before it gets too late. She is an old lady, after all, and kids are hard work.

With a pep in my step, I drop the empty basket at Chef's and make my way to my place, the sound of the twins' laughter still ringing in my ears. It's a beautiful sound—one I've paid for in blood, and one I'll spend a lifetime defending.

19

ROSALIE

The drive isn't nearly long enough to process my warring feelings. My shoulder angel and demon back at it again. Cirque du Noir is beautiful. Everything about it's stunning and maintained with pride. With every gentle nibble, a layer of the ice I'd frozen around my heart begins to thaw. It's hard to stay guarded when faced with the quiet, deliberate care he shows the animals.

Adriano continually makes me question my sanity. He's sweet and endearing, the image of chivalry. When he let me take center stage, giving me a taste of power I'd never dreamed of, he inspired feelings I'm not quite ready to address. The man I'd met at the auction doesn't match the man I'd spent all day with.

After a quick pit stop for food, I'm back at the motel. It doesn't take long for Martín's ringtone to hunt me down, demanding information.

"How's our favorite whore today? Did you learn anything useful about his weapon dealings?"

I couldn't fake indifference if I tried. "*Excuse me?*"

"Señor Devereaux. I'm certain he must've let his guard down after getting a taste of what's between those sexy legs."

Recovering, I try to find anything that can placate his salivating jowls. "He was tired from the show last night. He passed out right afterwards, and I couldn't stay long after he woke. But he did invite me back tomorrow. I'm sure I can get more information out of him then. Certainly, you understand."

He's still never admitted that he doesn't remember any-thing from that night when I drugged him. Male pride can be a powerful weapon when wielded properly. Martín's scoff rattles the line, displeased with my lack of information, but too proud to counter me; he lets me off the hook. "I expect a better update tomorrow."

Making myself comfortable on the motel bed, I lay out my feast of a burger and fries. Flipping through the limited channels on the boxy TV, I finally give up, tossing the re-mote to the side. My internal turmoil is too strong to be alone with my thoughts. Propping my phone, I call the one person who feels like home.

After a few rings, Anna's smiling face fills my screen. "Hey girl! Where've you been? We miss you!"

"I'm on the road, running some errands for Martín. How're you?"

"Better now! I thought I'd have to eat my dinner all by myself." The tables behind her are bustling with people sort-ing themselves like in a high school cafeteria.

"You're never by yourself. What are you talking about?" I pop a fry into my mouth.

"Phillips under the weather today. I figured I'd come get some fresh air, then bring him some soup afterwards."

"Gosh, hopefully it's nothing serious?" My brows crease with concern.

Waving her hand in a dismissive gesture. "Oh, I think he'll be fine. This happens seasonally every year. I keep tell-ing him to see a doctor, but you know men—stubborn to the core." She lets out a laugh, bringing a smile to my lips. "Who knows, it's probably just a bout of that pesky man-flu."

"You're telling me. Sometimes I swear they're a whole different species."

My mind wanders to Adriano. He's stubborn, demand-ing, imposing, but he also embodies the dichotomy of pas-sionate, caring, and sweet at the same time. I flop with a sigh; my body physically drained from the emotional roller-coaster I've been stuck on all day.

Anna squints, analyzing me with her all-seeing mom eyes. "Well, do you want to talk about it?"

I raise my eyebrows. "Talk about what?"

"Whatever it is that has you walking around looking like the weight of the world balances solely on your shoulders."

I don't know how she does it. *Maybe it's a mom thing?* I deflect, trying to avoid the conversation. "There's nothing to tell. It's just another day in paradise."

Anna waits, not pressuring me to talk, but providing space that if I need to then I can. She's always been such a great sounding board, providing the type of love and support I always craved from my own parents. Kind. Wise. Insightful. All things that make her perfect at giving judgement-free advice. After the last forty-eight hours, having a second opinion isn't the worst idea.

I take a bite of my burger, letting the juices drip while I try to figure out the best way to ask Anna her thoughts without giving away details about the auction and my unsanctioned rescue mission.

"It's about that guy..." I begin. "The one I mentioned might be involved in some lucrative activities. Well, he absolutely is. I should hate him; I *do* hate him, but the rest of me seems to have missed the memo.

"He's infuriating. Just when I'm convinced he's a horrible person, he spends all day acting like a good man, and I'm confused all over again. I'm not even sure if I'm making any sense." I ramble on, burying my face in my hands.

The weight of how I gave in to him so easily, my failure to find the twins, and lingering shame from my meltdown pile into a mountain of angst. Anna continues to listen as I spiral.

"He's disarming. Completely distracting. One minute he's super sweet, the next he's ruthless and distant. Despite knowing he's involved in sickening things, my pulse stutters every time he looks at me. It's electric. Magnetic. What's wrong with me that the only man to catch my attention also happens to be wrapped in danger and darkness? It's terrifying."

Anna leans closer to the phone. "Oh, sweetie, that is quite the conundrum." Her gentle demeanor takes the edge off my creeping panic. "Well, I sure can't tell you what to do, but I can tell you how I've dealt with something similar. Would that help?"

I nod and look away from the screen. It's too hard to hold her gaze when she looks at me with those knowing baby blues.

"Well, you know my Phillip. Many years ago, before we

first met, we were young and with different troupes. As you know, even though we never talk about it, circuses come with their own dalliances on the... darker side of things." She hesitates, glancing around to make sure she wouldn't be overheard.

"It was opening night; I was debuting a new routine. Our ringmaster had the brilliant idea that we should host a collaborative show with one of the groups from the next circuit over.

"I was halfway through my routine when the bar slipped. I'd held one of my flips tucked for a few seconds too long, and by the time I reached out, the bar had already swung away from me, just inches out of reach. I ate shit, landed on the net, and embarrassed myself—losing my confidence.

"Little did I know, but at the time, Phillip was watching my performance from the ground, and from the way he tells it, he fell in love at first sight.

"He found me before the next show, not to offer advice, but to give me his own kind of *encouragement*." She winks, fanning her face. "After one of the hottest kisses of my life, I was so focused on steadying my wobbly knees that I nailed the routine. I was hooked. I didn't even know his name, but within six months, we were married and performing our own high-flying duet."

My mind flashes to some of the acts that they've pulled off at Circo del Sol. At their age, you'd never know they were pushing mid-fifties. The way they twisted and swung with ease across bars spoke to years of practice and connection. It was obvious to anyone watching that they were one of the best trapeze duos out there.

"Our relationship was perfect. It wasn't until after my ringmaster had signed off on my transfer to Phillip's circus that I learned about their... *extracurricular* activities."

She hesitates, taking a breath as though the next part of her memory was painful to discuss. "I knew as much as the next carney that we have business outside the tents—it's how we survive. But I didn't know how deep Phillip was in it. He was part of a team that performed extractions, or as most people would call it: breaking and entering.

"It wasn't until he came home with a black eye and some deep cuts on his body that I began to question things. I let it go that night, cleaning his wounds, waiting for him to tell me what happened. But he never offered an explanation. He was hiding the truth, and it ate me alive for weeks. Finally, I got tired of waiting and cornered him, demanding to know what was going on. He admitted that his crew beat him pretty badly and left him to get caught by the authorities."

"No." My blood grows cold. Carnies were notorious for handling their issues among themselves, doing everything to leave the cops out of things. It was an unspoken rule; something about some honor among thieves and being united against a common enemy. So, for Phillip's group to abandon him was a huge deal.

"Yes." She lets out a shudder. "I thought it was them being petty, but eventually he caved and told me that the other group was involved with taking more than just... *things*."

My body goes rigid at her implications. My voice drops to a low whisper. "Anna, he wasn't involved in taking people. Right?"

She peers through her light curls, guilt pasted across her features. "He didn't want to be, but they gave him no choice."

The ice crystallizes in my veins. "What do you mean he had no choice! There's always a choice!" I snap.

"You don't understand. It was no different than defying Martín." Her sharp retort puts me at pause. She takes a calming breath. "I know how you feel. I had the same initial reaction. I told him to leave. I couldn't stand being around him. I spent weeks ignoring his pleas to let him explain."

This was making me wary of Phillip. Up until now, I considered him a strong, loyal, kind man—a pseudo father, really. My world crumbles. How can I trust them with my inner conflict around Adriano's trafficking involvement when they were involved themselves? That they might *still* be involved in?

"Eventually one of his crew took pity on him and came to talk to me." She continues. "It turns out Phillip had neglected to tell me everything when explaining his injuries. Yes, they were from his crew, but it was because they'd caught him trying to smuggle the girls to safety. To help them escape and warn them. Their leader had walked in as Phillip was handing a baby to its older sister instead of grabbing them."

The warmth seeps back into my bones. *Rescue. Phillip had been rescuing them.*

She pauses, the raw vulnerability tangible, overlaid with hope that her story could provide clarity for my confusion. "Sometimes, things aren't always what they seem, Rosa. A dangerous man doesn't always mean a bad one. It just means that he's surrounded by darkness. But if he chooses to fight it instead of being consumed by it. That, honey, is a man worth fighting for. Take your time to see if your man is the darkness or simply lives in it. Then you can decide what you're willing and able to live with."

After dropping that bomb, she leaves me to stew, wishing me a good night. My screen goes black and the motel room is once again filled with silence and the reverberation of my thoughts. My brain is working overtime to sift through the emotional wreckage. To come to terms and see Phillip in this new light. To ponder what kind of dangerous Adriano truly is, and to contemplate what I could live with versus what would eventually destroy me.

20

ADRIANO

Apparently, sleep only makes an appearance when I have a certain Latino dream as a body pillow. It's infuriating, but I can't help wishing she was in my bed again.

Rosa arrives mid-afternoon, immediately demanding to see the twins.

"This isn't a game, Adriano! I came here to find them and won't leave until I have."

I let out a low, amused chuckle. "Of course it's a game, ma chérie. A thrilling one. If you wanted a simple tour, you would've simply bought a ticket instead of breaking in. I already told you: They're perfectly safe and exactly where they belong. You'll find them if and when I decide it's time. Now, you wouldn't insult my hospitality by rushing the main event, would you?"

With her demands deflected and curiosity temporarily subdued, I lead the way to my favorite stop: Raj and Shiva.

Even though a few others help care for my striped cats, I'm the only one allowed in the enclosure with them. Putting on protective gloves, Rosa follows closely through the first set of doors, ensuring they seal behind us.

"You'll have to stay in this area, but meet Raj and Shiva, our two tigers." I slip past the second gate to see my babies. She watches in awe as two lanky cats prowl from their indoor enclosure to the outdoor section.

"Hey guys." I croon. They circle, rubbing against my legs

and bumping my palms with their massive heads. To the untrained eye, they're just oversized house cats, purring, demanding affection, and content to be left alone. The most obvious difference is when a small cat rakes its claws, it's inconvenient, but if a tiger lashes out, it results in a eulogy. So, even though we've worked together since they were cubs, I'm still cautious and give them exactly what they give me. Respect and space. The two fundamentals that make our relationship work.

Rosa gasps as Raj lets out a huge yawn, displaying a set of sharp, pearly whites and a long, sandpaper tongue. He stretches out, flopping his thick, orange and black stripes at my feet.

Rosa asks from beyond the steel mesh, "Are they dangerous?"

Nodding as I pet Raj's coarse fur. "Everything in this world is dangerous, ma chérie. But Raj and I have been together for over a decade, and Shiva almost as long. Besides, they secretly love the spotlight."

Shiva purrs in agreement, contentedly chewing on their newest bone as she lays across the paddock from Raj, her intelligent copper eyes tracking Rosa's movements. "They only do one or two tricks and then get all the meat they could ever want. They're basically free loaders." I laugh.

She ogles the magnificent beasts. "They're stunning."

We spend the next few hours wandering the grounds, giving her the full circus experience. Even though there weren't many people around, she seems to be in awe of Cirque du Noir's scale. I could watch her for hours without complaint, pride swelling in my chest with every compliment and wondrous glance.

Looking around at the deserted tents, she finally asks, "Where is everybody?"

"They're around. Everyone does their warmups early in the morning, so they get the afternoons off to run errands or do whatever they want."

"And the children?" she asks. "What do they do when they're left unattended?"

She was digging. I can see the wheels turning behind those intelligent eyes, the same ones that have been hunting for a trace of the twins at every turn. She's smart. Coy. But she's playing checkers with a chess master. She's so focused on her next jump that she hasn't noticed I've already mapped out the entire game.

I'm about to answer when a loud rumble pierces the air. The growing tension shatters instantly. Rosa's face turns a shade of pink as she places her hands on her abdomen, as though that'll muffle its vocal protests.

I snicker. "Are you hungry, cher?"

Her stomach answers in her place with a well-timed gurgle. "No, I'm fine." Stubborn minx.

I wrap around her from behind, placing my hands over hers and nuzzling close. "I've been listening to your stomach for the past thirty minutes. I don't want to be held responsible for a hangry woman on the loose."

She softly leans into my embrace. "Really, I had some coffee this morning and a muffin. I'm fine."

A growl rumbles from my chest at the thought of her going most of the day without food. A low, primal itch awakens, the raw instinct to provide and protect pushing its way to the surface. "That was hours ago. Come on, we're getting you something to eat."

Despite her protests, I change course and we head toward the cookhouse.

As we get closer, laughter and yelling greet us. In the center of the trailers, there's an open patch of grass filled with teens and kids of all ages. The trailers and tents surround the space, creating a courtyard that's been transformed into a temporary stadium. A soccer ball flies between the make-shift nets on either end of the grassy pitch, and a chorus of greetings meet us as we enter.

As I shout back at the youngsters, a quick red blur hurtles out of nowhere and plasters itself to my knees, almost taking me down.

"Woah! Hey there, champ." I greet the tiny koala. He lets out a whimper, causing me to immediately switch from playful to serious. I've always loved kids, and after losing Sammy, they help fill the void that permanently exists in my core. Tousling his hair and peeling him off my legs, I crouch to his level. "Hey little man, what's wrong?"

The little boy sniffles. "They won't wet me pway wit them." He's still young enough that his 'l's come out sounding more like 'w's.

"Awe, buddy, that doesn't sound right." Gathering him in

my arms, I tuck him against my shoulder and make some introductions. "Hey little man, this is my friend Rosa. Rosa, this is Luca."

He peeks up from my shoulder with a shyness I know is all an act. "Hi, Miss Wosa."

"Hey there." Rosa reaches out and shakes his little hand. "It's lovely to meet you."

He gives an impressive Puss 'n Boots imitation, his puppy eyes wide and glassy. "Will you pway soccer wit me?"

"Actually, we have to grab a—" Rosa interrupts me, halting my attempt to let him down easy so her stomach can be appeased.

"I'm not going to fade away, Adriano. Come on, we can eat after." She leaves no room for debate.

The hope written on Luca's tiny cheeks is too sweet to resist. "Alright. We can play for a little bit. You better get ready to run!" I tickle him, spurring a contagious belly laugh to burst out of Luca's little body. I turn, wagging my eyebrows at Rosa. "Well? You coming, little bird?"

21

ROSALIE

My ovaries have officially exploded.

The whirlwind turned out to be the cutest little boy with a bright red t-shirt and matching rosy cheeks. It should be illegal to be so stinkin' cute. Add in Adriano on his knees and it's a picture that could thaw ice off the deepest permafrost. He's so at ease with Luca. His demeanor is gentle and patient as he listens intently to every word that passes his little lips. It's enough to make a girl ovulate.

We claim a corner of the field between the picnic tables and where the older kids are playing. We form a small triangle. Adriano sticks close to Luca as we pass a white and blue soccer ball back and forth. Little Luca does his best to not trip over his short legs, putting his all behind every kick. Unbothered by the kid's lack of coordination, Adriano carefully returns the ball toward his tiny feet. His attentiveness has my heart melting into a permanent puddle.

Despite all my regular exercising, I must admit my foot-eye coordination is definitely lacking. It takes all my focus and concentration to get the ball to Adriano's feet without sending it too far or not far enough. The Louisiana heat beats down, adding to the beads of sweat building on my forehead. Before long, I'm a toasted and dripping mess. Squinting at the sun, I vow to never take the dry West Coast weather for granted ever again. Humidity is a bitch.

Seeing that I'm overheated and flushed, Adriano pauses the game. "Cher, if you're too hot, you can go wait at the picnic tables while I finish up. Is that okay?"

Despite stubbornly wanting to keep playing, I'm cooked. Conceding, "I'm calling it. I'll be over there. Take all the time you need, Tiger."

Adriano radiates satisfaction, puffing his chest out at the new nickname. It seems he likes it as much as I do, sending me off with one of his megawatt smiles. After meeting Raj and Shiva, the title fits him perfectly.

"Hey little man, you ready to join in with the big kids?" He scoops Luca up and places him on his shoulder. The tyke pumps his fists with a cheer, clearly excited to be included and to have Adriano joining with him.

Adriano hollers at one of the older kids playing. "Hey Tony, mind if we join in?"

"You're always welcome to play, old man!" The boy, who I'm assuming is Tony, shoots back with a grin. My pulse spikes. No way was anyone reckless enough to insult the ringmaster directly to his face. At Circo del Sol, even muttering behind Martín's back is considered risky.

Adriano just throws his head back, letting out a hearty laugh. "Old Man! Ouch! I'll show you old. Kick us off, kid!" He snipes, clearly not upset in the slightest by the friendly jab. They kick the ball in and resume running around. Adriano takes special care keeping an eye out for Luca. He hoists Luca onto his shoulders, securing his legs with his strong arms, and storms the goal. Moving with cat-like grace, he expertly dribbles the ball, spinning and kicking a perfectly placed goal into the corner.

They do a silly dance that they've clearly done before. FIFA has nothing on their victory moves.

"We did it! We did it!" Luca chants in triumph from his perch, while the other kids swarm them, jumping around and trading fist bumps. Adriano parades around the field like a conquering king, soaking in every bit of the boy's joy.

"Great job, little man!" Adriano congratulates. "I couldn't have done it without you."

Luca beams, making a whole different sensation wash over me. A piece of me pines for the scene before me. Everyone here doesn't just act like family; they are family. A true family. The kind that bickers and teases each other. Supportive. Loving. The kind of family I've always dreamed of. The kind I used to have before my cousin was taken.

It's such a stark contrast to how Circo del Sol operates.

Sure, we're a circus family, but we aren't really connected. I can't think of more than a handful, specifically Anna and Phillip, who I consider more than loose acquaintances. Martín is a fearsome ringmaster who rules with the type of incentives that inspire cowardice, not greatness. All the adults actively herd their children in the opposite direction when they see him coming. Hell, even I try to avoid him half the time.

Not at Cirque du Noir, Adriano and his family are the opposite. Clearly, everyone here is comfortable with him. He knows each person by name and cares about them. Kids flock to him, seeking his attention and approval. Despite being the intimidating Ringmaster Devereaux to the outside world, all day I've witnessed the Adriano that only those closest get to see—the steady, tender leader beneath the hard exterior he presents to the world. Nowhere can I find even a remnant of the ruthless man from the auction.

They continue playing until Adriano's ready to call it quits. Calling Tony to the sidelines, he mutters something under his breath that I can't quite overhear. The older boy nods enthusiastically, taking Luca by the hand and bringing him back onto the field with the rest of the group. The game resumes, the older kids clearly making an extra effort to include the boy. Adriano takes stock, watching them play for a moment longer. Satisfied, sweaty, and smiling, he heads straight for my bench.

Scooping me in a sticky hug, he draws an indignant shout from my throat. "Put me down, you animal! You're all sweaty!"

He smirks, pulling me in tighter before placing my feet onto the picnic bench. Dropping his hands to my waist, we're close to eye level. "I wouldn't mind being sweaty with you, ma chérie." He winks playfully. "But I'm parched. What do you say we grab a drink and something to eat?"

I nod in agreement. Candidly, I'm thirsty—in a few different ways—and could use some water to cool down. Helping me off the bench, he leads the way.

22

ADRIANO

Still sweaty, but filled to the brim with lightness, we enter the larger tent next to the makeshift soccer field. The tables and chairs inside match the additional seating Rosa was resting on outside. As always, it smells wonderful. Chef's loud humming reverberates throughout the hall.

A handful of people are already scattered among the tables. Some are eating, others playing card games, and some engaged in pleasant conversation. Near the kitchen, a few long tables wait, stocked with heat lamps and sternos. On nights like tonight with no evening show, Chef sets the hall up buffet-style; it ensures everyone can eat at their convenience, and no one goes hungry. That's Chef's version of a living nightmare: hungry souls in his kitchen. Nope. I've known him most of my life and can confidently say I've never seen anyone leave here anything less than full.

Palming Rosa's lower back, I guide her past the plates and utensils toward the kitchen. Chef always has something set aside for special occasions and guests. And that's exactly what she is, a special guest. My special guest. Ducking past the hanging pots and pans, I escort her into the bowels of the kitchen.

Chef is in his element, his large frame swaying between counters and trays. Eight different pots and pans boil and simmer on the stovetop. Cutting boards filled with uniformly diced vegetables line the counters, the oven bursting with chafing pots and dishes. It's chaos, but no meal is better than the delicious food he prepares. On the road, you'd think everything is fast food and grease, but Chef takes pride in using fresh ingredients and a shit-ton of spices to keep us healthy and coming back for seconds.

His burly arms dip a large ladle into whatever delicious stew or soup he has brewing. The music pauses briefly as he brings the spoon to his lips, sniffing deeply and slurping the liquid. Holding it in his mouth, he grunts with disapproval, then adds salt and a myriad of other spices. With a stir, he dips another spoon into the mixture, tasting it and letting out a hum of renewed approval. "*Magnifique!*"

Giving a slight cough, Chef spins around, spoon still in hand.

"Hey Chef, I wanted you to meet someone." A muscle jumps in my jaw as I fight a wider smile, forcing my shoulders down to keep from glowing with pride. I let a grin slip through anyway, trying not to look overly excited to show off this woman as mine.

Drying his meaty hands on the towel tucked in his apron strings, he greets Rosa. "Ah! A lovely lady! Welcome to my kitchen, I'm Chef!" His smile is genuine and friendly.

"This is Rosa. She's visiting from out of town." I introduce her, intentionally omitting the fact that she's a ringmistress at another circus. It's nice to pretend that she's a normal girl and I'm a normal guy spending the day together.

"Pleasure to meet you, Señor." She offers a sweet greeting, her fingers dwarfed by his. Seeing her warmth directed at someone else sours my stomach. I don't like hearing her call anyone else Señor or sharing her charm with other men. Those things should be reserved for me, and me alone.

Damping down my inner caveman, we continue the casual conversation. "I was hoping you might have something special tonight?" I raise my eyebrows toward Chef.

Quirking his eyebrows, a knowing glint reflects back. He knows what I'm really asking for. I want something to woo my date so she'll want to stay, maybe even come for a different kind of seconds. Catching my drift, his grin gets impossibly larger, his cheeks bursting as he studies me.

"Ah, of course, Adriano! I have a special dessert I whipped up this morning. A fine tiramisu for the fine lady." He snags a pre-dished plate from the fridge.

"Oh! I don't want to be any trouble! I can just have what everyone else is having, Señor." She gushes, her eyes darting between us, sensing the silent dialogue passing over her head.

"Nonsense. It would be an honor to have you be the first taster of the latest tweaks to my recipe! Besides, anyone as beautiful as you deserves a delicious dessert." He dismisses her concerns with a wave.

Passing her the plate and a fork, he leans in, muttering loud enough for me to catch it. "You must be a very special lady, Miss Rosa. Our Adriano doesn't bring just any woman around here. We're happy to see him find someone who brings him joy." A wary look clouds her face, the list of questions itching to jump off her tongue.

Sure, I've had women around before, but I've never once had them eat with us or even considered introducing them to Chef. Rosa was special; anyone who knew me well enough would understand that. Rosa, who's likely used to Martín's 'use and discard' mentality, seems shocked that I don't show just anyone around my circus.

Definitely not, I'm too busy for that shit. Besides, the only one I'm obsessed with seeing more often is her.

Giving Chef a wink and our thanks, we head back to the main dining area. Snagging a table, I drop her dessert and send her to the buffet line. We can't have her stomach rumbling for a second longer. Passing her a plate, she takes small portions of each dish. Removing the serving spoon from her, I pull her plate closer and add another scoop of mashed potatoes.

"Hey! I won't be able to eat all of this!" She protests.

Smirking, "You have to eat more, little bird. Otherwise, you won't have energy for all the fun I have planned for us later."

I set the heaping plates next to the tiramisu and leave Rosa to grab us cutlery, napkins, and drinks. Sauntering back, I shouldn't be surprised to find our previously vacant table bustling with girls from the show. Ava and Avery have joined, waving their arms in big dramatic motions while they regale Rosa with over-embellished tales of Ellie and Babar. Maddy observes quietly, a wallflower content to watch the boisterous girls claim the spotlight. Other acts have started gathering at nearby tables, listening in and adding their two cents.

Dropping my wares on the table, I take a seat off to the side, wanting to be close, but giving her space to socialize. Rosa glances my way before continuing to listen intently to Ava. As time passes, the rest of the circus family trickles in. Mothers call the kids in from the soccer field, and before long, the tables are packed. Laughter fills the air as everyone devours Chef's latest culinary masterpiece. Even Spike and some of the younger guys join in, taking turns asking Rosa questions and pitching which East Coast cities she should visit.

She glows, her smiles coming easier as the meal progresses. Luca and Tony join us, with Luca opting to eat his dinner from Rosa's lap. She's a natural, cutting his food into bite-sized pieces and pacing them so he can chew and participate in the conversation. She alternates between the veggies, potatoes, and barbeque ribs with ease, keeping him from fussing and having a wet napkin on standby for every missed morsel.

I've never considered having kids of my own. After seeing how hard it was to keep Sammy out of this life, and watching so many others be forced into it, it seemed selfish. No son or daughter of mine would be safe or free. Which one was worse depended on the day. Hell, until meeting Rosa I hadn't even considered wanting a woman long-term. It simply wasn't in the cards. Not for me.

Lately, that's been shifting. I find myself daydreaming about waking with my arms around her. After watching her with Luca, I see visions of her belly growing round with my child, waddling barefoot while I pamper her. I imagine a small bundle with her eyes staring back at me—a son, a daughter, fuck it, maybe one of each. The dream is so vivid I can almost taste it. Touch it. Then reality comes knocking, jolting me back to the thousand reasons it's impossible. A wife, a child, a true family... it's a pipe dream at best, self-imposed torture at worst.

For now, I allow myself to imagine how life could be if Rosa was truly mine in all the ways I desire. I envision her as a mother figure to the kids here, my equal, ruling the big top with her by my side.

The laughter slowly dies down and families usher their kids home for their bedtime routines. Many of the young adults head behind the tent to the bar with Spike to shoot the shit. Clearing our plates, I give her shoulder a gentle, firm squeeze.

Leaning down, my lips brush against her neck as I fight the growing urge to kiss her. "Time to say goodnight, *mon petit oiseau.*"

She looks up, the picture of contentment. "Oh, good-night, Tiger." She quips with a smirk. My little bird thinks she's hilarious.

"Not to me, cher. To everyone else." I urge, my hand slid-ing lower, finding the curve of her waist. I give her a heart-beat before I haul her flush against me. "Come on. It's time to finish our tour."

With a smile and a sigh, she waves goodbye, planting a sweet peck on Luca's cheek as he scurries off to his momma. The closing ceremony takes longer than I expect as she hugs, shakes hands, and says her parting words to everyone. Ap-parently, they're just as captivated with her as Chef and in the short time they've known her. She's won them all over like she's been slowly dismantling me.

23

ADRIANO

ack at my trailer, the door hasn't even clicked shut before I'm on her. "*Finally*, I thought I was going to have to share you for the rest of the night." I bend down, nuzzling into the crook of her neck.

She shoves at me halfheartedly. "Stop that. I'm all sweaty!"

"I know a better way we could get sweaty, cher." I drop my voice an octave, nipping at her exposed skin.

"Adriano! You're impossible!"

I kick the door shut behind us as I guide her backward into my domain.

"Don't you have more to show me?" She raises her eyebrows, her voice demanding. "Is the tour finished?"

I pause at her request, giving her a brief reprieve before hauling her closer, my palms resting on the curve of her hips, anchoring her while she braces against my chest.

"Hmm, there's plenty I can show you, cher, but I think we should get clean first. I don't want you to be uncomfortable, and I'm sure I reek." I give her a squeeze, my fingers digging in, kneading her plump peaches. "What do you say, chérie? Shall we get cleaned up before getting dirty all over again?"

She catches her lower lip between her teeth, a slow, seductive tug that snaps the last of my restraint. My little bird isn't just watching anymore; she's inviting the storm.

"It probably is a good idea to get clean." She says with a

giggle. "We can't have you stinking up the place."

That's all the encouragement I need. Sliding my hands under her tight ass to those strong thighs, I hoist her up, her legs wrapping around my waist. She throws back her head and lets out a laugh. Fuck, that sound is addictive. I'd do anything to hear it on a loop.

Her fingers interlocked behind my neck as I carry her to the small bathroom and set her on the edge of the sink. Sliding the glass door, I flick on the water, dialing it to a toasty heat. I pull my shirt off over my head in one fell swoop and toss it in a ball.

Rosa's breath hitches, her gaze tracking every dip and bulge of my muscles. I let her drink her fill. It's only fair, considering I plan to spend the rest of the night doing the same to her.

"Like what you see, little bird?" I tease.

Her gorgeous brown eyes dilate with excitement as her hands slide down my pecs toward the ridges of my abs. The heat radiating off her paints her cheeks an enticing shade of pink, matching the steam slowly curling around us.

The urge to unwrap her tight little body is overwhelming. I grasp the hem of her shirt and she lifts her arms, helping strip the layers away. Leaning in, I take her lips in mine, my tongue swiping at the seam, coaxing them open. She matches my ferocity as she fumbles to undo my pants, her dainty fingers trailing my stomach toward the button on my jeans. With a zip, the fabric gives way and sinks lower on my hips. Her touch stokes the fire building between us.

I dip my head, thumbing the lace of her bra aside to finally claim her. With a groan, I latch on. They're fucking perfect. Just large enough to fit in my palms with a little extra to squeeze. Her rosy nipples are erect, begging for attention I'm more than happy to give. With one nipple in my mouth and the other massaged between my fingers, I unclasp her bra and let it fall to the floor.

"Fuck baby, you're gorgeous." I let out a low growl of approval. Switching sides, worshipping both breasts evenly. She moans, her little noises the sweetest symphony I've ever heard.

She's so responsive, arching into my lips, pulling me closer until there's no air between us. With a hum of approval, I work my way south.

"Lift your ass, sweetness." She obeys, and I quickly peel those leggings that have been teasing me all damn day over her slim legs.

"So sexy. Did you wear these for me?" I slip my thumbs under her black lacy panties, discarding them on the floor.

Now that she's bare, I realize the view from the front is even more stunning than the reflection I'd been memorizing in the mirror. She's a masterpiece of soft curves and flushed skin.

Opening the shower door like a gentleman, I guide her into the steaming water. "Come on, dirty girl, let's get you all clean."

She hums in response, vibrating with lust. My little bird gets complacent when she's turned on. I place her under the hot stream, her dark curls flattening under the weight. After her hair's sufficiently wet, I spin her around, massaging her temples as I work my shampoo into her scalp. I'll do anything to keep touching her, loving that she'll carry my scent after this.

Her ass rests against my cock, my hard length perfectly wedged on top of her round cheeks. Rosa releases a throaty moan, causing it to twitch in response. She wiggles her hips, relishing testing my self-control.

My hands sink into her tight waist, spinning her around to rinse. She runs her fingers through her hair, chin tilted to the sky, water washing away the suds, while I pour soap onto a loofah.

Lathering her body in sensual strokes, I take my time, circling each perky breast. She's so short that she has to lift her legs one at a time for me to reach them, carefully balancing on my shoulders. With her front fully washed, I spin her around and repeat the process. Starting at her shoulders, I work my way south. She leans forward, bracing herself on the shower wall, arched and begging for my touch. I swirl the loofah up each inner thigh, avoiding her most sensitive spots, saving the best for last. Teasing. Savoring the intimacy. After a few more strokes, she thrusts her hips back, huffing in frustration.

"Something the matter, cher?" I ask amused.

"Yeah, you're being a fucking tease." She mutters, less than impressed by my strategic neglect.

"Well, I can't leave ma chérie unsatisfied, now can I? Tell

me what you want."

She whines in response. Arching her back so her ass is gliding along my shaft. My pointer trails her spine, weaving my fingers in her hair. "Use your words, little bird. What do you need?"

With a dramatic exhale, she caves. "More. I need more, Tiger. Please."

I'm already addicted to the sound of her desperation. "Since you asked so sweetly, cher. Your wish is my command."

Instead of thrusting forward, easily slipping into her soaked pussy, I kneel behind her, gifted with the view of her pretty pink lips and tight hole.

"Shit baby, you have the most beautiful pussy. The perfect dessert." Flattening my tongue against her lips, I lick in long strokes from clit to slit. "Goddamn, you taste delicious. I could feast on you for hours."

Rosa pushes back, desperately trying to control the pace and pressure on her clit. With a sharp smack, I spank her ass.

"Stay still. I told you I was hungry. Now let me eat."

Latching my lips on her clit, I begin to feast. Building pressure and speed. Alternating between long flat laps and short spearing thrusts. Shoving my tongue in and out of her pussy. I circle her clit as I fuck her with my tongue. Her moans spur me on as I hold her still.

Pulling back, I add two fingers to her tight channel, sucking hard and giving her time to adjust to the intrusion before curling them.

"Such a greedy little pussy." Plunging in and out, she tightens around me, moaning with every stroke against her sweet spot. Bringing my thumb to circle her clit, I give just enough friction to keep her on edge.

"Mmm, Tiger. Please. I'm so close." She chants a prayer of release.

I hold steady, adding my tongue back into the mix, licking and swirling around her tight ring.

"Ah! Not there!" She protests, but her body says otherwise, her pussy beginning to tremble around my fingers. My dirty girl.

"Come on, cher, give it to me." I growl, refocusing and pulling her sensitive nub between my teeth. I suck hard, fingers hitting that pleasure spot with every stroke. "Come for me."

"Fuckkk, Adriano!" Her body bows beneath the assault, the pleasure stimulating her nervous system. With a shriek, "I'm coming!" She clings to the wall for dear life as her orgasm hits, rolling through her in waves. Her sweet nectar explodes onto my tongue as I lap up every drop.

"You did such a good job." I praise. Withdrawing my fingers from her pussy, I place a kiss on her hood. "Such a good girl for me."

She hums, floating blissfully in her post-orgasmic haze.

While she gathers her senses and descends back to planet Earth, I wash my body quickly and run some shampoo through my hair so I'm no longer a sweaty mess. Turning off the water, I grab a fluffy towel, wrapping her up like a burrito after drying her relaxed body.

"Wow. Just wow." She catches her breath. "I don't think I've ever come from someone's mouth alone."

"Clearly, they weren't trying hard enough, little bird. You're so responsive and easy to read. Any man who hasn't gotten you there is no man at all."

Her glazed eyes and soft smile bring me to my knees. The tugging in my chest wrenches tighter with each content sigh. This girl is going to be the death of me.

Holding her tight, she nuzzles in as though there's nowhere else she'd rather be. If a human could purr, that's exactly the low rumble you'd hear from my throat.

Toweling off, we fall into my bed. I place one arm behind my head, as she burrows into my chest, her thin fingers fiddling absentmindedly with my dusting of hair there. I can't look away, like she's a figment of my imagination and if I blink, she'll fade away. She's real. She's here. And once again, I find peace in her presence.

Finally, she breaks the quiet. "It's so different here."

"*Mm?*"

"Everyone here is so friendly and welcoming. They seem.... Comfortable. Not fearful like..." She trails off.

"Like they are of Martín?" I prompt. She averts her gaze, suddenly extremely focused on twirling my short hair. "I'm glad you think that. We're a family and family shouldn't have to walk on eggshells around each other."

"We're a family too..." she protests. "It's just... different."

Raising her chin so I have her eyes. "What's so different,

sweetheart?"

"They trust you... They love you... They feel... safe."

"That's what the role of ringmaster is, cher. They trust me just as I trust them. I'm not perfect, but they know I'd do anything to protect them."

"I can see that." She whispers softly. "I wish that's how things were in the real world."

"This is the real world. It's my world." My heart aches at the lost tone in her voice. Clearly, she hasn't felt safe in a long time. The animalistic need to protect her burns from my soul. "Who hurt you, cher? Tell me, and you'll never have to worry about them again."

Rubbing slow circles on her back, her breathing slows. Just before she drifts off, I hear her murmur. "It was me who couldn't protect them..."

24

ADRIANO

Waking with a start, the weight on my chest shifts as the world comes into focus. Prying my lashes open, I find Rosa no longer tucked sweetly at my side but straddling me and pounding on my chest.

"Wake up, dammit. We have shit to do." She snaps.

Stretching my limbs, "What is it? What's fucking wrong?" I growl right back.

She has the audacity to look offended, like I'm intentionally playing dumb. How is it that she falls asleep so innocent yet wakes up as hellfire incarnate?

"We weren't supposed to fall asleep, dammit. Now there won't be as much time!" The urgency in her tone raises my hackles.

I'm officially confused. "Enough time for what? What the fuck are you talking about?"

"The twins! Don't think a few orgasms are enough to make me forget why I'm here in the first place! You promised me you would show me this "safe" place where you've hidden them." Her animated hands drawing air quotes as she speaks.

Ah, right. Daniel and Maribel. "Technically, I never promised that I would show you them. I simply said you were invited to visit, and I'd give you a tour. Which I absolutely did."

Her eyes narrow, leaning harder on her forearms. "You know that's not what we agreed on. Where are they? I need to know they're alright!"

Taking in her appearance, I note how beautifully disheveled she is. Her hair is curling every which way, her skins lightly flushed, though no longer sated. Her bewildered expression is teetering on the verge of panic.

"Jesus, woman, calm down. I already told you they're fine. Why would I lie?" Cupping her cheek, I try to soothe the fear pumping adrenaline through her veins. "Cher, seriously, after everything you've seen today, do you really believe I would hurt them?"

Her shoulders fold inward on themselves as though she could vanish if she were small enough. I hate how haunted she looks. My little bird should never be afraid. I pull her flush against me, wrapping my arms around her until there's no room left for her fear. As much as showing her the twins would be the easiest way to set her mind at ease, I won't risk exposing them to more danger. They're my responsibility. Mine to protect too.

My mind catalogues the day. The way her gaze softened watching the kids play. Her ease with the other acts, asking them thoughtful questions and genuinely caring about their responses. She cares for these people, these strangers. I wouldn't be shocked to see her take up arms for them.

Making a move, I take a calculated risk. "Do you trust me, Cher?"

Her eyes give her away, her internal conflict warring across her face. She wants to trust me so badly, but, rightfully so, she still has reservations. My good girl. Trusting her gut and being diligent. Just one more reason this woman is attractive as fuck.

Glancing away, tugging her bottom lip between her teeth, she answers shyly. "I want to, but I just can't... I watched you *buy* people... That isn't the kind of thing I can turn a blind eye to."

Making a decision, I roll us off the bed, haul on pants, a shirt, and toss her the bundle of clothes from the bathroom floor. She stands there, naked and stunned, not moving.

"Well, come on then, little bird. We'll have to be quick."

I know her truth now—she's a huge softie. Her hard exterior is just a front she shows to the world. I'm sure it's a coping mechanism, self-preservation at its finest. But my little bird has turtle-like tendencies that she hides in her shell.

I'm honored to catch a glimpse of her raw, tender heart when she finally spots the twins. From behind the trailer next to Baba's, we observe them from afar. Her sharp, calculating eyes scan them from head to toe, mentally checking them for injuries or signs of distress. Noting that they're not only unharmed, but that Baba is doting on them as though they were her own, her whole posture melts. I know keeping this much distance is difficult, but she plants her feet, abiding by my demand to stay in the shadows.

"They're still adjusting to life here." I whisper, keeping my voice low to avoid detection. "I don't want to risk them recognizing us together or disrupting their already fragile routine with too many new faces. Not yet."

She nods in acknowledgement. "They look happy." Rosa exhales, her voice thick with relief.

"Baba is an amazing mother. She's fostered many little ones over the years. She already loves those kids as if they're her own and will do anything to keep them safe."

Despite my gut telling me I don't have to shield them from Rosa, I'd be stupid not to enforce the line. She needs to know these kids are ours—untouchable. She won't be getting possession of them. Not now, not ever. Her protests about working for Martín feel genuine, but in this line of work, I can never be too careful.

We linger in the shadows. She seems content to simply observe them from afar.

"Will they stay here forever?"

"They're welcome here as long as they'd like. When they're older, if they want to join the circus, they can. If they want to choose a different path, then we'll let them go. But they'll always be one of us. Forever under my protection."

She scans my face as I let her see the sincerity of my claim. Julianna has already set up independent trusts and bank accounts in their names. If they want the world outside, they'll have the means to take it. If they want to run, they'll never have to look back at an empty plate or a cold bed. After their freedom was stripped away at such a young age, the least we can do is give them the keys to control their own futures.

As much as it'd be easier for them to stay here, where I

can better protect them, plenty of our kids have gone out on their own. Julianna still monitors them, but they're free. Free from the life. Free to find love and careers. Free to simply be themselves.

"But what about their home? Their families? Won't they be looking for them?" Her question is laced with concern.

"Unfortunately, we haven't been able to locate their family, but even if we did, it wouldn't be safe to send them back. Their country's known for kidnappings and even having families sell their children off intentionally. If we can find their real parents, then we'll evaluate the situation. But if we can't locate them, at least they'll have stability, safety, and love here."

Rosa must have found what she was searching for, seeing as she sighs softly and melts into my side. I throw an arm around her, pulling her head into my shoulder. She lets out a hum of approval, lost in thought.

"What's on your mind, cher?"

"Just taking it all in." She averts her eyes, her hands folded in her lap. "I-Um, I'm relieved... After the auction, seeing you bid so aggressively for all those girls, I've been struggling to combine that horrible man with the attractive one from earlier today..."

Placing a hand over hers to stop her twisting. "Cher, make no mistake, I am not a good man. I do bad things, but even bad men have lines they won't cross. Harming and selling children is one of them."

Her glassy eyes tear me apart.

"Everyone does bad things, Adriano. It's the reason why that matters most. And in this case, I'd say the ends justify the means." She beams with adoration. "You saved them. No bad man would spend millions of dollars to set someone free."

I can't take it anymore. Her softness. Those sweet words falling from those delicious lips. She's looking at me like I not only hung the moon, but each individual star surrounding it. I brush a kiss against her lips. Slowly at first, fully expecting it to be short and sweet. But as her fists clench my shirt, pulling herself closer, I give in.

My lips move against hers, desperate for more of a taste of her. Her mouth part, releasing a breathy moan, opening for me. My tongue slips into her mouth, granting me access as she meets me with equal intensity. It's even more perfect than the memories of our first kiss. The one I'm secretly hoping will be my last first kiss.

Breaking apart, she commands breathlessly, "Let's go to your trailer, Tiger." Her flushed cheeks and puffy lips make my inner caveman purr.

Taking off, I try not to drag her as I tow her toward my place. "Let's go, ma chérie."

25

ROSALIE

Throwing open the door, he closes the distance, the door slamming shut behind us. His large palm cups my cheek, caressing it. Pressing my forehead against his, I savor the knowledge that this man is a good man. Possibly a great man, even if he doesn't view himself that way. He's gone above and beyond what any normal person would to give others a shot at a life.

A pang of grief rings from deep inside. If only a guardian angel like Adriano was around to rescue Carmen. Pushing the guilt, grief, and sorrow away, I focus on the present. Focus on the ones that were given a second chance and the man responsible for it.

Our first kiss is slow. Sensual. Lighting a fire in my toes, it travels up my body, the flames licking every inch of my skin. He takes his time, moving his soft lips against mine, taking us deeper. The swipe of his tongue easily coerces me to open, letting him plunder every corner of my mouth. The heat builds steadily as we get lost in each other.

Stripping my shirt, he expertly unclasps my bra, pulling each nipple between his teeth. He gives a sharp nip before soothing them with his flat tongue. Reaching a corded arm behind his head, he heaves off his shirt, leaving his cut chest on full display. Dark wisps of hair dust his muscled pecs, thickening into a trail leading to his treasure trove.

Fuck, he's delicious.

His muscles ripple under my fingertips as I get lost in the sensations. His thighs brush against mine, guiding me until my knees hit the bed.

"Please tell me you want this. That you want us, cher..." Desperation laces his voice. "Because fuck. If we keep going, I won't be able to stop."

Large hands knead my ass as he waits for permission before stripping my legs bare, giving him access to his soaked prize. His need for consent connects deep in my soul.

"There's no one else I want more, Tiger." Husky lust coats my voice. "Please, fuck me, Adriano."

His tension releases like a spring as he rips my leggings off, taking my lacy panties with them. My skin smolders as he devours me with his eyes—a predator sizing up his prey.

A deep purr vibrates in his chest. "You're gorgeous, cher."

Sliding off the bed, I drop to my knees, the plush carpet cushioning them. I'm eye level with his member, his bulge bursting at the seams of his boxers.

I scrape my nails up the backs of his thighs, loving the tremble that travels through his body. Hooking my fingers into the waistband, I drag his boxers off. His cock springs free, jutting upwards toward my lips. Thick. Heavy. Obscene. Veins trace along his shaft, leading to a swollen head glistening with precum.

"Fuck," I whisper, wrapping my fingers around the base, struggling to close my hand around the sheer size of him.

Adriano's eyes burn as he watches me explore. Squeezing, I stroke once. Slow, then tighter, delighting in the low growl that rumbles from his chest. Dragging the tip to my lips and licking the salty bead, I moan as it melts on my tongue.

"*Mm*, God, you taste good." I swallow him deeper, my tongue tracing the underside of his cock as my lips stretch around his girth. He twitches in my grip. *I'm going to take every inch of this beautiful monster.*

"Good girl... Watching you take me like that—Christ, you're going to ruin me." His praise feeds my soul, making me wetter.

Bobbing and sucking hard, my hand moves in sync as I take him deeper. Inch by inch his cock stretches my lips until it hits the back of my throat. Fighting the urge to gag, I take a breath through my nose and swallow, sliding the tip down my throat.

His hands find the back of my head.

"Jesus, Cher."

Resuming a steady rhythm, I get lost in the sensations, burying my nose close to the base with each gulp. Pulling back, strings of saliva coat his massive length.

His hips twitch forward, clearly aching for release. Fingers tighten, gripping my hair as he tilts my head up.

"Give me those eyes, gorgeous." I look up, hollowing my cheeks, not missing a beat.

I can't wait much longer. I reach down, stopping at my beaded nipple to give it a pinch.

We lock eyes, his chiseled jawline clenched tight. "Go ahead, cher. Show me what you need." Moving lower, I circle my clit with fast, tight movements. My moans vibrate against him.

"More, ma chérie, show me how hungry that pretty little pussy is." Two fingers slide between my own legs. Circling. Plunging. He drives deeper into my throat until he jerks, and I know he's close.

"Good girl, now open wide, let me ruin these lips." Holding my head still, he moves faster, punishing my throat. The brutal pace makes me even wetter as I match his pace with my fingers, his grunts and groans spurring me on.

"Don't come yet, cher." He spits. "I want you on my cock when you come."

I almost combust on the spot. He growls, as my body trembles. "I said don't come."

He pops me off with a sharp motion and hauls me onto the bed. My pussy quivers, empty and aching. He expertly draws my fingers to his mouth, lapping them clean with the same brutal tenderness.

Teasing, I make a show of lying back, slowly spreading my knees, giving him a clear view of my glistening lips already coated in my slick.

He covers me, the press of him familiar and dangerous. His rod teases my clit as I line him up with my entrance. His lips possess mine, my faint taste on his mouth. Each massive hand is filled with one of my breasts, rolling and pinching my nipples.

"Mm, Adriano," I groan, arching toward the pressure.

"Tell me what you need, sweetheart. Beg for it."

Grinding against him, my need physically dripping from my aching pussy.

"Please, Adriano. Fill me." I beg, blubbering for release.

"Make me come."

He thrusts his hips forward, his dick piercing my tight channel. The sensation of fullness overwhelms my nervous system as I stretch to accommodate his girth.

"Fuck, you're tight." He groans, letting me adjust to his size. His kiss consumes me as he takes exactly what he wants, amplifying the sensations between my thighs. He starts to move. Slow, languid strokes graze each delicious ridge inside me. Every pump hits deeper.

He speeds up, snapping into deliberate, harder thrusts. Every drive pins my hips to the mattress; each withdrawal leaves me aching for more. The tempo ratchets—each hard thrust stealing my breath.

He clamps my hips in a punishing grip, likely to leave bruises tomorrow, but I don't care. I love that he's marking me, claiming me as his. The idea of having a physical reminder of how he possessed my body turns me on even more. My nails score his back as I meet his thrusts with equal enthusiasm, climbing higher as he ravishes me.

"Turn over." He snaps between gritted teeth, and before I can think, he flips me—swift, efficient—so I'm on my hands and knees. My heart thuds hard against my ribs as he admires the view—my shoulders trembling, the curve of my spine, the mark on my hips where his hands just were.

He positions himself at my entrance, one hand braced on the bed beside my shoulder, the other cradling my hip like an anchor. The next thrust is brutal and perfect, slamming into me from behind. The angle hits deeper, driving into places the slow movements never touched. My nails dig into the mattress as he hammers. Loud and punishing.

"Fuck, ma chérie. Look at you taking every inch in that sweet pussy." He continues pumping his monster inside me. I ride the waves he's making, hips bucking and chest heaving.

It's raw and relentless—pistoning. He slides a hand between us, seeking my clit, rubbing mercilessly with each powerful shove. The friction of his palm and the pound of his cock together build lightning in my belly.

"Come for me." He snarls. "Come all over my cock." His command sends me over the edge. My body folds, spasms, and breaks—an orgasm tearing from me with a scream. He keeps fucking through the tremors, relentlessly drawing another, deeper cry from me as my walls clench and roll around him.

He loses it—growing jerky and desperate. With a guttural roar, he fills me with ropes of release.

He keeps going until the tremor in his thighs dies, his breaths stuttering in ragged, satisfied puffs. His cock pulses as it pumps the last of his seed, coating the inside of my pussy.

Slowing, he grinds his hips in shallow circles—prolonging my pleasure as I ride out wave after wave. He pins me close, pressed against my back, and I let the lingering reverberations roll through me as he murmurs soft, half-French praises into my ear.

"Such a good girl, cher" He whispers. "You did so good."

He flips us, keeping his length inside me as I curl into him. Nuzzling closer, I let the small tremors rock through my pussy. I've never come so hard before, but two toe-curling orgasms in one day have my muscles sore and sated. My wild thoughts have quieted. Adriano's heartbeat steadies me, his scent on my skin.

There's nowhere else I'd rather find my peace.

26

ADRIANO

She's my perfect puzzle piece fitting flush against me; every curve of her well-spent body draped across mine. It's impossible to keep my hands off her.

Ma chérie. My little bird.

I trace circles absently along her back while she dips into a lulling sleep. Her deep breaths and cute snores quieting the chaos that constantly swirls in my soul. The break from the madness is an oasis, a safe haven I've never known.

Is this what heaven's like? I would have sworn fifteen minutes ago that it was sinking into her soft body for the first time. But this—the content aftermath, this was sanctuary. Peaceful. Gentle. Intimate.

Softening, I slide from her pussy, our combined juices trickling down her thighs onto mine. Despite wanting to lie here forever, I carefully shift her and slip to the bathroom for a warm washcloth. Taking care of Rosa is second nature. Instinct. I gently swipe the cloth along her lips and thighs, wiping away our release. I ditch the towel and crawl back in, pleased that even in her sleep she seeks me out.

I'd seen her naked before. In the shower I'd worshipped her, covering every inch of her frame with kisses and suds. But now, in the lulled aftermath, I notice a small tattoo peeking out from her inner wrist: Two tiny ravens, one flying after the other.

The ink must be special because, unlike mine which covers my whole arm, her body is otherwise unmarked. I knew the term little bird was fitting; I just didn't realize how accurately.

Sweet pecks work their way from my collarbone toward my stomach. No screaming. No pounding on my chest. Ever the early riser, she wakes first, my eager bird chasing her worm. And God help me, I'll never complain.

Blinking away the haze, I commit the vision before me to memory. She's an image. A goddess. Rosa, hair mussed from sex and sleep, sliding lower with a mischievous gleam. A siren draped across me, playful and wicked all at once.

"Having fun little bird?"

"Mhm. I was disappointed, waking up feeling so… empty." She pretends to pout, though her grin betrays her.

Such a sassy thing, my girl. Ma chérie. My cock hardens at the mere suggestion, stiffening as her fingers curl around the base and give a few lazy pumps.

"Well, we can't have you disappointed." My smirk deepens as I tug until she's straddling me, her perfect tits bouncing free, nipples flushed and tight. "Hop on, chérie. We can't leave you empty for long."

Her laugh is throaty. She guides me to her already slick folds, grinding against the tip before sinking lower an inch at a time. Her pussy clamps around me, a velvet vice pulling me to the hilt. A groan tears from her chest—and mine.

"Ugh, you're so tight, cher." My fingers bite into her hips, holding her still a beat as I wrestle my release back under control. Counting. Breathing. Anything to delay the inevitable.

When the surge retreats, I loosen my grip, rolling my hips upward, grinding her clit against me. Her breath stutters, soft gasps melting into husky moans as she rides me slow and steady.

"Better, baby?"

"Shit, Tiger. God—I'm so full." Her rhythm quickens, breasts swaying as she bounces, greedy for more.

"Oh yeah? Does that greedy little pussy like being stretched around my cock?"

"Yes—yes! Please, touch me. I need you."

I pinch her nipples, alternating between soft strokes and

sharp rolls, until she cries out, arching against me. She balances on my chest as she rides me. Every shiver tells me she's close. Her thighs tremble, the muscles in her legs struggling to keep pace. Her nails rake my shoulders, marking crescents in my skin. She bites her lip, but the moan that escapes is feral, raw.

Watching her unravel is intoxicating—my chérie taking me like she was made for it, fighting her pleasure and begging for more in the same breath. The power of it settles in my chest like fire: the sight of her taking me. Needing me. Losing herself to me.

"Come on, cher." I growl, brushing damp hair from her forehead. "Give it to me. Let me watch you fall apart."

She slams down harder, chasing that final edge.

"Take what you need." I encourage, my voice rough. Coaxing. Sweat coats her body as she works her pussy onto my cock over and over. Grabbing her hips, I help lift her up and down. Her head tilts back, a cry breaking from her throat as her climax rips through her. Her pussy grips me, milking me with each pulse.

She's stunning—flushed, slick skin, puffy nipples. Quivering as aftershocks ripple through her. I keep grinding shallow thrusts, prolonging every second of her bliss until she collapses against me, boneless.

Once she starts to descend from cloud nine, I take my turn.

"Hands and knees." I command, flipping her onto all fours. Admiring the perfect arch of her spine, her delicious round ass on full display. The very object of every man's fantasies—but this view is now mine alone. "Christ, cher—this view."

She presses her breasts to the sheets, wriggling her hips until her cheeks jiggle. "Please. Fill me up, Tiger."

I slam into her, hard and fast, chasing the release that's been clawing at me since I woke. She meets each thrust, shoving her hips back, her slick heat pulling me deeper with each stroke.

"Fuck, Rosa, this is heaven. You're perfect, sweetheart. All mine. Only mine."

"I'm yours. Please, I need your cum. Fill me."

Her begging breaks me. My balls tighten. My thrusts turn frantic. Reaching down, I rub her clit with furious circles.

"I'm so close." She gasps.

"Come on, cher. Give me one more. Be a good girl and come for me."

Her scream splits the air as she convulses, spasming tight, dragging me into the abyss with her. My growl is feral as I push through the aftershocks, jerking inside her as I spill deep, ropes of heat, filling her to the brim. Her body quivers beneath me, wrecked and beautiful.

It's as though knowing the twins are safe destroyed any barriers holding us apart. I've never met someone so easy to talk to. Our conversation flows easily between topics as we get to know each other. My little bird is as intelligent as she is beautiful. A cunning little fox. Her tales of manipulating Martín and growing up in Mexico add color to my image of who Rosa is.

Tracing the ink swirls on my arms absentmindedly, her fingers lightly trail the side of my neck. "Do they all have meaning?" She asks.

"Some of them do." I shrug. "Others were added to fill the blank spaces in between."

"Certainly, they must mean something." Her eyes glint in the morning light. "Empty space is still a choice. What about this one?" She taps the purple top hat wrapped in Mardi Gras beads on my forearm. Its once-vibrant colors have faded to lighter pastels outlined in dark tribal lines.

"My first one. I was sixteen and had been traveling with the circus for years. My family had moved away, and I wanted to keep a piece of them close."

"Why the beads?" She pries deeper, a polite curiosity mixing into her tone.

"We're originally from Louisiana. Mardi Gras is huge there," I explain. "It's home... or at least the closest thing to it. It's a reminder of my roots. Of who I was before all this. The perfect blend of my real family mixed with my circus family."

Her pointer drifts higher, brushing the faint scar on my bicep. "And this?"

The room fades. I'm eighteen again, knuckles bruised

and a blurred parade of bloodied faces flashing before me.

I blink back to her face. Silent for a beat. "That one isn't a tattoo."

She studies me quietly, asking permission to know more.

"I'm not a good man, cher." She waits for more of an explanation. I could lie, but her trusting gaze invites truth.

"I already told you I was chosen to be ringmaster. My predecessor, Armond, wasn't kind. He ran Cirque du Noir with an iron fist. Relentless. Harsh. Demanding.

"I was young when he first started training me to sharpen the skills I'd need to be ringmaster someday. "Often it involved fighting. In the beginning, I'd get beaten so badly I could hardly stand. He insisted that no progeny of his would be weak. Vulnerable. So he trained me the only way he knew how."

Her grip tightens around my arm, her nails digging into my skin as if she could reach back through time and claw his eyes out.

I continue, acknowledging her touch with a squeeze of my hand. "Many of these scars were from training. From learning to defend myself against full-grown men. Later on, the marks came from being the bigger beast. The first time I won a fight, he promoted me from punching bag to his goon. Anyone he needed intimidated, I did it. Anyone he deemed worthy of punishment, I delivered it."

For a heartbeat, the circus is gone and I'm standing over two men in a filthy living room, Armond's hand steady on my shoulder as blood pools beneath their bodies.

I pull her closer, burying my face in her hair. "Every mark on my skin is a story. Some I'll tell you. But some you're better off not knowing."

She holds me tight, stroking my back gently while I absorb her comfort, her scent grounding me.

Pointing to her wrist, I press a kiss to it. "What about you? Why does my little bird have a tattoo of two little birds?"

She glances away, retracting into her little shell. I give her a squeeze. "If you don't want to tell me, that's okay. I wasn't trying to pry." I give her a way out. As much as I want to know what caused those shadows to dance behind her eyes, I can't stand being the source of her discomfort. Not anymore. Not after we've shared so much.

"It's okay... I-I want to tell you." She swallows hard. "I've just never told anyone before..."

I do my best to provide silent support while she composes herself.

27

ROSALIE

"After my cousin was taken... things changed. I changed. I was angry. Really fucking angry. Angry at the world, at my family, at those who took her. Hell, sometimes I think I was even a little mad at her. As twisted as that is, she left me. It wasn't her choice, obviously, but being young, it was... difficult to process it all."

TEN YEARS EARLIER

Lights flashed. Loud Spanish beats thumped through the club. Drinks flowed cheap and easily. I had no business being at a club on a school night, but realistically, my parents had checked out a long time ago. So I was free. A teenager in every sense of the word, trying to numb my pain and emptiness in any way I could.

School was dull, my family distracted and distant, and life a black hole that was sucking me dry. So, I did what all teens do best: make questionable decisions.

Stumbling out of the club, I took the familiar route through the city. Wandering between unoccupied alleys and corner shops until my feet stopped. Every night for the past few weeks, I kept finding myself buzzed outside of a small tattoo shop. The designs covering the windows entranced me, their dark curves and clean lines drawing me back.

Tonight, I was tired of looking. Instead of staring

forlornly at the storefront, I wandered inside, the bell ringing quietly as I crossed the threshold.

You're probably envisioning some dank shop with a bearded biker giving piercings and questionable tattoos in a back room, but this place was the exact opposite. The glass counter was spotless, no fingerprints or smudges in sight. Large three-ring binders sat in perfect order across the top, filled with different artwork and doodles.

The artist, Maria, was soft spoken, her designs vibrant and neat. I spent hours lost in her books, letting the buzz fade as I traced the lines on the pages. She let me hang around, supplying me with water and letting me process my feelings. The tequila had stripped me bare—leaving me raw, vulnerable, and with no verbal filter. I must've talked her ear off for hours, complaining about my family, crying soft tears at the hole where Carmen once lived. The secrets of my guilt and shame that I never dared share at home came tumbling out.

Maria simply listened, her calm demeanor an invitation to let go. She doodled while I vented. Before long, I was sober, emotionally drained, and ready to go home. Maria closed the shop, insisting on walking me home, and with how depleted I was, I let her.

It was the beginning of an unlikely friendship. I visited Maria often, sober this time.

I wanted something in honor of Carmen; a visual tribute to her memory and a mark of the invisible scars that I'll carry for the rest of my life. So, I went to Maria. She was more than happy to help, pulling out the small notebook filled with doodles from the night we first met. Some were generic swirls and spirals, but the corner of the page had a delicate silhouette of a flying bird. A raven.

"You described your cousin with raven hair. A caged soul who needed to break free." She explains. "I thought it might be nice to set her free, give her wings to fly away, even if it wasn't in this life."

An ode to Carmen. An ironic, liberating embodiment of how I wanted to save her and how I wished I could be free too.

"After processing some of the grief and guilt, my friend

Maria gave me one raven, in honor of my cousin who was taken."

Adriano remains still, waiting for the rest of the story to surface.

"And the second one, little bird?" he asks, softly prompting me as he tenderly tucks a wild curl behind my ear.

"The second one is for the other girl I couldn't save." My eyes mist at the memory. Unlike with Carmen, where others grieved her too, this was a burden my soul bore alone. I never had intentions of ever sharing the load until Adriano. But if anyone would understand, it was him.

Finding strength in his arms, I recount a failure that still haunts me.

"I swore to avenge Carmen. To save others from the same horrific fate. My mentor, Joaquín, spent hours honing my skills: Muay Thai, Krav Maga, Jiu-Jitsu—everything to turn me into a fighting machine.

"I'd caught wind of an auction nearby with a small-time cartel. I swiped my parents' keys and headed into the desert. Sticking to the shadows, I crept around the abandoned movie theater. The windows were no longer transparent; they were translucent at best. The desert sand had scratched the glass beyond repair, everything coated in a layer of dust. Unable to enter, I figured I could tail one of the vehicles to a place with less security.

"The rear theater doors swung open, a large man stumbling out with a young girl in his meaty grip. He dragged her to a van, throwing her unceremoniously into the back before hopping into the driver's seat. It was my chance. I was convinced that I could take out one man. But after following the van lights from a distance, it slowed, the side door sliding open and the poor girl's body slumped out into the sand. The van slammed the door shut and carried on, driving off with a cloud of dust.

"It was too late. I was too late."

Adriano squeezes me, lending me the strength to continue.

"I hadn't noticed the other men or even considered they wouldn't keep her for long. Carmen had been held for years. This poor girl didn't even last a few hours. It was the first dead body I'd encountered. My stomach emptied its contents as I set to work figuring out what to do with the girl's body. She didn't deserve an unmarked grave in the desert, but I couldn't move her without making things worse.

"Eventually, after crying more tears than I'd thought possible, I called Joaquín, who immediately instructed me to leave and assured me that he would take care of it. How he disposed of her body, I'll never know. But when I trekked out the next day, it was as though nothing had ever happened.

"The other smaller bird is for her, a token for the girl the world forgot. The girl I failed." I choke up. "That's when I swore to never fail again."

"Oh, my little warrior." Adriano's lips press against my temple, brushing away tears that I hadn't realized were trickling down my cheeks. "I'm sorry you had to experience all of that pain."

He pulls me in tighter. My lips are dry, my voice hoarse. His thumb rubs my wrist, acknowledging the two little birds etched into my skin—permanent marks for the stories already inked on my soul.

28

ROSALIE

Pulling into the parking lot behind Cirque du Noir, I wander in search of Adriano. A few ladies greet me politely. Tony waves from his unicycle, slowing his wild pedaling to give me a fist bump. Luca leaps into my arms and clings like a baby koala, hitching a ride while I make my rounds.

Ironically, after such a short time, it's already more like home than Circo del Sol ever was. The camaraderie. The genuine care. It's wild how quickly these strangers claimed me as their own.

Luca babbles about how he's been learning to juggle with Tony. His little hands flap wildly as he demonstrates his throw - catch, throw - catch sequence he's been practicing. His excitement's contagious with his pink tongue sticking out as he concentrates on catching the imaginary scarves.

With Luca still perched on my hip, I listen intently, loving his giggles as he shares his day with me. I'm so focused that I don't notice a certain towering man lumbering up from behind. His calloused hands on my waist jolt me out of our conversation, as he leans in, placing a sweet peck on my cheek. Luca's face scrunches into a grimace.

"Eww! That's icky! Girls have cooties," he exclaims.

Adriano simply chuckles, ruffling the little boy's hair. "They may have cooties, but I'm willing to risk it." He winks, placing Luca's wriggling body on the ground so he can scramble away, his squeals inciting laughter from us both. Now child-free, Adriano spins me into his embrace, kissing me properly.

"Mm, I could get used to this, Cher." He whispers.

"I think you already have, Tiger." I playfully bat at his chest. "No spreading cooties in public!"

A sexy smirk teases his lips. "With you looking so delicious, I can't help myself. What can I say? I'm a weak man."

Our playful banter has become second nature. Exchanging quips and teasing is definitely one of the lesser-known love languages. I plant a kiss on his lips, short, but sincere. "It's good to see you too, handsome."

"I have a surprise for you." He says, intertwining our fingers.

"Oh? And what could that possibly be?" Raising my eyebrows, my mind runs wild with dirty fantasies.

"Not that kind of surprise, my dirty bird. But I think you'll enjoy this one. Come on." He guides me through the maze of trailers to a familiar tent. He halts at the beaded curtain covering the entrance.

"I think they've finally adjusted enough, and Baba's kept the kids on a pretty strict schedule, but I know the language barrier is hard for them." He shuffles his feet, shifting with uncharacteristic nervousness. "You don't have to, but I thought it might be nice for them to meet someone else who speaks Spanish... They're inside if you're interested?"

This man is full of surprises. His thoughtfulness. Placing the twins needs first and helping them adjust to their new home. I ignore the pangs as I slip deeper in love.

Launching myself at him, I leap into his arms, unable to contain my excitement. "Are you serious? I can meet them?" I press tiny kisses all over his face. "You, sir, never cease to surprise me."

His grip tightens around my waist in response, lust curling around the corners of his eyes.

"Only if you want to, cher. I spoke with Baba, and she agreed that it could be helpful for them."

Placing me on the ground, I do a little happy dance before recomposing myself.

"Yes, please. I wouldn't miss this for anything."

Reaching through the retro divider, he holds the beads back and follows me into the tent. Baba's in her makeshift kitchen, filling two plastic bowls with goldfish and grapes. The twins are playing quietly on the shag rug in the living room, seemingly content.

"Hey Baba! I brought the visitor we discussed earlier." He announces our arrival.

Her bangles jingle. "Welcome, welcome. Please, come in! Make yourselves at home." She grasps my hand in both of her wrinkled palms. "You must be Rosa. You're such a lovely flower, like your namesake." She greets enthusiastically.

"It's wonderful to meet you, Baba. Thank you for letting us come by."

The crinkles deepen around her eyes as she smiles. "Oh, sweet girl, these kids need all the love we can give them. Thank you for coming and loving on them. They're shy, but kindhearted."

She passes me one of the snack bowls and calls out to the twins. "Daniel, Maribelle, you have a visitor; *Mijos, tienen una visita.*" Their blue eyes flick up, Daniel moving closer to Maribelle in a protective stance that only softens when he spots Adriano behind me.

Curious.

Adriano crouches as he greets them. "¡Hola, amigos! How are my little friends today?"

Maribelle slowly approaches, handing him a stuffed pink unicorn. "*Mi unicornio. Mi nuevo amigo.*"

"She's trying to tell you this is her new friend, the unicorn." Baba translates easily for Adriano. He scoops up the toy and opens his arms, waiting for her to close the distance before pulling her onto his lap. He makes the stuffy prance around on her arms before the unicorn gives her a plush fake kiss on her cheek. Maribelle's giggle melts my heart further.

Clearly, he's spent ample time around these kids. They're wary of strangers, rightfully so, but for Daniel to drop his guard and Maribelle to willingly share her treasures, he's had to work for their trust.

"He's been coming by twice a day every day since he brought them here." Baba whispers softly. "It's taken some time, but he's been patient—bringing gifts, learning silly Spanish words, and simply letting them adjust. They've warmed right up to the big goof." Her gleam speaks to her pride in their progress.

"He really has a way with kids." I agree, my eyes glued to them.

"Little *amigos*, I want you to meet my *amiga*, Miss Rosa."

He tells them, waving me over. "Miss Rosa, meet my little *amigos*, Daniel and Maribelle." He holds the unicorn with a snicker. "And Monsieur Unicorno."

I lower myself beside Adriano and slip into my native tongue, introducing myself. "*Hola, amigos. Me llamo Rosa. Mucho gusto.*"

Daniel lights up, the language barrier vanishing as he dives into full conversation. "*Hola, me llamo Daniel y mi hermanita se llama Maribelle.*" He leans closer. "*Somos gemelos, pero soy tres minutos mayor.*" He holds up three small fingers and smirks, making sure I know that despite being twins, he's a whole three minutes older than his "little" sister.

Maribelle protests, as only a younger sibling can, letting out a string of rapid Spanish, adamantly disputing his claim. We slip into an easy rhythm, chatting about their favorite colors, animals, and foods. They share a whirlwind of short stories about Señor. Unicorn and all the imaginative adventures he's been on this week.

Their innocence and creativity is inspirational, pulling me away from the circus for a while.

Daniel and I play with blocks, while Baba relaxes, and Adriano sits on the floor with Maribelle on his lap. He periodically passes her a grape or goldfish while she plays.

They seem happy—truly relaxed. Significantly less tense than the first time we'd spied on them from behind the trailer. Their English has been rapidly improving too. Baba spends time daily reviewing the basics and they're absorbing it like sponges, already proficient in "Span-glish."

Before long, an hour and a half has passed, and the twins are yawning from all the excitement. Taking our cue to leave, Adriano and I say our goodbyes, promising to visit again tomorrow to continue our games. Tiny arms tug on my pants and I look down to see Maribelle's precious blue eyes holding mine. She spent most of her time sitting with Adriano, playing with Señor Unicorn. She summons me to her level, bringing her hands to my face as she puts her mouth against my ear and whispers in Spanish, "Miss Rosa, are you our new friend too?"

My heart breaks at the raw courage it took for her to ask. Smiling softly, "Of course, my little *amiga*. I would love to be friends."

She grabs my cheeks between her sticky little palms.

"Yay! ¡*Mi amiga* Rosa!"

Squishing her tiny body, I give a quick hug before stepping back with a wave. "*Hasta luego*, little one."

As we're leaving, my phone rings, Martín's Darth Vader ringtone echoing in the night.

Adriano lets out a chuckle. "You better answer than."

"It can wait, really." I tuck the phone back in my pocket.

He leans against a nearby trailer. "Answer it, Rosa. I insist." His voice drops, leaving no room for argument.

Pressing the green icon, I put the phone to my ear. "The fuck, Rosa? You get too distracted spreading your legs to check in?"

I outwardly cringe, before schooling my features. Feeding him some lines about being busy seducing Adriano and how I'm digging around while he isn't looking. Hanging up couldn't come quick enough.

When the call disconnects, Adriano's frame shifts as he pushes off from the trailer and saunters closer. "Anything interesting to report, Miss Rosa?"

"Nothing noteworthy." I pocket the phone, embarrassed that he knows Martín wants me to seduce him for information. "Martín's just fishing. I won't give him anything he doesn't already know."

"That won't satisfy him forever," Adriano says, his voice low. "He's not a patient man."

"I'll come up with something. Don't worry about it."

"I'm not worried at all, *mon petit oiseau*." Mischief gleams in his eyes. "But I'm happy to help with the script. Think of it as a new act for our show, something to keep him at bay—at least for a while."

29

ROSALIE

Peace and joy blossom in my soul with each visit to Cirque du Noir. But today is different. Today, my stomach twists with each bend in the road as our last day together begins.

As excited as I am to see Adriano, I'm already dreading the inevitable heartbreak that will come tomorrow. Circo del Sol will begin heading west, while Cirque du Noir heads in the opposite direction, taking my new-found family and heart with them.

I shove the pending storm down, locking it up for the day. *Don't let this spoil today. Enjoy this last chance to be together for a while and deal with the fallout later.*

Instead of spending time with the rest of the carnies milling about, I make a beeline for his trailer, quietly slipping inside and locking the door behind me. The steady rush of water tells me he's still in the shower. *Perfect.*

I strip—slow and deliberate—leaving a trail of clothing from the door to his bed. Each piece falls away until only the lingerie remains. Red, wicked, and unforgettable. If this is our last time, he'll remember it every time he closes his eyes.

The water shuts off, followed by the creak of the door. Steam pours out, curling around his shoulders as he drags a towel across his body. Thank goodness for quality mirror placements, because I can enjoy the show from here. Droplets cling to the ridges of his abs before he brushes them away, his movements unhurried, unintentionally teasing. Draping the towel around his shoulders, he musses his hair to mop up the remaining moisture. He finishes drying, his muscles shifting under golden skin before his gaze snags on me in the mirror.

He freezes.

The sight of me sprawled across his dark sheets has him rooted in place. Scarlet lace bites into my tan skin. Crimson straps and gold chains glint under the lamp. I'm upside down. My legs are propped against the wall, hair spilling across the sheets, lips curved into a catlike grin. I let him drink me in.

When he turns, his eyes are molten, dragging down the line of my body. From my crossed ankles to the garters biting into my thighs to the belt hugging my hips. His gaze lingers on my breasts, sheer lace framing hard nipples linked by a delicate gold ring. My tongue flicks out. Seductively tracing the outline of my mouth before teasing my lower lip between my teeth, daring him closer.

His groan fills the room, low and guttural. I'm grinning wider than a Cheshire cat. I love that my body can rile him up without a single touch or word. He's already swollen to a hardened point, bobbing with every step like his body refuses to wait.

Closing the gap, he kneels, mouth crashing against mine, tasting, taking, devouring.

"God, you're a vision." He growls. "What did I do to deserve such a gift?"

I purr back. "A gift? You haven't even seen the best part, Tiger."

His mouth falls open slightly, his breath sputtering as I spread my thighs. The lace parts to either side of my lips, revealing my glistening heat, dripping and ready for him.

"Fuck." He mutters, dragging a finger through my slit. "Christ, Cher, you're soaked."

Bringing it to his lips, he sucks his digits clean with a groan. "Mm, such a delicious surprise."

The praise burns through me, my nipples tightening in response. I tug him closer, tongue tracing the underside of his length before sliding to his swollen tip. Pulling him into my mouth, he shudders. Hips jerking.

His fingers stroke deeper, teasing, and curling. His mouth finds my clit, sucking and flicking while I gag around him, refusing to let go. The room fills with wet sounds— slurps, gasps, moans. His tongue, his fingers, and his cock all own me, stretching me, until I'm nothing but sensations.

I quiver. Shaking. Aching. Needing more.

Gathering my juices and swirling them lower, he teases a more forbidden hole. Pooling spit and slick, his thumb presses past my tight barrier. So full. Stretched. All three of my holes filled with him. He worships me. My body no longer my own, but his. His to use. To own. To please.

The pressure builds fast. My body strains against itself as he plays me like an instrument. His rough pads curl against the perfect spot while his tongue works in relentless circles. My breath shatters into broken cries, muffled around the thickness filling my throat.

It hits like lightning. My toes curl. My back bows off the bed, every nerve ending detonating at once. I scream around him, the vibration making him groan as he bottoms out. He doesn't stop—doesn't let me come down—hurling me through orgasm after orgasm until tears stream down my face. My vision whites out. I'm overstimulated, broken open, and wrecked—gasping with incoherent sounds while he wrings me dry.

His thrusts grow erratic. Desperate. As though my convulsing body triggers his own climax. He fists my hair, holding me in place. Using me. Hard. Fast. Breathless. His whole body locks as he explodes with a snarl, his cock pulsing hot jets down my throat. I swallow greedily, choking on the force, but still begging for more. I suck harder, milking every drop until his thighs tremble and his hips jerk weakly.

When he tries to pull back, I don't let him. I lave my tongue along his length, cleaning him thoroughly, savoring every inch like he's the sweetest thing I've ever tasted. Only when he slumps against me, spent and shaking, do I release him, lips swollen, smile feral.

It was flawless. A shattering release. The perfect memory of us. As much as I didn't want this to be our last time, we didn't know when we'd cross paths again. If this was the end, then there was no better way for us to spend it than lost in each other's bodies.

It's wild how in such a short period of time, I've shared more with this man in a week than I have with any other soul in a lifetime. Maybe after I've avenged Carmen, I can see about switching roles to Cirque du Noir. They're already family and I'm going to miss them too, not just Adriano's dick. The whole package.

As always, I'm awake before my handsome ringmaster. The morning rays trickle through the windows, casting an angelic facade on his features. My avenging angel, one who walks in the darkness to lead others to the light.

I drape my body across his, enveloped by his scent and warmth. I can't remember a time when I've felt more safe or cherished.

Carefully untangling myself from his limbs, I pad to the bathroom. Cleaning myself, I creak the door open to rejoin Adriano when my gaze catches. I've admired the posters hanging in his trailer before, but never closely examined the pictures that line his mirror. This one stands out from the others. It's old, the edges worn and creased as though it has been folded and unfolded many times.

Inspecting it closer, I realize it's less like a photo and more like a postcard. A ringmaster poses as though he's announcing the next act while two acrobats swing from in the background. The man hangs by his knees, arms outstretched for a woman whose silver leotard sparkles in the light, her body twisting mid-air as her crown of light brown curls spills toward the floor. Squinting, I do a double take. These faces look familiar. Far too familiar.

Adriano's deep voice rasps from the bed. "Cher?"

"Right here, Tiger. Just had to pee." I tiptoe to the bed, crawling into the nest of blankets. "Mm, I wish this never had to end."

"Me too, cher." His eyes closed. "Stay. Martín doesn't deserve you, and I need you."

My mind pictures what things could be like if I stayed. The boisterous dinners, playing with the kids, maybe even finding my own role in the show. Most importantly, spending evenings tangled up with this amazing man.

The guilt swarms in as I lose myself in the fantasy. I can't have that yet, not until I've eliminated everyone responsible for Carmen's death. I won't let her loss be in vain, not if I can help it.

"I wish I could stay, but I can't just leave Circo del Sol... not yet." My words thick with regret.

He escorts me to my car, his hand steady on my back, oblivious to the fact that I'm carrying a piece of his past in my pocket. The guilt is sharp, but my need for the truth is sharper. I may have swiped his postcard and stashed it in my pocket. I need to confirm my suspicions before confronting him about it.

What I wasn't ready for was everyone at Cirque du Noir to be waiting to say goodbye. While some were packing gear, every single person took the time to give me a wave, nod, or hug. Luca insists on being held while he hugs my neck, little tears sneaking out at the prospect of not seeing me every day. Tony shuffled his feet awkwardly, as only a teenager can, trying to act too tough for hugs. Pulling him into my embrace, his soft sniffles shook both of our shoulders as he indulges me.

"You'll be coming back, right?" he asks meekly, clearly not sure if he's allowed to ask.

"Hopefully. I'm sure our circuses will be close by again one of these days." I try to reassure him.

"But that's a whole year away. Can't you just stay?"

"I wish I could, but not this time." He shuffles away; shoulders hunched in defeat.

Baba taps my shoulder, swinging me around into her grandmotherly arms. "You best be coming back soon, *mija*. I know true love when I see it, and honey, you two won't stay apart for too long."

"Oh no, we're not—" I open my mouth to protest, but she interrupts me.

"Our Adriano needs you, just like you need him." She whispers. "Your demons aren't as strong when you're together."

She slips off one of her bangles and slides it onto my wrist. "When you're ready, we'll be here waiting. You'll always have a home and family here."

Everyone slowly disperses, continuing to load trailers, until only Adriano and I are left in the parking lot. His hands are shoved into his pockets as he watches me with those dark eyes.

"So... uh, I guess this is it, huh?" I force out.

Backing me to my car door, he dips, mashing his lips to mine. His body says all the things neither of us are ready to verbalize. Panting, our foreheads touch, the gesture tender and raw.

He slips my phone out of my back pocket, flipping it open and programming a number in. His number. His phone rings. He silences it without looking, then passes my phone back.

"It's not goodbye, cher. Never goodbye." He rasps. "I'll talk to you soon, okay?"

"Okay, Tiger." He opens my car door, checking that I'm buckled and giving me one last smooch before closing me in. "Talk soon."

"Drive safe, ma chérie."

And with that, I pull away, leaving what very well might be the love of my life in the rearview.

30

ROSALIE

Every mile marker makes the ache in my chest intensify. Leaving Cirque du Noir was one of the hardest things I've ever done—and I've done my fair share of hard shit.

Hours later, the sharp sting has gone numb. I cut the engine and collect my thoughts, the crinkled postcard I swiped burning a hole in my pocket. Peering past the well-worn creases, I can't help but see the resemblance. The same curly hair. The prominent cheekbones. Even the physique is a match. Add a few years and it's like peering through a time machine.

Gathering my belongings, I make my way toward my trailer, already behind on packing. Passing the training grounds, I spot Phillip perched at the top of a ladder, dismantling rigging and bars. Below him, Anna is coiling the disconnected ropes into neat, round piles.

"Rosa! We've missed you! Someone's been staying out late." Anna grins, a mischievous glint in her gaze. "More escapades with this mystery man of yours?"

At least it's Anna and no one else noticing my late arrival.

"Something like that," I reply, plastering on a big smile, trying to keep the melancholy at bay. But even the best actors and actresses can't hide from Anna's mom-eyes. She drops the rope mid-coil and rushes over, wrapping me in a tight bear hug.

"Oh sweetie, I'm sure you'll see him again." She encourages. "If it's meant to be, then the distance won't change a thing."

Taking a deep breath, I soak in her motherly embrace. It's exactly the reminder I needed that this is home too. Our family is small, but Anna and Phillip are all I need. It's enough. It has to be.

"Hey, I actually wanted to talk to you about something..." I slip the tiny sheet from my pocket and press it into her palm. Unfolding the edges, Anna falters, the color draining from her face.

"W-where did you get this?" she demands, her voice dropping to a harsh whisper.

Her reaction wasn't at all what I had expected. Sure, I thought it might be a photo from their glory days, but I wasn't trying to scare the poor woman. Her whole body is rigid, her fingers trembling as she fights for control.

Gingerly, I try to set her mind at ease. "I might have stolen it from my mystery man?" My jovial tone isn't helping to calm her nerves. "I thought it looked remarkably similar to you and Phillip. Figured the odds you had doppelgängers running around were pretty low and maybe it was you two from the younger years."

Shadows darken in the corners of her eyes. She glances around, calling to Phillip. "Honey, can you come down for a second?"

He finishes tying off another bar, hollering over his shoulder. "Sure thing. Just a second, Dear."

"Phillip." Her voice is sharp, the urgency clear. "Now."

His head snaps up, his eyebrows knit together as he actually looks at his wife. "Shit," he mutters, dropping everything and hurrying over. "What is it, baby? What's wrong?" He wraps an arm around her, turning her so she's facing him.

Anna darts her eyes left and right, checking the coast is clear. She slips him the postcard. Matching shadows cloud his expression as he scrunches his nose. "Fuck."

"Rosa found this at her mystery man's place." She grabs his arm, a silent conversation happening between them. I start to back away, feeling like I'm intruding on an intimate moment. Not getting far, Anna snags my wrist, dragging me back into their tiny circle. Phillip's deep voice takes over. "We need to talk. Somewhere... private."

"Oh, um, sure. Okay," I stammer. "Is everything alright?"

"Shh. Not here." Their cagey behavior sets off every alarm. "Meet us in our car. Ten minutes."

"Uhm, okay, yeah. I can do that." I'm officially freaked out. This wasn't how I expected the conversation to go at all. I was wondering if they'd ever met Adriano and figured we could reminisce about their time at Cirque du Noir. Possibly even seek advice about long-distance circus relationships. I never would have guessed I'd trigger an emergency protocol.

They hurry away, tending to who knows what before I'm expected at the meeting point.

Wandering through the trailers, I pretend I'm packing—pretend my mind isn't racing at a million miles per minute. My watch blinks; it's time. They pull up just as I step into the parking lot. Anna rolls down her window just enough to bark, "Get in."

Sliding into the backseat, I buckle up, hoping I didn't accidentally stumble upon a Bonnie and Clyde serial killing duo. *They seemed so normal. My gut instinct can't be* that *wrong. Right?*

We drive for at least twenty minutes, winding down backroads at exactly the speed limit, getting further away from civilization. Finally, the car grinds to a halt in the middle of nowhere. And I do mean nowhere. Other than a few sparse trees, it's flat and barren, not a house or headlight in sight.

"Leave your phone here." Phillip instructs, leaving no room for argument.

They both hop out, not checking to see if I'm following as they stride deeper into no-man's land. *Shit, this isn't where I'm going to die.* My imagination whips together a new, worse outcome with each step. By the time we come to a stop, I'm starting to sweat from the mix of Texas heat and cold dread.

Cross-legged on the ground, we sink into silence. The strain in the air is palpable.

"Rosa, honey, we need you to tell us everything." Anna starts, still shaken but more poised than earlier.

"I already told you. I found it at my man's place. I thought it looked like you two."

Their faces don't relax at all. Phillip takes over. "This mystery man have a name?"

Dammit. I'd been hoping to keep that one a secret. "He does, but I don't see why it matters..."

"It's important, Rosa. We wouldn't be asking if it wasn't."

Anna presses. "Who is he?"

Running through my options, I finally land on the best one: the truth. "Adriano." I fist my shirt, twisting the fabric. "Adriano Devereaux. He's the ringmaster at Cirque du Noir."

Relief visibly washes over them as though hearing his name was enough to set their souls at ease. "So, Adriano's your mystery man?" Phillip's tone softens.

"Yeah... he's who I've been meeting for the past few weeks." It's like being scolded by my parents for seeing a boy without their approval, except in the middle of a desert.

Philip holds up the photo. "And where did you find this?"

"In his... uhm... trailer." The embarrassment rolls through me. This must be what the "sex talk" is like. Color starts to return to Anna's flushed cheeks.

"Oh, thank God." She says more to her husband than to me.

I fidget awkwardly. "So... why all the secrecy? What's going on?" My mind picks up momentum. "Wait—Is this actually you guys? Do you guys actually know Adriano?" *Holy shit, what if they do know each other?*

"I guess you're owed an explanation. In short, yes—this was us, from many years ago." Phillip resigns, letting his guard drop. "And yes, you could say we... *cough*... know the ringmaster of Cirque du Noir."

"What? How? When?" The questions tumble from my mouth.

Anna chuckles, placing her hand on Phillip's bicep. "Well, since forever? I mean, I would think that a mother would know who her own son is."

My mouth gapes, the bomb of information she dropped absorbing into my brain. "You mean... that he's your *gulp* son?" I scrunch my eyes closed, wishing I was invisible.

"Our first born, yes."

Mortification is only one of the many emotions colliding in my chest. I've spent the last few weeks talking to Anna about my mystery man and how amazing the sex is. Sex I've been having with her *son*. Hiding my face in my hands and curling in on myself isn't making me small enough to escape the embarrassment.

"Oh, God," I groan.

Peering between my fingers at them both, I can see it. The resemblance they have to Adriano. He definitely takes more after his father with his tall, dark hair and deep brown eyes. But those curls and his skin tone are all Anna. Had I been looking for it, I could have placed it sooner, but why would I be?

"I am so sorry! I didn't kno—" Their laughter cut me off.

"Oh, honey, there's nothing to be sorry for. I knew my son would pick nothing less than the best woman to be his." Anna's kindness melts away a layer of embarrassment. "Besides, we already think of you as our adopted daughter."

The sentiment fills a small crack in my heart—a void that has spent a lifetime searching for a family who could truly love and accept me. Sure, my parents loved me in their own way, but verbal confirmation from the people I viewed as my "adopted" parents healed some of my internal scars.

"Wait—you were part of Cirque du Noir?" Confusion floods me. "Why on earth would you leave and join this shit show?"

Anna laughs softly. "It wasn't our first choice. But we can't complain."

"What are you talking about? They're a completely different class of circus! It's like stepping out of the lion's pride and into the lion's den."

Sigh. "We know, sweetie. It's a little more complicated than that." Anna gets a misty, far away look. "We didn't leave by choice... and we didn't return by choice."

My hackles rise. "What do you mean, 'by choice?' Did someone force you? Did Adriano make you leave?"

"Not exactly." Phillip interjects. "It's not as black and white as that. You see, back then, it was simple. We loved the circus. Had two healthy sons who also loved the life. That man in the middle here." He points to the older gentleman, "Armond wasn't a great man, but he wasn't as horrible as the other ringmasters. He gave us a home. A family. He let Anna join us without question when I'd asked his permission. He was ruthless, but generally fair."

Anna softens as she thinks about her baby boy. "Our Adriano was a handful. Even though we wanted him to find a normal act, he tried a bunch of options in his younger years, but he didn't find his calling until his teens. The trapeze genes must have skipped him, and all went to his younger brother. But even as a boy, he could always hold an audience's attention with ease. He was commanding, confident, and the perfect temperament for a future ring-master. So naturally, Armond took an interest and took him under his wing as a protégé."

It made sense. From what I'd witnessed, Adriano was all those things and more. A natural born leader, the kind of man who people stopped to listen to. And he obviously loved the circus and his family.

"But why did you leave? Adriano wouldn't have forced you to go. Was it Armond? Did he force you out? I'm sure Adriano would've taken you in after he took over..."

My wheels were turning, but the gears were grinding. Something wasn't adding up. *Why would they leave Cirque du Noir? And why wouldn't they have gone back?*

Despite being clearly proud of their eldest son, a mixture of shame and grief coats the air.

"We never wanted to leave," Anna says, her voice thin. "We loved the circus, our home, our family. But we couldn't stay. There was an... incident. Our other son, Sammy, was beaten, and Adriano lost his mind. I guess he'd received a threat. People were starting to test the strength of the future ringmaster of one of the largest underground arms trades. Adriano was already shadowing Armond, but we didn't real-ize how deeply involved he'd gotten until it was too late to get him out." A shudder ripples down Anna's spine.

"Fucking assholes," Phillip tacks on. "Threatening a boy just to see if the big brother blinks."

"We tried to convince him that it would be alright; that empty threats couldn't scare us off," Anna says. "But he and Armond had already made a deal. We had no choice but to follow Armond's orders."

"Why didn't he come with you? Why didn't he leave too?" My heart aches for little Adriano. For the pressure and adult choices life forced him to make at such a young age.

The puzzle pieces are slowly falling into place from our conversations. How he treats the circus kids, his fierce pro-tector streak, and that air of loneliness about him even in a crowded room. Even with the circus family, he missed his actual family. His blood.

"We begged him to, but we were too late." Phillip's eyes go flat. "The deal had already been struck. His promise to become ringmaster in exchange for our freedom and the re-sources to disappear."

"By the time we were told of the deal and Adriano's plan, there was nothing more we could do. Our boy was lost to us, so we did the only thing we could do to protect them both. We took Sammy and disappeared." Anna's defeated tone was enough for me to reach out and clasp her hand in mine.

I shake my head, the irony tasting like copper. "I hate to break it to you, but you're kind of on a pretty public stage performing with Circo del Sol."

"We stayed off the map for years. Sammy had as close to a normal childhood as we could provide." A sigh leaves Anna's deflated body. "But about a year ago, we started getting strange letters. Someone had found us. They were trying to blackmail us to get to Adriano again."

She looks at me, her eyes pleading for understanding. "We obviously took the threat seriously, but we couldn't put him in danger. Not after all he's sacrificed for us already."

My voice drops. The edge in my tone pointed and sharp. "Threats? Who threatened you?"

"That's the thing, we still don't know." Anna lets out a shaky breath. A thick silence permeates the air, as though just speaking about the threat might make it appear.

Lowering my voice to a whisper. "What did they say?"

"Nothing explicit at first... but they escalated, becoming pretty explicit, but never making any direct demands. Notes appeared everywhere—our jobs, the house, our cars. Nowhere was safe, so we went into hiding.

"Circo del Sol seemed like the perfect cover. No one would expect us to go toward the world that threatened us, especially a competing circus. We always wear masks to keep our identities hidden. It was Phillip's idea, and honestly, it was brilliant."

"And Sammy?" My heart races. They've never even mentioned another son.

"We dropped him off at college," Anna says. "One that would keep him close to Adriano, but out of harm's way. Then we cut off all contact with him, trying to build as many layers of separation as possible to keep him safe."

It was a desperate kind of brilliant. Hiding in plain sight, dividing and conquering, and up until now, it's worked. No one has figured out who the dynamic duo truly are.

"We hate to ask, but you didn't show this to anyone else, right?" They hold out the postcard as though it could burn them.

"N-no, you're the first people I've seen since getting back... so no one else knows." I stutter.

"Thank God." Anna grasps both of my hands in hers. "Please, we need you to keep this a secret, especially from Adriano."

The sting from her doubt is quickly soothed by them entrusting me with their truth. "Your secret's safe with me, I promise. You're family." I wrap her in a warm hug. With that handled, it was time for the next order of business.

"Now tell me everything you can about these threats. No one threatens my family and gets away with it."

"I can do you one better." Anna's expression curls into a vicious smirk. "I saved every letter. You can see them for yourself."

31

ADRIANO

The last few weeks I've become a grumpy mother-fucker. Even Julianna has noticed my irate temper and irritability from afar. I'd love to say it's work-related, but honestly, I miss New Orleans. I miss the wholesome afternoons with my little bird and evenings spent losing myself in her.

It was too easy for us to fall into a routine. Morning practice, afternoons a perfect mixture of hanging out with the rest of the gang before sneaking off to bury myself in her before the evening shows. Despite usually only having one-night stands, there were times when I've kept the same girl for the week we were in town. But with Rosa, everything was different. I looked forward to seeing her, not just for sex, but to actually spend time together. Watching my family take her in and claim her as one of our own made my chest bubble with pride. Her kindness and motherly instincts with the kids had me constantly battling a hard-on at the worst possible times.

As the circus life goes, it was shorter-lived than I had hoped. Before we knew it, both Circo del Sol and Cirque du Noir had to move on to our next destinations. We've spent the past month working our way through Arkansas and Georgia, then up through the Carolinas—spending a week in each state. The show went on without a hitch, our acts performing their hearts out with crowds that enthusiastically praised us. But the high I usually felt after a performance had dimmed, leaving me horrible company to be around.

The first few weeks apart, we texted relentlessly. Every morning started with a "Good morning" text and every evening ended with a "Goodnight, cher." I found myself checking my phone constantly, even during morning training, just to catch a glimpse of what she was up to.

The playful banter kept my spirits light, and we quickly graduated to phone calls and video chats. The lack of sleep was well worth our conversations into the wee hours of the mornings.

The frequent calls and surprise selfies of her in those tiny show outfits got me through the day. They also helped keep my libido in check. It turns out my little bird can be quite the sexy operator—happily putting on scandalous shows for me at night while I commanded her from my bed, exactly the way she liked.

We talked about anything and everything. Her childhood before the tragedy of Carmen's disappearance, the loneliness of being a teenager with disengaged parents, her passion for martial arts and homemade enchiladas. In return, I gave her pieces of my own youth, how my parents were attentive, and Armond took me under his wing to keep me out of trouble.

Some topics were still off-limits— specifically my parents' current whereabouts, or anything related to Sammy. But even then, the silence on those fronts didn't seem to matter. Despite the hundreds of miles between us, I felt the space shrinking. For the first time in my life, I wasn't just wanting a woman, I was becoming anchored to one. Our late-night whispers stitched us together in a way that made the physical distance feel like a temporary inconvenience.

Suddenly, it all stopped. Each day, she pulled a little further away. Her texts became short and sporadic. My calls were declined or went straight to voicemail. No more video chats. *Poof.* She was gone like a ghost. Hence my shitty mood.

Thankfully, I've had enough work to bury myself in. With Julianna still on the road with Sammy tracking my parents, the backlog of paperwork and admin has piled up. With our stint in Virginia starting next week, I've spent my afternoons reviewing DOD bids and CIA contracts, prepping for a slew of meetings. It's the perfect excuse to hide away in my trailer, avoid the outside world, and spare them my misery.

For the first time in weeks, I almost feel normal. The familiar scents of grease and hops greet me. It's a refreshing change of pace after my miserable ass has been moping around for weeks. Despite my schedule being jam-packed, anytime we're near D.C., I always make time to meet my buddy Bryce outside of the CIA's stuffy boardrooms.

Bryce Langdon has been a field agent for as long as I've been ringmaster, possibly longer, and he'll soon be the new head of the Special Activities Center (SAC).

Bryce in and out of the office is like Dr. Jekyll and Mr. Hyde. At headquarters, he's always in a tailored suit paired with a watch with an outrageous price tag. Out here, in the wild of our favorite pub, he's just a guy sporting a casual t-shirt, well-worn jeans, and shit-kicker sneakers. His ability to switch effortlessly between corporate and off-the-clock Bryce was a skill the CIA probably recruited for all on its own.

Moseying to our usual corner booth, I'm greeted by his megawatt smile and a sweating pint of beer.

"Adriano! How ya been?" He claps my shoulder as I meet him halfway for a bro-hug.

"Bryce, hey man! I've been pretty good. How're you?"

"Oh you know, the same shit, different day. Doing my best to stay busy so I don't get roped into the latest Washington drama. The usual." He shrugs noncommittally, his contagious grin makes mine grow tenfold.

"You? Stay out of the drama?" I let out a dry laugh. My mind flashes to the last time we'd met for beers. His crazy ass had been elbow-deep in some international, tin-foil-hat cult, and he was loving every second of it. To Bryce, life was a game, a challenge that he took in stride better than anyone else I've ever met. I was convinced the CIA invented missions just to keep him entertained enough to stay out of trouble.

"Well, mostly anyway." He takes a short pull, draining the last few sips of his beer before setting the empty glass at the edge of the table. Right on cue, the waitress flits by, dropping off two fresh pints of frothy golden goodness.

"Figured I'd save us some time and order ahead." He

motions to the new round between us.

"Thanks, buddy," I raise my glass toward him. "Cheers—to no drama." Our drinks collide with a hearty *clink* in celebration of our annual reunion.

"Cheers to that." He chuckles, taking another healthy swig of his beer. He eyes me up and down, his gaze shifting into his professional setting—analyzing, calculating. "How's circus life treating you?"

"You could always come and see for yourself. You know you've always got two tickets on hold at the box office."

He waves a hand dismissively. "One of these days I'll make it. I'm just always finishing a mission or catching up on the pleasures I missed while deployed." His eyebrows wagging suggestively.

"Shouldn't be a problem now then, not with that fancy new title and office they're giving you."

If anyone deserves to be head of SAC, it's Bryce. Under that fun, outgoing exterior is a man who possesses more intelligence than a majority of the other intelligence agencies combined. He's quick-witted, resourceful, and has a sixth sense for reading people. That, plus his healthy dose of paranoia, makes him the best.

"Ah hell, we'll have to see." He says, leaning back. "It doesn't officially take effect until early next month, but I'll try to make the time."

"Excited?"

"Yes and no. I'll miss the action, but I'm excited to see what new shit I can stir up from the top." Checking over his shoulders, he drops his voice an octave lower. "Really though, how are you? You look wrecked, brother. Like you haven't been sleeping, and not for the fun reasons."

Running my fingers through my hair, I give him a high-level overview of the last few weeks, knowing full well that he won't drop it until his curiosity is satisfied. I focus on Rosa, mentioning some vague family drama without touching on specifics. As far as the Agency knows, my parents and Sammy are dead and buried. Some skeletons are meant to stay in the closet, and that is one of them.

Bryce listens patiently, absorbing every detail and filing it away. "Shit, man. That's rough. If you decide you want help tracking this chick down, let me know. You know I'm happy to help."

"Nah, I appreciate it, but I'm sure she's either busy or ghosting me on purpose." My ego deflates at the admission. As much as my every thought revolves around her, it's entirely possible she's already moved on. My chest feels like a hollowed-out cavity, but I respect her too much to hunt her down. If Rosa wants space, then space is what she'll get.

"Well, the offer stands if you change your mind." He shrugs, switching gears entirely as we chat about sports, the weather, and other dude stuff. By the time we're done shooting the shit, I'm a little lighter. Between the company and beers, I hit my mattress with a flop and finally get a few hours of dreamless sleep.

32

ADRIANO

Typically, I don't mind dressing up. Hell, it's a staple part of my job as ringmaster to wear jackets and finery designed to woo the crowd. Even then, the way a crisp suit can make me feel like a caged animal is impressive. I tug at the starched collar of my shirt, unable to leave it alone. Some might mistake my discomfort for nerves, but I just prefer my boots to loafers and my purple coat to a suit jacket.

Passing under the high archway and through the sliding glass doors, I cross the familiar shield and star emblem, framed by the words *Central Intelligence Agency, United States of America* in bold gray and white lettering. Striding between the bland pillars, I swipe my guest badge to open the glass gates blocking the entrance to Langley's headquarters from the general public.

Navigating the halls with ease, I make my way toward the familiar boardroom where Director Thomas Vance, the nearly retired head of SAC, and I always handle business. Unlike the building's exterior of off blue glass panes and concrete, the interior is a tomb of dark mahogany tones and lush carpet. No one can see in or out. It's a vacuum of state secrets and high-end security. The familiar camp of black leather chairs surrounding a massive oak table greet me as I enter the room.

Vance's gaze lifts from a stack of paperwork; he's been awaiting my arrival for a while now. Years of military training make a man insanely punctual—the kind of punctual that is labeled extremely early by society's standards. Despite being older, his neatly trimmed haircut and thick-rimmed glasses give him a sharp Clark Kent look. He's fit and commanding, a man who refused to let the grueling hours hunched at his desk soften his edges.

Bryce is already settled in, his attention buried in his phone. Typically, it's just Vance and me, but with their upcoming transition, they're using today to hand off the contractor accounts.

Nodding politely to Bryce, I give a firm handshake to Director Vance. "Director, it's a pleasure to see you. Thanks for taking the time to meet."

"Always a pleasure, Mr. Devereaux." He dips his head respectfully, returning the greeting. "The Agency values your support. I'm sure our partnership will continue to thrive as Special Agent Langdon takes the reins."

Bryce and I exchange a professional greeting, feigning the distance of mere acquaintances. It's better if the Agency doesn't know how close we are.

Taking a seat, we dive right in, conducting a thorough retrospective analysis—discussing last year's performance, highlighting what went well, and reviewing any complaints or issues with the merchandise. My weapons are top-notch and highly sought after, so finding a buyer has never been a struggle. The CIA just happens to have deeper pockets than the average thug, and every deal like this helps move Cirque du Noir one step closer to a legitimate portfolio.

Director Vance and I move contract by contract, ensuring no detail is overlooked, while Bryce flips open a laptop and taps away.

"The Sig Sauers and Glocks were perfect, as always." Vance says. "Next year we'll need to double our count."

I scribble a note on my copy of the contract. "Not a problem. When do you need those in by?"

"Ideally, ASAP. We have escalations stirring with a new warlord in North Africa. Work with SnoDex Logistics to get them dropped directly at our base in Morocco."

"It'll double the shipping costs, but I'll work with Jin to coordinate the delivery," I reply. "How'd the experimental tactical vests work out?"

"They worked well for the cold, but they weren't great

for the heat. We'll renew for the same quantity as last year, but we need something better suited for the desert. Do you have anything lighter that breathes easier?"

"We have a new lightweight ceramic plate carrier," I offer. "It's modular and built for high-heat endurance. It'll fit your standard kits without the bulk."

"Perfect. Bryce, pull the paperwork together for a sample order."

"Got it." Bryce says without looking up. "Want those delivered to Langley?"

"Yes, let's get them here for testing." The director continues working through his list.

The hour blows by and we've got our takeaways to prepare for our next meeting. "Any other issues with the merchandise we need to cover?"

"No. They were on time and high quality, as usual." Vance extends his hand. "Special Agent Langdon will have the updated paperwork pushed through the proper channels by Friday. Let's reconvene at the same time next Wednesday."

"See you then." I close my folder, a million dollars in new equipment orders tucked under my arm. "And congratulations on the retirement, Vance. This place won't be the same without you."

The Director lets out a rare, genuine laugh. "Don't encourage me. My poor wife has been waiting for me to get out of this building for far too long. She's already booked back-to-back cruises for the next four months."

33

ROSALIE

After learning Anna and Phillip *Devereaux's* true identities, it took a day for everything to sink in. My two favorite people at Circo del Sol are not only on the run, but they also happened to be the parents of the only man to ever unravel me.

Putting aside my embarrassment, I get to work doing what I do best: fixing and planning. I'd meant it when I said no one messed with my family. Blood or chosen, it doesn't matter. Family is family, and they are part of my tribe.

So the hunt begins.

Digging through the nondescript shoebox, we spend the drive between cities dissecting every letter they'd received. Anna was smart to keep them bundled together, scrawling the dates they were found across the envelopes for reference.

The notes were all the same: matching sheets of heavy cream paper with centered text typed in a generic font. At a quick glance, it could easily have been mistaken for a bill or a piece of junk mail. It was a calculated blandness—the kind that let a death threat sit on a kitchen table without drawing a second look.

After poring over the content for hours, I hit a wall. Then I saw it.

"Holy shit! I think there's an emblem or logo here!" I slide the sheet over to Anna.

She examines the cream-colored paper, leaning in and squinting at it like Velma without her glasses. "I don't see anything, honey. It looks blank to me."

"Here, look." I point to the bottom righthand corner. "You have to rub over this spot."

There's no signature, but if you carefully inspect the corners, each letter carries the same faint, embossed ridges. It isn't pronounced enough to see with the naked eye, almost as though the notes were sealed leaning against another object with that shape. A stamp, a seal, or a desk plate that pressed its identity into the grain of the paper.

Anna skims her fingertips across the page, tracking the ridges like she's reading braille. "You might be right. I think something is there." She digs in her purse like a madwoman, pulling out a piece of scrap paper and a half-melted restaurant crayon.

Laying the blank sheet over the note, she starts to rub the crayon over top. "When the boys were young, they were obsessed with mysteries and pretending to be detectives. They had read that you can reveal the imprint of something written on a pad of paper by coloring lightly over it." She keeps scribbling gently, her arm wiping in slow linear sweeping motions. "It wasn't so funny when I came home to the entire trailer covered in crayon—they might have forgotten the part about putting a piece of paper on top first. But, if we're lucky, it could work."

A round emblem starts to form, a thin circle surrounding a vague shield. It's hard to make out the details, but it resembles a crest of sorts with an animal perched above it. It isn't much, but it's a start. Wherever these letters originated, this mark is associated.

My afternoons that were previously consumed by Adriano, are now substituted for hours of online research. It's like hunting a needle in a haystack, except my haystack consists of the entire internet. Scouring and scrolling through endless crests and emblems is mind-numbing. The problem isn't that I couldn't find anything, it's the complete opposite. I've found hundreds of possibilities. Without a clearer reference, I'll never be able to narrow it to a single image.

My phone buzzes on the desk, the vibration rattling against the wood like a warning. I don't need to look to know who it is. I've memorized the rhythm of his persistence.

Adriano.

I stare at his name lighting the screen, the weight of a thousand unspoken words pressing against my chest. My thumb hovers over the green icon, aching to hear the rough velvet of his voice. But I can't. I promised Anna that I'd tell no one—especially him. A promise I fully intend to keep. Besides, if he knows I'm in this deep, he'll pull me out to keep me safe—or worse, he'll get involved himself trying to help.

Not trusting myself to not let something slip, I swipe left, sending him to the void of my voicemail for the second time today. The deafening silence that follows amplifies the ache in my chest, leaving his string of unanswered messages cluttering my homescreen.

In desperate need of a break—and a way to drown out the guilt—I switch tactics and try to meet with Sammy. Maybe he has additional ideas on what might be after his parents. I book a flight and take a day trip to Louisiana.

Visiting his university proves unfruitful. No one has seen or heard from him. It's as though he vanished into thin air. His dorm room is already overrun by his roommate's stuff, and not a single professor has marked him present since last month. It's suspicious.

Tracking down people was something I could do. Tapping into my network, I call Joaquín.

"¡Hola Rosita! It's been too long. How're you, *mija*?" His melodic voice bubbles through the line.

"Hola, Joaquín. I'm good. You?"

"Good, good. Too hot here, as always, but I'm doing fine." We spend a few minutes catching up on his MMA gym and gossip from the old neighborhood. It's a dance we both know by heart.

Finally, the pleasantries taper off, and it's time for business.

"Joaquín, I need a favor."

"Anything for my favorite girl. How can I help?" *God, I miss him.* His candor's a refreshing reminder that I'm not alone.

"It's a big ask," I say. "I need to find someone, a close friend's son."

Joaquín's breath hitches, a signal of the shift. Years in the service built a wall of paranoia around him thick enough to warrant a system of coded speech, even on secured lines. He doesn't ask *what*. He asks *how bad*.

"Code Red?" He clips, flipping into military mode. *Abduction. Trafficking.*

"I don't think so, but I'm not sure. More of a Code Amber situation." *Missing, but unconfirmed foul play.*

He continues his line of questioning. "When and where were they last seen?"

"Not 100% certain. At bare minimum, a month ago at his college in Louisiana."

"A month? *Mierda*, Rosa. He could be anywhere by now." I can hear the frustration in his growling response.

"I know, I know. But I have to try. His parents have been Code Black for months now." *Living under the radar.*

"I see. Send me what you've got, and I'll put out feelers. I'll be in touch."

"Wait!" I call out, gripping the phone tighter. "I have one more thing."

"Yes?"

"I'm sending a picture of a logo. It's only a partial, but I haven't had any luck identifying it."

He chuckles, the sound a fleeting warmth. "I'm always up for some light reading, *mija*. Send it, and I'll take a look."

The line goes dead a heartbeat later, the warmth of his voice already fading. Code Red, Code Amber, Code Black. The colors of my life lately.

Practice was brutal. My body is sore from the new poses that Martín demanded I hold during different acts to "enhance the audience's experience;" a crock of shit considering I was offstage for ninety percent of it. Each week he pulls me further from the spotlight, relegating me to the corners and shadows. It pisses me off, but Martín is a man who gets what he wants and right now he wants less of me.

The spray of hot water thaws my tense muscles, as the drain whisks away the sweat and grime. The fumes I've been running on finally catch up to me. I sink to the stall floor. *Ahh, this is heaven.* The steam curls around me in a protective cocoon, while the water drops pelt my skin to a flushed rosy color. My mind wanders off before having to focus on more research. Tipping my head back, I let my hands follow where my mind goes—a sweet memory of Adriano and our last shower together.

My palms slide down my body, tweaking my nipples

lightly as they move further south. My knees spread; feet planted wide as the water cascades along every dip and crevice. I pretend my hands are his— Adriano's—as he softly warms me up before overwhelming me with pleasure.

His tall, hard body presses against mine. His sweet accent whispers sweet praises into my ear.

Such a good girl....

Look at you taking me so well...

Fuck sweetheart, you wreck me...

Even in my dreams, his voice brings me to my knees.

Lightly scraping my nails on my inner thighs, I hone in on that delicate bundle of nerves under the hood. Applying pressure in tight little circles, just above my needy holes. Dripping. Aching to be filled.

His thick, long fingers dip inside me. Swirling the moisture around, coating his fingers and parting my core. Sliding in and out the way he does, I curl my fingertips against the rough ridge that has me panting.

I add another finger, pretending the stretch is from the intrusion of his delicious cock. My mouth waters as my back arches, head back, moaning his name as my release coats my thighs.

It's been this way for weeks, living day-to-day off the mental spank bank content we created together. It's not enough to fill the emptiness that's taken up residence in my chest, but I welcome the brief mental escape.

Wrapped in a fluffy white towel, I twist my hair and make my way toward the dresser. I stop short. A note sits squarely on my pillow, the plain white envelope a stark contrast against my gray sheets. "Rosa" is typed across the center. Simple. Direct. Clear.

The air in the trailer turns brittle. Someone was in here while I was in the shower and left this for me to find.

My hand trembles as I open the edges, carefully separating the glued corners, revealing cream paper inside. My breath hitches. I know this paper. It's the same kind that I've spent hours analyzing for clues.

My heart leaps into my throat. I carefully pull out the tri-folded sheet, pinching it delicately between my forefinger and thumb. I brace myself as the paper unfolds. Like every other letter, the text is typed and centered. The only thing on the large page.

'Seems being at the center of one circus isn't
enough for a greedy girl like you.
It's time to step out of the limelight or we'll remove
you forcibly.
It's your choice, Rosalie.'

Swallowing hard, my fingers brush the bottom corner, praying the familiar round ridges aren't present, but expecting nothing less. Raised bumps meet my fingertips. *Shit.* I scramble to my desk, snagging a paper and pencil to make an imprint of the design, watching as each charcoal stroke reveals the same mystery logo.

34

ADRIANO

A petite female agent intercepts me in the lobby, insisting on an escort. Taking the elevator down, she leads me through winding corridors that feel less like an office and more like a bunker. She swipes her badge, unlocking the heavy door, redirecting me from our normal boardroom to a smaller, dim room.

"Please wait here. Someone will be with you shortly." Her tone is thick with strange remorse as she shuts the metal door behind her.

Bland gray walls make the room seem smaller than it actually is. A sterile, metal desk and two chairs occupy the space. I slide into the chair facing the door, not wanting my back to the entrance.

The thumb drive in my pocket contains all the information that Director Vance requested in our last meeting. It had taken me countless hours and more video calls with Julianna than I'd care to admit to gather all the necessary documents. Usually, Julianna handles it, but with her still on the road, she worked some tech-voodoo magic to set up a secure connection and guided me through the more complex parts. With how many shell companies we are buried under, it's difficult for anyone except her to keep it all straight.

After waiting over a half-hour, the door swings open and a shrewd man barges in, taking the seat across from me. Unlike Vance and Bryce, who exude serious but calm energy, this man feels darker, more akin to the criminals I deal with. The atmosphere around him is heavy, coiled tight with a singular obsession. He sits quietly, observing me with a harsh stillness. His face is set in a neutral mask, except for the two deep, permanent creases running from the sides of his sharp nose to the corners of his pressed mouth.

I wait, refusing to disrupt the silence first while watching his green eyes assess me.

He breaks first. "Adriano Devereaux. What a pleasant surprise."

"It seems you have me at a disadvantage. You know my name, but I don't know yours. And you certainly aren't Director Vance or Special Agent Langdon." I jab, hoping to unsettle him. This room, the wait, the lack of professionalism, it all screams overcompensation.

"Ah, yes. Of course." He leans back. "You can call me Special Agent Brandon. I'll be taking Director Vance's place today."

I place my elbows on the table, pasting on a bored expression. "If the Director is too busy to meet, we'll reschedule. No need to waste your precious time, Special Agent."

I stand to leave, pulling out my phone to shoot Bryce a quick message.

"If you leave now, there won't be a next meeting." Brandon sneers. "You see we've run into some complications."

I pause, my interest piqued. "And what might those be?"

Brandon slides a thick file across the table. "Your last shipment didn't pass internal inspections. Signs of tampering. Missing product. It appears that your business can't fulfill its end of the contract, making you ineligible for renewal."

My gaze narrows. There's no way any of our products would've been missing or messed with. My crew stationed near Langley holds higher clearances than most people in this building. They're all loyal veterans who would never damage or ship damaged goods.

"My products are the highest caliber and none of my team would have tampered with them. We run tighter security than your whole alphabet soup," I retort.

Brandon puffs out his chest. "All the evidence says otherwise." He points to the file.

I scan the contents, flipping through the folder. Pages

upon pages of damage reports fill the crease: missing bills of ladings, tampered crates, claims of damaged slides on the latest shipment of Sig Sauers and Glocks, delays on shipments that we'd sent in months ago. A myriad of issues that don't match the invoices I'd reviewed with Vance and Bryce days prior. Something was off. The top of the page has the correct logo and business name, but the dates and orders don't line up.

"Special Agent Brandon, this is clearly a misunderstanding, but I'll only speak with the Director. When he returns, we'll get to the root of these accusations." I close the file, tucking it under my arm and refusing to return it. This information is coming home with me.

"I already told you, the Director will not be meeting with you moving forward." His tone is the only indication that his nerves are fraying.

"Then there's nothing more to discuss. My team will conduct an internal investigation. Thank you for bringing me your concerns." I leave the thumb drive in my pocket and head for the door.

"Mr. Devereaux," Brandon calls after me. "I expect to see you here next week. If you don't return with substantial proof of innocence, you'll be charged with destruction of government property and held until a full investigation is completed." His green eyes sparkle at the blatant threat.

"Of course, Special Agent."

35

ROSALIE

Since the ominous letter made its appearance, I've closely watched Martín's every move. He's always been a shady character, but between the note and him forcing me out of more acts, he was the prime suspect in my investigation.

He doesn't love Adriano, but I wouldn't go so far as to say he hates the guy. To Martín, business is just that—business. It's rarely personal. He doesn't see people; he sees dollar signs and opportunity. What I can't piece together is the why. Why would Martín target Adriano's family, then willingly let them join Circo del Sol? What's his angle?

One benefit of my minimized time in the spotlight is that I now have extra time to snoop while Martín is guaranteed to be busy. Anna keeps watch, monitoring Martín's whereabouts, and sending an SOS text if he's done early. With my early warning system in place, I casually stroll to Martín's trailer. Discreetly palming my tools, I easily unlock the door with an inaudible *click*.

Stepping into the dark space, I fumble around until the light switch flicks, illuminating everything in a soft yellow hue.

Unlike Adriano's trailer, where everything is neat and cozy, Martín's trailer is disorganized and lavish. Bright red silk sheets are bunched and strewn across the king-size bed. The vanity is littered with sprays and glass bottles, making the place reek of stale cologne and cheap desperation. Laundry overflows from the basket, the floor surrounded by socks and rumpled clothing. You could compare the after photo of a hotel room trashed by a high rockstar and Martín's quarters and find nary a difference. Hell, the rockstar might actually be voted the tidier of the two.

His desk is no cleaner. The ornate cherry wood dominates the space, almost too big for the room. Stacks of papers, receipts, and food wrappers are piled high, a perfect advertisement for why some people require housekeeping services. Scrunching my nose and intentionally breathing only through my mouth, I start sifting through the largest piles for anything to pop out.

Bills, invoices, magazines. He really needs a filing system. I fight every OCD bone in my body to not start sorting or alphabetizing them. Moving to the next stack, I skim for any abnormalities. Nothing stands out. *Something must be here.* Determination fuels my veins.

My gaze catches on a single cream sheet. *Jackpot!* Tugging it loose, the familiar font appears.

Ships rest in the southern shelf by the sea.
24 @ 01:00
CUF 100k

It must be some kind of code. I snap a quick photo with my phone before shoving it back exactly where I found it. I can decipher the message later. The clock is ticking and I don't want to leave any stone unturned.

Pulling out drawers, I continue strategically tearing through the other stacks of papers and checking every other possible hiding spot. The rest of the clutter is just noise. There's nothing else in this mess that whispers of a conspiracy. I'd say it might be on Martín's computer, but he's so oldschool that he barely knows how to send emails—let alone manage the cybersecurity protocols an illicit online business requires. So hard copies are my best bet.

Exhausting my options, I double-check that everything is in its original home and exit the same way I came in. Martín should be none the wiser.

Keeping my distance, I tail Martín through the maze of tents. He weaves between them with entitled confidence, ignoring the other circus folks like the peasants he believes we are. Approaching his trailer, he casually clears his left and right, as though he's ensuring no one is watching him before swiftly entering and locking it behind him.

After finding that suspicious letter on his desk, I'm paranoid and invested. Martín is up to something, and it's only a matter of time before I unravel the mystery.

Sneaking closer, I duck under one of his windows, listening intently for any movement. He rustles around briefly, but nothing sounds out of the ordinary.

Just as I'm about to throw in the towel, he cracks the window above me, likely seeking air circulation to combat the stifling California heat. His phone chimes with a distinct, unfamiliar ringtone.

"Hello?" He answers, the other person muffled by his ear against the receiver.

"Yeah, tonight at 01:00."

"You better be on time. This is your last chance, or you're out."

"Just make sure your crew isn't packing heat and we shouldn't have a fucking problem." *Packing heat? This must be some kind of drop. He only ever focuses on security when he's handling international deals and drops, not for normal meetings.*

"Yes, be ready and waiting at the south entrance." *Holy shit! I think he's talking about the docks! Or could it be a warehouse? Dammit, there are so many options.*

He hangs up with a vicious grunt. "Fucking morons."

Still crouched in the bushes, I scroll my gallery, checking my photo of Martín's letter to see if I can narrow down the location. I already have the date and time. Only one last piece of information, and I'll crack the code.

With my car tucked away from street view, my keys twist in the ignition, cutting the engine. Flipping a quick text with the address to Joaquín, I silence my phone.

By the docks, I wait a safe distance from a massive, unmarked warehouse—the kind of scale that leads you to assume Amazon or Walmart operate out of it. Rows of empty bay doors are lined up, ready and waiting for deliveries. The parking lot has enough lamp posts to be brightly lit—or it would be, if half of them weren't burnt out, leaving only a few remaining bulbs to pierce the dark.

I glance around, hoping I didn't decipher Martín's code wrong. In head-to-toe black, I stick to the shadows. Binoculars hang loosely around my neck. Sweat trickles down my spine, the tiny beads of moisture doing little to quench the heat.

Prowling closer for a better vantage point, I scout a clear view of the doors and main entrance, and raise my binoculars to hone in on any activity. So far, all I've seen is a few men going in, but no one has returned. No boxes. No crates. Empty hands and a locked door. *Suspicious.*

I'm still uncertain if this is a drug drop or something worse, but judging from the lack of activity and men, I'm leaning toward drugs. *Boring.* If we're working with new suppliers, I'm not entirely surprised I was left out of the loop. Martín continues to isolate me from circus operations. I figure after my afternoon rendezvous with Adriano and the pitiful intel I'd fed him, he might finally be suspicious of where my loyalties lie. Usually, it wouldn't matter and I would've been included anyway. Martín is one thing above all else, lazy. If he can avoid doing the work or can make someone else do it, he absolutely does. So, it's out of character for him to be so involved with a delivery.

Every slow, shaky breath has me on edge, the sharp precipice of breaking the code tentatively within reach, but still so far away.

My watch blinks: *1:00 AM*.

A nondescript box truck pulls in and backs flush to the receiving bay. I strain to catch a glimpse of the driver, the cargo, or anything more than the white panels of the trailer. Having no luck, I'll have to get closer to see what's going on. Zipping my black jacket tighter, I make my way around to one of the side entrances.

Luckily, these industrial shells house dozens of businesses under one roof. I jimmy the lock on a neighboring unit and slip inside. No guards. No cameras. It's almost too easy.

The interior is a cavern of silence, illuminated only by the ghostly crimson of emergency exit signs. High ceilings disappear above the rows of metal framework. I follow the wall until I reach a break in the space—a large industrial door.

I worry that activating the sensors—or worse, the buzz of the canvas rolling up, will trigger a safety alarm. In these places, safety relies on the very things I can't afford: bright flashing lights and piercing sounds. For me, stealth is critical.

Instead of approaching the large door, I spy an air duct that connects the warehouses. Using the metal beams as a ladder, I wedge my way into the larger than average crawl space. *Thank God for industrial HVAC systems, or I'd never fit.*

Shimmying, I inch my way through the metal tunnel toward the bright lights. Reaching the metal grate, I peer through the angled slats, listening for signs of life. Silence. *Phew.* I'd made it into the correct warehouse without being caught. I ease the grill open and carefully slide through, avoiding dropping to my doom. Now, to venture further into the belly of the beast.

Staying between the metal racks, I nudge my way around the stacked boxes and pallets. Soft voices guide me through the maze of rows until I'm close enough to discern random voices and phrases.

"Hmm. These are quite nice."

"Damn! Look at the grip on those."

"Shut up, you'll get us in trouble."

A heavy *thud* is followed by a hissed curse. "Ow, dammit. Watch where you're going fucker."

I risk a peek from my hiding spot. Two men are inspecting a large wooden crate while a handful of others unload more heavy totes from the truck. My stomach drops. The dimensions are way too big for drugs. They're twice as long as they are wide, but only a foot deep.

The two men standing over the open crate are dressed way nicer than everyone else. On one side, a man in a form-fitting dark suit with matching gloves inspects the merchandise. His whole demeanor screams "mean and ornery," with deep creases that testify to his lack of humor.

The other man wears a light suit, his pale gloves a stark contrast to his slicked-back black hair. He looks vaguely familiar. Analyzing his features, I try to place him until the realization clicks: the shorter Mexican closely resembles none other than Martín Gonzales. Maybe he's a brother? A cousin? Whoever he is, he's clearly up to no good. A smarmy smirk coats his lips as he peruses the crate's contents.

If they were off to the side just a hair more, I'd have a decent view of the crate's contents, but since their parents weren't glassmakers, I'm stuck guessing. I wait as they haphazardly close the lid, issuing a series of commands before walking off—likely to finalize payment. At this point, the truck is mostly empty. The crew has shifted from unloading to driving the crates deeper into the warehouse. This is it. The moment where I can choose to play it safe and retreat to my car or venture further and try to solve the mystery of what's in the box.

My teeth worry my bottom lip while I assess my options. As easy as it would be to turn and run, this opportunity might not come again. Other than a few ominous letters, I have no other leads to pursue. This is it—my needle in the haystack that actually panned out. It's a chance I can't pass up.

With ninja-like grace, I drop between the stacks of crates, landing softly on the concrete. My glorified ballet slippers allow me to move without a squeak or creak as I slide as close as possible along the stacks while staying hidden.

With everyone distracted and no one expecting me, I have one shot to get a closer look before the bossmen return. Crouching low, I wait until the henchmen are shuffling the heavy pallets deeper into storage. Seizing the opportunity, I skate across the floor like a kid on hardwood in socks.

My momentum slows as I reach the base of the box. The top's ajar just enough that I can hook my fingers on the rim and peer inside without having to lift it. With my face half-hidden behind the case, my eyes widen as dark, heavy metal gleams back at me. I count dozens of guns lining the crate, half-buried under shredded paper.

With a whole trailer load, this buyer must either be a massive redistributor or preparing for a war. I shudder at the idea of Martín meeting a new dealer. Is he replacing Adriano? Everyone knows weapon distribution is exclusively his market, and he won't take kindly to anyone bringing in competition.

My mind spins scenario after scenario, stalling as a new worst-case forms. *What if Adriano is behind the threats to his family?* Is the seller one of his men? I don't recognize him from Cirque du Noir, but it's plausible, if not extremely likely that he has others running deliveries.

Taking a mental picture, I turn to scramble back to my hiding spot when two large goons block my way. Their bulky arms are crossed over massive chests, forming a human barrier between the crates and the stacks, leaving me fully exposed.

I skid to a squealing halt. "Well, um, hey guys. Don't mind me, I'm just running something to the boss." I nervously chuckle, throwing my thumb over my shoulder in what I pray looks like a relaxed, natural gesture.

Tweedledee and Tweedledum swap a quick glance with raised eyebrows, clearly not buying my story, before they close in. Spinning on my toes, I sprint around the crate and dive for the nearest aisle. Gripping the post, I launch myself around the corner with the Tweedle-brothers in pursuit.

Turns out, you should really watch where you're going when trying to run away. I swing around the corner, making what I think is a clean escape until I slam into a wall of muscle. Large hands grip my arms, locking me in place.

"Well, well, well. Look what we have here."

My spine snaps to attention as I come face-to-face with none other than Mr. Broker and Mini Martín. Mr. Broker's foxy gaze skims me from head to toe, letting out an obnoxiously loud laugh as I struggle to create space, but his grip only tightens. He hauls me closer to his cologne-drenched body, forcing the air out of my lungs.

"Mr. Gonzales, it seems we've caught ourselves an intruder." Mr. Broker breaks out into a grim smirk. "*Tsk*. And here I was assured you had the highest level of security in place."

Mini Martín's expression drops. "Señor, I swear we have guards patrolling the area and monitoring every door."

Mr. Broker raises his eyebrows, his tone half-teasing, but deadly serious. "If I can't trust this outfit's security standards, then I'll take my merchandise elsewhere. I don't do business with incompetent buyers."

Panic bubbles from Mini Martín. "Please, Señor. Martín will kill me if this deal goes sideways. Besides, we've already unloaded and paid for everything." He stammers between trying to exude confidence and hyperventilating at the prospect of Martín's wrath. "I'm sure we can come to an arrangement."

Mr. Broker feigns bored indifference, as though the

conversation is a waste of his precious time. More focused on me, he continues his perusal as I struggle to escape, his tight grip causing my fingers to tingle with numbness. "I'm listening."

Mini Martín glances around frantically, in search of anything that might interest Mr. Broker enough to overlook his infraction. You can almost see the lightbulb flicker over his dumb head. "What about the girl? You seem to like her. We'll give you her as a gesture of good faith—a little incentive to start our partnership on the right foot."

Mr. Broker seems to ponder Mini Martín's offer, amused by my ever-growing scowl.

"I am not for sale." I snarl at them both, my temper reaching meltdown temperatures.

"Do you know who this woman is?" Mr. Broker asks, dismissing my outburst and directing his question only to Mini Martín.

Mini Martín scrubs the back of his neck sheepishly. "Umm, no? Am I supposed to know her?"

Mr. Broker's tongue clicks, a clear sign of disapproval. "Oh Hector, Hector, Hector. I'm amazed Martín lets you conduct any of his business. *This* happens to be your brother's ringmistress, Ms. Rosalie Martínez. I'm not too sure how happy he'd be to find out you've sold her off to save one measly deal."

My eyes widen. This man knows who I am—who I *really* am. He used my real name, Rosalie, not just Rosa. Dismayed, I turn to Hector, ready to tear him limb from limb the second I get free.

Hector studies me, his eyes roaming my face in an attempt to jog his memory. Finally, he opens his mouth. "If she were available... and if Señor Gonzales agreed to it... Would she be enough compensation to ensure we continue having profitable relations?"

My heart rate skyrockets at the idea of being a prisoner. Joaquín has my location, but he won't be concerned for at least a day or two.

Mr. Broker does another slow appraisal. "Hmm."

"Please, Señor. She's quite a beauty. I'm sure she'd be a great addition to your collection." Hector pleads.

"Consider it done. But this is a warning. Cross me or show up with shitty security again and we're finished—with additional consequences." Mr. Broker's words have me vibrating from a cocktail of fear and rage.

Hector simply nods, flipping open his phone and stalking off as he contacts who I assume must be Martín himself.

"Let. Me. Go." I hiss. Mr. Broker doesn't seem irked in the slightest. His green eyes are impressively light for a man who had his weapons deal interrupted.

He shakes his head, leaning in closer with his smoky breath. "Oh, Rosalie, you should have heeded my warning. But here you are, making the next step in my plan that much easier to execute."

Hector makes his way back to us, a slimy smirk in place as he pretends to dust off his hands in a dramatic motion. "Well, Señor Martín is more than happy to do whatever it takes to keep business moving. Consider her a peace offering."

I start fighting with all my might, catching Mr. Broker by surprise and dislodging my arms from his fists. I sprint toward the stacks, my head swimming with information as I desperately try to connect the dots while searching for an escape. A door to the receiving bays comes into view. I pump my arms harder, my chest burning as I race toward the exit.

My fingertips brush the doorknob when a large shadow passes over me, tackling me to the ground. Sprawled like a baby deer on ice, I thrash to get free, but the weight on my back renders me immobile. Tweedledee must have been waiting for his boss's signal, knocking the wind out of me with his pounce. His forearm wraps tightly around my throat until spots dance in my vision.

"*Tsk, tsk,* Rosalie. You should've known better than to run." The soft clack of Mr. Broker's shoes reaches my ears. A sharp prick pierces my neck. My muscles go limp and my eyelids grow heavy as the world spins out of focus. I descend into darkness, hearing his final, whispered promise: "Don't worry, pet. It'll all be over soon."

36

ADRIANO

An unfamiliar number flashes on my phone. Strange, but it isn't unheard of for Julianna to use a burner. "Hello?"

Silence beats on the other end. Just as I'm about to hang up, a soft, familiar voice echoes through the line. "Hey, honey, it's me."

Now it was my turn to be silent. *What the fuck? Is someone playing a prank?* There's no way that voice is actually coming through the receiver. I growl, pissed at the tease of getting to finally hear a voice I've missed for years. "Excuse me, who the fuck do you think you are?"

"Honey, Adriano, it's really me. I'm sorry I wouldn't be calling you if it wasn't an emergency. It's really me. It's momma."

My heart drops, the anger swirling at the surface immediately retreats, being replaced by protective instinct. "What's wrong, Mom?" She takes too long to respond. "Mom, seriously. What the fuck is wrong? Are you in trouble? What do you need?"

"We're okay, honey, well... sort of. Your father and I are making do. I-It's our friend... she's in trouble, and we didn't know who else to call."

My anger resurfaces.

"You mean to tell me you disappear for months— *MONTHS*! No note. Nothing. Sammy shows up at my show and you aren't even calling for yourselves? Seriously!"

"I know we have a lot of explaining to do. It isn't safe, though. Please, we have to talk in person. I don't know who's listening or is in on it, but we need your help, baby." She pleads.

"I don't have time to meet, Mom." I answer coolly. "Besides, I've already helped you both, and what good did that do?"

Her voice turns desperate. "I know you're upset, and I promise to explain everything. We just need to see you. It's urgent. We wouldn't have called if it wasn't life or death. *Please.*"

The wist and concern lacing her voice tugs on my heartstrings. I haven't heard from either of my parents in over a decade so for them to reach out, out of the blue, it must be serious. My schedule is chaotic. I'm drowning in meetings, juggling Agent Brandon's accusations while maintaining the shows, but family first. If I must, I can make time.

With a sigh, I relent. "Fine, one hour. That's all I can spare, and this better be fucking important. Life-or-death important."

"Oh, honey! Thank you, thank yo—" I interrupt her rejoicing. "One hour, Mom. Le Petit Cafe in Richmond at 1:00 PM tomorrow. You have five minutes to show or I walk. Don't make me wait."

"I'll be there." She rushes, as though the offer before her would expire. Who knows, maybe it would. I'm mildly volatile today, so anything is possible.

"Gotta go, see you tomorrow at one."

My thumb hovers over the red button as I hear her whisper. "Thanks honey, I love you."

Click.

Scrubbing a hand over my face, I take a breath as I process what the fuck just happened. Hopefully, this complication doesn't have anything to do with the bullshit on Capitol Hill. I wouldn't exactly phrase it as "life or death," but technically anything dealing with weapons has the potential to be exactly that.

I've had Julianna trying to track my parents for weeks with her facial recognition software and zero hits. None. Nada. Zilch. It's impossible since she can find anyone, anywhere. Unwilling to call it luck or coincidence, I hit her contact and wait.

"Hey, Jules. What are the odds you have a location for our MIA parents?"

Her keyboard clacks rhythmically in the background. "Nothing yet. They're still in the wind, but I've got the programs running facial rec on every feed for a match."

"Well, my mom just called. I'll be meeting her downtown tomorrow. You can stop searching. They'll come to us."

The typing stops. Her voice quickly grows serious, fully focused on our conversation. "Are you sure it's them, Adriano? Do you need backup?"

My mother's voice loops in my mind. The sheer panic couldn't be faked, and I'd know her voice anywhere. "It was her, Jules. I'm not sure what's going on, but she's the one who asked for a meeting. I'll let you know if anything changes, but I shouldn't need backup for this one. How are things going with Sammy? He driving you crazy yet?"

She pauses for longer than usual. *Weird.* "He's a pain in the ass, but it's nothing I can't handle. I'll let you know if anything comes up. I promise."

Her partial truth hangs subtly. I don't have the time to play mind games with her. This isn't the time to dig for full truths versus half-truths. I just have to trust her and leave it for now.

"Alright. Let me know if anything changes. I mean it, Jules. If you need help, you fucking call."

"Yeah, yeah. You've got it, A."

THE NEXT DAY

Passing the hunter-green awning and white wiry patio furniture, the bell rings as I enter Le Petit Cafe. It's a quaint hole-in-the-wall on the outskirts of Richmond with decent coffee and unbeatable privacy. The scent of fresh-baked pastries and coffee grounds greets me as I find a seat amongst the handful of other patrons. Snagging one of the tables, I set my too large frame on the wiry chairs.

I check my watch: *12:59.* The jitters kick in as I wait for the surprise caller to arrive. Julianna's text late last night confirming her program flagged an 'Anna Jones' passing through airport security, wasn't enough to steady my nerves. My confidence fades as self-doubt slowly takes over.

Fuck, it's been years. What am I doing sitting out here in the open like a goddamn amateur? I wish Julianna or one of our enforcers was around to watch my back, but I ordered everyone to stay clear just in case it really is my mother. Even after a decade, my first instinct is to protect her anonymity.

The hands of my watch click to the top of the hour, hitting 1:00 on the dot. Grunting in frustration, I drain the last sip of my espresso. I'm ready to throw in the towel when the bell rings. A familiar frame slips through the door, a hat pulled low on her brow. She scans the room, her face lighting up at the sight of me.

Ignoring the baristas, she approaches my corner table with grace and determination. With a wave of my hand, I gesture for her to sit, like a king summoning his servants or granting an audience. Her slim build finds her chair, and I sit back as I take stock of the woman before me.

She looks almost exactly how I remember her. Chestnut hair frames her face in loose curls, and her bright blue eyes are just as expressive as ever. The only signs of aging are the faint crows' feet at the corners of her eyes and a few wisps of silver at her temples. She's aged beautifully, forever a looker.

"Oh, honey." Her baby blues brim with tears as she gives me a once-over. "It's so good to see you."

I nod, doing my best to remain impassive and emotionally detached. After this, she'll be disappearing again for her own safety, and I don't know if I can handle losing her a second time. So, despite my desire to wrap her in a bear hug, I refrain from an overly touchy-feely reunion.

"My God, you're the spitting image of your father. We've missed you..." She begins.

Cutting her off, I interject before we get too far down memory lane. You know what they say, rip off the Band-Aid. So I grab and pull. "You said on the phone this was urgent. As good as it is to see you, we have to keep this short." I do a quick scan of the cafe to ensure no one is eavesdropping. "What matter was so pressing it had to be discussed in person?"

She pulls her bottom lip between her teeth. "Oh Adriano, it's horrible!" she lowers her voice, leaning in close. "We have this... friend... who I'm pretty sure has been taken."

I cock an eyebrow at her. She comes from circus life and knows all about Armond's sordid involvement in trafficking circles. Hell, that's where we "adopted" Julianna from.

"And what makes you think this friend of yours is missing? Couldn't they just be running an errand or taking a vacation?"

"She wouldn't have run off. We're her only family and she doesn't take time off." She looks down at her hands, now folded on the table. "She was... looking into some stuff for your father and I. We've been facing some... challenges lately..." her voice trails off.

"Things like uprooting your lives again? Enrolling Sammy in a program we explicitly agreed not to put him in? Disappearing from your cookie-cutter fake lives?" I snarl, agitated. They have the gall to ask for help for this "friend" after deliberately placing their own son in danger?

"Adriano, honey. Something came up..." She shifts uncomfortably, the wiry chair scraping against the floor. "Your father and I tried our best to handle things on our own... but it doesn't seem to be working."

"Such as?" I pry. After the last few weeks of searching for them, I'm owed at least a decent explanation.

If I took the time to analyze my frustration, I'm hurt. Hurt that they didn't come to me until now. That they weren't comfortable enough to reach out when they were clearly scared and running. *Fuck*, they didn't even tell me they were leaving. After all I've sacrificed for them, haven't I proven I'll do everything in my power to help them? To protect them.

"It doesn't matter. What matters is finding our friend." She retorts, finally growing a backbone and dismissing my inquiry.

"I'd say it does matter, Anna. If I'm supposed to track and likely protect this friend of yours, I'll need all of the information about what she might have stumbled upon while 'helping' you."

Her hands start to tremble, a forlorn mist clouding her eyes. A sigh of defeat leaves her lips as she recounts the journey.

"A little over a year ago, your father found an unmarked letter in the mailbox. No postage. No return address. Just... nondescript scribbles. We didn't think much of it, but then each month, we'd find another. Vaguely veiled threats. Eventually, things escalated. Letters at work.

"It wasn't until we found one stuck in Sammy's back-pack—a particularly graphic threat to Sammy and you that we realized we had move. Up until then, they were so vague and never mentioned you. We thought it was some punk kids playing a prank, but so few know of our connection... we got scared. I'm sorry we didn't tell you, but we didn't want to make things harder for you."

My blood pressure spikes at the confirmation of a real threat. "You should have come to me, Mom. I would've helped you."

"We couldn't risk it. We didn't want to accidentally play into their hands by confirming our connection. So, we did what we thought was best. We sent Sammy to a college where, if we hadn't fixed things within a year, he would show up on your radar. It was a fail-safe we hoped would never be needed."

"And you and Dad? Where did you go?" I ask.

She twiddles her thumbs. *Shit.* I wasn't going to like whatever came next.

"Your father and I joined Circo del Sol. Figured we'd hide in plain sight for a while." *Yup. I didn't like that one bit.*

"What?" My jaw drops, the shock temporarily overriding my anger. "Are you serious? What the fuck? Why would you go back to the circus?"

"No one knows us on the West Coast. We wear masks in the show. It was the safest option, but that's beside the point! We need your help, Adriano! Rosa is missing and Martín wasn't concerned about it when we asked."

My pulse sputters to a stop. "Wait. Hold on. Rosa—*my* Rosa? As in Rosa, the ringmistress for Circo del Sol? That's your missing friend?"

Anna looks extra sheepish now. It's the first giveaway that she might have a clue as to what Rosa means to me. That we know each other. That we're... more than just friends.

"Yes, honey. Your Rosa."

Time stands still, the blood rushing past my ears, my heart beating in poignant thuds. My worst nightmares seem determined to come true. In less than fifteen minutes, I'm reunited with my on-the-run mother, who tried to hide my baby brother, while the woman of my dreams is missing.

The universe is taking the saying, 'kick him when he's down' a little too literally.

My chest constricts, my vision tunnels as I fight the impending panic attack.

"No... no, no, no!" The panic controls my mind. "She was fine. I spoke with her a few weeks ago."

Pain flashes across her face, the possibility of Rosa missing causing her the same stabbing sensation I'm experiencing. "I'm sorry, honey. It's been over twenty-four hours since we've last saw her. And we usually see her multiple times a day, unless she's visiting you."

The last barb pierces my armor. "Why would she disappear? Surely she's just off doing something. Right?" My bullshit-meter's going wild. "What aren't you telling me?"

She starts wringing her hands together, her age showing more as the conversation wears on. Clearly, she's still withholding information. Locking eyes, my voice drops an octave. "Mom. Why is *my* Rosa missing?"

The nerves vibrate off of her, the mix of concern and shame painting her expression. Breaking our stare, her eyes downcast as she whispers. "She was looking into some stuff for us. Trying to find who was sending the threatening notes. We told her not to, but she refused to listen."

Tears well in those baby blues. "Honey, I'm so sorry. We didn't know she would take things so far until she'd already started digging. By then, it was too late. She's like a dog with a bone. All we could do was watch out for her while keeping quiet."

The words tumble out of her mouth, desperate to erase the truth of what she's saying. Rosa is gone because she was trying to help my parents with a mess they were too afraid to bring to me.

My chest aches. On one hand, I'm proud of my girl for being such a noble vigilante. On the other, I'm nauseous at her disappearance coupled with white-hot rage. So much anger. Anger at my parents. Anger at whoever had the nerve to snatch Rosa. Anger at whoever threatened my family. The temperature on my already short fuse is at risk of going nuclear.

My head feels like a cartoon with smoke billowing from my ears as my face turns various shades of crimson. A ticking time bomb waiting to explode.

My poor mother looks defeated, guilt riding her hard. I'm sure the amount of stress she and my father have endured hasn't been easy. No easier than their decision to finally involve me.

"Don't worry. I'll find her." Conviction swells in my chest, I curl a fist around my mother's shaking hands with my own lethal resolve. "They'll pay for this. They'll all pay."

37

ROSALIE

gh. My body aches. My head pounds. Everything hurts. My mouth feels like I've swallowed a cotton ball. Dry. Swollen.

My eyelids refuse to lift as I fight against their weight to pry them open. When my crusty lashes finally part, I instantly wish I hadn't. A thin stream of light pierces directly into my skull. I bring my hands up to shield my face, but they stop halfway. Closing my eyes, I slip back into the darkness.

Time is a man-made construct. As consciousness slowly returns, I slowly take mental stock of my body. My temples still throb worse than a hangover from hell, even just my thoughts make my temples pound. The base of my skull aches while I force my brain to focus.

Dry. My mouth is so fricken dry. I try to swallow, failing and triggering my gag reflex as my swollen tongue touches the back of my throat.

Raw. My throat's scraped and rough, like I've been screaming for hours, even though I've only just woken up.

Water. I'm desperate for it. My body's so dehydrated that salt has crystallized in the corners of my tear ducts since I'm too wrung out to produce actual tears.

Pushing through the haze, I continue the check-in. My muscles are stiff and sore, but nothing feels broken. I wiggle my fingers and toes, working my way to my wrists and ankles, only to find heavy resistance.

Needing to see what was holding me back, I squint, doing my best to let in just enough light for me to peek. Fighting to focus, blurred shapes finally start to make sense around me. A thick rope binds my wrists together, preventing them from moving freely. They're connected by a heavy-gauge chain that loops through an eyehook in the floor. The other end of the steel is padlocked to the rope bindings at my ankles, keeping me pinned in a tight, permanent crouch. I can move, but not a lot. Every time I try to adjust my arms, the rope tugs at my ankles; every time I move my feet, it jerks my wrists down. Each movement contorts me into strained positions to find slack for my other limbs.

I'm all alone in the small, barren room. A few miscellaneous eyehooks stick out among the peeling yellow walls. The cool concrete against my skin sends a shiver through my bones. The tiny basement window doesn't have a screen or glass, just a few rebar bars built directly into the foundation, covered by a solid piece of plywood.

Ugh. I shut my eyes, savoring the slightest reprieve from the light.

Where am I? I try to remember what happened last. Digging deeper through the haze until memories click into place. The warehouse. The messages. The strange crates. It all comes flooding back. Followed by the heavy thud as someone knocked me out from behind.

No wonder my head is screaming. I was clobbered by a giant.

Tuning into my surroundings, I listen carefully, documenting every distinct sound and scent. Every crime documentary and training session with Joaquín has prepared me for this situation. Be observant. Be smart. Be patient. I would earmark two out of three as my strong suits. But all three at the same time are a challenge, especially with this damn headache.

I try to slow my breathing, but even the air in my lungs is so damn loud that it's hard to hear. It's too quiet. A faint dripping echoes from afar, but there are no obvious signs of life. No birds or crickets. No hum or honks of cars. Just deafening silence.

As much as I should be trying to escape, the seduction of

darkness calls to me. It promises the illusion of a few minutes of peace if I just let go, something I'm in desperate need of if my head's ever going to quit. Giving in once more, I slip back into the abyss.

Harsh whispers jolt me awake. Men's voices grow closer, the jumbled vibrations slowly sharpening into decipherable words with their approach. My binds groan as I shimmy to face the heavy, metal door. As much as I'd love to position myself with a wall against my back, the hooks have me anchored in the center of the room. Before long, the footsteps halt as the voices continue to argue. Spanish—I'd recognize my mother tongue anywhere.

My prison door creaks as one of the voices shoves it open. Blinding light floods in as two silhouettes enter my quarters, their shadows stretching across the concrete floor toward me. I bite back a whine, the sudden flash sending pins and needles piercing through the back of my eyes.

"Ah, she's finally awake!" The shorter of the two exclaims in Spanish, clearly thrilled I'm no longer unconscious. Both men have a permanent tan most native Mexicans sport, paired with gelled dark hair. Shortie has a greasy, unkempt mustache and a pudgy belly, the kind only a dedicated bar patron could gain.

I try to pin down the accent. Shortie's lilt and drawl have the right cadence to place us close to Central Mexico, but who the heck knows anymore. People migrate too often for me to be sure where exactly here is. I could be across the border or just in a basement in East L.A.

The taller bloke is leaner and meaner. A distinct, jagged scar cuts through his eyebrow, his expression locked in a permanent, lethal scowl that could make a hitman flinch. He stalks around me like a hawk circles its prey, his perusal making my skin crawl. He grunts at Shortie.

"I agree. She'll do more than nicely. A sweet piece of ass like this will fetch a pretty penny." Shortie replies, clearly the conversationalist of the group.

Fetch. My blood runs cold. I'm not just a prisoner; I'm inventory.

Scarface completes his appraisal, grabbing my chin with

his meaty paw, examining my features. I shake my head, doing my best to dislodge his grip, but he squeezes tighter, his smarmy smirk making my stomach flip.

"Feisty." He agrees with his partner. "It'll be fun breaking this one." Disgust and fear possess my body as I process their implications.

"I am not for sale." I spit through gritted teeth, needing to assert any ounce of control over the situation.

Their cackles bounce off the walls. "Oh, princess." Shortie maliciously voices. "You're whatever we say you are. We own you."

Their words, designed to demean me just further incite my temper. Letting a snarl loose, my attitude is met with a swift *smack.* The back of Scarface's hand connects sharply with my jaw. My teeth chatter as the sting spreads across my cheek. He fumbles with his belt. "Should we put that smart mouth to better use?"

"Dammit! Not the face, you idiot. Can't damage the merchandise." Shorty scolds Scarface, clearly not upset that he hit me, but that it landed somewhere visible. "Besides, no samples. You heard the boss. He wants this one untouched."

"Whatever." Scarface grumbles. "She shouldn't be so mouthy then." He re-buckles his belt, adjusting his pants. I glare at him, but keep my mouth glued shut. There is no way in hell he's getting me to open for him.

Shorty heads toward the door, no longer acknowledging me. "Come on, let's check out the others quick before lunch."

Before following his buddy out, Scarface delivers a swift, sharp kick to my ribs. "I'll be back, princess."

My ribs scream, the bruises likely already beginning to form black and blue pools. Waiting with bated breath until the door is shut and secured by the *click* of the deadbolt, I let out an irate exhale. *These fucking assholes!* Some men can be such fricken pigs. Thinking women are property or just toys to be used and disposed of. The same type of assholes who took and abused Carmen.

Forcing deep breaths—in through the nose, hold, exhale through the mouth, and repeat. My boiling blood returns to a normal simmer. The ache in my side finally subsides. I have to get out of here. There is no way I'm going to be auctioned off like a goddamn animal. Not if I can help it.

Formulating a plan for my escape, I'm interrupted by the

growling of my stomach. Shortie's words echo in my head. *The others.* They were going to visit others. Other girls? More women like me?

This throws a wrench in my plans. I can't leave if others are trapped. *Ugh.* Operation Rescue Rosa and company begins.

38

ADRIANO

Tearing out of the cafe, my phone is pressed to my ear before I even reach the sidewalk. Dialing Rosa, I hold my breath while it rings, going straight to voicemail. *Fuck.* I know we haven't been talking as much. It's been over a week since she went radio silent. I flip a quick text telling her to call me ASAP, but I don't expect a reply.

By the time I reach the car, my adrenaline has surged into a tremor. My hands are shaking too hard to dial, so I ask Siri to get Julianna on the line.

Her relaxed voice fills the vehicle. "Hey A, long time no talk. What's up?"

"We've got a fucking problem." I cut the pleasantries short. My only priority is finding Rosa and getting her to safety.

"Shit." Her playful tone instantly switches to serious. "What do you need from me?"

This is why she's the best right-hand anyone could ask for. At the first signs of trouble, she's ready to roll up her sleeves and help in any way she can. Hack the dark web? Done. Hide a body? No questions asked. Her loyalty and resourcefulness never cease to amaze me.

"I need you to find Rosa. My mom thinks she's been taken. That the same people who have been harassing them might be who snagged her." I spit out in a single breath.

"Wait. Your Rosa? Like Rosa from Circo del Sol—that Rosa?" The clicking of her keyboard picks up in the background.

"Yes. My Rosa." I growl.

"And what about your mom? Rosa's been chasing the same assholes that I've been hunting for weeks, A. I'll do what I can, but shit... I'm not sure where to even begin." She releases a big sigh, the frustration seeping through the phone. Jules hates not delivering results. This puzzle has had her and Sammy gallivanting all over the country chasing phantom threads for months.

"Apparently, she likes to play detective and may have landed herself in some trouble. Anna said they asked Martín about it, but he brushed it off. He might be a good starting point." My knuckles whiten on the steering wheel at the mention of the scumbag's name.

"Hmm... that might just work." Her gears are already turning. "Give me some time. I'll make a few calls and see what I can scrounge up."

"...Thanks, Jules"

Her voice softens, her fingers pausing on the keyboard. "Hey, I've got you, A. We'll find her." The clacking resumes, and the call disconnects.

I know we'll find her. There isn't a stone I'll leave un-turned until I do. I just hope it isn't too late.

━━━•◦●◯●◦•━━━

While Julianna sifts through the shadows and back doors of the interweb, I do the only thing I can: call contacts the old-fashioned way.

My first suspect—Martín Gonzales. I press the green icon. It rings a few times before redirecting me to voicemail.

'Hola, I can't get to the phone right now. Leave a message and I'll call you back!'

I jam my finger on the red button. Redialing right away. "Come on, pick up, asshole." I mutter, needing him to an-swer the fucking phone.

"Hola, Señor Devereaux! To what do I owe the pleasure?" Martín's chummy voice connects to my car's speakers.

"Martín." My tone leaves no room for misinterpretation. "Where is Rosa? ."

"Right now?" He chuckles. "Oh, you know, she's been off doing her own thing lately. I'm sure she's just running errands. Why do you ask?"

I gnash my teeth, his carefree act grating on my nerves. "She hasn't been answering my calls. When's the last time you saw her?"

"Well, is it possible she's just tired of you? What is it the kids call it these days.... Ghosting? Is it possible she's just ghosting you?" Ever the comedian.

"Very funny, Martín." My instinct to jump through the phone to throttle him flares. "When did you last actually see her?"

"Hmm, maybe two days ago?" I can picture him running his stubby fingers over his waxy mustache while he pretends to remember.

"And that doesn't bother you?"

"We've been busy packing. So it isn't unreasonable for her to be floating around until we're settled." He goads. "I'm sure she's around here somewhere."

He's definitely lying, but as my mom mentioned, he doesn't seem to care. "I see. Well, when you see her, let her know I was looking for her."

"Si, yes of course, Señor. I'll pass your message along, but you know women, even then, she might not call you."

Unable to listen to more of his bullshit, I cut the line.

Well. That wasn't the answer I was hoping for, but his non-information is more informative than he realizes. *Fuck.* Martín might actually be behind Rosa's disappearance. If that's the case, then she's in serious trouble. Martín's method for getting rid of "problems" has the limited range of death or sale—a fate worse than death.

Canceling my meetings on the Hill, I clear my schedule to go hunting. Instead of wasting time playing politics with a hack like Special Agent Brandon, I have my girl to save.

39

ROSALIE

My wrists are raw from trying to loosen the rough cords tethering me to the floor. Despite my efforts, the knots are so well done that I've only managed to loosen them a fraction. Every time I make progress on one, the other three nooses tighten, making it virtually impossible to escape without losing one of my limbs. Thankfully, the circus makes you flexible, so I'm at least able to find positions that relieve the constant pressure of being folded like a pretzel.

The concrete maintains a consistent cool temperature. I used to pray for an escape from the heat and humidity, but now I'd give anything to feel the sun on my skin. They must have stripped me of my black catsuit when I arrived. When I woke, I'm barefoot, wearing thin cotton panties and a loose t-shirt. I'm covered, but barely. The flimsy fabric and chill from the cement have my body on the constant precipice of a shiver.

I've lost track of time. The lights in the hallway never shut off, shooting thin beams through the cracks under the door and into my dark cell. The only time the lights turn on is when someone delivers scraps of water or to torment me. Scarface and Shortie have been back a few times to "visit." They mostly taunt me, but a few times Scarface has gotten excited, leaving me with at least a few bruised ribs.

The heavy deadbolt jolts as someone slides a dog bowl of water through a rudimentary slot in the bottom of the door. The first time they delivered water, I was wary—convinced it was laced with something. I held out for what felt like eons, but was likely only an hour. I glared at the dish like it was the enemy, furious it was there at all. But eventually, my thirst and desperation won out and I drank it all. The relief of the lukewarm liquid sliding down my raspy throat was akin to nirvana. It cooled my swollen tongue and cleared the phlegm just enough that if I wasn't already so dehydrated, I would've cried from happiness.

Periodically, someone switches out the bowl, refilling it with more liquid gold. Now, I am more intentional, taking small sips to keep the scratchiness at bay while I nurse my hangover. When only the last dregs are left, I cup my hand to scoop them out, washing the dust from my face—desperate to feel clean in any way possible. I try to keep track of the hours, scratching the number of water deliveries into the dust on the floor, but the concept of time eludes me. Between deliveries, I spend the hours of darkness resting, my body still working overtime to purge the drug-induced haze.

The whole door quakes and creaks. The lights flick on, blinding my night-adjusted vision. Squinting, the slim silhouette of a woman in baggy clothes materializes with a bucket in hand. She hugs the contours of the wall, dropping the galvanized bucket with a hollow echo in the corner of the room. Approaching cautiously, she produces a key, unlocking the padlock from my ankles and unlooping the chain from the eyehook. My muscles scream in agony as blood rushes to my extremities. Pins and needles shoot up my feet as I struggle to stand for the first time in who knows how long. Using the metal chain as a leash, she escorts me to the rusty bucket.

Wordlessly, she points at it and waits. Despite the two bowls of water my bladder is barely full. My body had absorbed every drop of liquid in a desperate attempt to rehydrate. Privacy was a luxury I'd lost back at the circus. Not sure when I'd get another chance to go, I slid my thin panties over my knees, squatting just over the pail. Without any toilet paper, I do my best to shake and air dry before resecuring the fabric.

The girl seems too frail to be entrusted with moving a prisoner like me. Her skin hangs on her petite bony frame.

Her neck is encased in a thick metal collar, a seamless circle locked by a small pinhole. Her wrists don similar "jewelry." Heavy irons are clamped around each wrist, the skin beneath irritated and puffy from the weight shifting against her with every movement. Her eyes are vacant and dull, like any spark of hope was snuffed out ages ago. Anger and remorse surge through my veins as I take in the poor creature.

She leads me back to the center of the room, bending to re-secure the eyehook to the floor. Peering over her shoulder, I spy no one waiting for her or guarding the door, but I keep my voice low just in case.

"Where are we?"

Her eyes widen as they briefly make contact with mine. Panic oozes off her as she spins away, shuffling to the door. She shakily returns with a plastic tray with a single piece of bread on it. Warily, she places it on the ground within my reach. Careful to maintain her distance and avoid further eye contact, she drops the food, grabs the bucket, and rushes out of my cell, the heavy door sealing with a clang behind her.

40

ADRIANO

Two days. Two whole days of dead ends and unanswered questions. I'm exhausted, but closing my eyes only leads to nightmares; vivid visions of the horrors Rosa might be enduring.

Chef has been delivering meals to my trailer, since even a minute's break is time my girl can't afford. Forcing food down, I continue scouring the internet for any hints of who is after my parents. So far, my only clues are the cryptic note from my parents' house and what my mom told me.

The words on my laptop screen blur as my bleary eyes finally quit on me. I rest my head in my hands, my fingers tugging on the roots of my hair. The sharp sting helps ground my racing mind. My eyelids droop shut.

Buzz, Buzz.

My cell jolts me awake, dancing across my desk as it sings Julianna's ringtone. Before I can get a word out, her voice streams through. "I've got a lead!"

I shake off the grogginess. "Huh?" A feeling dangerously close to hope flutters to life in my chest. "Where? What is it?"

"I got a call from a contact in Mexico. I've never worked with him directly, but my people vouched for him. There are whispers of an auction in Mexico City with a 'featured item' being sold... It could be her."

Fuck. I knew it was a possibility, especially with Martín involved, but I naively hoped she was just laying low while whatever shit she'd stumbled upon blew over.

"Send me the details." I say, already rummaging for my passport in my desk. "I'm taking the next flight south."

"I'll do you one better. I've already got a pilot on standby at Dulles. You're wheels up in an hour."

I grin for what feels like the first time in weeks. Julianna really does think of everything.

A half-hour later, I'm hitting the tarmac, climbing the rolling stairs two at a time into the belly of the jet. A duffle hangs from each shoulder. One is filled with clothes. The other is stuffed to the brim with weapons, burners, and enough ammunition to be considered a small arsenal. That's the benefit of flying private, fewer questions and even fewer security checks.

The flight takes off in under an hour, putting me ahead of schedule. Glancing at my phone, I cross my fingers that this "Joaquín" guy speaks decent English. Otherwise, we're in for a long, painful game of charades. The nine-hour flight feels more like a century, the seconds stretching into minutes stretching into hours. I'm teetering on the edge of insanity, the worry for my girl plaguing my mind. Popping a few sleeping pills, I force my body to shut down to catch a few hours of rest before we touch down.

The pilot navigates us expertly through the air, gently gliding onto the Tijuana runway. As he finishes his post-flight checklist and protocols, I'm already grabbing my bags and rushing off the plane. A black, tinted SUV is waiting at the bottom of the stairs, idling directly on the airstrip.

A burly Mexican is leaning casually against the grill. His dark hair is trimmed short and neat, aviators reflecting the bright sky, and his arms crossed as he waits. Blue jeans hang comfortably from his hips. He reaches to meet me, his biceps and chest stretching his white henley to the max. His presence is sharp. Aware. Deadly. Despite being dressed as a civilian, his military roots are obvious in the way he carries himself.

Adjusting the bags on my shoulders, I extend my hand. "Adriano."

His scarred hand engulfs mine in a firm handshake. "Joaquín. Thanks for coming so quickly." A thick Spanish accent coats his perfectly fluent English. "Get in." I send up a quick thanks that we won't need a translator.

Soon, we're cruising down the highways of Tijuana. The lack of traffic laws and organization makes it feel closer to a car chase than a normal drive. Bikes and vehicles that could easily be mistaken for scrap metal thread in and out between lanes and lights. Everyone pretends that blinkers and speed limits are suggestions. Joaquín shifts smoothly between gears as he bobs and weaves around traffic with stunt driver-like ease.

Peeling off the main drag, we bounce down backroads. The SUV's high clearance easily navigates over the massive speed bumps at the tops and bottoms of each street. Before long, we're turning off the paved paths onto a dirt road. The dust kicks up behind us as we snake between cacti, following a road that is mapped only in Joaquín's head.

We're a decent way south, past the main city streets and barrios when he rolls to a stop at a tall corrugated fence. The weathered metal sheets create a nine-foot barrier decorated with large palm trees planted every ten feet. To anyone driving by, it's just a fence. In our line of business, it's camouflage. The rundown appearance makes me slightly worried our final destination will be a shitty shack. It wouldn't be my ideal accommodations, but for Rosa, I'd spend a hundred nights facing the elements if it meant getting her home safely.

Pressing a small button on his sun visor, the unpainted gate groans open, the rust-covered chain creaking under the strain. The SUV glides through, waiting for it to shut behind us before we continue our journey. The landscape transitions from red desert dirt to fine white sand as we wind up the stone drive toward a little cottage. It feels out of place for this part of the coast. The cottage gives off a proper Key West beach house vibe. White siding and pale blue shutters cover the single-story home. A wooden porch runs the length of the house with a matching blue hammock strung between two of the posts. It's quaint. Small, but meticulously maintained. Clearly, Joaquín's crisp style extends to more than just his wardrobe.

Throwing the SUV into park, Joaquín heads to the back and grabs one of my duffle bags, tossing the other to me. "No one really visits, but any friend of Rosa's is a friend of mine."

He gestures to the cottage. "Welcome to mi casa."

The salty ocean breeze fills my nose, my lungs appreciating the fresh air over the thick dust of the drive. Seagulls squawk overhead, and beyond the rear fence, the sound of lapping waves drifts into this tiny oasis.

The security measures don't match the house's aesthetic at all. At first glance, I'd describe the place as a sweet Airbnb that college kids would rent for spring break. But if you really scanned the area, you'd notice the traces of defensive hardware seamlessly integrated into the space. Joaquín enters a PIN into a panel on the front door, scans his thumbprint, and waits for facial recognition to register. The door swings open with an audible click, and we enter his humble abode.

The interior embraces the term *open-floor concept* to a "T." The living room has a small breakfast nook nestled against the far wall. A well-loved tan couch separates the living area from the kitchen. White cabinets line the kitchen as it wraps in an L-shape around appliances. Only two doors break the layout. Joaquín drops my bag on the couch before heading deeper into the space.

He nods toward the first door. "Bathrooms there. And that one's my room." Joaquín points back to the couch. "You can sleep here as long as needed. It isn't much, but it's secure."

I fight a grimace at the prospect of the couch. It isn't that I mind sleeping on one, it's just painfully obvious that my six-foot-one frame is either going to hang off the edge or I'll be imitating some of our contortionists to fit. *Anything for Rosa.*

"Thanks. So, you mentioned you're a friend of Rosa's. How do you two know each other?"

I slide into the breakfast nook while Joaquín gathers stuff from the cupboards.

"Ah, Rosa and I met some time ago. She was young, lost, and itching to learn to fight."

Without his sunglasses on, it's easier to see he's an older guy. Silver flecks the hair at his temples, but the frame underneath is fit and capable. My eyebrows furrow with concern at the idea of my little bird getting into a brawl with Joaquín's bulk. "Fight? Why would she want to fight you?"

"Oh, no." He lets out a hearty laugh. "She didn't want to

fight me specifically. I own an MMA gym in town."

My eyes widen in recognition. "*You're* the one who taught her to fight. She's mentioned you."

"I used to only train men. But she rolled up in her teens demanding to learn and wouldn't take no for an answer. So, I took her in and taught her everything I know." He beams with the pride of a father. "And your girl? She's spent more time on the mats than my professional fighters."

"I'm not surprised. She can be quite relentless when she wants to be." I chuckle, relaxing at the fact that Rosa wasn't getting beaten up. I can see it, a younger Rosa, her dark curls bouncing behind her as she barges into Joaquín's gym, demanding he train her. My little bird can be quite a spitfire.

"And you? How do *you* know Rosalie?" He turns the question around on me.

Fuck. How do I even describe our relationship? It isn't like we met under normal circumstances. Our history hinges on scandalous encounters forged in the kind of shadows the circus doesn't advertise—not sweet dates and dinners.

"We met through a mutual business partner." Technically, it isn't a lie. "I'm the ringmaster of Cirque du Noir. We occasionally work with Circo del Sol."

Joaquín's eyes narrow. "What kind of work?" His gaze lasers in on my expression as though he's trying to catch me in a lie.

"Mostly trading." My vague answer doesn't land as I'd hoped. His body visibly stiffens, his fists clenching at his sides.

"Trading what exactly? Be explicit or get the fuck out." An aggressive, lethal edge coats each word. The proud papa replaced by a calculating operative.

I recoil at his tone. No one takes that tone with me and lives to tell about it. Not Adriano Devereaux. No fucking way. Swallowing my pride, I make an exception to my rule. This man has information about Rosa, and more importantly, he cares for her. Without him, I have no other leads.

"Weapons and drugs, mostly. Sometimes counterfeit goods or information."

Silence permeates the house. Joaquín doesn't blink, his eyes locked on mine as he sifts through the half-truths. "No people?"

Holding his gaze, I take the calculated risk and tell him

the truth. The kind of truth that could ruin everything. My operation. My reputation. All of it. "I don't trade skin—despite what you might hear."

He studies me intently, seemingly appeased by my statement. "Who is Rosa to you?"

"She's mine." The words are out before I can think to filter them—sharp and territorial. "We're together. At least… we were before she disappeared."

His eyebrows shoot up. Apparently, that wasn't the answer he'd been expecting. "Funny. She's never mentioned you before."

"It's new. And complicated." I growl, pissed at his implications. "But make no mistake—she's mine. And I'll do anything to make sure she's safe."

Thankfully, Joaquín seems to believe me. Content with my answer, he pulls open a drawer, grabs a thin folder and drops it on the round table in front of me. "Good. Now enough small talk. This is what I've got."

We flip through the folder, getting brought up to speed on all things Rosa. There isn't much, just the ghost of a trail: a few cell tower pings, a handful of addresses, and some miscellaneous receipts and call transcripts.

"Rosa checks in once a week, every Sunday without fail. So when she didn't check in last week, I knew something was up. I tried calling and texting, but it went straight to voicemail. She checks the burner at least once a day, so after twenty-four hours, I started digging. Here's everything I could find or that she sent over the last few weeks."

He lays out a map with cell triangulations and a radius expanding partially over the ocean. "These are the last towers that her phone pinged. All of them indicate she was near the harbor."

He points to the industrial block, a labyrinth of shipping containers and warehouses. "She texted me an address nearby before she went MIA, but it's more than a few clicks to the south. I'm not sure why the fuck she'd be hanging around the port. But I know in my gut it isn't to catch some waves."

"I think I might know part of the reason." I let out a heavy sigh. "She was helping my parents investigate an issue they've been having. I don't know what she found, since I had no idea she even knew them. But my best guess is whatever trail she was following led her to those docks."

"There's whispers on the dark web about a pretty assassin being auctioned off at a special event in Mexico City." He adds. Disdain and disgust wash over both our features. "Based on the description, it sounds like it could be her."

"Wait. Assassin?" I repeat the word like it's in a foreign language. My mind stalls, trying to reconcile the woman I held in my arms with someone who hunts in the shadows. "My Rosa?"

"You need to get to know your girl better." He deadpans, not wasting time with extra explanations. "It's reliable, but I'm not sure if it's her or not. Technically she's more of a vigilante than assassin, but I couldn't find anything else that sounds even remotely like her. Right now, it's our best bet."

The trickle of hope tangled in sorrow flickers a beat in my chest. "Alright. What's our plan?"

"Locate the auction, infiltrate the holding cells, and break Rosa out." Joaquín says, laying it out efficiently, like a simple extraction mission is second nature for him.

"If she's the feature, they'll have her under lock and key." I point out. "What if we just buy her? We get tickets and go in as bidders. Do it so we don't have a Mexican cartel breathing down our necks afterwards."

He ponders my proposal, analyzing every scenario and outcome. "It's bold, but it just might work. If I cash in a few old IOUs, I might be able to get us through the front door."

I'm confident that between Julianna and Joaquín's contacts we can get an invite.

"And once we're in?" Joaquín asks.

I grin. "That's my specialty."

Joaquín peers at me with confusion. His broad arms folded across his chest. "I thought you didn't trade people."

"I don't trade them." I say, my voice dropping an octave. "But I never said I don't buy them."

41

ROSALIE

The bread is better than it has any business being. I guess going long stretches without food and minimal water can turn anything into a Michelin star meal. Nibbling at the corners, I try to stretch out my snack. The tiny crumbs barely register in my rumbling stomach, but they give me something to focus on.

My new routine continues, bowls of water alternating with bread and supervised potty breaks. My body aches from sleeping on the hard floor, my muscles stiff from being contorted in whatever position my chains allow. My brain is functioning at half capacity due to a lack of nutrients, but the half that is working has been busy. Plotting. Scheming. Wracking my brain for ideas. I need information before I can plan: where are we, who else is here, and how long do I have before it's too late?

The frail girl who delivers my "meals" has been tough to crack. Every time she brings water or food, she keeps her distance, making it nearly impossible to communicate. The bathroom breaks, however, were a different story. Each time she unlocks the padlock from the floor, I speak soft words to her. English, Spanish—anything that might solicit a response. Based on her reactions and the small, black barcode inked just behind her ear, I've deduced two things: she doesn't speak English, and she isn't here of her own free will. Beyond that, she's a stone wall, refusing to answer me and avoiding eye contact.

The lights flick on, the sudden, harsh brightness making it difficult for my retinas to adjust. Her small frame enters the room with the tiny key. This time, the bathroom break is different. Her grip shakes as she misses the lock on the first try.

"Mexico." Her whisper is so soft that even straining, I almost miss it. Her lips barely move, her gaze still fixed on the lock.

My brain kicks into gear, celebrating the small milestone of success. *So we're in Mexico. Good to know.* "Is anyone else here?" I ask her quietly as our backs turn toward the bucket.

She tucks her chin slightly, almost imperceptibly. Her eyes dart around searching for signs we've been caught communicating. *Yes.*

"Who? Who else is here?" I urge, desperate for more information.

She side-eyes me, not willing to offer me more. Trying again, I embrace the rules of Twenty Questions and ask only yes or no questions.

"Are there more girls like me?"

Her chin tucks again. *Yes.*

Okay, now we're getting somewhere.

"Are there more than ten?"

Nod, *yes.*

I take my time, multitasking my mini-interrogation while relieving myself. I need to maximize every second for more information. "More than twenty?"

Her pupils track left, then right. *No.*

Shit. That's more girls than I hoped for, but it isn't as many as there could be. Less than twenty others to rescue in Mexico. *How hard could it possibly be?*

I drag my stiff panties back up, my face crinkling into a grimace. God, I miss the feel of clean clothes. Days' worth of filth and grime are caked into my skin, a layer of grit that twenty measly bowls of lukewarm water can't scrub away. My keeper leads me back to the middle of the room. I refrain from asking more, in case her paranoia holds merit. She's hanging by a thread as it is, and if she snaps, my only window into this place slams shut with her.

This time, when the door shuts—the familiar *clack* of the deadbolt sliding into place, I stay awake. Biding my time. Plotting. Planning my next move. Now that I've started getting answers, the real fun begins.

Chatter echoes from the hallway, the sound bouncing off the concrete walls and ricocheting into my cell. I'm still re-adjusting my position, trying to get closer to upright than curled like a sideways shrimp when the door swings open with a violent clang. My stomach drops as Shortie waltzes into the room—alone. His presence sets my nerves on high alert. Adrenaline floods my bloodstream.

"Rise and shine, *chica*. It's showtime." He sneers, wrenching me by the arm. He unlocks the contraption trapping me to the floor and hoists me upright. My nerves short-circuit, sending jolts of raw, stinging daggers shooting up my legs. He jerks me through the door, my heels dragging on the cold floor as I catch my first glimpse of what lies beyond my holding cell.

A long, narrow hallway stretches before me, bathed in the hum of industrial fluorescent lights. Staggered iron doors, carbon copies of mine, line the walls. They're all latched shut, secured with matching deadbolts, making it impossible to tell which rooms are occupied or not. I count each one as Shortie pulls me along. Sixteen doors, including mine. I scurry to do the math, remembering my keeper's in-sight. *More than ten, less than twenty.* If there's only one girl or room, then I'm hopeful there are only fifteen girls to save. Fifteen souls to liberate. Fifteen reasons to make it out of here alive.

Shortie keeps his tight grip on my arm, more dragging than guiding me through the corridor. I carefully catalogue each twist and turn for later, slowly building a mental map of the building's layout—a left, two rights, until we finally reach a polished wood door. He shoves me across the thresh-old, and I hit the floor hard. My limbs are useless, weak from days of dehydration and starvation. A hit of vertigo from the manhandling leaves me light-headed and slow.

This room is a sprawling contrast to my personal hell—I mean, cell. The deep red furniture is closer to the back room at a strip club than the desolate, barren space I've grown used to. A tall man in a tan suit stalks closer, his authority filling the space as he assesses me with a predatory gaze. Based on the tailored suit and matching fedora, he's dressed too sophisticatedly to be a mere underling. This is the boss, the *Jefe*.

His sharp eyes skate over my barely clothed body. My dirty panties and the thin fabric of my shirt do nothing to hide my curvy frame. My skin crawls with every inch he covers. I wrap my arms tightly around my waist, too weak to rise to my feet but refusing to shrink under his inspection.

Shortie guards the door, his hands folded professionally behind his back as he pretends to be a disciplined soldier waiting at attention. A pathetic masquerade.

"Hope you're enjoying your stay, Rosa." Jefe's smooth, accented voice coats the air. "Seems you've pissed off some very powerful men."

My eyes narrow. I hadn't expected him to address me directly. Usually, men like him think of women as merchandise, objects, barely better than dogs and certainly not as people. I hold my tongue, unsure what the appropriate response is without understanding the rules of his game.

He continues, as only a man who enjoys the sound of his own voice can. "And it's such a pity, a sexy thing like you. I promised I'd make sure you disappeared, but I think I can offer something much more... agreeable."

My eyebrows furrow in confusion, and I give in to my sassy nature. "Ah yes, because I'm in such a rush to make deals with men who abduct women and treat us worse than prisoners."

Regret floods my system as the words cross my lips. *Who in their right mind provokes their captor? Apparently, this girl.*

Jefe's face drops for a split second before he bursts into laughter, the sound jarring and uncomfortably loud. "Ah, there's that fire I've heard so much about."

His lack of offense puzzles me further. He reaches out, grabbing my chin in a possessive manner. I press my lips together, clenching my teeth, determined to keep my mouth sealed from his possible intrusion. His thumb and forefinger stay clamped in a punishing grip, threatening bruises as he forces me to hold his gaze.

"Contrary to what you may believe, I'm a man who can appreciate a good flame. I find pleasure in getting close enough to get burned before taming it until it's a harmless candle." Jefe says. "Instead of being auctioned off to the highest bidder, I'll offer you a one-time deal: be mine. You'll have anything you ask for, within reason, and in exchange, you'll pledge your services, your loyalty, and your body to me. Only me. All you have to do is agree, and all of this can stop."

I barely contain my physical revolt as I recoil on instinct. The idea of any man owning me—controlling me—makes me nauseous. The bread crumbs and water threaten to make an appearance at his implications. Hell, they aren't even implications; they're demands.

My mind drifts to the rough pressure of Jefe's hand, comparing my current revulsion to the memory of the one man who inadvertently owns me. Body, mind, and soul. How his touch, while demanding and controlled, incites heat and safety—not the fear and disgust this man provokes.

"I already told Shortie over there." I swing my eyes toward the door. "I'm not for sale."

"You seem to be under the illusion you have a say in the matter. Very well. Decline my offer. I'm sure whichever capo or gangbanger purchases you will be significantly less benevolent."

He releases his grip, standing and brushing his lapels as if my filth is contagious. "Send Nina in," he sneers, strutting away with the hollow arrogance of a bully who's never met his match.

The heavy door slams behind him. Shortie snatches my arm, hauling me into an adjoining room. I'm greeted by a group of women in various stages of being primped. An older woman, who must be Nina, orders the others to continue while she waltzes toward us with confidence and grace.

"Another one? I'm full up. You'll have to bring her back later." She waves her hand in dismissal.

Shortie grunts. "This one was sent directly by the boss. You'll make time."

He doesn't even look at her as he speaks. *I guess it's good to know his disrespect extends to all women and I'm not just an exception.* Nina is unbothered by his shitty attitude and over-inflated sense of self-importance. She points to a sad line of folding chairs leaning against the wall where a group of scared girls huddle closely together.

"Fine. Put her over there. I'll put her next in line."

Without another word, Shortie pushes me toward the chairs and turns to leave. Falling onto the cold metal seat, I'm grateful to no longer stand or kneel. The relief on my joints is a welcomed reprieve after so many hours curled awkwardly on the floor and being tossed around like a ragdoll. The space is bustling. Women shuffle frantically, moving the other girls through a brutal assembly line of cleaning and beautification.

Knowing better than to converse with the other girls, I simply observe their current state. All of them are dressed like me—thin dirty shirts, some oversized, some fitted, paired with various boyshorts. Their hair is tangled and matted, likely from sleeping on the floor, and their skin's coated in a familiar layer of dirt. I'm older than all of them by at least a decade, many of them looking to be in their early teens.

Before long, I'm ushered to a large stand-alone sink. A woman with elbow-high rubber gloves leans me back until my head hovers over the basin. Hard streams of water penetrate my matted curls and tickle my scalp. Her expert fingers work shampoo into my roots, coating the ends with conditioner to loosen my tangled mop. The dust and grit wash away in a rush of euphoria, the sheer sensation of getting clean overriding the fact that the salon is in a dungeon.

Hurrying me to the next station, two women bark orders to strip and get into a tub. It's nothing fancy, just a large vat big enough to kneel in. Cool jets of water pelt my skin as the first woman hoses me off. The temporary chill is worth enduring just to watch the muddy brown water circle the drain. The other woman dips a loofah on a stick into a bucket of soapy water, making it feel more like a car wash than a bath. At their instruction, I raise my arms and spread my legs so she can scrub off the grime. The scratchy material of the sponge chafes my skin, turning it red from the friction. Every crevice is thoroughly scoured and rinsed before they finally order me to step out of the bucket. A rough towel is thrown at me, the sad fabric pushing the water off my body more like a squeegee than absorbing it. I'd have been happier if they chucked a roll of paper towels at me instead.

Washed and dried, Nina is waiting in the clothing department, her fingertips tapping her crossed forearms as she directs a team picking outfits from a mobile rack. Moving efficiently, like designers prepping for fashion week, they hold various outfits against my frame. Her *tsk* dismisses the current outfit, and the next option appears in its place. After a few tries, she goes to the rack herself and finds a style that meets whatever criteria she has in mind.

Her assistant shoves the dress into my hands and waits for me to put it on. The sleek fabric easily slides over my head, stretching and molding to my curves. Unlike the other girls, who are in white virginal slips, I'm in a form-fitting black and red dress. The top of the dress sports a blood-red "V" of fabric that accentuates my breasts and waistline. It makes me look dangerous. Formidable. Not quite a black widow, but definitely arachnid-inspired.

The assistant spins me around for Nina's final inspection, and with a hum of approval, I'm quickly moved to the hair and makeup stations. Despite years of effort wasted trying to tame my hair, my wet curls still live in a permanent rebellion—doing everything except the desired outcome. My faith that they can make anything mildly presentable with my rat's nest is limited at best.

I recognized the girl at this station as the meek woman who delivered my bread and water. Her heavy irons match the other attendants, excluding Nina. Sitting on a rickety chair in front of her, I try to stay still as she gently brushes out each tangle. After what feels like forever, her fingers part my locks into thirds and thread them together in a long, loose braid. I do my best to catch her eye, but she's determined to avoid me. Her nervous energy shakes the air around us. Subtly patting her hand, her face flashes up to mine. The deep pools of sorrow and regret drown us both. I can't risk talking, so I settle for a soft smile, hoping the sincerity gives her some semblance of comfort. Despite her working here, when I'm free, I vow to try to save her too.

A different girl approaches with a handful of brushes. She paints my face, focusing on my eyes and lips. I'm never given a mirror, but I can only imagine how I look now that I'm clean and all dolled up.

I'm put in a line, shoulder to shoulder with the other girls, each of us in our new outfits. Cold seeps from the damp concrete through the soles of our feet. Apparently, finding clothing was significantly easier than finding shoes. Nina marches down the line, inspecting each of her creations with hums of approval. Every few steps, she snaps her fingers and an attendant rushes forward to tweak a hairstyle or add a smear of makeup. But overall, she's pleased with her work.

Counting the girls, I confirm fifteen plus my helper. More than I had hoped, but less than the last auction. There has to be a way to contact the outside world for backup. Le Fantôme would know exactly what to do, but only if I can get a message out.

After Nina stamps her invisible seal of approval, they swap our rope handcuffs for metal restraints, locking the manacles around our wrists and linking them together with a long, heavy chain. I'd expected to be ushered back to our original cells, but instead, they herd us through a secondary door to a different holding area.

The room is surprisingly clean and bright. A large mat, like ones I've spent countless hours training on at Joaquín's gym, lines the floor. We crowd into the space, the heavy chain forcing us to stay clumped together. The door closes behind us with a metallic *clunk,* trapping us again. But this time, we're alone, guarded only by the shadowed boots visible beneath the door. It's the opening I've been waiting for. It's time to get the other girls on board and figure out how we're going to escape.

42

ADRIANO

As always, Julianna comes through. Her confirmation of our invitations to the auction brings some much-needed relief, though my cortisol levels are off the charts from the phantom pressure of the clock ticking.

Joaquín has been indispensable. I can see how Rosa easily befriended him. We've worked tirelessly, tracking any possible leads to try and confirm if she is actually at this auction. The last thing I want is to flag the wrong person's radar and have them move her, or worse, sell her off in advance. Discretion is key, but it makes fishing for information a slow, grueling process.

We've been granted two tickets—one for me, posing as an up-and-coming businessman, and one for Joaquín, acting as my dedicated security and translator. My Spanish is lacking, and his finesse is essential for navigating the tumultuous waters ahead.

After a few nights in Tijuana, Julianna books us a private flight. Avoiding security, we load our gear into the aircraft and depart for Mexico City. A brief four-hour flight later, we land on a private airstrip and start prepping for the auction.

A few hours later, we're dressed to impress and armed to the teeth.

Joaquín cleans up nicely. He's lost the sunglasses, leaving his obsidian eyes on full display—sharp, intense, unwavering. The charcoal suit stretches taut across his broad shoulders, a silent testament to the raw strength beneath, yet the cut is precise enough to maintain an air of upper-echelon sophistication. Regardless of the outfit, his aura hasn't changed. He's still just as imposing, lethal, and disciplined as ever.

Joaquín's rolodex of contacts pulls through, securing a rush-ordered custom navy suit that fits like a glove. My tall, lean frame has always been a nightmare to dress; off-the-rack suits are always too loose or too short. Joaquín's tailor is nothing short of a miracle worker, creating enough room for my muscular arms to move uninhibited—a necessity if this comes to blows.

The invite explicitly states no weapons allowed. Guards will be stationed at every entrance and exit—not to ensure safety, but compliance. This doesn't prevent us from loading the rented SUV with enough firepower to start a small war. Everything from knives and guns to grenades and a small rocket launcher is strategically tucked into the vehicle.

Joaquín passes me a seven-inch blade before sticking a matching one in his sock. I raise an eyebrow. "Metal detectors?"

He just shrugs. "Polycarbonate. They won't set them off, but are still sharp as fuck."

Sheathing the knife, I tuck it against my ankle. Now, we're ready.

No different from auctions in the US, we park at an ostentatious mansion nestled in the rolling hills outside the city. The smooth stucco walls reflect the intense Mexican sun, contrasted by the warm baked red and orange hues of the terra cotta roof. The high archways and intricately carved doors are painted a rich brown. Delicate iron grills frame the bottom half of each window. Some hold boxes of bright pink and red native flowers, while others overflow with luscious ferns sticking through the metal designs.

Guards surround the estate, stoically positioned at every opening, their hands resting on the automatic rifles draped across their chests. Joaquín and I approach, handing them our invitations and passing through the metal detectors with ease. Spreading our arms like we're passing through airport security, they pat down our pockets and nod—letting us through.

We follow the crowd through the house to a large courtyard. The floor is paved with elegant, patterned tile-work, surrounded by stone arches, the perfect alcoves for armed men to loiter. Columns support a shaded walkway that hugs the inner perimeter, creating a continuous pathway that connects every wing of the mansion.

A makeshift stage dominates the courtyard, the platform sitting just three steps above the tiles. It's a one-way runway designed to herd the girls through like cattle—a human chute that channels them up one side and down the other.

Ignoring the senseless chatter around me, the Spanish blending into gibberish, I scope out the space—making note of every entrance, exit, window, and guard. My goal is to confirm Rosa's here and place the winning bid. Money isn't a limiting factor, and this rescue mission will be significantly easier if I play by their rules and buy her outright. But in case shit hits the fan, I'm ready to burn the house down.

Joaquín, however, is listening attentively. He's feigning disinterest, but his ears are tuned to the crowd mingling around us. After a few minutes, he tugs my sleeve and jerks his head toward the platform. The auctions about to begin, and we want to make sure we have the best seats in the house.

Everyone settles in as the auctioneer takes the stage, joined by a man in a crisp tan suit. While he delivers a passionate welcome in Spanish, I scan the crowd. As the spiel wraps up, Joaquín noticeably stiffens, his spine going rigid and shoulders jutting back. I raise my eyebrows in silent question. His subtle chin dip settles my nerves, but then he leans closer, whispering under his breath.

"He said they'll debut the special item last. That'll be her."

Returning his sharp nod, I settled in for the long haul.

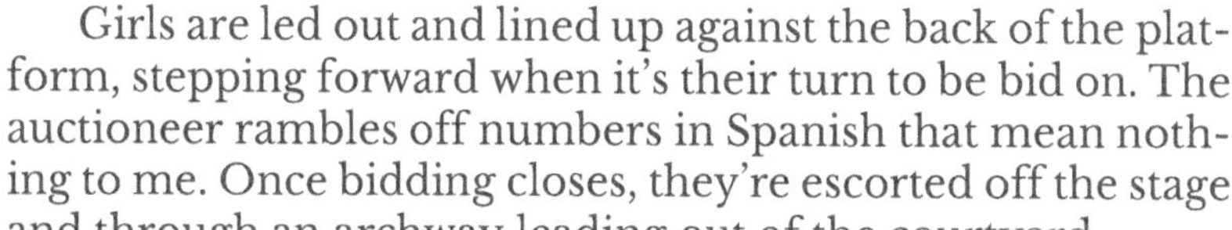

Girls are led out and lined up against the back of the platform, stepping forward when it's their turn to be bid on. The auctioneer rambles off numbers in Spanish that mean nothing to me. Once bidding closes, they're escorted off the stage and through an archway leading out of the courtyard.

The wait is killing me. The anticipation a vice around my heart, tightening with every girl who crosses the stage. Each one is clothed in white innocence, wearing more makeup than a girl their age should ever know.

Events like this always suck, but waiting to bid exclusively for Rosa is proving harder than I'd expected. Typically, everyone knew not to fuck with me, and I won dozens of girls with ease. But in Mexico, the rules are different. I'm not as well known or half as feared. This auction isn't like the others I've attended. Instead of the elite pretending to be sophisticated, everything here is more raw. Primal. Like we're the hunters cornering vulnerable prey.

The last girl crosses the stage and vanishes through the archway. The man in the tan suit retakes the mic from the auctioneer.

"Ladies and Gentlemen, it's time for our final sale of the night. The renowned *Cuervo Libre* herself!"

A hush falls over the crowd as two guards escort out the featured girl. My nails dig into my palms so deeply that tiny droplets of blood bead along their arced indents.

Paraded toward the stage is none other than my Rosa. I want so badly to call out her name. To catch a glimpse of her gorgeous brown eyes. To reassure her that the cavalry has finally arrived. Instead, I stay quiet, refusing to break the stoic persona I've donned for the night.

Despite the shackles and bare feet, she's a vision. Her curves are accentuated by the flair of a red hourglass centered on tight black material. The guards support her weight as her head lolls, her glassy eyes squinting at the crowd as she passes.

Jolts of relief and anger rip through me. We've found her. If it weren't for Joaquín's ear to the ground, I'd still have no idea she was even out of the country. My palpable relief is short-lived as the auctioneer opens the floor. The flurry of bids flood in as everyone opens their wallets. Rosa's reputation precedes her, speaking to their twisted fantasies of breaking her spirit and owning her body and mind.

Joaquín jumps into the war, bidding with no spending limit. I'll pay whatever it takes to bring my girl home. The numbers climb, higher and higher, until the number of participants thins to a handful. Before long, it's just Joaquín and one other slimy fellow. He peers at us from the other edge of the stage, trying to stare me down while my eyes narrow in retort. He squirms under my gaze, slowly lowering his paddle and letting the auctioneer call the final bid.

"Ten million—going once... going twice..."

The gavel is descending. A triumphant grin is fixed on Joaquín's face, when a sharp, insistent ringtone slices through the air. The auctioneer freezes, his hammer inches from the podium. Every eye in the courtyard shifts to the man in the tan suit as his phone vibrates violently in his grip.

He holds a dismissive finger to the stage and snaps into the phone in rapid Spanish. His face, initially annoyed, goes pale, then tightens into a mask of professional subservience. He ends the call, his gaze landing on Rosa as she sways between the two guards.

He strides back to the mic, his voice now loud and authoritative.

"Ladies and gentlemen, a change in circumstances. *El Cuervo Libre* will not be sold to the highest bidder tonight." He pauses, staring directly at Joaquín. "To the gentleman who offered $10 million, thank you for your enthusiasm. But the goods are no longer available. We look forward to doing business together at the next sale."

A low murmur ripples through the crowd, Joaquín's grin replaced by stunned rage.

"What the fuck is going on?" I growl, grabbing Joaquín's arm.

He slams his bidding paddle onto the stage, the plastic snapping under the force. "We were the highest bidders! You can't do this!" He yells in Spanish, then switches to English for my benefit. "This prick is selling her out from under us!"

Before the man could offer a smug reply, the guards holding Rosa seize her manacles. Instead of taking her to the other girls, they drag her the opposite direction, back to the darkened archway she'd emerged from.

"Wait a second! Where are they taking her?" I snap, my pulse hammering against my throat.

She was within reach—so close I could almost feel the heat off her skin. Then the floor dropped out. What the fuck?

43

ROSALIE

Waiting backstage, my escape plan fizzles as they auction off the others before me. There's no chance to intercept them or help while I'm being held under lock and key. Isolated—again.

Jefe approaches, sporting the same tan suit as earlier. "Damn, mamacita. It's a shame you didn't take me up on my offer. Your new master won't be half as generous as I would've been."

He grips me by the throat, applying firm pressure on the sides of my neck. It's almost like he already knows who's buying me. Jerk. Staring him down, I refuse to look away. The auctioneer finishes, forcing Jefe to break his hold and waltz to the microphone.

Just as the last of the girls exit the stage, a sharp prick pierces my neck. Whipping around, Scarface's menacing smirk greets me—empty syringe poised between his sausage fingers.

"Don't worry, princess. This'll only numb you for a little bit. You'll feel everything once your new owner gets their hands on you." He cackles. Shortie snags my one arm and Scarface the other as they drag me between them onto the blinding light of the stage.

My vision spots with black, a tingling sensation spreading across my skin from whatever sedative they've pumped into my bloodstream this time. The auctioneer's words bleed together. The spotlights are a wall of light, making it difficult to see past the edges of the platform. Squinting, I try to see past the blur, but the crowd keeps morphing between blobs and dark silhouettes. A familiar face comes into focus. *Joaquín! Is it really him?* His paddle flicks, a towering figure hovering behind him. *Adriano.* I'd recognize those dark locks anywhere. *He's here!* Hope blooms inside, a violent spark at the prospect of freedom.

The auctioneer's words dissolve into static as he takes bids left and right. Everything moves in speedy slow motion as the world fades in and out of focus. So many paddles. Each one belonging to some sicko who thinks you can buy people like this is a goddamn farmer's market. My arms stiffen, the shackles weighing me down like cinder blocks. If it weren't for Shortie and Scarface pitching me upright between them, I'm sure I'd be facedown by now.

Just when my knees can't stay locked for a second longer, I'm lugged off stage in the wrong direction. My head is too heavy to rotate around. I limp along without much resistance as they escort me to the Jefe.

Ignoring my noodle-like form, Jefe focuses on my captors. "Forget the holding pens. Take her out the back. There's a van waiting."

Shortie's eyebrows shoot up as he and Scarface exchange silent glances. Clearing his throat. "Uhm, Jefe? Wouldn't she be loaded out with the others?" He drops his gaze submissively to avoid his boss's gaze.

"Ha! No, I've made a special arrangement with Señor Vasquez to have her shipped directly to his estate in Bogota. He'll be expecting her to be hand-delivered."

Something wasn't adding up. *Bogota? Why would they be sending me to Colombia?* Confusion worries my forehead as I try to understand what's happening.

Before I can sort it out, I'm hauled through a hallway, down a flight of stairs, and into a servant's tunnel tucked in the wall. Small lanterns light the path as I'm half walking, mostly dragged down the narrow corridor. The floor tilts up as we ascend a set of creaky stairs, the dust forcing a sneeze from my lungs as we disturb the clearly abandoned route.

Scarface grunts as he throws his shoulder into an older door, the wood creaking under the force of his weight. The night sky opens above us, tiny glinting stars sparkling across the Mexican sky, Mother Nature blissfully unaware of the turmoil and horrors occurring beneath her dark cover.

Shortie gives me a hard shove. My hands fly up, barely

avoiding smashing my face into the dirt. The van's beams illuminate our silhouettes as the goons circle the rear and swing me inside like a sack of potatoes. My body lands with a thud, the sedative muting the impact. But I know the aches and pains will find me later in full force. The sliding door slams shut, my world spinning. Shortie and Scarface jump up front, their doors shaking the entire vehicle.

I bite back a groan, my ribs bruised and limbs still heavy. The rumble of the engine is the last thing I feel before darkness consumes me.

44

ADRIANO

Following Joaquín, my insides are hollow. My heart left with Rosa while my body remains frozen in place. My pulse hammers against my ribs, my soul heavy. I send up a quick prayer to the powers at be that Julianna and Sammy can work some magic to free the other girls. Usually, I'd be the first to help, but I'm so focused on rescuing Rosa that everything else is white noise.

The other girls are lined along the mansion wall—waiting for their buyers to pick them up. Scanning the group, my chest tightens. Rosa isn't in the line. She isn't even with the guards who were manhandling her earlier. My tongue is stuck, the words wedged in my throat as I tap Joaquín's shoulder.

"Where is she?" The gruff edge to my voice forces him to turn around.

He glances around, reaching the same jagged conclusion. Rosa's missing. He spins away, barking questions in Spanish at the nearest guard. I assume he's asking the same question.

The guard ignores us, staring blankly ahead as though Joaquín hadn't said a word. Just as I'm about to get involved, Joaquín storms to the front of the line. The money man is at a folding table with a cash box and card reader. Don't think that just because it's illicit or illegal it isn't a high-tech industry. It just means that tech skills are in high demand and highly compensated positions, whereas business used to favor physical enforcers to collect owed funds.

Joaquín jams his pointer finger into the shrewd man, the smattering of Spanish punctuated as he holds the terrified man's collar in a clenched fist. The guy sputters in fear, answering bleakly and pleading with Joaquín. I don't catch everything he says, but my peripheral vision catches movement.

In the distance, a dark van idles, its headlights off as it loiters in the night. Shadows shuffle under the cover of darkness, the interior lights turning on as they open the side door and toss something inside. I'd recognize those curls anywhere. *Rosa.*

I race to Joaquín, who is now arguing with the smarmy man who was running the show earlier. Clearly, he's trying to calm Joaquín, who is now inches from tearing him a new asshole.

Grabbing Joaquín roughly, I spin him around. "They just threw her into a van. What the fuck is going on?"

Joaquín's eyes narrow, the vein in his temple pulsing. He swings back toward the boss, his hands slicing the air as he snarls a final, jagged string of Spanish. He whips around, hooking my arm and dragging me along as he marches toward the parking lot.

"Why isn't she with the other girls?" I ask, my voice sharp.

Joaquín growls. "It seems our host was kind enough to sell her to a more *international market*. He worked out some backdoor deal with a goddamn Colombian cartel leader who took a personal interest in her."

My mouth gapes in shock before pressing into a thin line.

"They're likely on route to the airport as we speak." He continues, lengthening his stride into a power walk. "If we don't catch them before takeoff, she'll disappear."

We reach our SUV, jamming the keys in the ignition and skidding out of the parking lot. White-knuckling the "oh shit" handle and the center console, I hang on as Joaquín peels toward the highway at a rate of knots.

"Grab guns from the back." He commands. "I'm not sure what this'll come to, but we'll have to get close enough to try and stop them."

I stabilize myself on the headrest and reach for our arsenal. Passing a Glock and some grenades forward, I tuck a pistol into my waistband, choosing a feisty AK-47 for the heavy lifting.

"I saw them loading her into a black van." I say, my voice steady. "They shouldn't have much of a lead."

Joaquín guns it. "We should be able to catch them."

Taking the corners like we belong on a track instead of the guts of Mexico City, Joaquín expertly navigates the bumpy streets. It doesn't take long for the van to flicker into our sights. I roll down my window, the humid air slapping my face as I lean out and balance the barrel on the mirror.

"Think you can take out a tire?" Joaquín shouts over the wind.

"Get me closer and I'll give you a flat," I yell back. Joaquín's lead foot closes the gap until the van's tailgate fills my vision. Aiming for the tires, I fire off a couple of shots. The van swerves, doing its best to avoid the bullets. Squeezing the trigger, I take a few more shots. The bumpy pavement is a curse. Most of the lead peppers the tailgate with a hollow ring, missing the rubber I desperately need to hit.

"Get down!" Joaquín bellows. Lunging across the center console, tugging the back of my shirt and pulling me inside as one of the guards returns fire. Sporadic shots spray the front of our SUV.

"Dammit! Don't put any holes in the fucking car." Joaquín swears under his breath, swerving out of the line of fire.

We jockey back and forth, exchanging shots, while doing our best to minimize damage to either vehicle. The last thing we want is for the van to crash or flip with Rosa inside. They tear onto the highway on-ramp with us hot on their tail. Traffic thickens. A sea of taillights appears, forcing us to weave through traffic.

Ducking inside, I huff in frustration. "We can't keep shooting at them with all these people around."

Joaquín nods, both hands gripped tightly on the wheel as he focuses on navigating through the gaps. Refusing to give up, we keep hunting for a clear shot, but the wall of cars stays in the way.

Aeropuerto Salida 2.5 km - Airport Exit 2.5 km

"We can't let them reach that plane!" I snarl.

Joaquín's jaw grinds. I can practically see the smoke pouring out of his ears. The congestion thickens as we close in on the departure gates. Ahead of us, the van blows through an intersection at the last second. Horns blare as oncoming traffic slam on the brakes, tires shrieking. Boxed in, the cars in front of us block our way, the drivers deciding to finally abide by traffic laws and obey the red light. We're stuck in the gridlock, watching the van disappear.

"Fuck!" He slams the steering wheel.

A sports bike idles loudly beside us, its engine thundering, echoing my racing heartbeat

"I've got an idea. You keep going. I'll meet you there." I leap out of the SUV, snagging the handlebars and shoving the motorist onto the asphalt. With the AK-47 safely secured to my back, I swing my leg over and twist the throttle. The engine roars. Navigating along the dotted lines, I squeeze between the barricade of vehicles and rip through the light. I bob and weave through the chaos, rapidly closing the distance.

In seconds, I'm pulling alongside the van. Inside, the guards are arguing, one waving a pistol as he yells at his partner. The driver frantically checks his rearview mirror, searching for the SUV. I don't even try to hold back my vindictive smirk as I watch the passenger's eyes grow wide. Glock locked and loaded on the driver, my fingers squeeze the trigger—once, twice, three times.

The glass shatters with the first round, crashing in on them. The driver pitches forward as my second shot hits him in the temple, his whole body slumping and veering the van toward my bike. *Shit.* My third shot clips the passenger, his howl of pain audible over the hum of the bike's engine and the whipping wind.

Clamping the brakes, the bike nose-dives, slowing just enough for the van to narrowly miss clipping my front wheel. Skidding across multiple lanes, the van bounces up the concrete curb, onto the grassy median, and slams to a halt, the bumper crumpling as it hits a massive palm tree.

Ditching the bike, I sprint toward the van, my pistol still pulled but aimed at the ground. I approach the smoking vehicle. Confident the driver is either dead or incapacitated; I clear the passenger seat. He's breathing, but unconscious, a nasty gash staining his forehead red as he slumps against the airbags.

Not wasting a second, I tug on the rear door, the metal creaking its resistance. It's either locked or jammed. Snarling, I reach through the shattered passenger window, ignoring the shards of glass piercing my skin, and jam the unlock button. Taking a deep breath, the door handle nestled in my palm, I yank with all of my might. It heaves, groans, and slowly slides open, revealing a teenage girl curled up inside. The crash had tossed her around the empty metal walls, her small, battered body covered in bruises. She's shackled and cowering in the shadows.

It isn't Rosa.

My heart stops. A cold wave of disappointment washes over me, but I don't have time to drown in it. This girl isn't mine, but she still needs help. Tucking my gun away, I cautiously approach the wreckage with my hands raised, palms open and empty. Keeping my voice low and steady, I try to coax the trembling teen out of the steel tomb.

Just as I finally start making progress with her, Joaquín's SUV jumps the curb and he vaults out. The girl recoils, diving deeper into the van and peering around stiffly. Joaquín rushes over, expecting to see Rosa in my arms. His expression hardens into a thin line as his gaze clashes with the teen.

"That's not her." Joaquín states flatly.

"Obviously," I snap. "We must've followed the wrong van. Let's go. We might be able to make it before they leave."

He nods toward the terrified girl. "What about her?"

"Bring her with us. I've been trying to get her out of the damn vehicle, but she doesn't understand shit. Can you explain to her what's going on?"

Joaquín rocks back on his heels, bringing himself to her eye level. He speaks softly in Spanish. Whatever he's saying must resonate because she finally nods. The brave girl shuffles toward him, hands still bound, and climbs stiffly into Joaquín's backseat.

Hopping behind the wheel, Joaquín mutters, "What should we do with her?"

My phone is already out, my fingers flying over the keyboard. "I'll call in a friend. She'll be able to get her somewhere safe."

We rip toward the airfield, dust spitting out under our tires. Following the signs to the private airstrip, we finally spot it. The black van is parked on the tarmac while we're stuck on the wrong side of the chain link fence.

"We've got to get in before it's too late." My mouth's suddenly dry, like I'm chewing on cotton balls. The idea of losing her when she's within reach carves a crater in my chest. Hollow. Sharp. Visceral.

Joaquín points at the runway. The two goons who'd detained Rosa at the auction are just reaching their vehicle, dusting off their hands at a job well done.

Despite the wire mesh being see-through, we couldn't be further apart. Frantically searching for a way past the barbs, I'm helpless as I watch the plane take off, taking my soul with it.

Desperation claws at my throat. A wounded cry of anguish parts my lips as my worst nightmare comes true. We were too late. She's gone and headed to Colombia. I'd failed her.

Pulling out my phone, I rasp. "Bryce... I'm gonna need a favor."

45

ROSALIE

My head jolts as it makes contact with a hard panel, the sudden, sharp pain chasing away the drug-induced fog. The world shudders into focus as I'm jarred awake. *It'll be a miracle if I'm able to escape my chronic concussed state when this is all over.* My dark humor fails to distract me from the reality of my situation.

I peer around expectantly for Adriano. He was at the auction. I swear I saw him. But instead of his dark brown eyes, I'm greeted by new, strange faces, different guards from the goons who'd held me captive in Mexico.

The cabin is luxurious and spacious, yet I'm cramped into a single, economy-sized seat. My wrists and ankles ache under the bite of the metal shackles. In the seat next to me, a round-faced man with a short mustache is engrossed in an in-flight magazine. Others are lounging around the cabin, scrolling on their phones, unbothered by their involvement with a hostage.

A muffled voice patches through the intercom. "We'll be landing shortly. Fifteen minutes and we'll officially be in Colombia."

The transition is swift and clinical. The plane shudders to a halt and the cabin door hisses open. Not surprisingly, we're parked in the middle of a private airstrip. No bustling throngs or border security waiting, just a short paved runway, a single tower for traffic control, and a whole lot of empty space. No witnesses. No bystanders. No one to rescue me.

I'm led down the rolling stairs and immediately

transferred into a sleek, tinted helicopter. We lift off in a whirl, the world dissolving into a dizzying blanket of green jungle. My gut sinks. This isn't a standard criminal operation—this is organized wealth.

A heartbeat later, we settle onto a manicured lawn. The estate is so vast it makes the Manoir Hotel look like a shack—a fortress disguised as a tropical mansion. The air is heavy, thick with humidity and the scent of foreign blossoms. Towering palms stretch over us, casting shadows across the chopper. The entire villa screams of obscene wealth.

The guards, whom I've affectionately named Goon One and Goon Two, usher me past a deep blue pool and through a concrete archway. We weave through a maze of spackled corridors decorated with gaudy art before reaching what can only be described as a dungeon. The room's sparse, yet strangely not as repulsive as my last accommodations. A barred door with a mocking resemblance to prison is the gatekeeper to my new hell. The Goonies unceremoniously dump me on a simple mattress set directly on the concrete before locking me in with a loud, final *click*.

I slide down the wall, my head swimming as I try to absorb every detail of the last hour. My adrenaline fades, replaced by a cold dread. No one will be rescuing me. No one even knows this place exists. My new owner remains a mystery, yet everything about this place—the precision, the isolation, the sheer wealth—screams *ominous*. Martín was a chauvinistic pig, but this man is a predator.

46

ADRIANO

Bryce pulled through big time. Within a few short hours after my plea for help, Joaquín and I were cleared and loaded onto a military C-17 cargo plane that's transporting one of their special ops teams to Bogota. Apparently, being next in line for CIA director comes with perks.

We pass operatives strapping themselves into the jump seats lining the walls. Crates are strapped down in the center aisle, swallowing most of the cargo hold. Joaquín settles in with familiar ease, leaning back against the rough interior with a show of comfort that hints at his years in the service. Without our gear and bags, we're stuck standing out, our suits a stark contrast to their black tactical outfits. There's no blending in with our civilian clothes. Joining Joaquín, I pull off my jacket, the adrenaline finally crashing from the angst of the day.

"You good, amigo?" He points at the streaks of red marring my white buttonup. "You're bleeding through your shirt. Let me take a look." He pulls my arm over, twisting my wrist in the process.

"I've got it." I yank my arm back, fumbling with the buttons to roll up the sleeve when a sweet voice interrupts my struggle.

"Excuse me. Perhaps I can help? I'm our team's medic." A flash of recognition flickers across Joaquín's face, instantly hardening to a rigid, hostile glare at the petite woman kitted out in all black with a small first-aid kit in tow. The look he shoots at her would've sent most men retreating, but she just returns his glare before softening her gaze back to me. *Interesting.*

For nothing more than my own amusement of seeing Joaquín's reaction, I hold out my arm. "If you wouldn't mind, I'd appreciate it. Can't have anything slowing me down once we land."

She nods politely before finishing rolling my sleeve and getting to work. She's all business. Professional. Efficient. Knowledgeable. She dresses and bandages the deeper gashes, carefully cleaning them for residual glass. Joaquín's eyes never leave her, his jaw locked in a rigid clench. Once she's finished, she snaps her kit shut.

"Make sure to keep it clean and covered until you're back stateside. Infections are easy to catch in the jungle."

"Thanks, Doc." I smile warmly, admiring her handiwork.

"No problem." She smirks and returns to her seat, completely immune to Joaquín's pissy attitude. His scowl made tolerating her poking and prodding worth it.

Leaning back, I try to doze off, wanting to be fully rested when we hit the ground. But my mind refuses to yield. The guilt of letting Rosa slip through my fingers—not one, but twice—churns in my gut like acid. I run through every scene and scenario, agonizing over everything I could've done differently to protect her. Relentlessly, I replay the failure until I'm exhausted, finally falling into a shallow, restless sleep.

When the cargo ramp finally hisses open, we're unloaded onto the tarmac in Bogota. A stern man in command meets us by the cargo ramp. He doesn't offer a handshake, only points a gloved finger toward the first in a line of idling vehicles.

"You two are first out." He states, his voice flat and military crisp. "We'll drop you at your final destination before proceeding."

Grabbing our gear, we're loaded into one of the nondescript SUVs and head deeper into the concrete labyrinth of Bogota. The leader pulls up to a dilapidated row of colorful attached houses.

"This is your stop, boys." He points to the two-story yellow house. Blue-trimmed windows are covered by drawn curtains. White security grates bar the lower windows and the front door. It's run-down and unremarkable, just like every other home on the block.

"Are you sure you've got the right place?" I ask incredulously. "I thought we'd be meeting some wealthy cartel leader or warlord? Not the neighborhood watch."

Joaquín just shakes his head with a smirk. "It's the right place."

"Knock twice. They're expecting you." The commander nods, extending his arm through the SUV window. "Best of luck. We'd stay and help get your girl if we didn't have other orders."

I shake his hand, genuinely grateful for the lift and their sincere wishes. "You've done more than enough. Thanks for the lift."

The SUV doesn't wait for us, pulling away from the curb immediately. Joaquín stares at the house before stepping onto the cracked pavement and knocking twice. The door cracks an inch and we're greeted by the dark barrel of a pistol held by a pissed-off bearded man.

Joaquín jumps back in a hurry, hands raised. "Whoa! We were told you were expecting us?"

A voice cuts through the tension. "Easy, Gunner. They're friendlies." The door swings wider, revealing a familiar face—one I'd never expected to see outside a bar or boardroom—Bryce.

"Holy shit!" I ignore Gunner's predatory stance, crossing the threshold to embrace Bryce in a fierce bro hug. "What the hell are you doing here?"

He chuckles, radiating pure, chaotic energy. "Well, someone called in a favor to rescue a special lady. I couldn't pass up one more field op before I'm chained to a desk for eternity." He wags his eyebrows. "Besides, I wouldn't miss the chance to meet the girl who has the great Adriano all smitten."

Peering over my shoulder, his grin grows wider. "Hot damn. I didn't expect to see you again in this lifetime." He clasps Joaquín's forearm, pulling him into a hug.

"B, didn't realize you were the one Adriano called for backup. Good to see you."

"Thought you were out of the game?" Bryce asks.

Joaquín returns the smirk. "Is anyone ever truly out?"

Bryce pulls back from Joaquín, gesturing at the still-scowling Gunner by the door.

"Speaking of backup, this pleasant peach is Gunner. Gunner, meet Adriano," he says, giving me a hard slap on the back. "And this smooth operator is Joaquín."

Gunner just nods curtly, crossing his arms over his barrel chest. He doesn't look impressed, but no longer looks like he's about to shoot us.

Bryce glances between us, visibly energized by the unique circumstances. He rubs his hands together with a manic sort of glee. "Well, boys. What do you say we infiltrate a cartel compound?"

He leads us through the safehouse to the upper level. One room is a basic bedroom, but the other, which he unlocks with a heavy key, is a vault. The space is sparse, housing a single twin mattress on a wiry metal frame. Bare. Simple. Functional. Two large duffels sit beside the bed, overflowing with weapons. Bryce already has a myriad of firearms laid out in an orderly fashion across the mattress.

"We've got all the essentials: guns, grenades, flash bombs, and smoke bombs. You name it, we likely have it." He gestures toward a stack of familiar tactical vests beside the bags. "Some of the finest in cutting-edge technology. Courtesy of Mr. Devereaux himself." He winks.

Joaquín eyes me briefly before running his hands over the lightweight, flexible material. Letting out a grunt of approval, he shifts his gaze to me. "We need a plan. We can't just suit up and storm the gates head-on."

"Never said we wouldn't have one," I reply. "Just needed to know what we were working with before we made one. Bryce, you've been on the ground here before. Any suggestions?"

Bryce's shaggy locks shake as he laughs. "As much as I've always wanted to blow up this asshole, I figured we'd want a plan that didn't involve death by cartel. Come on, I've got some ideas."

He carefully relocks the makeshift armory and leads us back downstairs. The first floor is just as simple as upstairs. A dated kitchenette bleeds into the small living room with a round folding table and a few mismatched chairs. We gather around the table as Bryce conjures a large roll of blueprints, unfurling them across the tabletop.

"According to my contacts, it sounds like your girl was bought by Jorge Vasquez." Bryce's tone hardens, losing its playful edge. "He's a mean fucker. Likes to play with his pets before finishing them off. A real animal. Rumor has it he's more bloodthirsty than Pablo Escobar was."

Bryce taps a finger on an open space on the map. "There's minimal cover at the entrance. But we can flank around and enter from the west side. Intel shows he's a cocky motherfucker, so we're in luck. He hasn't had a threat on Colombian soil in quite a few years, so security's gotten pretty lax: minimal guards, regular perimeter sweeps, sparse cameras."

Bryce gets more wound up with each point, his hands dancing over the blueprints like he's conducting a symphony of violence. It's easy to see how the man was born for this. He's the full special ops package: detail-oriented, prepared, and a charismatic leader who thrives in chaos. He easily absorbs and creates mayhem in the same breath. It's times like these I'm relieved that we're on the same team.

We spend the next couple hours solidifying our plan of attack, reviewing it until Bryce is satisfied that our success is a mathematical certainty. Gunner, the silent shadow in the corner, volunteers to be our driver while the three of us extract Rosa.

Joaquín and I shed our business slacks and stuffy button-downs, changing into the functional tactical wear Bryce brought. Armed, he tosses each of us a vest, we load into Gunner's SUV and head out for Vasquez's compound.

47

ROSALIE

The bars clank as the Goonies waltz in. I scoot off the mattress, edging toward the wall, refusing to leave my back exposed to them. They yank my chains, leading me out into the gaudy labyrinth of corridors. The new twists and turns disorient me, ruining any chance I have of mapping the estate. Many blind turns later, I'm tossed into another bedroom. This one has fewer bars and more amenities. Two female servants are waiting inside, their faces masks of indifference. One scurries to the door, muttering something to Goon One, who fumbles in his pocket and produces a single key. The girl shoos him away before clicking the manacles off for the first time in weeks.

They herd me into the bathroom. One girl holds out a basket for my clothes while the other runs the bath. The temptation of warm water is too strong to resist, but the lack of weight makes me stumble as I lift my leg into the tub. I'd grown so used to shackles restricting my movement that I feel more exposed without the chains than I do without the dress.

The girls primp and preen, operating with silent synchronized efficiency. Their spa treatment is the most kindness I've received in weeks. By the time they're done, I'm barely recognizable. My dark curls are tightly pinned, straightened into a sleek frame around my face. A thick leather collar encircles my neck, buckled tight around my throat, and a skin-tight latex dress leaves nothing to the imagination. My wrists are decorated with a new set of chains, the iron shackles on my ankles remain gone, but the display of ownership is the same.

The guards return to escort me to the dining room, abandoning me just past the threshold. Overhead, an opulent crystal chandelier casts stark, white light that reflects off a dominating, long mahogany table. At the head of the table, a high-backed chair sits like a throne, making all other chairs along its length feel insignificant.

Amidst the aggressive display of wealth presides a middle-aged man. He isn't handsome, but he is intimidating. His face is broad and his jaw heavy-set. His tailored white linens and gold accessories are a picture of extravagance, an expensive mask for the violence beneath. Arrogance rolls off him in swaths, everything from his outfit to posture screaming entitlement. He stands, circling and inspecting his acquisition from all sides. I keep my eyes locked on him, my lips sealed shut, rooted in the place his goons left me.

"So, this is the infamous *Cuervo Libre.*" He sneers. "You've caused me a great deal of grief with your *activities.* Had I known my problem was this beautiful, I would've just kidnapped you years ago and saved my supply chain the agony."

He steps closer, running a hand through my locks. He licks his lips, a glassed-over infatuation taking hold as he drools over his "prize." He inhales deeply, exhaling with a soft sigh as he crowds me, the sheer gall of his proximity makes me queasy.

"Welcome to Colombia, pet." He points to the floor near his gilded chair. "Sit."

Choosing to play along, I bury my pride, summoning the cold seductress that once made me Rosa the ringmistress. Kneeling with catlike grace, I position myself at his feet while he perches on his throne. While this man might believe he's a predator, he has no idea who he's dealing with. Larger men have fallen for my whims, and him showing interest just gives me the upper hand. He's too comfortable. Too relaxed. Too complacent.

He isn't a complete idiot. My wrists are still bound, but my feet are free from their chains, leaving me more mobile than I've been in weeks.

A stiff butler enters the dining room. "Señor Vasquez, dinner is served."

Vasquez. As in, *the* Jorge Vasquez, leader of the Medellín

Cartel? This is worse than I thought. Over the years, I've rescued countless Colombians from Mexican rings. He's widely known for his involvement with drug trafficking, but his appetite for sex trades is no secret. *I have to get out of here. Fast.*

Jorge waves in the staff, and they hustle to get the silverware placed with trembling precision. The glutton devours a full four-course meal with no pause. His buttons threaten to burst against the white linens as he washes down the last of his dessert with a gulp of red wine.

"Let's continue getting to know each other elsewhere." He reaches down, his grubby hands grabbing a fistful of my curls, and roughly tugs me to my feet. "Come."

I stumble, but quickly find my balance as he leads the way. Servants rush around, gathering the dishes as we exit. Cautiously, I nick a slender steak knife from the table as we pass, tucking it against my wrist.

A few strides ahead, Jorge carelessly steers us down the hallway. The Goonies have split, leaving only Goon Two trailing close behind as we exit the dining hall. I have to escape. There's no way I'm letting Jorge "get to know me" better. Not today. Not tomorrow. Not ever.

Rounding the corner, I strike. With succinct precision, I swing both bound fists, stabbing Goon Two. A few rapid punctures and he's a goner. Jorge doesn't even register a disturbance until Goon Two slumps to the floor.

I lunge forward; my weapon leveled at Jorge's throat as he spins to face me. He doesn't flinch. Instead, his gaze roams the crimson splatters decorating my skin, practically purring with satisfaction.

"Your bloodlust lives up to the hype, pet. I must say, red looks good on you."

48

ADRIANO

Gunner drops us close, barely a half-mile from our breaching point. We reach the perimeter of Vasquez's compound, reliant on the cover of dusk to mask our movements. Silently, we trek to the west side, moving through the brush like ghosts. Bryce's gadgets allow us to easily scale the wall, evading any guards. Despite never working together, we move cohesively, methodically progressing as a unit.

Clearing the way, Bryce holds up a clenched fist. My pulse stutters as we come to a halt. Mere yards away, my Rosa stands like a warrior princess. Fierce. Her bound wrists not wavering as she points a small blade at her captor. Pride and panic war inside me at the red spurts sprayed everywhere. One man is already collapsed at her feet, but the other, who I can only assume is Jorge Vasquez, appears delighted. Unhinged. Delusional. My girl holds her ground, undeterred by the uneven odds in her pursuit of freedom.

Following Bryce's plan, our party splits. Joaquín and I slink off in opposite directions, flanking Vasquez. We move through the shadows of the adjoining rooms, eyes locked on the target and the woman holding him at bay.

"Stay back." Rosa growls at Vasquez.

He belts out a laugh, clapping a slow round of applause. "Yes! This is the Cuervo Libre I was promised: sassy, spicy, entertaining. And here I was worried you'd already been subdued." He steps in closer. Her spine straightens, elbows braced. "This just makes taming you that much more allur-ing, pet."

It takes every ounce of control to rein in my fury and wait for Bryce's signal. Time slows as the scene unfolds. Rosa steps back, eyes still locked on Vasquez as she creates more distance between them. His frame overlays hers, blocking a clear shot. She's almost to the corner when a guard yanks her into a headlock, his height lifting her to her toes.

Bryce's hand twitches, and we leap into action. He hits Jorge with a strategically placed shot to the calf, the crack of the suppressed round sending the kingpin to his knees and creating an opening to take out the guard. Rosa doesn't hes-itate, arcing the small knife down, plunging it into the guard's thigh before spinning, swiping it across his jugular in a fluid, practiced motion. As the guard collapses, she drops into a crouch, ready to pounce—her ire turning my direc-tion.

"Cher," I croak.

She jolts, the red haze seeping from her glare as she takes stock of her surroundings.

"A-Adriano?" She shakes her head, her eyes searching mine as if trying to confirm her mind isn't playing dirty tricks. "H-how?"

Joaquín emerges from the shadows; her reaction a mix-ture of surprise and delight.

Bryce clears his throat, awkwardly drawing our attention to him. "Not to be a buzzkill, but we've got to move unless we want more company. Joaquín and I took out a handful of other guards, but who knows how many others are lingering. Gunner's at the rendezvous, but we've got to get there first."

Leading the way, we fall in line: Bryce, Rosa, myself, with Joaquín picking up the rear. Despite being handcuffed and barefoot, Rosa is no damsel in distress, keeping pace with Bryce's long strides without complaint.

Bryce sprints ahead, pulling a compact grappling hook from his kit. He flicks a switch and the hook launches si-lently, catching on the top of the concrete wall with a soft *thunk*. He tests the line, then gives Rosa a firm look. "Go. Fast."

Without a word, she grabs the line and scales the wall with ease, her lack of footwear no hindrance. As she clears the top, Bryce shoves me toward the rope, then Joaquín, before hauling himself up last and retracting the line, erasing our trail.

Gunner skids to a stop and we pile in, zipping back to the safehouse. Squished between Joaquín and I, Rosa begins to tremble, her adrenaline finally crashing. Unable to keep my hands off her any longer, I hoist her onto my lap, curling protectively around her soft body.

"I'm covered in bloo—" She protests.

"Shh, Cher. Let me have this." I bury my face in her hair, inhaling her scent. Instead of protesting further, she leans closer, finding her own comfort in our closeness.

Gunner slows to a normal driving pace, prioritizing stealth over speed as we blend into the other taillights. Rosa shifts, letting out a low, pained groan.

"What is it, ma chérie? Are you hurt?"

"My side... it's sore. I'll be fine." She whispers, biting her lip. I gently probe her ribs and wince, counting at least two that feel severely bruised, if not cracked.

We get back to the safehouse, giving Rosa a chance to wash the iron and blood from her skin before the long flight home. Once she's feeling slightly more human, Bryce checks her over, taping her torso tightly while Joaquín returns our gear. I hold Rosa's hand the entire time, unable to bear any physical distance. Before the hour is up, we're on the move again. Gunner drops us directly onto a private airstrip where the jet's engines are already whirring.

"I owe you more than a few favors for this, Bryce." I pull him into a brief hug at the bottom of the gangway. "And Gunner, you ever need anything, just call."

Gunner tips his hat, a man of few words. Joaquín claps Bryce on the shoulder, their goodbye a silent exchange of respect.

"I'll handle the clean-up here and make sure this whole operation disappears," Bryce assures us, then turns to Rosa, offering a genuine, if slightly too wide, smile. "Welcome back, Rosa. Give 'em hell."

We board the jet. The long flight home to DC is quiet, save for the hum of the engines. Rosa sleeps in my arms, medicated and exhausted. I finally relax my guard and watch her breathe as the weight of the last few weeks lifts from my shoulders.

She's safe. She's coming home.

49

ROSALIE

"I'm fine, Adriano! I already told you they just need time to heal."

"No way, cher. You're getting checked out by an actual doctor. It's non-negotiable."

I cross my arms, letting out an involuntary grunt when my ribs shift. "I promise, I'll be okay. You don't just get to order me around."

Adriano's eyes darken. He steps closer, wrapping me in a gentle embrace that barely grazes my injuries. "Please, ma chérie. I thought I'd lost you. I watched you get kidnapped only to find you covered in blood. Set my mind at ease and let a professional check you."

His soft plea warms my heart. I spent so many hours in that cell dreaming of his face.

"We don't have time, Tiger. We've got to get back to Mexico. We left all those girls—"

He interrupts me with a growl. "Cher. You are *not* going back there. I just got you back."

"We *have* to! We can't just leave them!"

Sighing deeply, his shoulders droop in what I expect is defeat when he surprises me.

"It's not my secret to tell, but if I can assure you everyone at the auction has or is being rescued, will you drop it and see a damn doctor?"

I bob my head. He pulls out his cell, and dials a number.

"Hey, A. What's up?" A woman's voice crackles through the speakerphone.

"Need an update. Rosa's worried about the girls."

"She doesn't believe in Le Fantome? I'm hurt." The female voice answers. "We've got all but one out and safe. Should be wrapped up soon."

"I haven't told her about you yet."

"Seriously? She might as well be looped in. We already know she's the Cuervo Libre."

Le Fantôme? Adriano knows who they are?

"Need assistance?" Adriano asks.

The indignant huff passes through the phone. "Really? You know I'd ask if I did. Besides, Sam's proven more useful than expected."

My grip tightens on Adriano's arm. "Sam?" I whisper.

Turning away from the phone, he glances down at me, nodding as he speaks. "My younger brother. He's there with Julianna."

"Wait. Sammy isn't missing... and Julianna is Le Fantôme—*the* Phantom?"

"Yup," Julianna answers in his place. "Nice to finally meet you, Cuervo Libre. Welcome to the family."

Shocked and speechless, I let Adriano wrap up the call. My world tilts on its axis.

Sammy is safe. Julianna is Le Fantôme. They're together and rescued all the girls in Mexico. And everyone knows who I am.

We pull up to a nondescript building—a mobile hospital Bryce set up in Virginia to keep me under the radar. I can't help but be impressed. Adriano managed to find me, get us home, and arrange private treatment, all to keep me safe.

A petite woman in scrubs enters, her demeanor professional but warm. "Welcome, Ms. Martínez. How are we feeling?"

"Sore. But alive." I answer.

She smiles, checking her tablet. "Your tox-screen came back clear. Aside from a nasty concussion and those pesky ribs, you're in remarkably good shape. You'll need to increase your fluids and ease back onto full meals, but otherwise you're all set."

I look at Adriano, whose jaw's tight with lingering fear. I reach out, threading my fingers through his. "See? I'm fine. Now take me home."

50

ADRIANO

For the first time in months, I slept through the night with Rosa's warm body pressed against mine. But the first night was tough. I woke to her flailing violently, slick with sweat, and tears silently streaming down her face. Her breath came in shallow, frantic gasps.

"Cher, hey, sweetheart." I murmured, pulling her gently toward me, securing her so she wouldn't hurt herself. I let my heat and presence pull her back from to me. "You're safe, ma chérie. I've got you."

Her eyes flew open, wide and dark, seeing the van, the cages, the blood—anything but the ceiling of my trailer. Her fists clenched against my shirt. "They took them," she choked out, her voice a raw whisper. "They took them all. I couldn't—"

I leaned down and pressed my lips to her forehead, doing my best to be a steady anchor in her storm. "You're safe, my fierce little raven. You saved yourself, and the others are safe." I reminded her, my hand resting firmly over the rapid thrumming of her heart. "It's just a bad memory. It's over, cher. No one will ever take you again."

It took minutes for the tension to bleed out of her. Her rigid shoulders slumped as she collapsed against my neck, breathing in the scent of my skin until her pulse finally slowed. I held her, rocking her gently until she drifted back into an exhausted sleep. I stayed awake for the rest of the night, reassuring myself as much as her that she was safe. I spent hours calculating her captor's demise. Nothing would stop me from ensuring the men who haunted her suffered.

I wasn't the only one thrilled to have Rosa at home. Luca, Tony, Baba, and the twins welcomed her with open arms. Chef even prepared her favorite meal, homemade enchiladas, for her first dinner home.

She's it for me. Where she goes, I'll follow. There's no letting her go now. Rosa is mine. And there's no way she'll slip through my grasp again. She's the missing piece that brought my family together. My real family, plus a few welcomed additions. So, when she agreed to move in with me and stay at Cirque du Noir, I practically whooped with joy.

Joaquín said his goodbyes at Dulles, heading back to Tijuana. We video called my parents, who were relieved beyond words to see her safe. They'd already risked so much to contact me initially that we couldn't risk them flying out again. As far as we could tell, their cover at Circo del Sol was still intact and their plan of hiding in plain sight is effective against whoever is threatening us. So much to my disdain, they remained on the West Coast.

As much as I wished I could shield and lock her away while we neutralize the pending threats, she refused to be sidelined. Joaquín reminded me she's the fiercest person he's ever trained—even including his special ops soldiers. My girl is skilled. Determined. Fierce. And I wasn't going to be the one to clip her wings.

We finally agreed: she could help investigate the threatening letters, but strictly from under the radar. As painful as it was to let her into the line of fire, her beaming smile was a balm to my wounds. I was in trouble. I knew I'd do whatever it takes to keep her happy.

For now, we waited. Julianna was tracking down whoever was involved in Rosa's kidnapping. Then we would strike.

We were ready for war, but for tonight, we just have to heal.

EPILOGUE

ROSALIE

With Martín's involvement with my kidnapping, Adriano refused to let me return to Circo del Sol. I was worried the poor man was going to break out in hives, thinking I'd refuse his order to stay at Cirque du Noir. But there was no way I was going west, not when I finally had the chance to rejoin my new family.

Everyone welcomed me with open arms. The hardest adjustment was the hovering. Adriano's protective instincts had shifted into overdrive, transforming him into a looming, beautiful shadow. If he wasn't glued to my side, he ensured someone else was. My days were filled with a rotating roster of "babysitters." I spent hours chatting with Baba, watching the twins, and reading to Luca.

It's been over a month since I was rescued. My wounds are healed, my ribs stitched together, and my headaches are less frequent. Everything is perfect; well, almost perfect.

Adriano refuses to touch me.

His warm embrace anchors me through the nightmares and cold sweats, letting my brain and body heal at their own pace. But somewhere along the line, he also decided I was fragile and made of glass.

At first, I appreciated it. But now I'm frustrated.

Every night he teases me with his sexy body as we get ready for bed. His muscles on full display as he throws on those deadly gray sweats and snuggles under the blankets. His kisses drive me wild. Always tender and sweet, but halted before they could become deeper, all-consuming. The flitting of his palms hold the promise of pleasure, but never take things far enough before he rolls over and turns off the lights. Anytime we tread too close to the heat of passion, he pulls back.

This madness is going to end. I've officially had enough. I am healed and primed. Needy and insatiable. Desperate and committed. My man needs to set aside his protective bullshit and realize that by cutting me off, he's the one hurting me. Determination courses through my veins as I shower and shave, preparing to seduce my man.

The first rays of sweet morning sunlight trickle through the trailer window, painting stripes across the queen-sized bed. Adriano is fast asleep, his body still, except for the low, steady rumble of his snores.

I trail my fingers down the center of his chest, following the taut lines of his sexy V-muscles—the dark trail disappearing beneath the waistband of his sweatpants. He's rigid beneath the thin gray material, a testament to his hunger.

Gently, I slide the fabric down, liberating his morning glory. It springs free, thick and hot, immediately demanding attention. Salivating, I lean in. *It's been too long.* The salty, faintly metallic scent of his cock is home, as right and familiar as the beat of his heart against my ear.

Clenched at the base, I give a few languid strokes, the sheer size of him heavy in my hand. I ease him past my warm, wet lips, taking him with a soft, hungry moan. Adriano groans in his sleep, his hand finding my wild curls and threading the strands loosely through his fingers, a primal, unconscious sign of possession.

He wakes with an inhale, his eyes flashing open, instantly alert. He doesn't pull away; he arches into the sensation, his hands tightening.

"*Mm*, cher." He groans, his voice rough with sleep and pleasure. "You should be resting." He tries to sit up, his abs displaying a ripple of disciplined muscle, but I stop him.

I pull off him with a loud, wet pop, leaving his member slick and throbbing. I hover over him.

"I'll stop when I've had my fill, Tiger. Now stay still and let me play." I shove him playfully against the pillows, using my knee to hold him in place. My control absolute.

Licking, suckling, fondling—I worship him. Every swipe of my tongue and bob of my head sends an electric charge down my spine, pooling the heat between my legs.

My panties are too much. Reaching between my thighs, I push the lace aside, rubbing the pads of my fingers across my sensitive, engorged nub. My breathing choppy, matching the fierce, rhythmic pace of my mouth.

Adriano's fists clench, his fingers knotted tight in my hair, holding me in place. An indicator of his sheer restraint—the agonizing discipline it's taking to give me control when his body screams for release.

I worship him until my own need becomes unbearable. Tearing my panties aside, I climb over him, hovering over his cock. Pushing him back, I demand compliance.

"I don't want to hurt you, cher." He grates out, torn between desire and restraint.

"You're hurting me by stopping. I need you, Tiger." I sink down, guiding his erection home. He grips my hips as I dictate the pace, riding and grinding until he can't survive the passive pleasure any longer. With a primal growl, his last strands of control snap. He holds me steady and thrusts up, meeting my momentum. We move with a ferocious rhythm, the friction burning away the lingering trauma of the last month. The world dissolves in a blinding wave as we find our pleasure together.

"I love you, Tiger." I breathe as the first waves of release crash through me.

He drives into me one last time, joining me in bliss. "I love you more, Cher."

We collapse into a tangle of limbs, sweat cooling on our skin.

"I'm sorry," he whispers. "I was terrified of hurting you."

"You gave me exactly what I needed, Tiger." I kiss his damp shoulder. "But if you ever withhold sex again, we'll officially be fighting."

He chuckles, the sound muffled against my neck. "Understood, ma chérie. My apologies. Your safety will always come first, but I'll make sure your pleasure is my second priority."

Pulling me close, I curl into his chest, his length still nestled inside. We wallow in the quiet, shared warmth until he softens enough to slide out, leaving us hollow and satisfied.

We'd just finished showering when Adriano's phone rings from the other room. Julianna's ringtone fills the trailer. He puts it on speakerphone, motioning for me to join him.

Before he gets a chance to greet her, she's jumping down his throat, all business. "Hey, I think I found them."

This was it—the news we had been waiting for! Jules finally got a hit that could lead us to whoever was behind all our pain and threats.

"Fuck, where?"

Julianna's serious voice fills the other line. "New York. In our own fucking backyard."

"Shit. That's too fucking close." Adriano mutters.

"What's the plan, A?" Sammy's voice comes through the speaker.

Lowering his voice to a menacing growl. "We show him what happens when you fuck with our family."

Curious about who is threatening everyone Adriano loves? Want to know more about Julianna and Sammy's adventures?

Look for *Cirque du Noir Book 2: The Phantom's Retribution* (Coming Soon)

ABOUT THE AUTHOR

Raised in the heart of New England and transplanted to the Canadian Rockies. As an avid reader from a young age, Sara is still often found with her nose buried in a book.

The Ringmaster's Revenge is brought to life out of a creative writing assignment from her high school days. Upon re-earthing the manuscript from an old flash drive over a decade later, Adriano and Sammy's stories needed to come to life.

A little more about me:

Sara lives in Canada with her real-life book boyfriend (husband) and their dog. When she isn't writing, she can be found traveling and frequenting the dog park.

CONNECT WITH ME

If you enjoyed this story, let me know! Please consider leaving a review on Goodreads or Amazon.

www.ingramcontent.com/pod-product-compliance
Lightning Source LLC
Chambersburg PA
CBHW071557030726
47593CB00001BA/205